Chloe

charmz

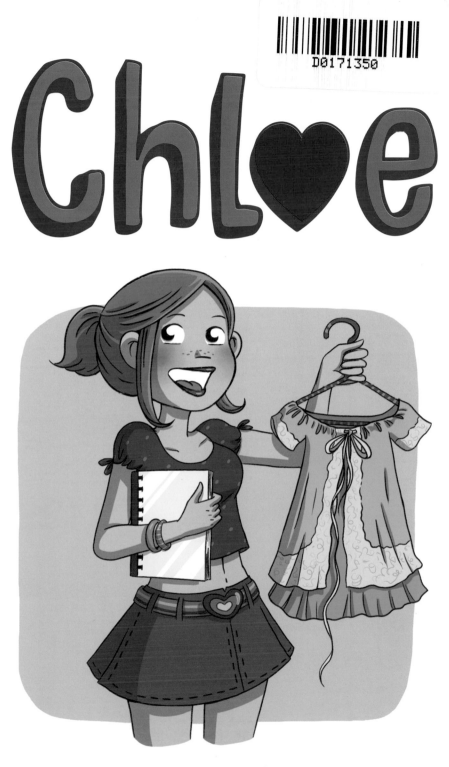

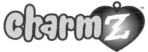

MORE GRAPHIC NOVELS AVAILABLE from Charmz™

COMING SOON!

COMING SOON!

STITCHED
MARIAH McCOURT
AARON ALEXOVICH
The First Day of the Rest of her Life
charmz

STITCHED #1
"THE FIRST DAY OF THE REST OF HER LIFE"

STITCHED
MARIAH McCOURT • AARON ALEXOVICH
Love in the Time of Assumption
charmz

STITCHED #2
"LOVE IN THE TIME OF ASSUMPTION"

PATRICIA LYFOUNG
The Scarlet Rose
charmz

SCARLET ROSE #1
"I KNEW I'D MEET YOU"

PATRICIA LYFOUNG
The Scarlet Rose
I'll Go Where You Go
charmz

SCARLET ROSE #2
"I'LL GO WHERE YOU GO"

Greg Tessier and Amandine
Chloe
The New Girl
charmz

CHLOE #1
"THE NEW GIRL"

Greg Tessier and Amandine
Chloe
The Queen of High School
charmz

CHLOE #2
"THE QUEEN OF HIGH SCHOOL"

ALL-NEW Graphic Novel by Greg Tessier & Amandine
Chloe
Frenemies
charmz

CHLOE #3
"FRENEMIES"

Sweeties
CHERRY SKYE
charmz

SWEETIES #1
"CHERRY SKYE"

GFFs
GHOST FRIENDS FOREVER
charmz

G.F.F.s #1 "MY HEART LIES IN THE 90s"

Ana and the COSMIC RACE
AMY CHU
KATA KANE
THE RACE BEGINS
charmz

ANA AND THE COSMIC RACE #1
"THE RACE BEGINS"

Charmz graphic novels are available for $9.99 in paperback, and $14.99 in hardcover. Available from booksellers everywhere. You can also order online from www.papercutz.com. Or call 1-800-886-1223, Monday through Friday, 9–5 EST. MC, Visa, and AmEx accepted. To order by mail, please add $5.00 for postage and handling for first book ordered, $1.00 for each additional book, and make check payable to NBM Publishing Send to: Charmz, 160 Broadway, Suite 700, East Wing, New York, NY 10038.

Charmz graphic novels are also available wherever e-books are sold.

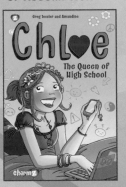

Chl♥e

Frenemies

Story by Greg Tessier
Art by Amandine

NEW YORK

Because sharing your passion is the most beautiful of gifts, thanks to the trainers and instructors who, through their motivation, bring so much happiness to their students. Have amazing internships!
Because putting your heart into your work is always right, thanks to everybody who make being kind and attentive their philosophy of life!
—Greg

It's almost 10 years since I left college—and 10 books later, thanks again, again, and again to Jean-Louis Chazelas!
A thousand thanks to Pierre for his precious and fabulous presence near the scanner! And to Kaouet for the coloring help!
And mountains of thanks also to my family for the wonderful, attentive support, KitKats, and sparkling water that go so well during nights of work!
—Amandine

CHLOE #3
"Frenemies"
Mistinguette [CHLOE] volume 5 "Mission Relooking" and
Mistinguette [CHLOE] volume 6 "S.O.S. Coeur en Détresse" © Jungle! 2015
www.editions-jungle.com. All rights reserved. Used under license.

English translation and all other editorial material © 2018 by Papercutz.
All rights reserved.

GREG TESSIER — Story
AMANDINE — Art and color
AMANDINE — Cover
JOE JOHNSON — Translation
BRYAN SENKA — Lettering
JEFF WHITMAN — Assistant Managing Editor
JIM SALICRUP
Editor-in-Chief

Charmz is an imprint of Papercutz.

ISBN HC: 978-1-62991-859-4
ISBN PB: 978-1-62991-858-7

Printed in China
February 2018

Charmz books may be purchased for business or promotional use.
For information on bulk purchases please contact Macmillan
Corporate and Premium Sales Department at (800) 221-7945 x5442

Distributed by Macmillan
First Charmz Printing

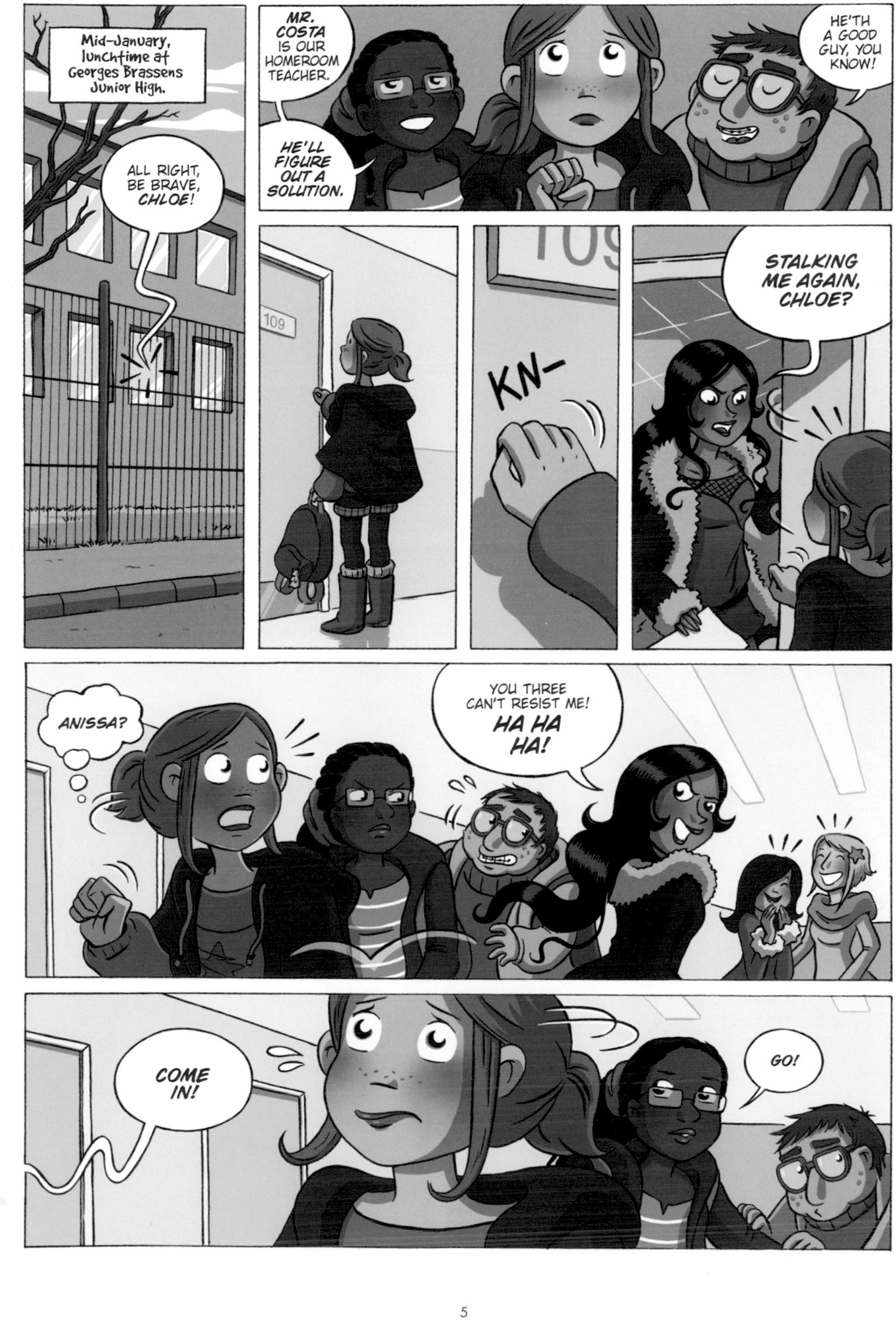

Mid-January, lunchtime at Georges Brassens Junior High.
ALL RIGHT, BE BRAVE, CHLOE!
MR. COSTA IS OUR HOMEROOM TEACHER.
HE'LL FIGURE OUT A SOLUTION.
HE'TH A GOOD GUY, YOU KNOW!
109
KN-
STALKING ME AGAIN, CHLOE?
ANISSA?
YOU THREE CAN'T RESIST ME! HA HA HA!
COME IN!
GO!

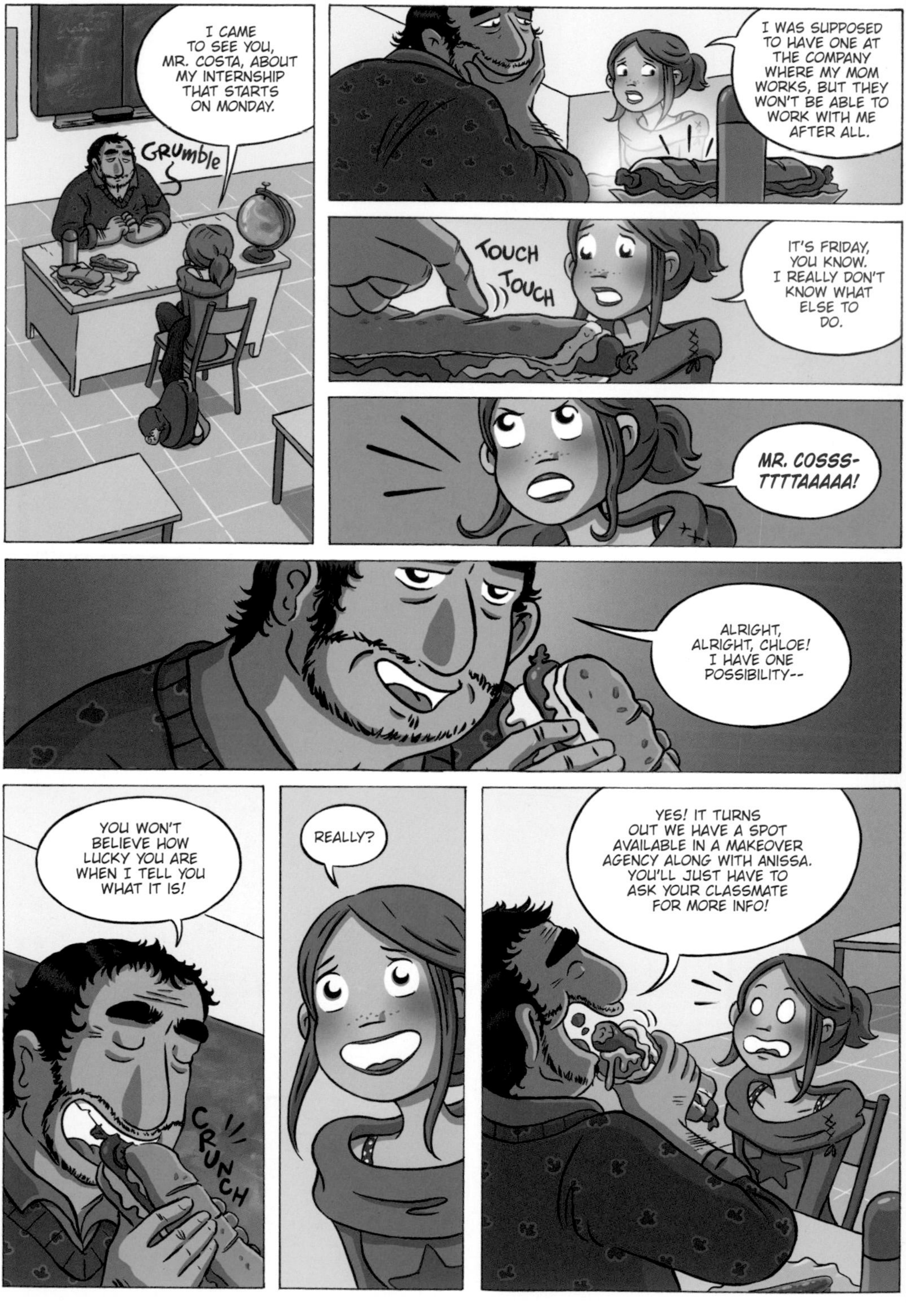

I CAME TO SEE YOU, MR. COSTA, ABOUT MY INTERNSHIP THAT STARTS ON MONDAY.
GRUMBLE
I WAS SUPPOSED TO HAVE ONE AT THE COMPANY WHERE MY MOM WORKS, BUT THEY WON'T BE ABLE TO WORK WITH ME AFTER ALL.
TOUCH TOUCH
IT'S FRIDAY, YOU KNOW. I REALLY DON'T KNOW WHAT ELSE TO DO.
MR. COSSS-TTTTAAAAA!
ALRIGHT, ALRIGHT, CHLOE! I HAVE ONE POSSIBILITY--
YOU WON'T BELIEVE HOW LUCKY YOU ARE WHEN I TELL YOU WHAT IT IS!
CRUNCH
REALLY?
YES! IT TURNS OUT WE HAVE A SPOT AVAILABLE IN A MAKEOVER AGENCY ALONG WITH ANISSA. YOU'LL JUST HAVE TO ASK YOUR CLASSMATE FOR MORE INFO!

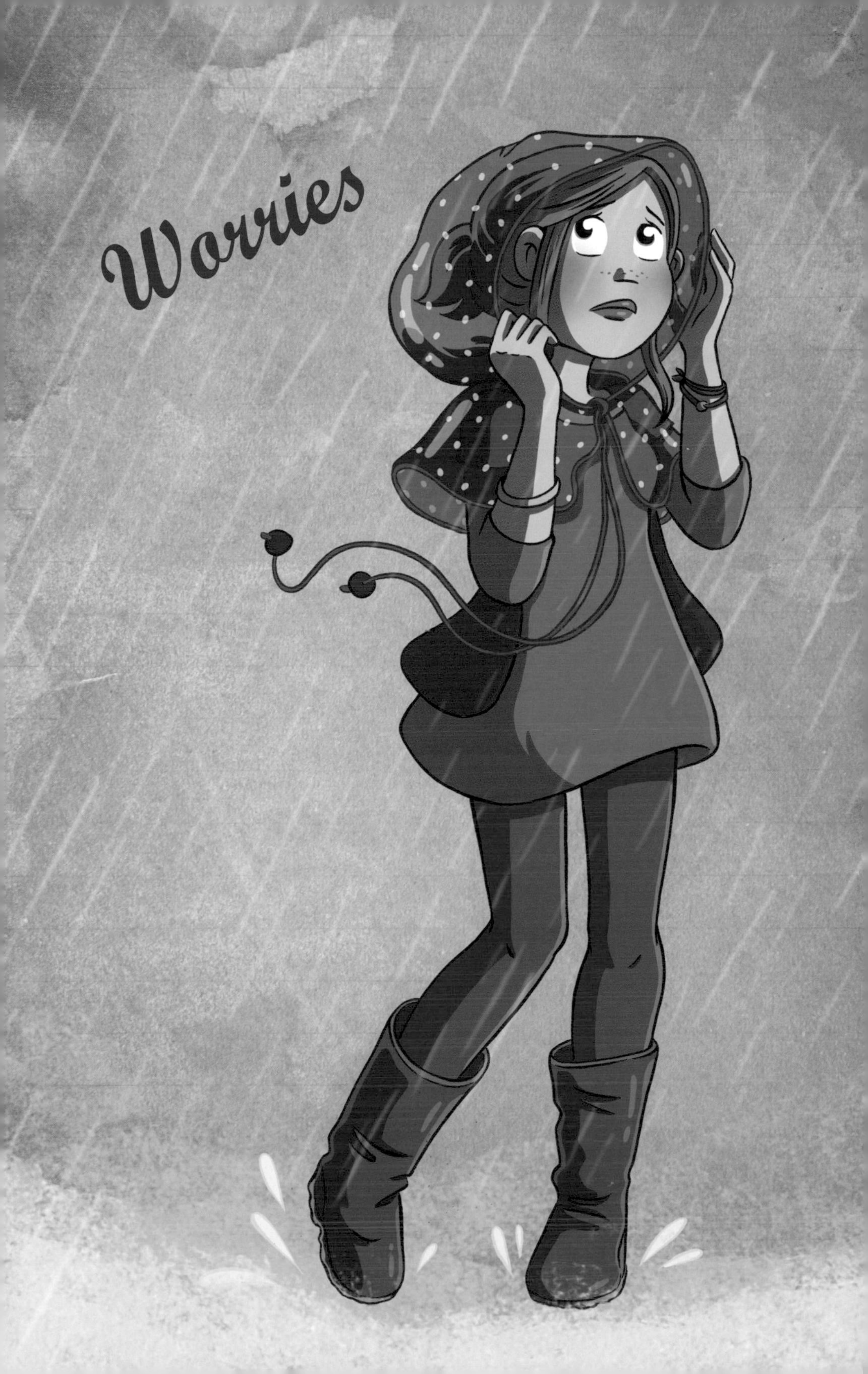
Worries

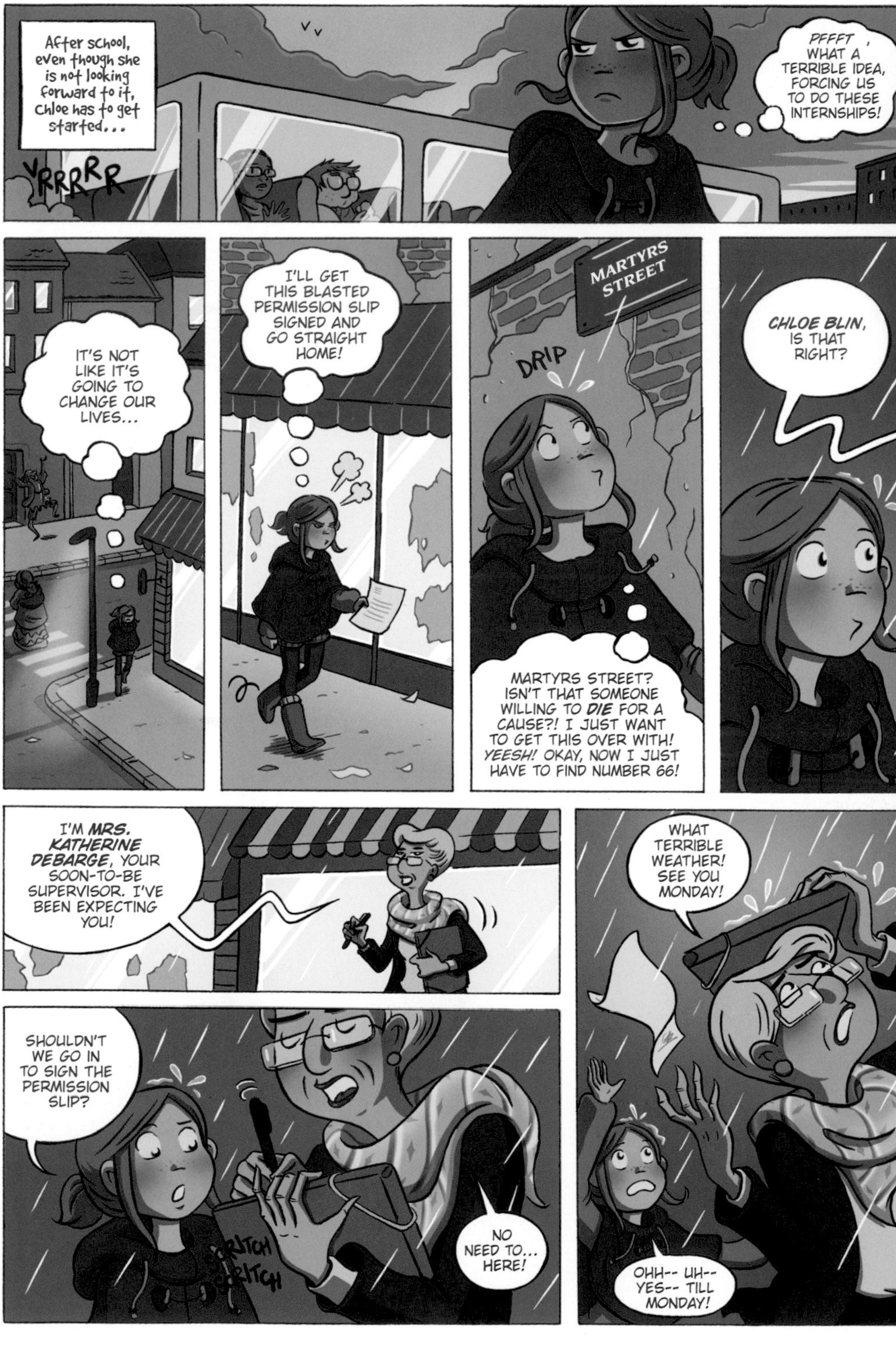
After school, even though she is not looking forward to it, Chloe has to get started...
VRRRRR
PFFFT, WHAT A TERRIBLE IDEA, FORCING US TO DO THESE INTERNSHIPS!
IT'S NOT LIKE IT'S GOING TO CHANGE OUR LIVES...
I'LL GET THIS BLASTED PERMISSION SLIP SIGNED AND GO STRAIGHT HOME!
MARTYRS STREET
DRIP
MARTYRS STREET? ISN'T THAT SOMEONE WILLING TO DIE FOR A CAUSE?! I JUST WANT TO GET THIS OVER WITH! YEESH! OKAY, NOW I JUST HAVE TO FIND NUMBER 66!
CHLOE BLIN, IS THAT RIGHT?
I'M MRS. KATHERINE DEBARGE, YOUR SOON-TO-BE SUPERVISOR. I'VE BEEN EXPECTING YOU!
SHOULDN'T WE GO IN TO SIGN THE PERMISSION SLIP?
SCRITCH SCRITCH
NO NEED TO... HERE!
WHAT TERRIBLE WEATHER! SEE YOU MONDAY!
OHH-- UH-- YES-- TILL MONDAY!

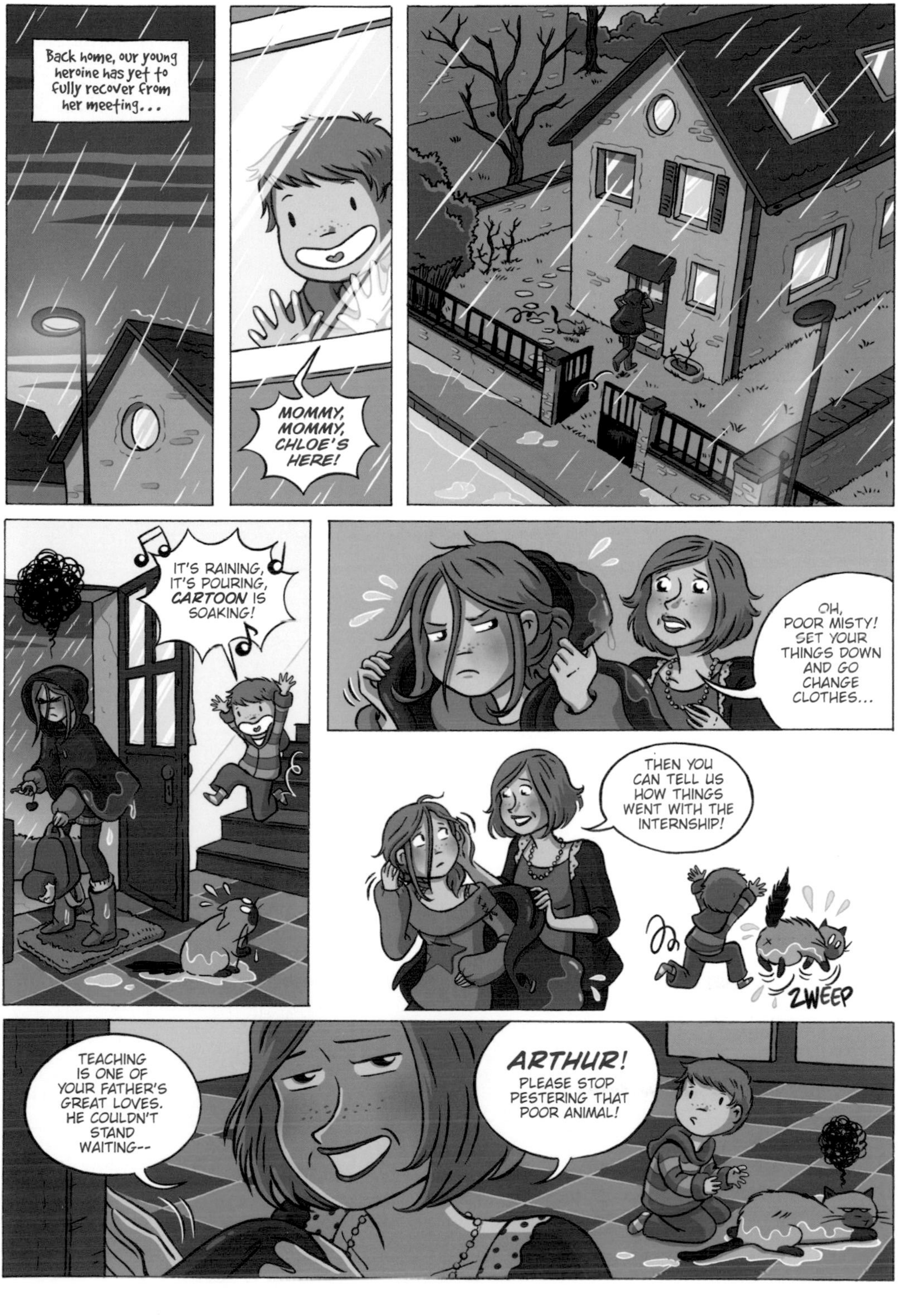
Back home, our young heroine has yet to fully recover from her meeting...
MOMMY, MOMMY, CHLOE'S HERE!
IT'S RAINING, IT'S POURING, CARTOON IS SOAKING!
OH, POOR MISTY! SET YOUR THINGS DOWN AND GO CHANGE CLOTHES...
THEN YOU CAN TELL US HOW THINGS WENT WITH THE INTERNSHIP!
ZWEEP
TEACHING IS ONE OF YOUR FATHER'S GREAT LOVES. HE COULDN'T STAND WAITING--
ARTHUR! PLEASE STOP PESTERING THAT POOR ANIMAL!

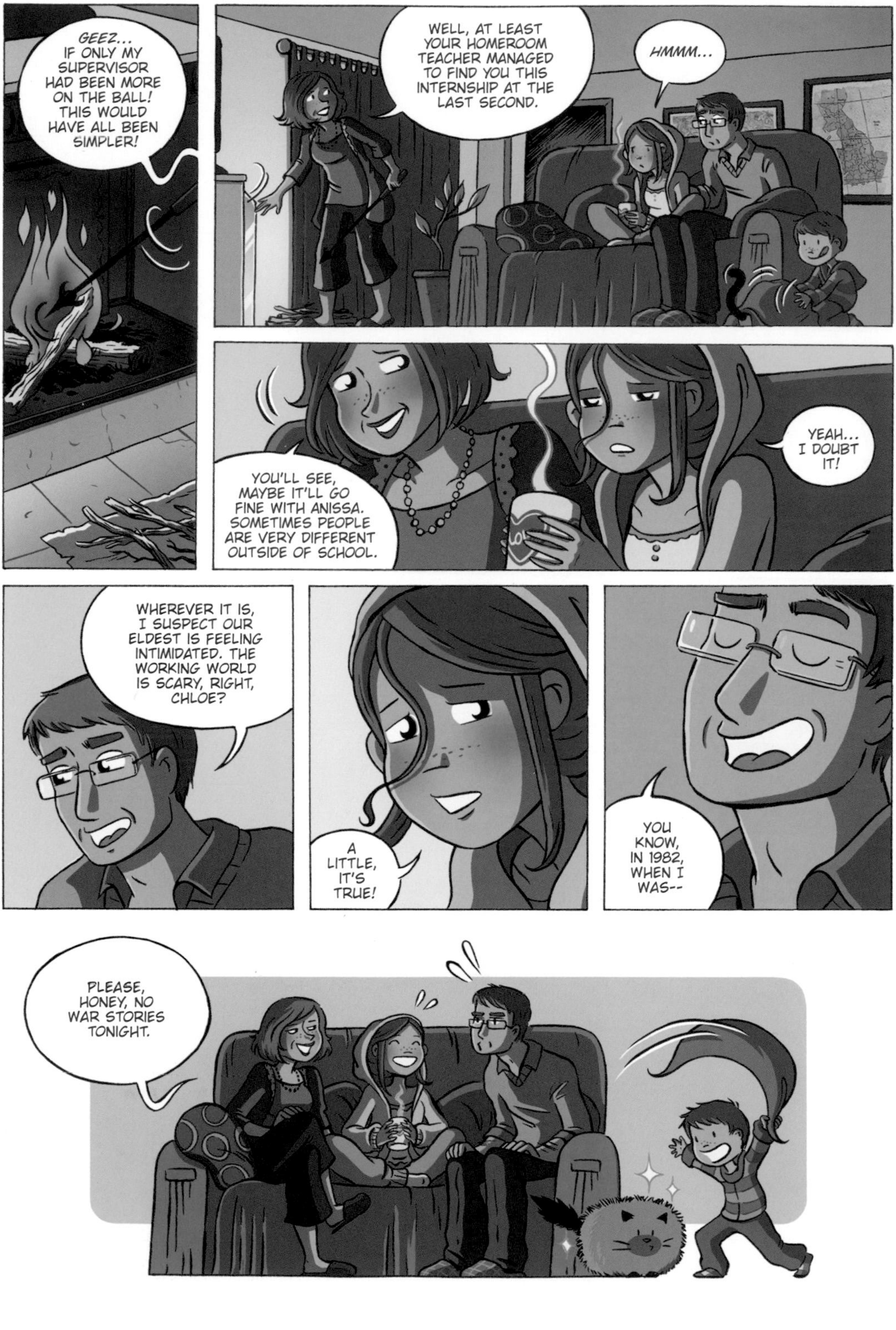
GEEZ... IF ONLY MY SUPERVISOR HAD BEEN MORE ON THE BALL! THIS WOULD HAVE ALL BEEN SIMPLER!
WELL, AT LEAST YOUR HOMEROOM TEACHER MANAGED TO FIND YOU THIS INTERNSHIP AT THE LAST SECOND.
HMMM...
YOU'LL SEE, MAYBE IT'LL GO FINE WITH ANISSA. SOMETIMES PEOPLE ARE VERY DIFFERENT OUTSIDE OF SCHOOL.
YEAH... I DOUBT IT!
WHEREVER IT IS, I SUSPECT OUR ELDEST IS FEELING INTIMIDATED. THE WORKING WORLD IS SCARY, RIGHT, CHLOE?
A LITTLE, IT'S TRUE!
YOU KNOW, IN 1982, WHEN I WAS--
PLEASE, HONEY, NO WAR STORIES TONIGHT.

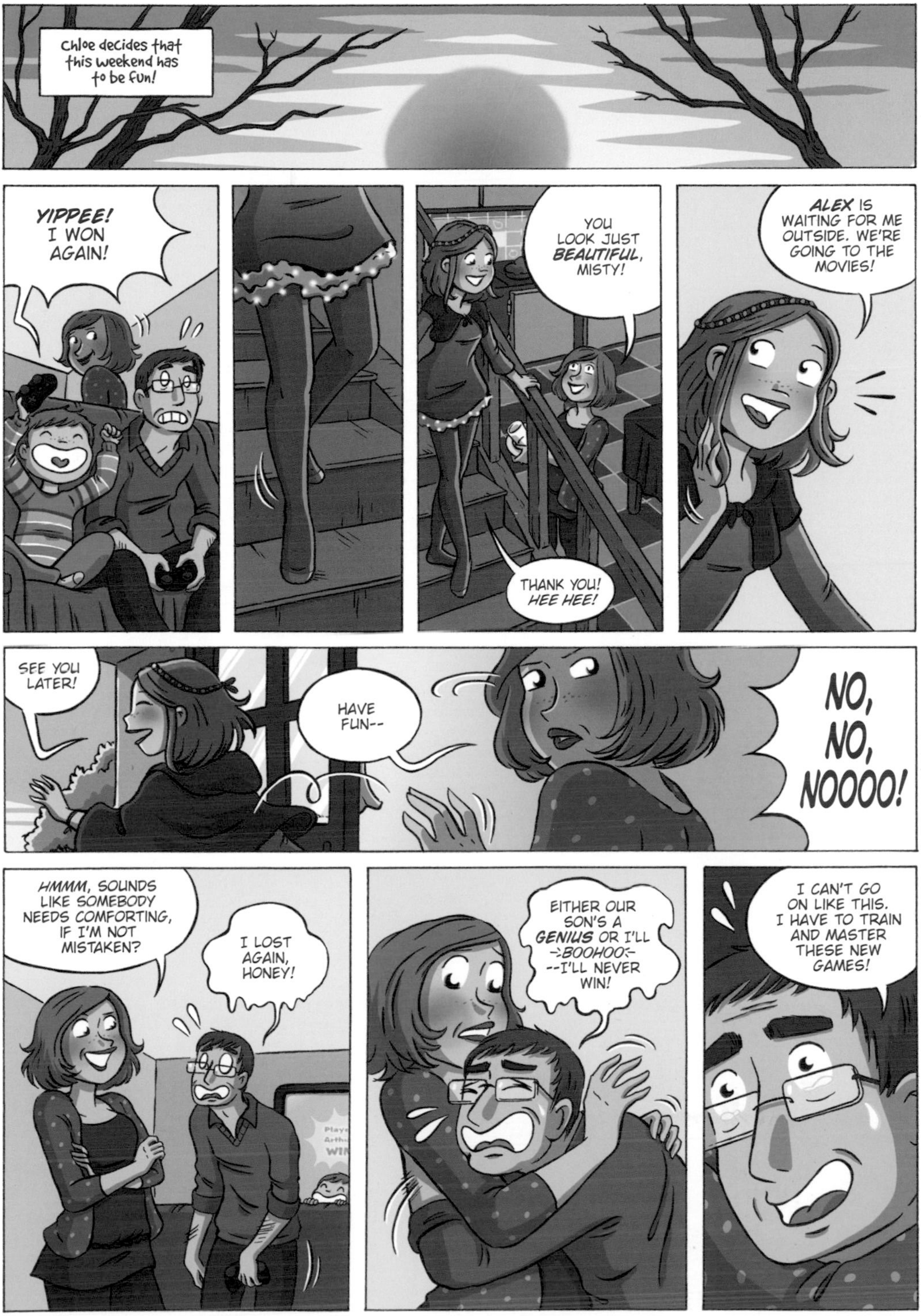
Chloe decides that this weekend has to be fun!
YIPPEE! I WON AGAIN!
YOU LOOK JUST BEAUTIFUL, MISTY!
THANK YOU! HEE HEE!
ALEX IS WAITING FOR ME OUTSIDE. WE'RE GOING TO THE MOVIES!
SEE YOU LATER!
HAVE FUN--
NO, NO, NOOOO!
HMMM, SOUNDS LIKE SOMEBODY NEEDS COMFORTING, IF I'M NOT MISTAKEN?
I LOST AGAIN, HONEY!
EITHER OUR SON'S A GENIUS OR I'LL -BOOHOO- --I'LL NEVER WIN!
I CAN'T GO ON LIKE THIS. I HAVE TO TRAIN AND MASTER THESE NEW GAMES!

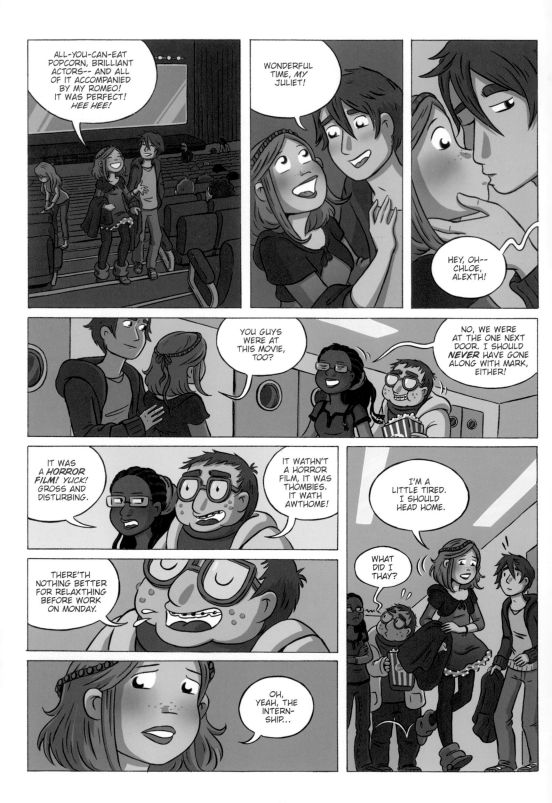

ALL-YOU-CAN-EAT POPCORN, BRILLIANT ACTORS-- AND ALL OF IT ACCOMPANIED BY MY ROMEO! IT WAS PERFECT! *HEE HEE!*

WONDERFUL TIME, *MY JULIET!*

HEY, OH-- CHLOE, ALEXTH!

YOU GUYS WERE AT THIS MOVIE, TOO?

NO, WE WERE AT THE ONE NEXT DOOR. I SHOULD *NEVER* HAVE GONE ALONG WITH MARK, EITHER!

IT WAS A *HORROR FILM!* YUCK! GROSS AND DISTURBING.

IT WATHN'T A HORROR FILM, IT WAS THOMBIES. IT WATH AWTHOME!

THERE'TH NOTHING BETTER FOR RELAXTHING BEFORE WORK ON MONDAY.

I'M A LITTLE TIRED. I SHOULD HEAD HOME.

WHAT DID I THAY?

OH, YEAH, THE INTERN- SHIP...

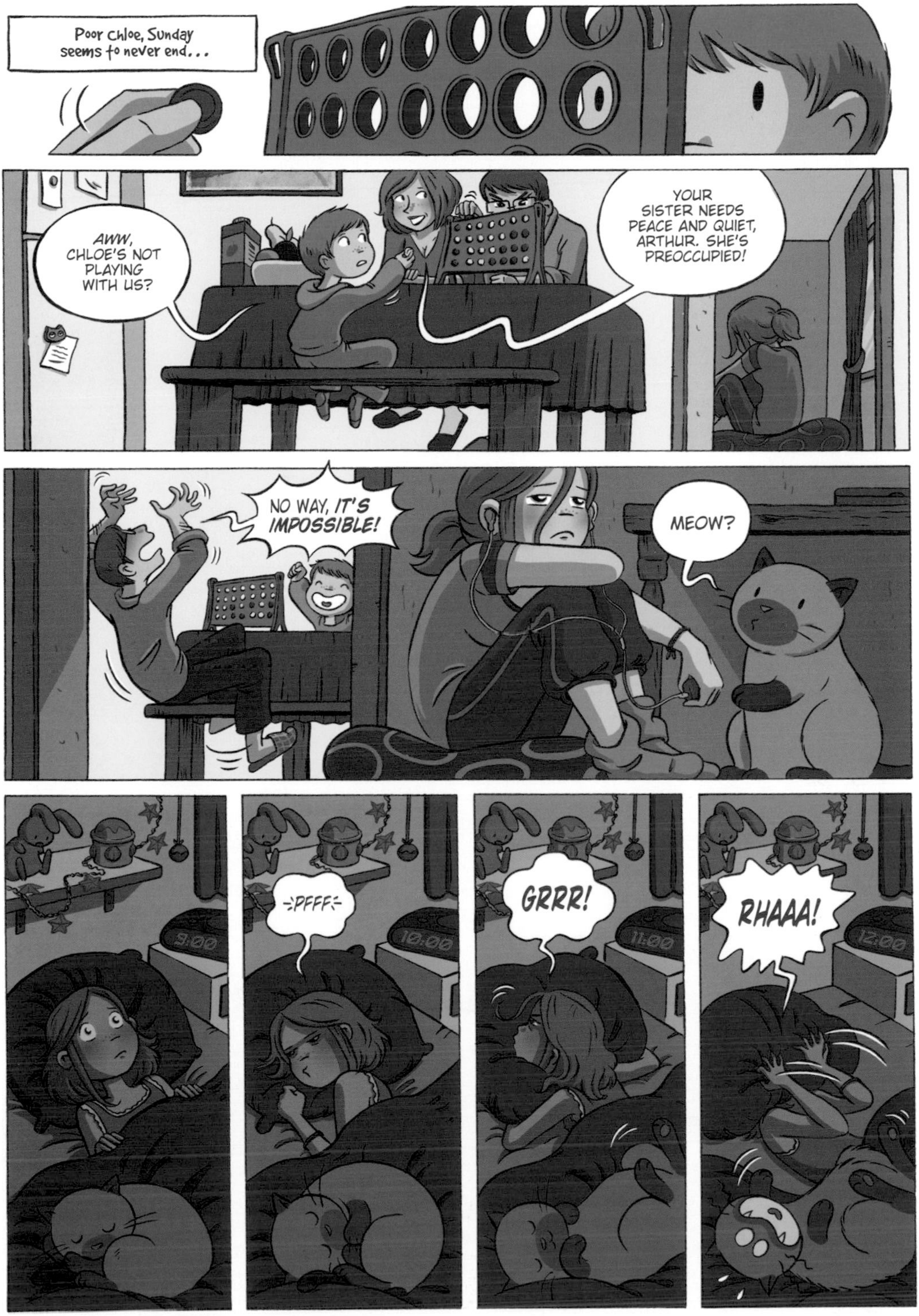
Poor Chloe, Sunday seems to never end...
AWW, CHLOE'S NOT PLAYING WITH US?
YOUR SISTER NEEDS PEACE AND QUIET, ARTHUR. SHE'S PREOCCUPIED!
NO WAY, IT'S IMPOSSIBLE!
MEOW?
9:00
PFFF
10:00
GRRR!
11:00
RHAAA!
12:00

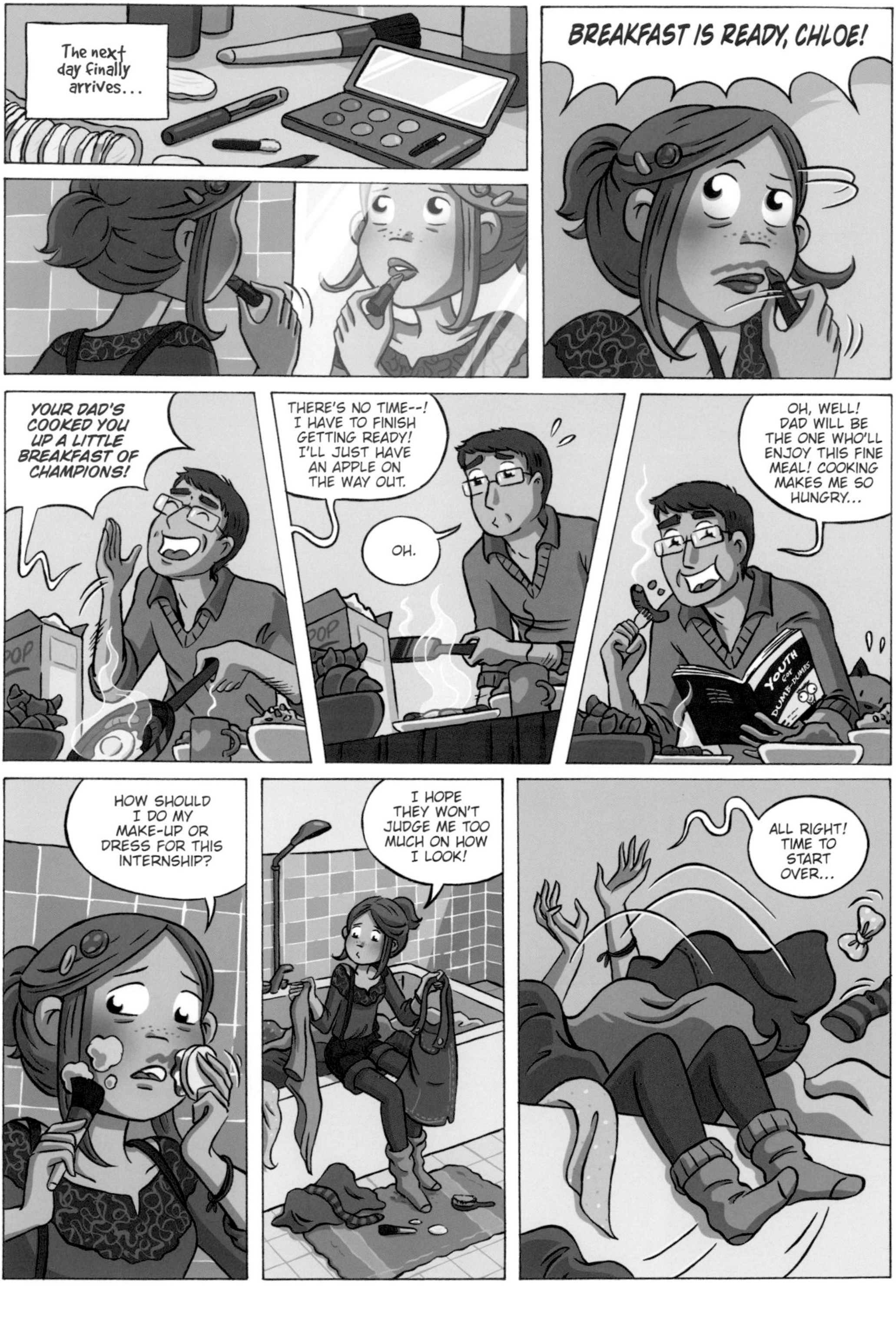
The next day finally arrives...
BREAKFAST IS READY, CHLOE!
YOUR DAD'S COOKED YOU UP A LITTLE BREAKFAST OF CHAMPIONS!
THERE'S NO TIME--! I HAVE TO FINISH GETTING READY! I'LL JUST HAVE AN APPLE ON THE WAY OUT.
OH.
OH, WELL! DAD WILL BE THE ONE WHO'LL ENJOY THIS FINE MEAL! COOKING MAKES ME SO HUNGRY...
POP
YOUTH for DUMB-DUMBS
HOW SHOULD I DO MY MAKE-UP OR DRESS FOR THIS INTERNSHIP?
I HOPE THEY WON'T JUDGE ME TOO MUCH ON HOW I LOOK!
ALL RIGHT! TIME TO START OVER...

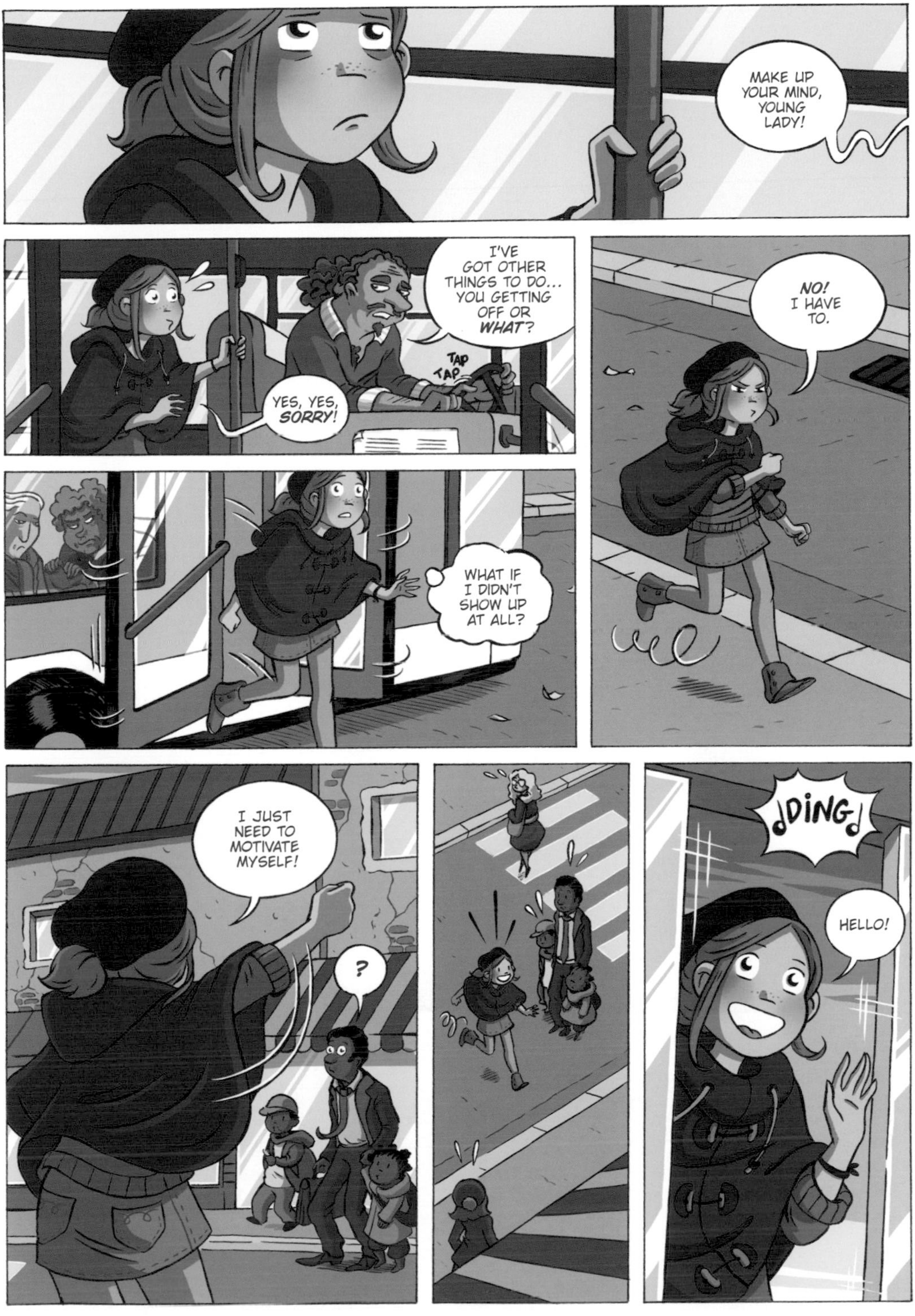
MAKE UP YOUR MIND, YOUNG LADY!
I'VE GOT OTHER THINGS TO DO... YOU GETTING OFF OR WHAT?
TAP TAP
YES, YES, SORRY!
NO! I HAVE TO.
WHAT IF I DIDN'T SHOW UP AT ALL?
I JUST NEED TO MOTIVATE MYSELF!
?
DING
HELLO!

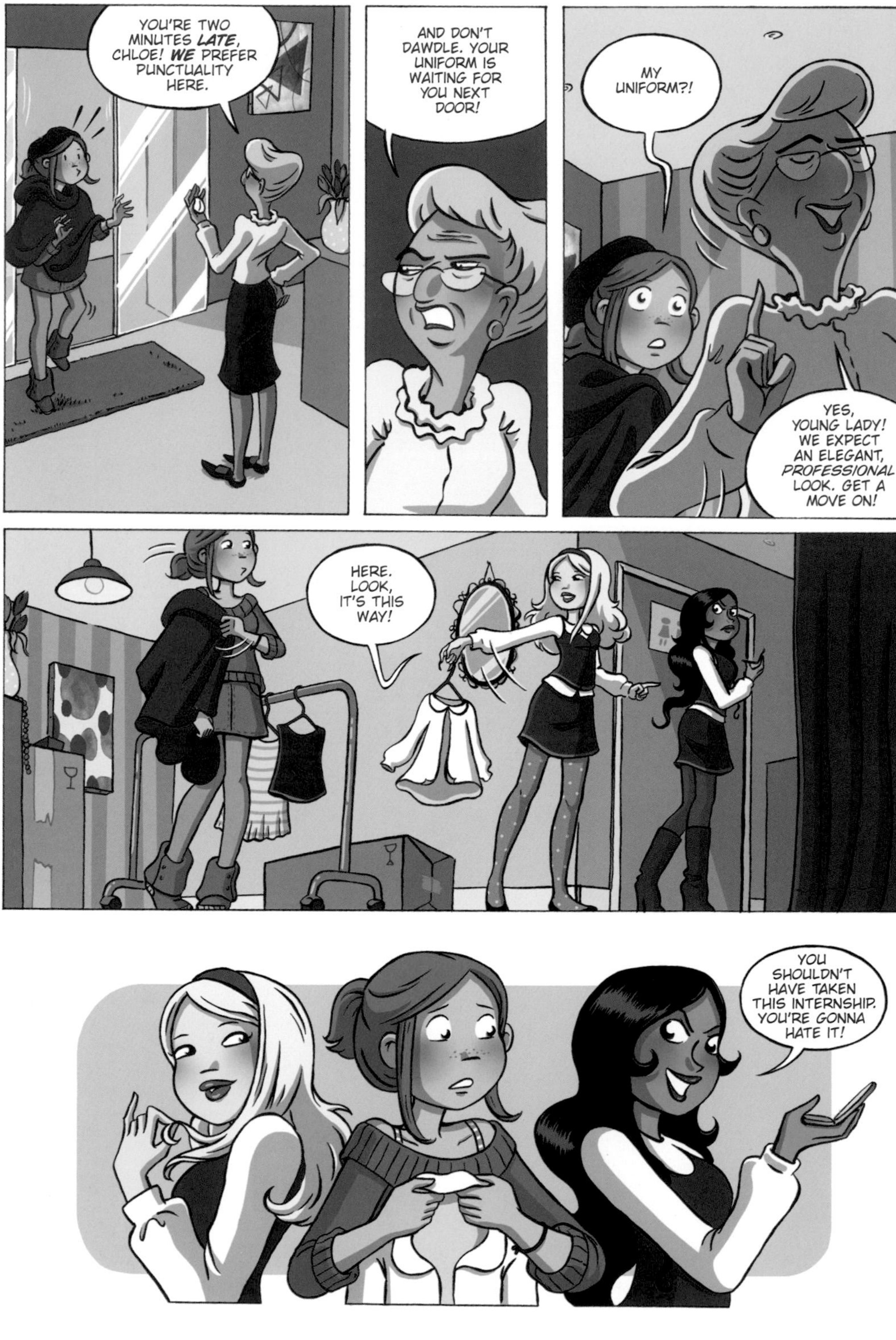
YOU'RE TWO MINUTES LATE, CHLOE! WE PREFER PUNCTUALITY HERE.
AND DON'T DAWDLE. YOUR UNIFORM IS WAITING FOR YOU NEXT DOOR!
MY UNIFORM?!
YES, YOUNG LADY! WE EXPECT AN ELEGANT, PROFESSIONAL LOOK. GET A MOVE ON!
HERE. LOOK, IT'S THIS WAY!
YOU SHOULDN'T HAVE TAKEN THIS INTERNSHIP. YOU'RE GONNA HATE IT!

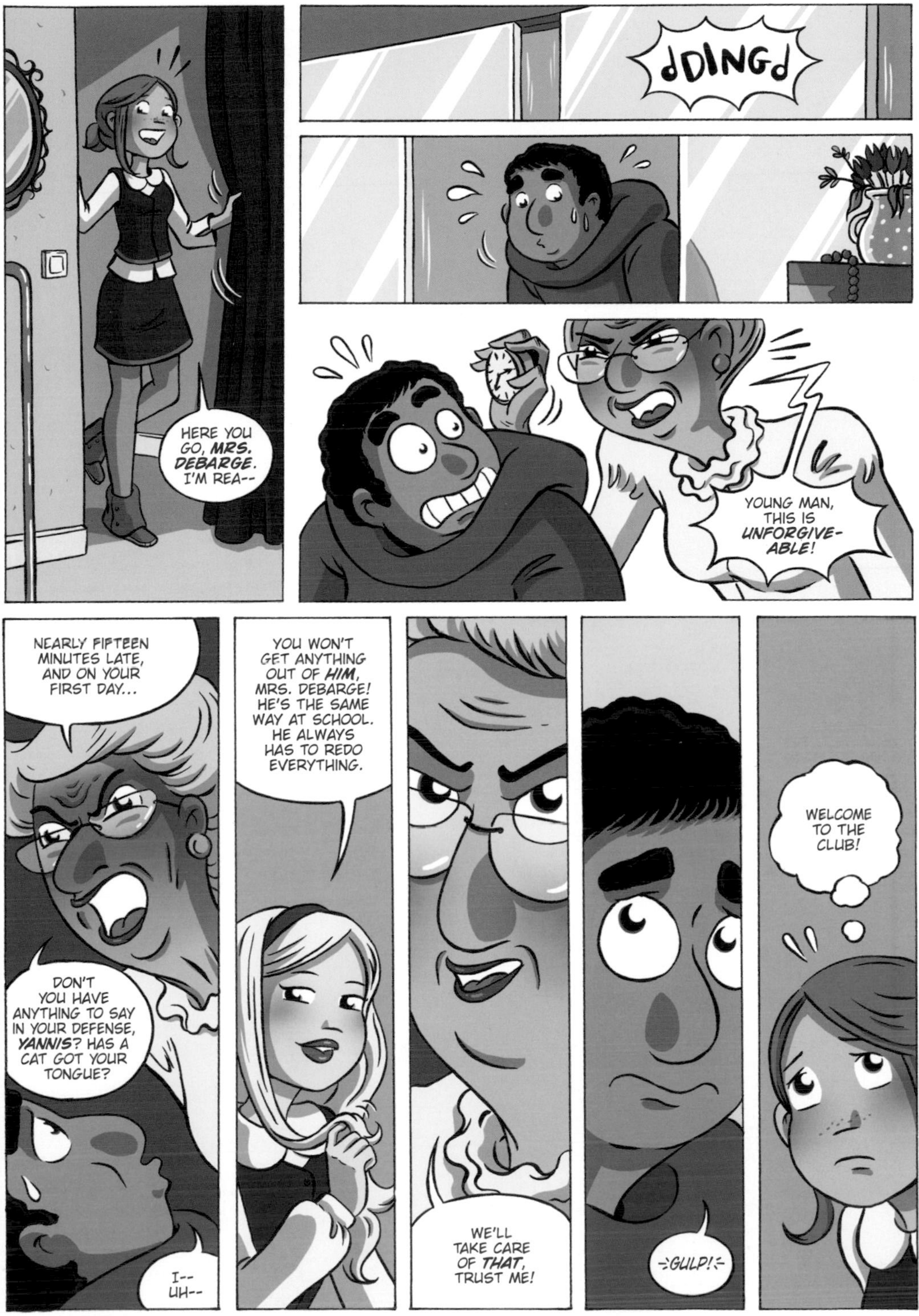
DDING
HERE YOU GO, MRS. DEBARGE. I'M REA--
YOUNG MAN, THIS IS UNFORGIVE-ABLE!
NEARLY FIFTEEN MINUTES LATE, AND ON YOUR FIRST DAY...
DON'T YOU HAVE ANYTHING TO SAY IN YOUR DEFENSE, YANNIS? HAS A CAT GOT YOUR TONGUE?
I-- UH--
YOU WON'T GET ANYTHING OUT OF HIM, MRS. DEBARGE! HE'S THE SAME WAY AT SCHOOL. HE ALWAYS HAS TO REDO EVERYTHING.
WE'LL TAKE CARE OF THAT, TRUST ME!
GULP!
WELCOME TO THE CLUB!

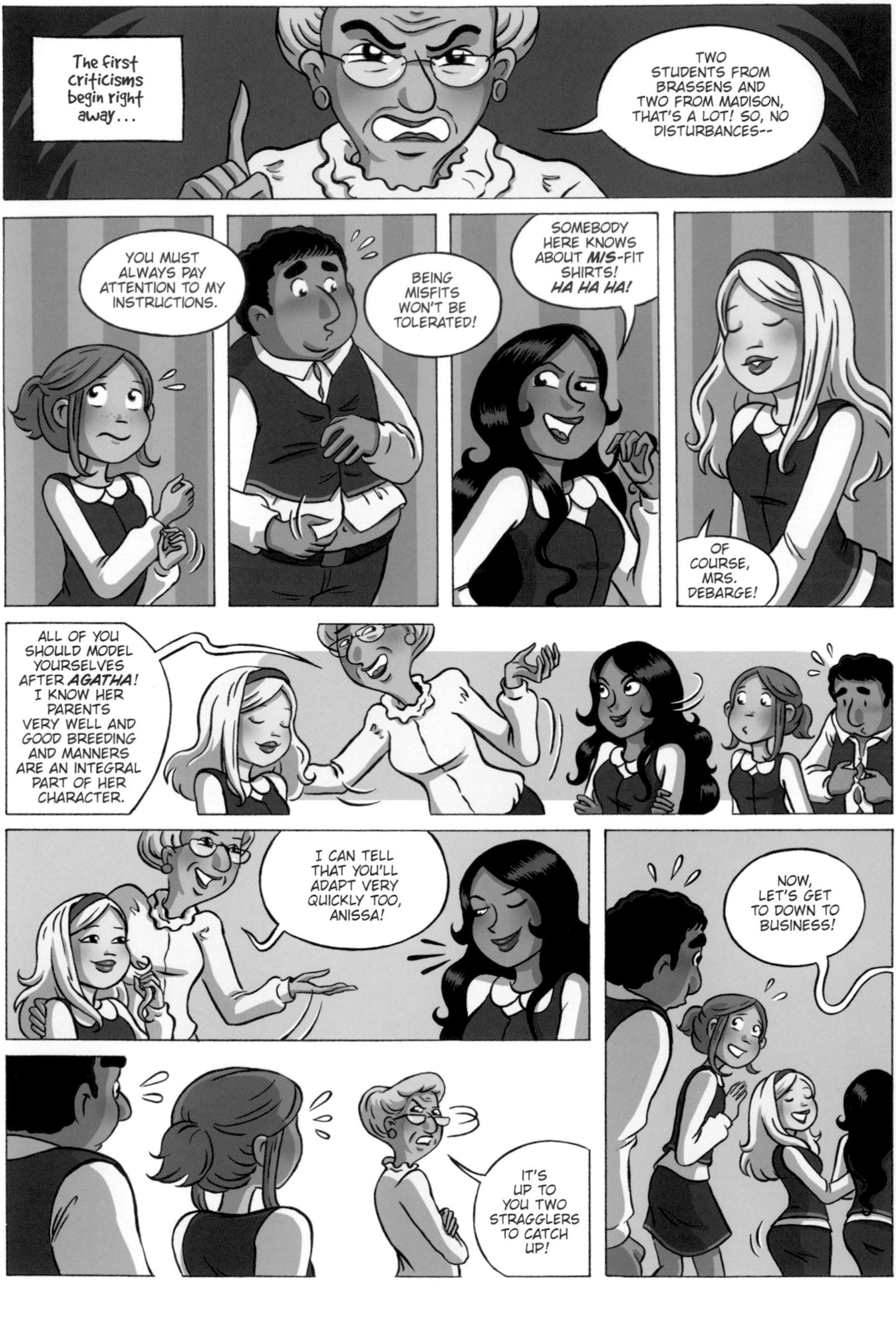
The first criticisms begin right away...
TWO STUDENTS FROM BRASSENS AND TWO FROM MADISON, THAT'S A LOT! SO, NO DISTURBANCES--
YOU MUST ALWAYS PAY ATTENTION TO MY INSTRUCTIONS.
BEING MISFITS WON'T BE TOLERATED!
SOMEBODY HERE KNOWS ABOUT MIS-FIT SHIRTS! HA HA HA!
OF COURSE, MRS. DEBARGE!
ALL OF YOU SHOULD MODEL YOURSELVES AFTER AGATHA! I KNOW HER PARENTS VERY WELL AND GOOD BREEDING AND MANNERS ARE AN INTEGRAL PART OF HER CHARACTER.
I CAN TELL THAT YOU'LL ADAPT VERY QUICKLY TOO, ANISSA!
NOW, LET'S GET TO DOWN TO BUSINESS!
IT'S UP TO YOU TWO STRAGGLERS TO CATCH UP!

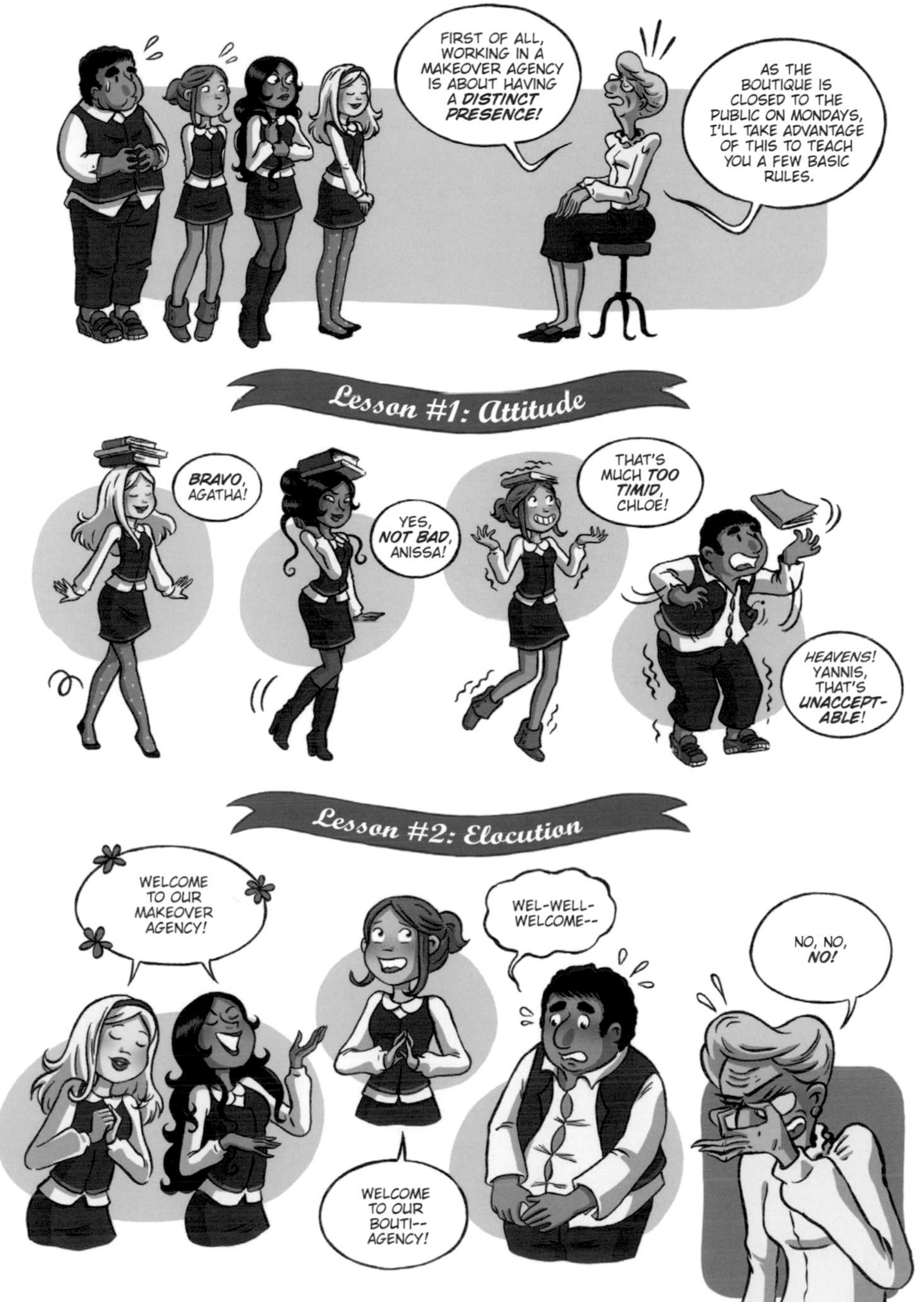
FIRST OF ALL, WORKING IN A MAKEOVER AGENCY IS ABOUT HAVING A DISTINCT PRESENCE!
AS THE BOUTIQUE IS CLOSED TO THE PUBLIC ON MONDAYS, I'LL TAKE ADVANTAGE OF THIS TO TEACH YOU A FEW BASIC RULES.
Lesson #1: Attitude
BRAVO, AGATHA!
YES, NOT BAD, ANISSA!
THAT'S MUCH TOO TIMID, CHLOE!
HEAVENS! YANNIS, THAT'S UNACCEPT-ABLE!
Lesson #2: Elocution
WELCOME TO OUR MAKEOVER AGENCY!
WELCOME TO OUR BOUTI-- AGENCY!
WEL-WELL-WELCOME--
NO, NO, NO!

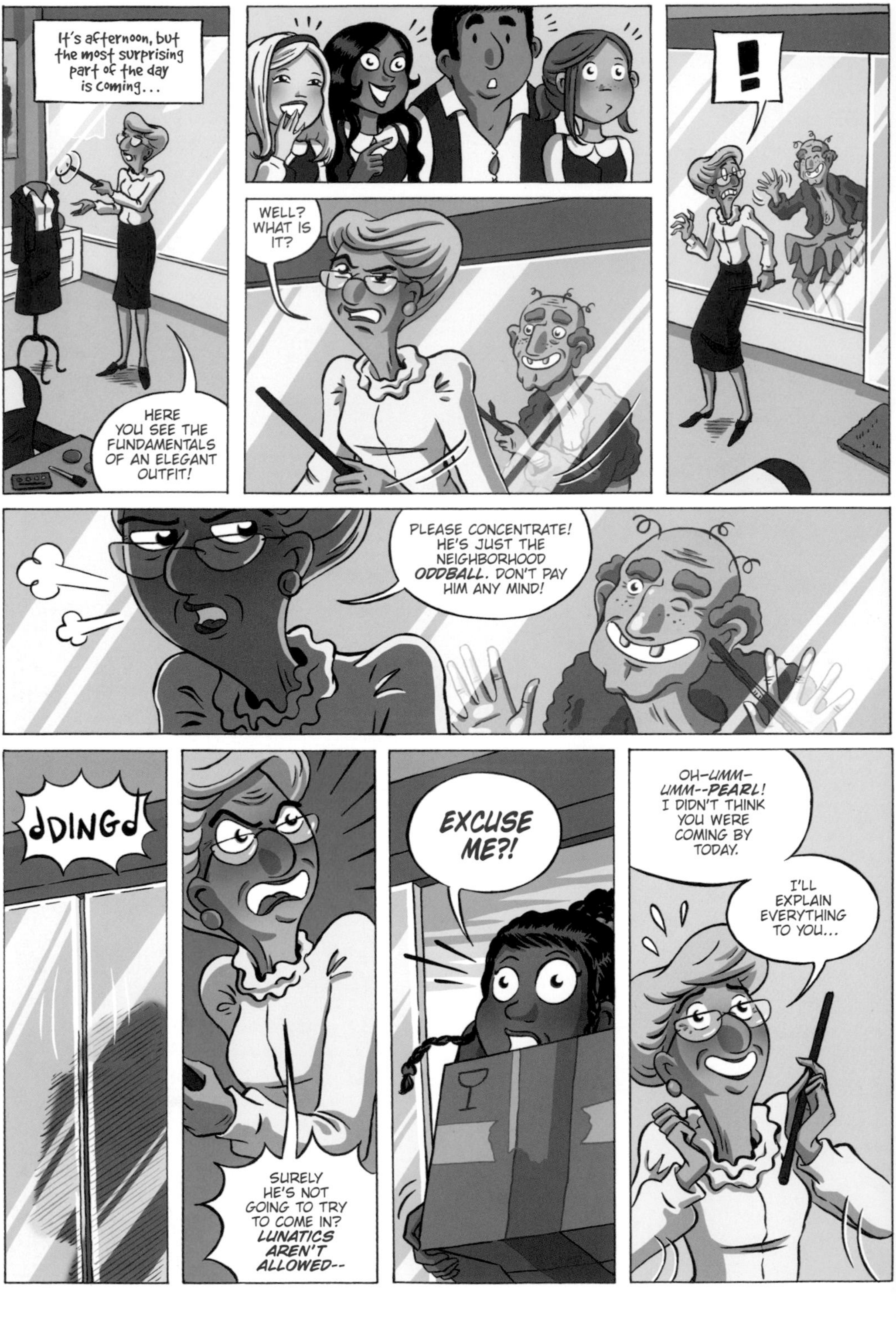
It's afternoon, but the most surprising part of the day is coming...
HERE YOU SEE THE FUNDAMENTALS OF AN ELEGANT OUTFIT!
!
WELL? WHAT IS IT?
PLEASE CONCENTRATE! HE'S JUST THE NEIGHBORHOOD *ODDBALL*. DON'T PAY HIM ANY MIND!
DING
SURELY HE'S NOT GOING TO TRY TO COME IN? *LUNATICS AREN'T ALLOWED--*
EXCUSE ME?!
OH-*UMM*-*UMM*--*PEARL*! I DIDN'T THINK YOU WERE COMING BY TODAY.
I'LL EXPLAIN EVERYTHING TO YOU...

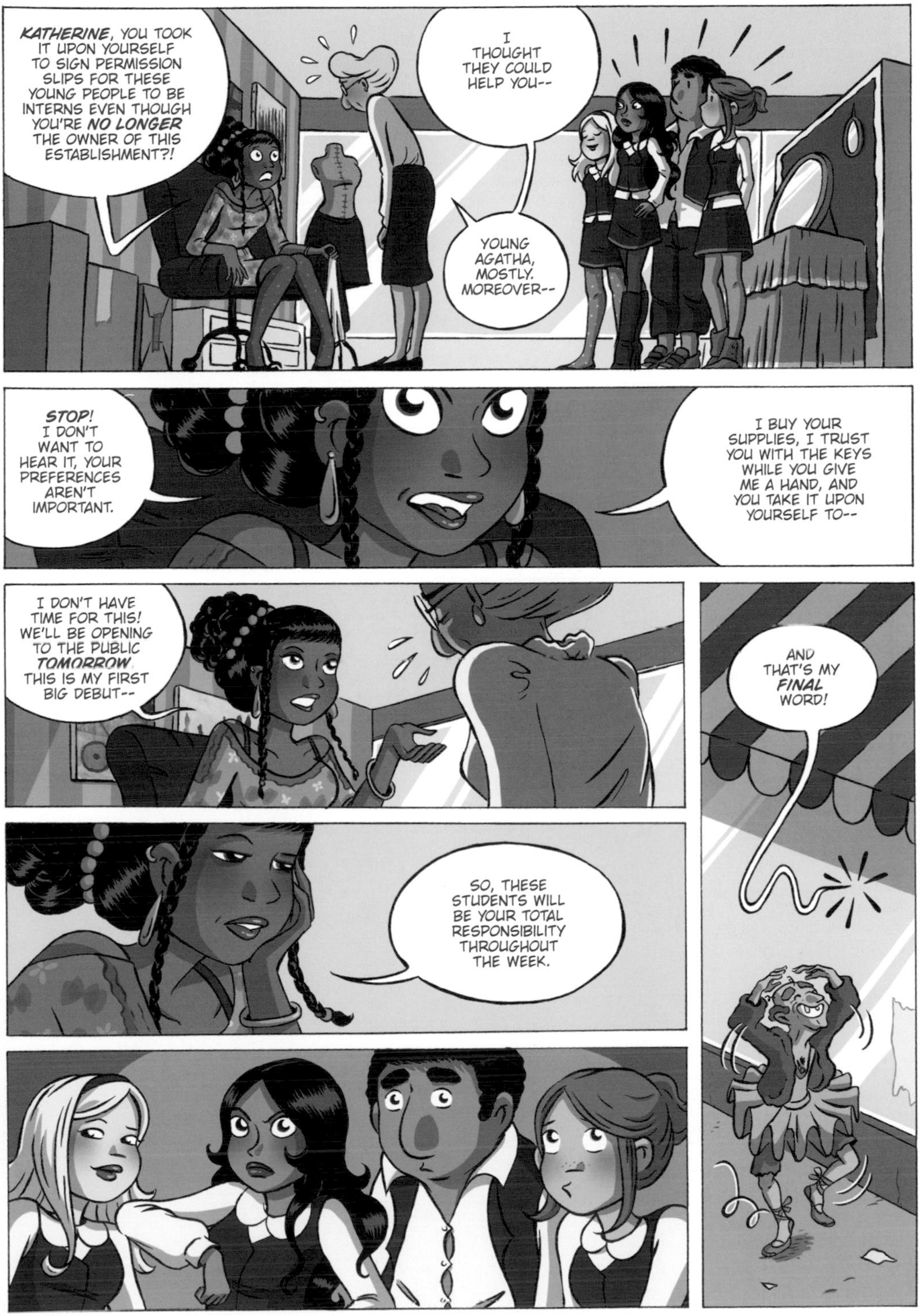
KATHERINE, YOU TOOK IT UPON YOURSELF TO SIGN PERMISSION SLIPS FOR THESE YOUNG PEOPLE TO BE INTERNS EVEN THOUGH YOU'RE NO LONGER THE OWNER OF THIS ESTABLISHMENT?!
I THOUGHT THEY COULD HELP YOU--
YOUNG AGATHA, MOSTLY. MOREOVER--
STOP! I DON'T WANT TO HEAR IT, YOUR PREFERENCES AREN'T IMPORTANT.
I BUY YOUR SUPPLIES, I TRUST YOU WITH THE KEYS WHILE YOU GIVE ME A HAND, AND YOU TAKE IT UPON YOURSELF TO--
I DON'T HAVE TIME FOR THIS! WE'LL BE OPENING TO THE PUBLIC TOMORROW. THIS IS MY FIRST BIG DEBUT--
SO, THESE STUDENTS WILL BE YOUR TOTAL RESPONSIBILITY THROUGHOUT THE WEEK.
AND THAT'S MY FINAL WORD!

Last name: BLIN
First name: Chloe
Grade: 9th grade, Group B

Internship Report

School: G. Brassens Middle School
~~Internship supervisor~~: Mrs. DEBARGE
DICTATOR

Topsy-Turvy

Internship site introduction:
The "Topsy-Turvy" boutique is a makeover agency. Recently created, it offers to clients personalized support concerning fashion and style.

↳ *if they manage to get any.*

Examples of makeovers:

before/after by Miss Pearl

before/after by Mrs. Debarge

Facilities description:
Located at 66 Martyrs Street, the agency's facilities include a main room with a reception desk, ~~a large sele~~ction of clothing, as well as a mirrored space for hairstyling and make-up. There's a kitchen nearby for lunch and a stockroom.

HELL Simply put!
↓
Total AGONY ... Brrr!

The facilities:

clothing
kitchen
restroom
reception desk
curtain
entrance
hair dresser
martyrs street

The ~~martyrs~~ Interns

Anissa
Agatha
Yannis
Me...

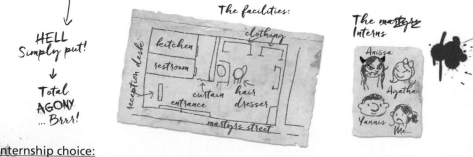

Internship choice:
There was no choice. I had to accept this CURSED job without complaining. My first experience in the working world looks like it'll be horrible!

Habits

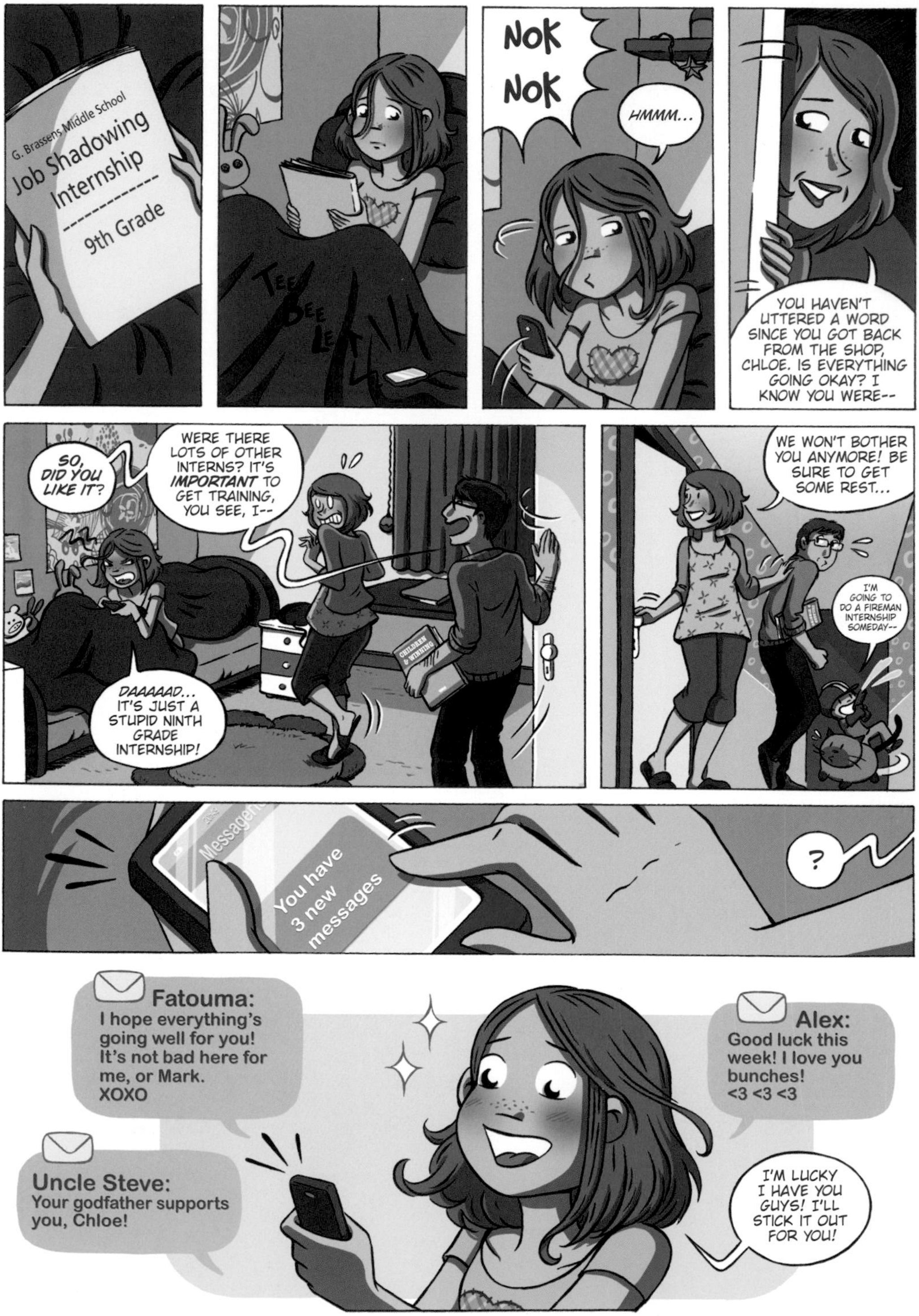
G. Brassens Middle School
Job Shadowing Internship
9th Grade
NOK NOK
HMMM...
YOU HAVEN'T UTTERED A WORD SINCE YOU GOT BACK FROM THE SHOP, CHLOE. IS EVERYTHING GOING OKAY? I KNOW YOU WERE--
SO, DID YOU LIKE IT?
WERE THERE LOTS OF OTHER INTERNS? IT'S IMPORTANT TO GET TRAINING, YOU SEE, I--
DAAAAAD... IT'S JUST A STUPID NINTH GRADE INTERNSHIP!
CHILDREN & WINNING
WE WON'T BOTHER YOU ANYMORE! BE SURE TO GET SOME REST...
I'M GOING TO DO A FIREMAN INTERNSHIP SOMEDAY--
Messages
You have 3 new messages
?
Fatouma:
I hope everything's going well for you! It's not bad here for me, or Mark. XOXO
Uncle Steve:
Your godfather supports you, Chloe!
Alex:
Good luck this week! I love you bunches! <3 <3 <3
I'M LUCKY I HAVE YOU GUYS! I'LL STICK IT OUT FOR YOU!

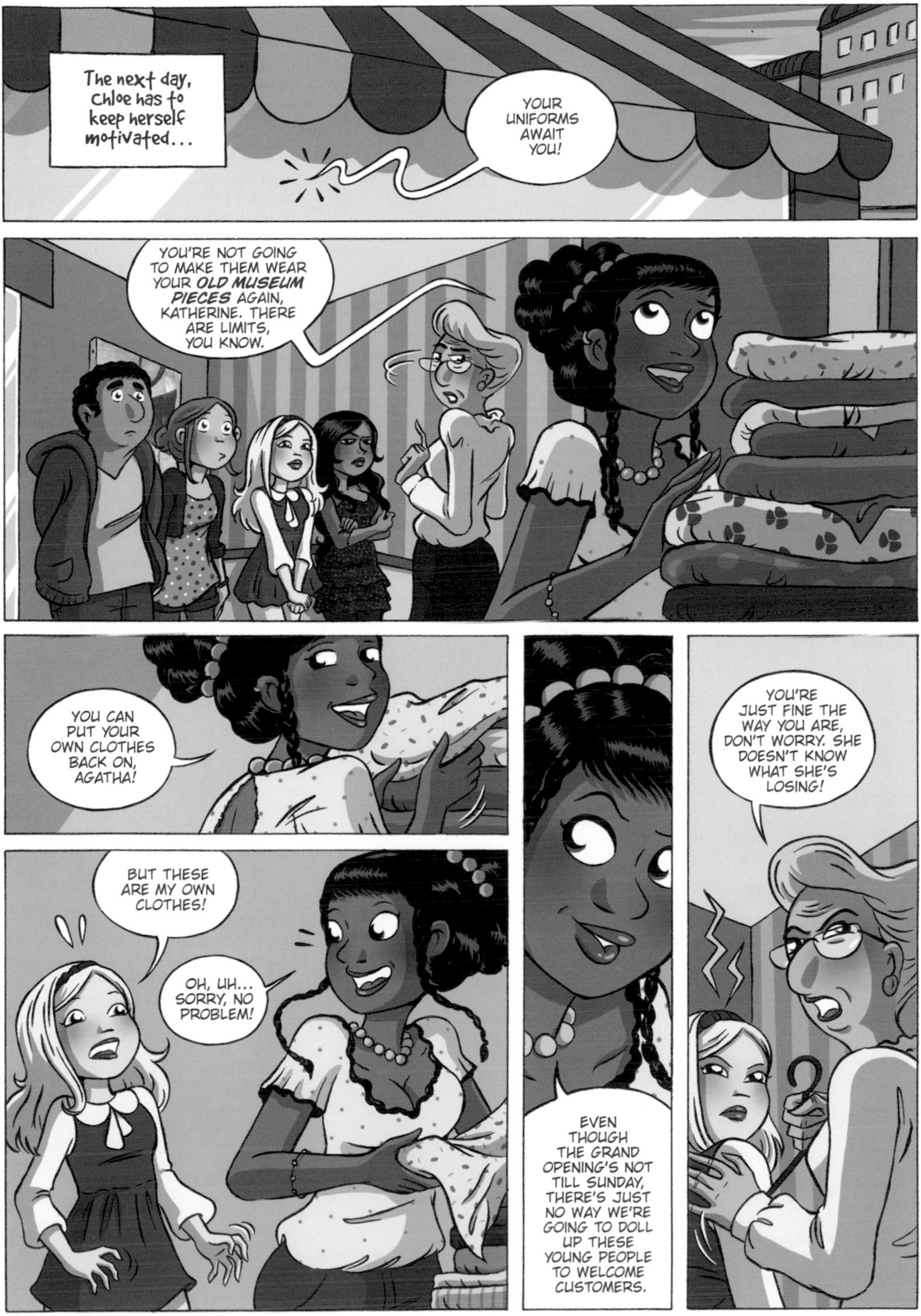
The next day, Chloe has to keep herself motivated...
YOUR UNIFORMS AWAIT YOU!
YOU'RE NOT GOING TO MAKE THEM WEAR YOUR OLD MUSEUM PIECES AGAIN, KATHERINE. THERE ARE LIMITS, YOU KNOW.
YOU CAN PUT YOUR OWN CLOTHES BACK ON, AGATHA!
BUT THESE ARE MY OWN CLOTHES!
OH, UH... SORRY, NO PROBLEM!
EVEN THOUGH THE GRAND OPENING'S NOT TILL SUNDAY, THERE'S JUST NO WAY WE'RE GOING TO DOLL UP THESE YOUNG PEOPLE TO WELCOME CUSTOMERS.
YOU'RE JUST FINE THE WAY YOU ARE, DON'T WORRY. SHE DOESN'T KNOW WHAT SHE'S LOSING!

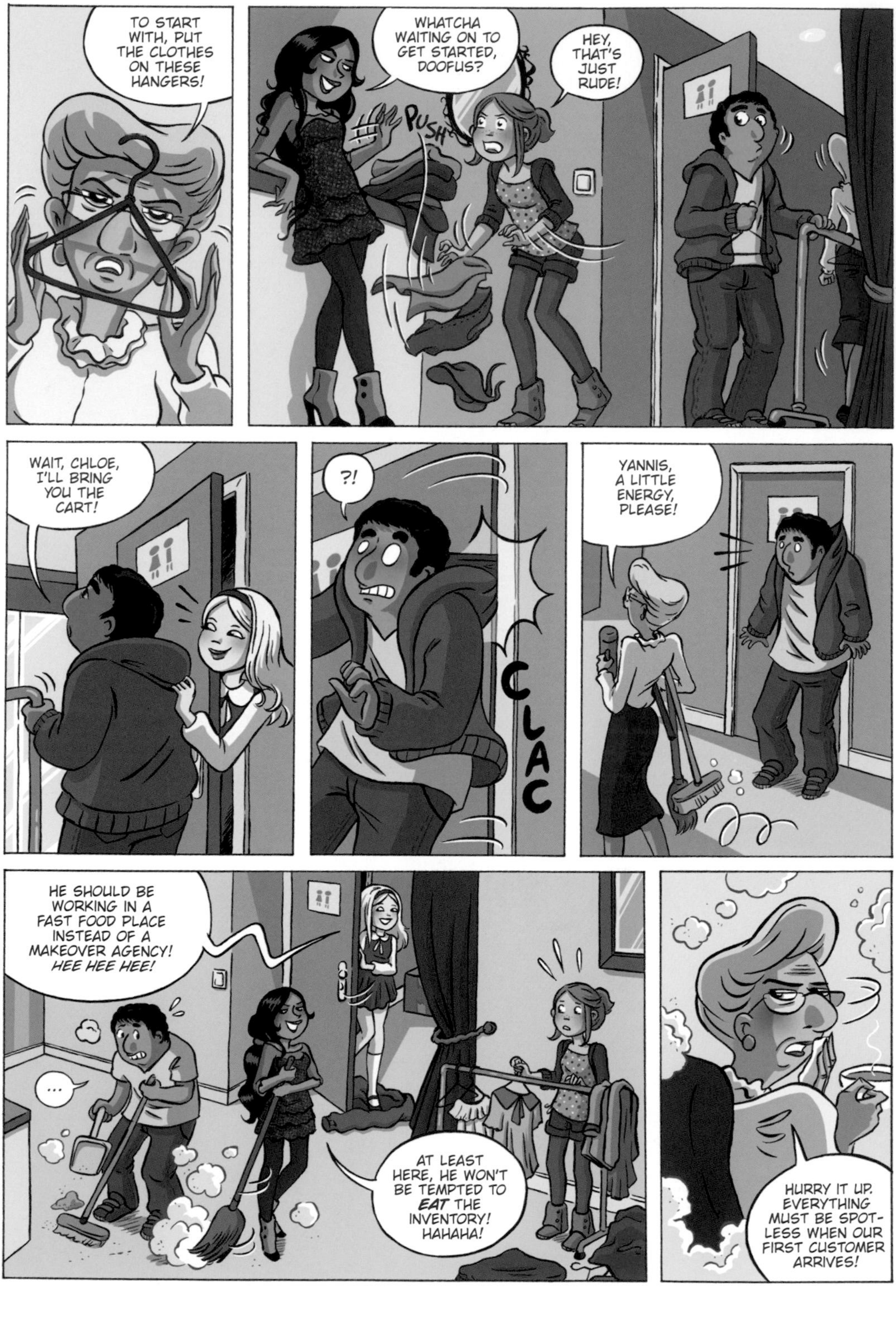
TO START WITH, PUT THE CLOTHES ON THESE HANGERS!
WHATCHA WAITING ON TO GET STARTED, DOOFUS?
PUSH
HEY, THAT'S JUST RUDE!
WAIT, CHLOE, I'LL BRING YOU THE CART!
?!
CLAC
YANNIS, A LITTLE ENERGY, PLEASE!
HE SHOULD BE WORKING IN A FAST FOOD PLACE INSTEAD OF A MAKEOVER AGENCY! HEE HEE HEE!
...
AT LEAST HERE, HE WON'T BE TEMPTED TO EAT THE INVENTORY! HAHAHA!
HURRY IT UP. EVERYTHING MUST BE SPOTLESS WHEN OUR FIRST CUSTOMER ARRIVES!

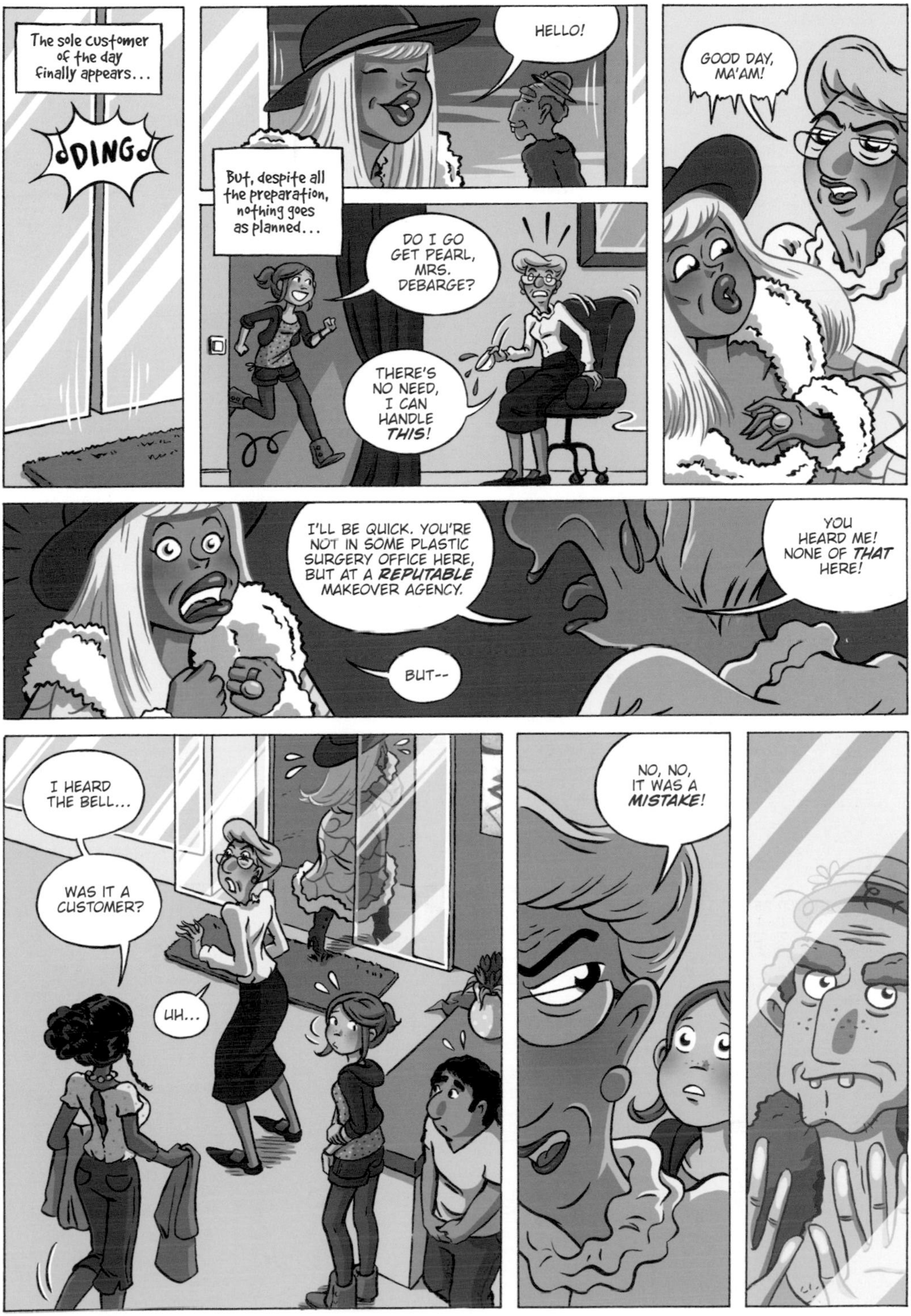
The sole customer of the day finally appears...
DING
HELLO!
GOOD DAY, MA'AM!
But, despite all the preparation, nothing goes as planned...
DO I GO GET PEARL, MRS. DEBARGE?
THERE'S NO NEED, I CAN HANDLE THIS!
I'LL BE QUICK. YOU'RE NOT IN SOME PLASTIC SURGERY OFFICE HERE, BUT AT A REPUTABLE MAKEOVER AGENCY.
BUT--
YOU HEARD ME! NONE OF THAT HERE!
I HEARD THE BELL...
WAS IT A CUSTOMER?
UH...
NO, NO, IT WAS A MISTAKE!

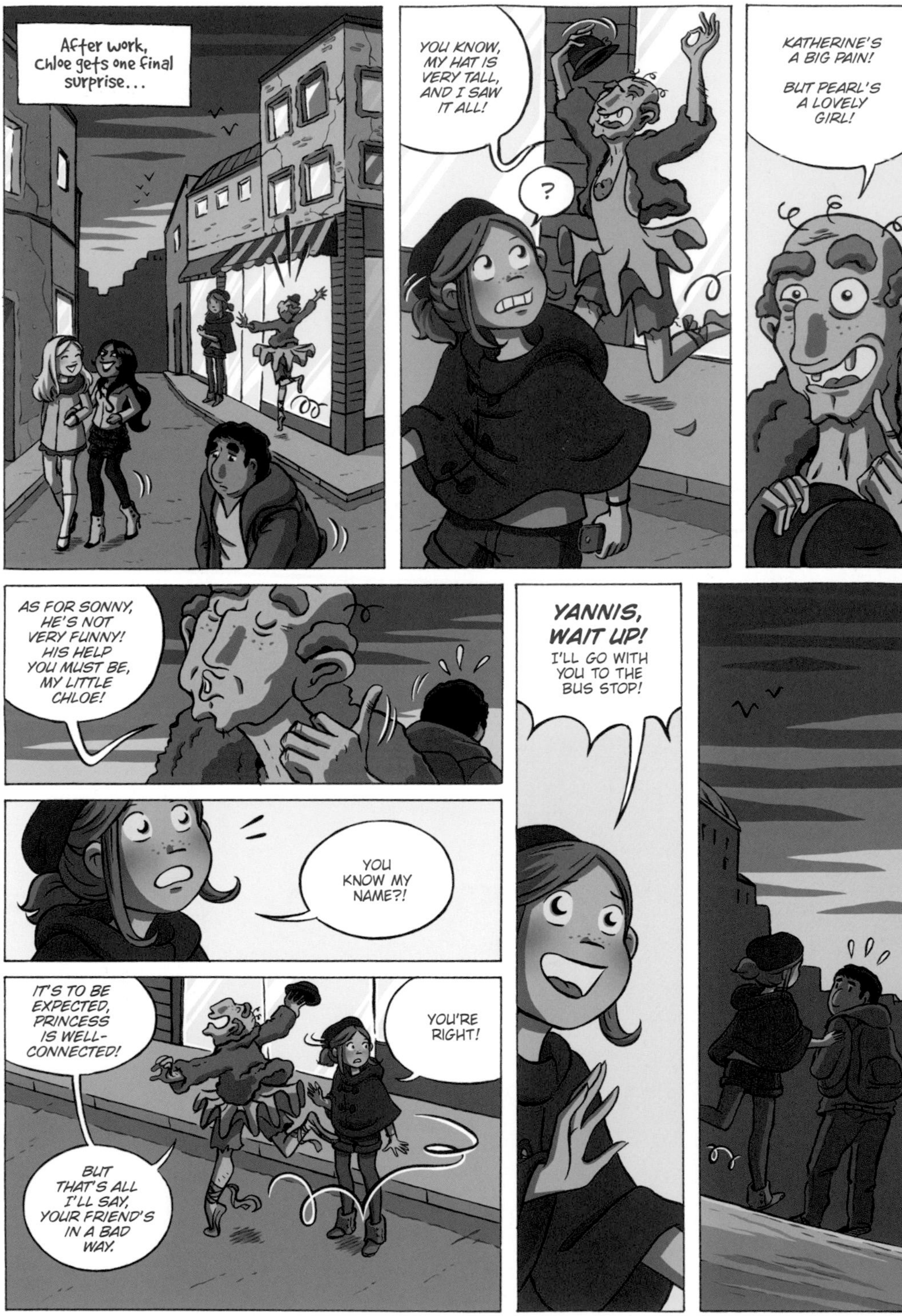
After work, Chloe gets one final surprise...
YOU KNOW, MY HAT IS VERY TALL, AND I SAW IT ALL!
?
KATHERINE'S A BIG PAIN!
BUT PEARL'S A LOVELY GIRL!
AS FOR SONNY, HE'S NOT VERY FUNNY! HIS HELP YOU MUST BE, MY LITTLE CHLOE!
YOU KNOW MY NAME?!
IT'S TO BE EXPECTED, PRINCESS IS WELL-CONNECTED!
BUT THAT'S ALL I'LL SAY, YOUR FRIEND'S IN A BAD WAY.
YOU'RE RIGHT!
YANNIS, WAIT UP!
I'LL GO WITH YOU TO THE BUS STOP!

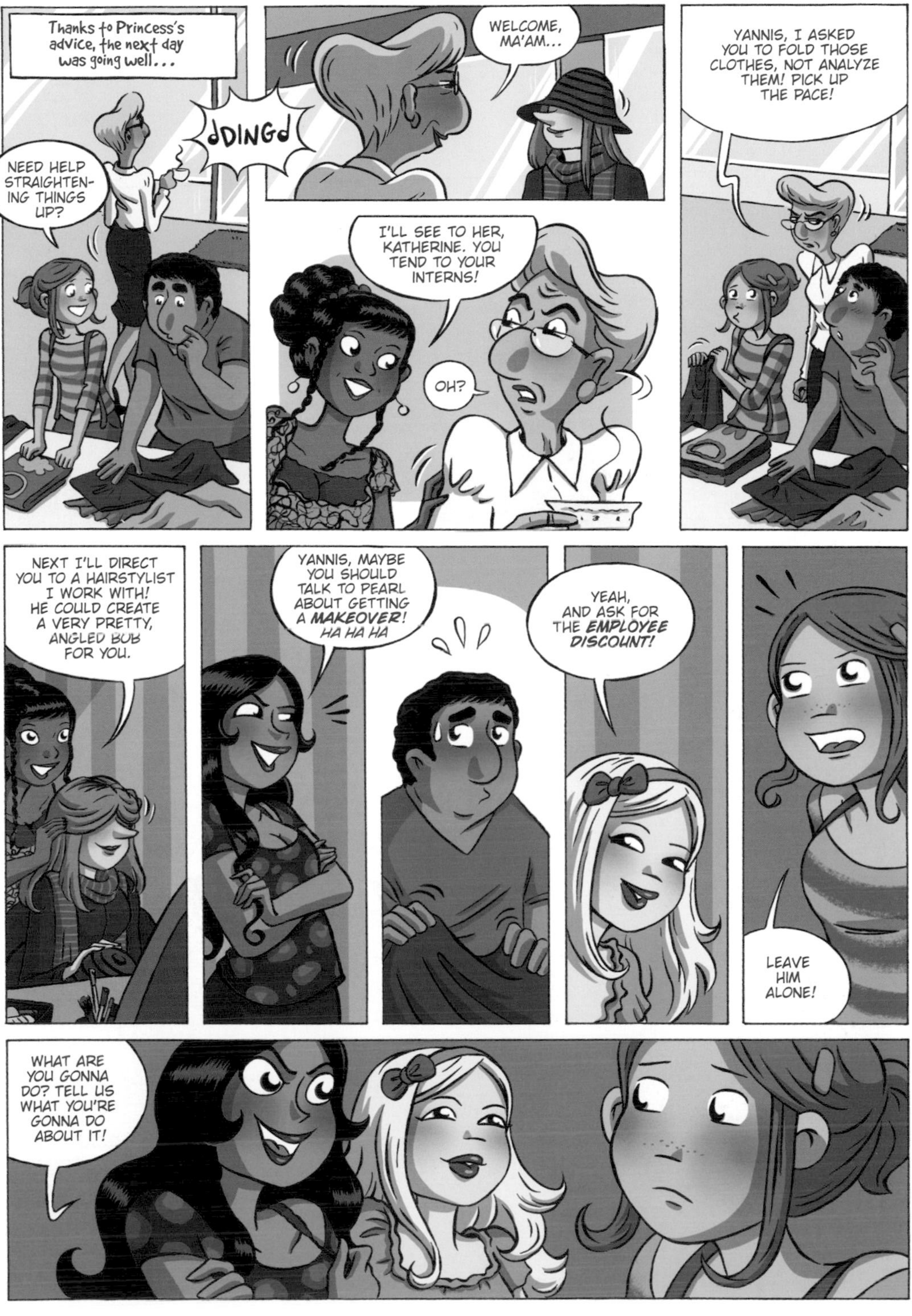
Thanks to Princess's advice, the next day was going well...
NEED HELP STRAIGHTENING THINGS UP?
DING
WELCOME, MA'AM...
I'LL SEE TO HER, KATHERINE. YOU TEND TO YOUR INTERNS!
OH?
YANNIS, I ASKED YOU TO FOLD THOSE CLOTHES, NOT ANALYZE THEM! PICK UP THE PACE!
NEXT I'LL DIRECT YOU TO A HAIRSTYLIST I WORK WITH! HE COULD CREATE A VERY PRETTY, ANGLED BOB FOR YOU.
YANNIS, MAYBE YOU SHOULD TALK TO PEARL ABOUT GETTING A MAKEOVER! HA HA HA
YEAH, AND ASK FOR THE EMPLOYEE DISCOUNT!
LEAVE HIM ALONE!
WHAT ARE YOU GONNA DO? TELL US WHAT YOU'RE GONNA DO ABOUT IT!

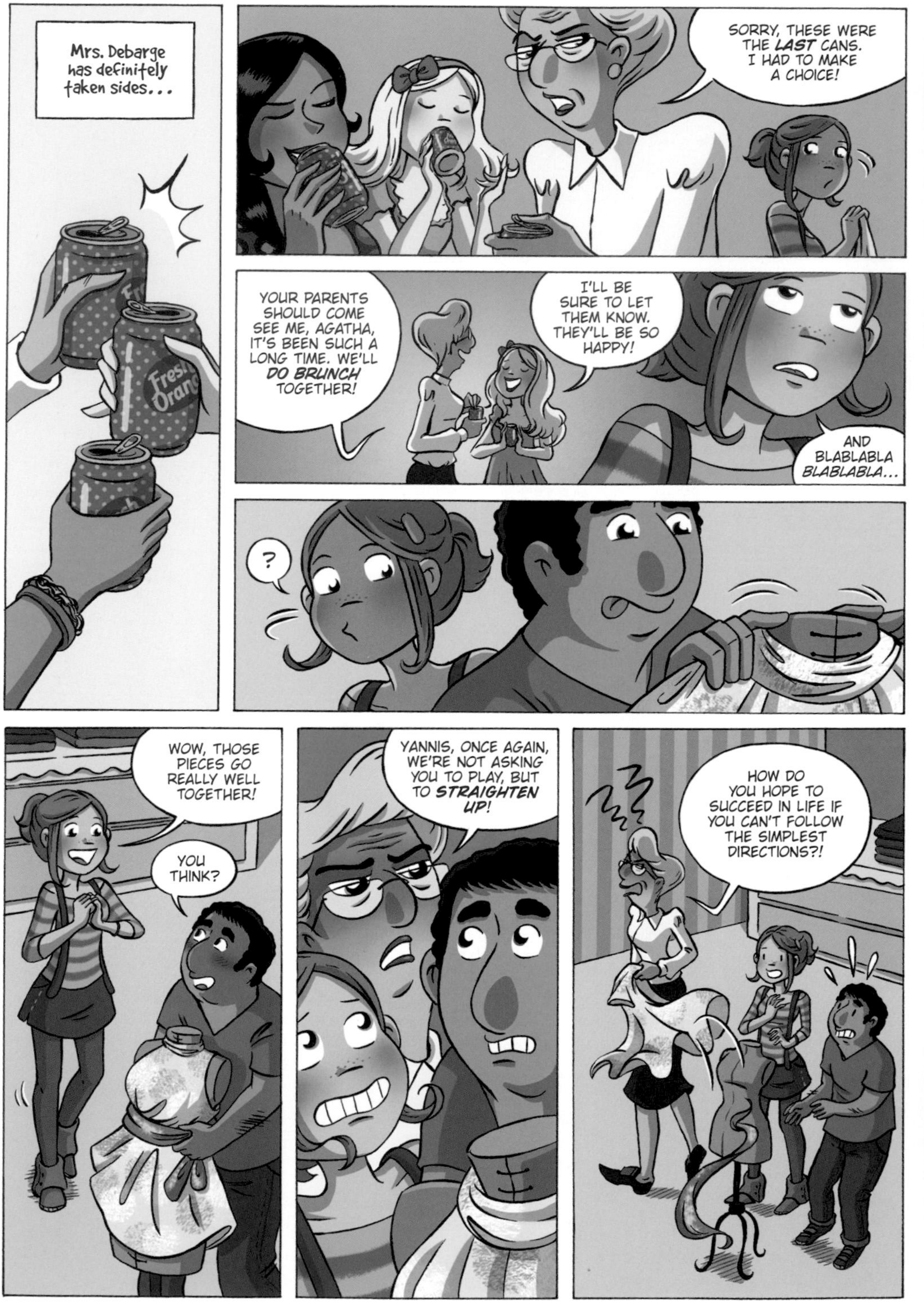
Mrs. Debarge has definitely taken sides...
Fresh Orange
SORRY, THESE WERE THE LAST CANS. I HAD TO MAKE A CHOICE!
YOUR PARENTS SHOULD COME SEE ME, AGATHA, IT'S BEEN SUCH A LONG TIME. WE'LL DO BRUNCH TOGETHER!
I'LL BE SURE TO LET THEM KNOW. THEY'LL BE SO HAPPY!
AND BLABLABLA BLABLABLA...
?
WOW, THOSE PIECES GO REALLY WELL TOGETHER!
YOU THINK?
YANNIS, ONCE AGAIN, WE'RE NOT ASKING YOU TO PLAY, BUT TO STRAIGHTEN UP!
HOW DO YOU HOPE TO SUCCEED IN LIFE IF YOU CAN'T FOLLOW THE SIMPLEST DIRECTIONS?!

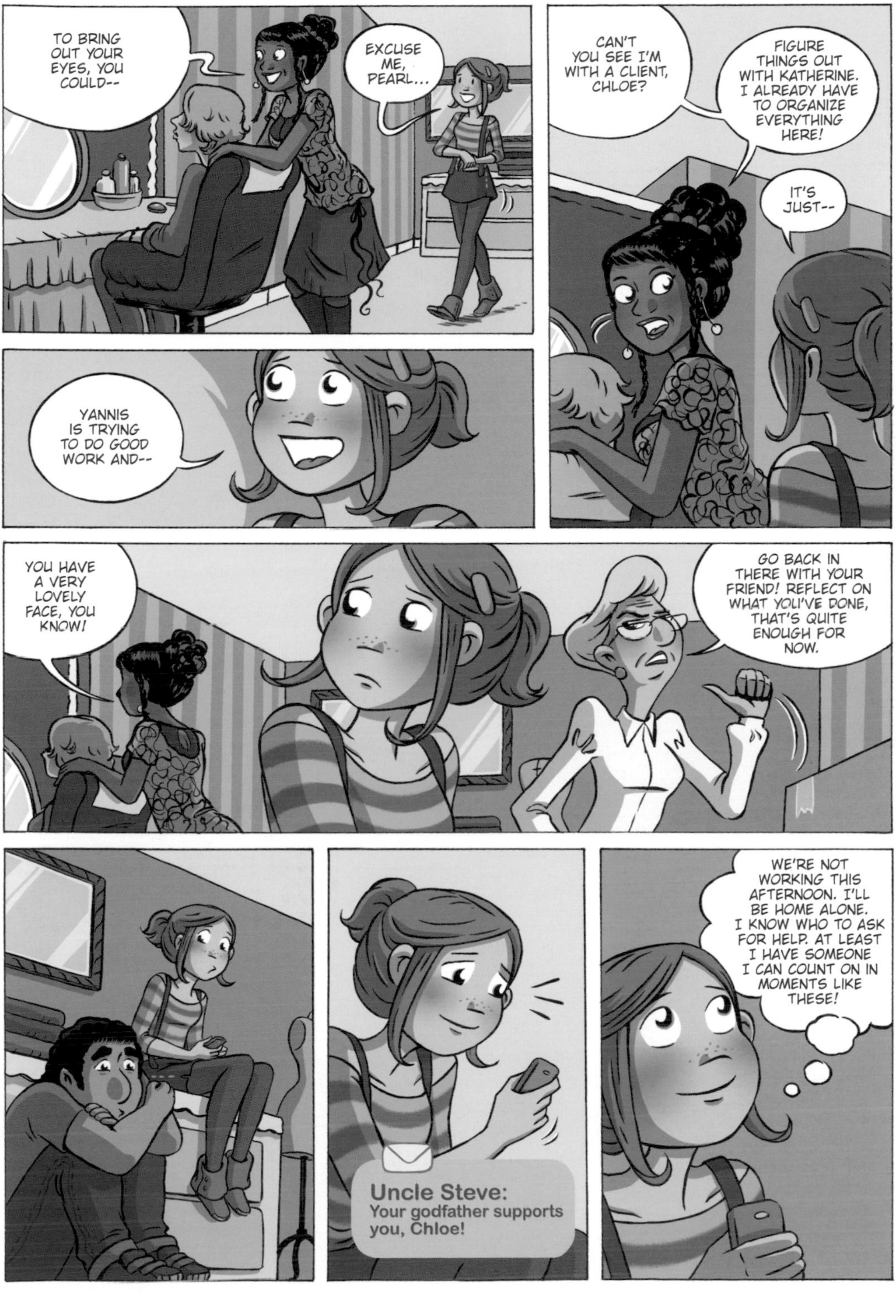
TO BRING OUT YOUR EYES, YOU COULD--
EXCUSE ME, PEARL...
CAN'T YOU SEE I'M WITH A CLIENT, CHLOE?
FIGURE THINGS OUT WITH KATHERINE. I ALREADY HAVE TO ORGANIZE EVERYTHING HERE!
IT'S JUST--
YANNIS IS TRYING TO DO GOOD WORK AND--
YOU HAVE A VERY LOVELY FACE, YOU KNOW!
GO BACK IN THERE WITH YOUR FRIEND! REFLECT ON WHAT YOU'VE DONE, THAT'S QUITE ENOUGH FOR NOW.
Uncle Steve:
Your godfather supports you, Chloe!
WE'RE NOT WORKING THIS AFTERNOON. I'LL BE HOME ALONE. I KNOW WHO TO ASK FOR HELP. AT LEAST I HAVE SOMEONE I CAN COUNT ON IN MOMENTS LIKE THESE!

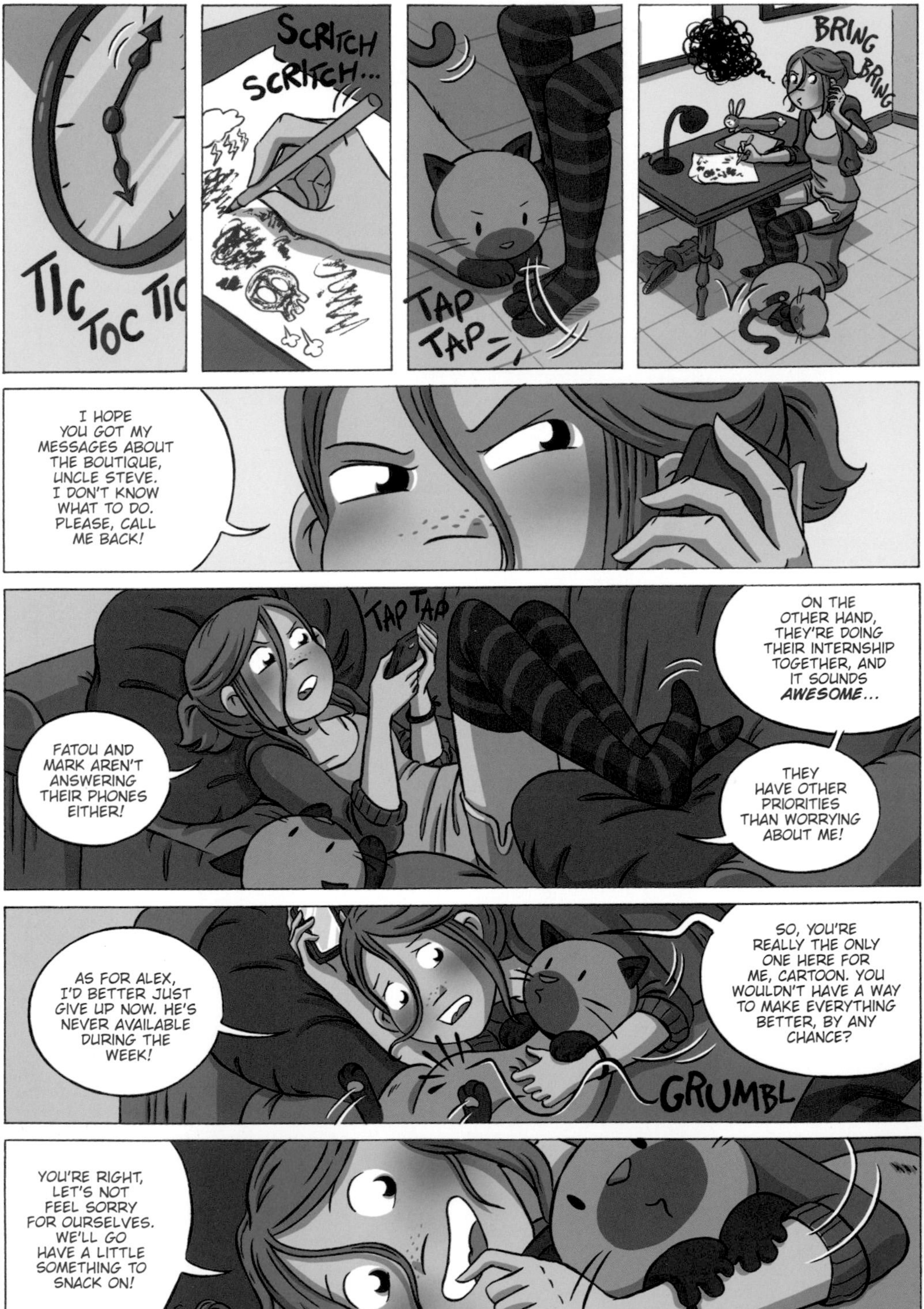

TIC TOC TIC
SCRITCH
SCRITCH...
TAP
TAP
BRING
BRING
I HOPE YOU GOT MY MESSAGES ABOUT THE BOUTIQUE, UNCLE STEVE. I DON'T KNOW WHAT TO DO. PLEASE, CALL ME BACK!
TAP TAP
FATOU AND MARK AREN'T ANSWERING THEIR PHONES EITHER!
ON THE OTHER HAND, THEY'RE DOING THEIR INTERNSHIP TOGETHER, AND IT SOUNDS AWESOME...
THEY HAVE OTHER PRIORITIES THAN WORRYING ABOUT ME!
AS FOR ALEX, I'D BETTER JUST GIVE UP NOW. HE'S NEVER AVAILABLE DURING THE WEEK!
SO, YOU'RE REALLY THE ONLY ONE HERE FOR ME, CARTOON. YOU WOULDN'T HAVE A WAY TO MAKE EVERYTHING BETTER, BY ANY CHANCE?
GRUMBL
YOU'RE RIGHT, LET'S NOT FEEL SORRY FOR OURSELVES. WE'LL GO HAVE A LITTLE SOMETHING TO SNACK ON!

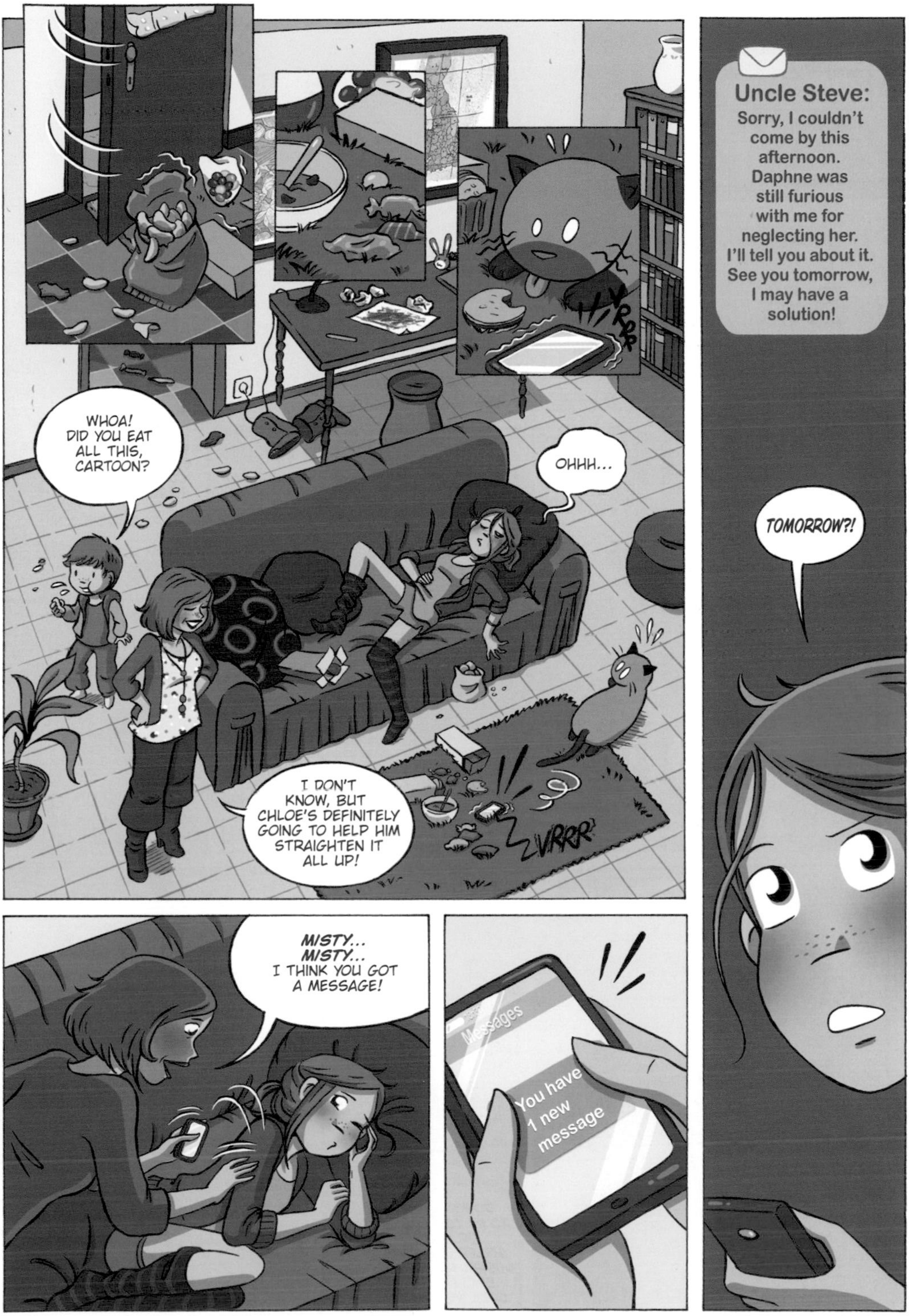
VRRR
WHOA! DID YOU EAT ALL THIS, CARTOON?
OHHH...
I DON'T KNOW, BUT CHLOE'S DEFINITELY GOING TO HELP HIM STRAIGHTEN IT ALL UP!
VRRR
MISTY... MISTY... I THINK YOU GOT A MESSAGE!
Messages
You have 1 new message
Uncle Steve:
Sorry, I couldn't come by this afternoon. Daphne was still furious with me for neglecting her. I'll tell you about it. See you tomorrow, I may have a solution!
TOMORROW?!

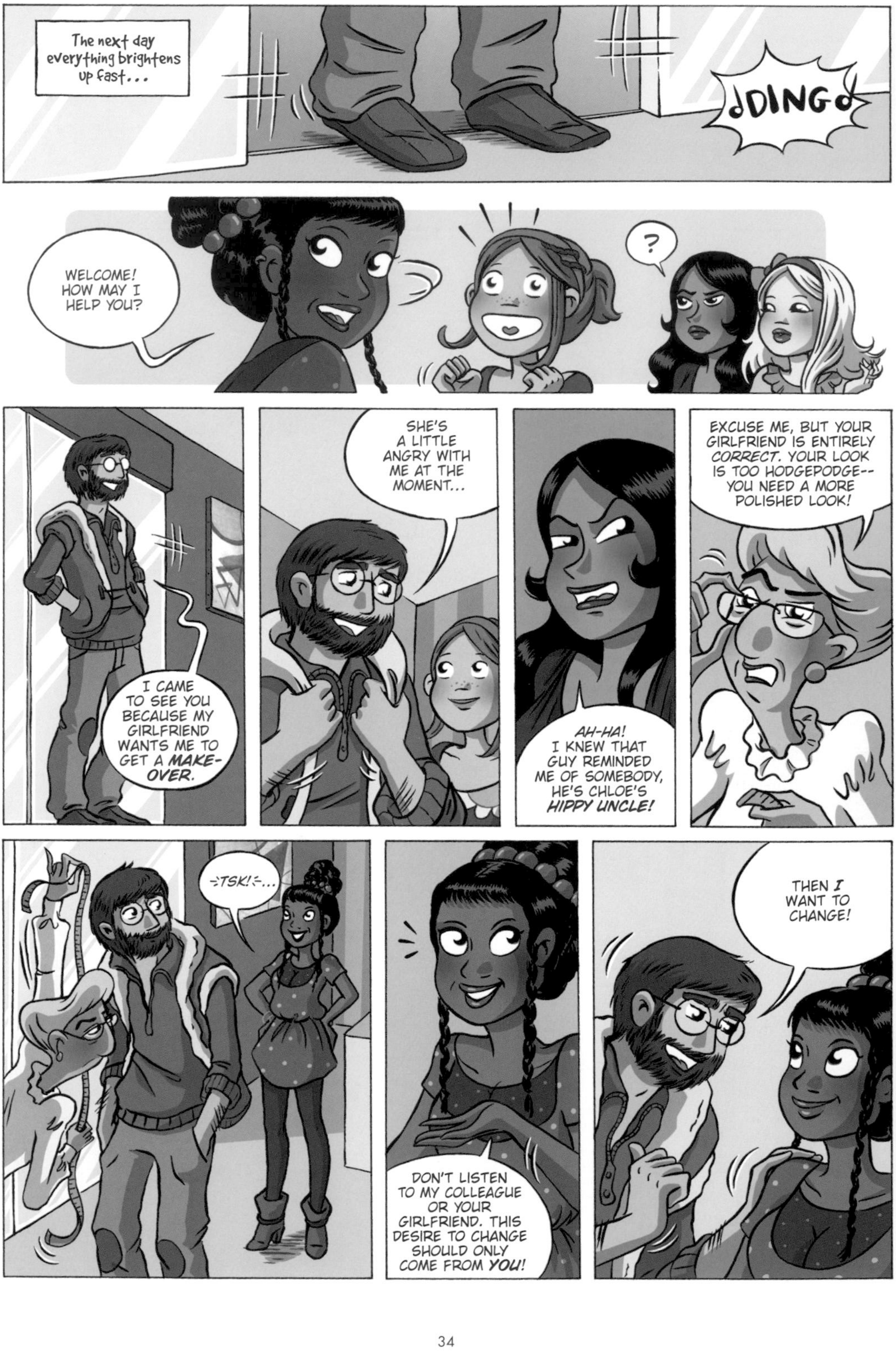
The next day everything brightens up fast...
DING
WELCOME! HOW MAY I HELP YOU?
?
I CAME TO SEE YOU BECAUSE MY GIRLFRIEND WANTS ME TO GET A **MAKE-OVER**.
SHE'S A LITTLE ANGRY WITH ME AT THE MOMENT...
AH-HA! I KNEW THAT GUY REMINDED ME OF SOMEBODY, HE'S CHLOE'S ***HIPPY UNCLE!***
EXCUSE ME, BUT YOUR GIRLFRIEND IS ENTIRELY *CORRECT*. YOUR LOOK IS TOO HODGEPODGE-- YOU NEED A MORE POLISHED LOOK!
TSK!...
DON'T LISTEN TO MY COLLEAGUE OR YOUR GIRLFRIEND. THIS DESIRE TO CHANGE SHOULD ONLY COME FROM ***YOU!***
THEN *I* WANT TO CHANGE!

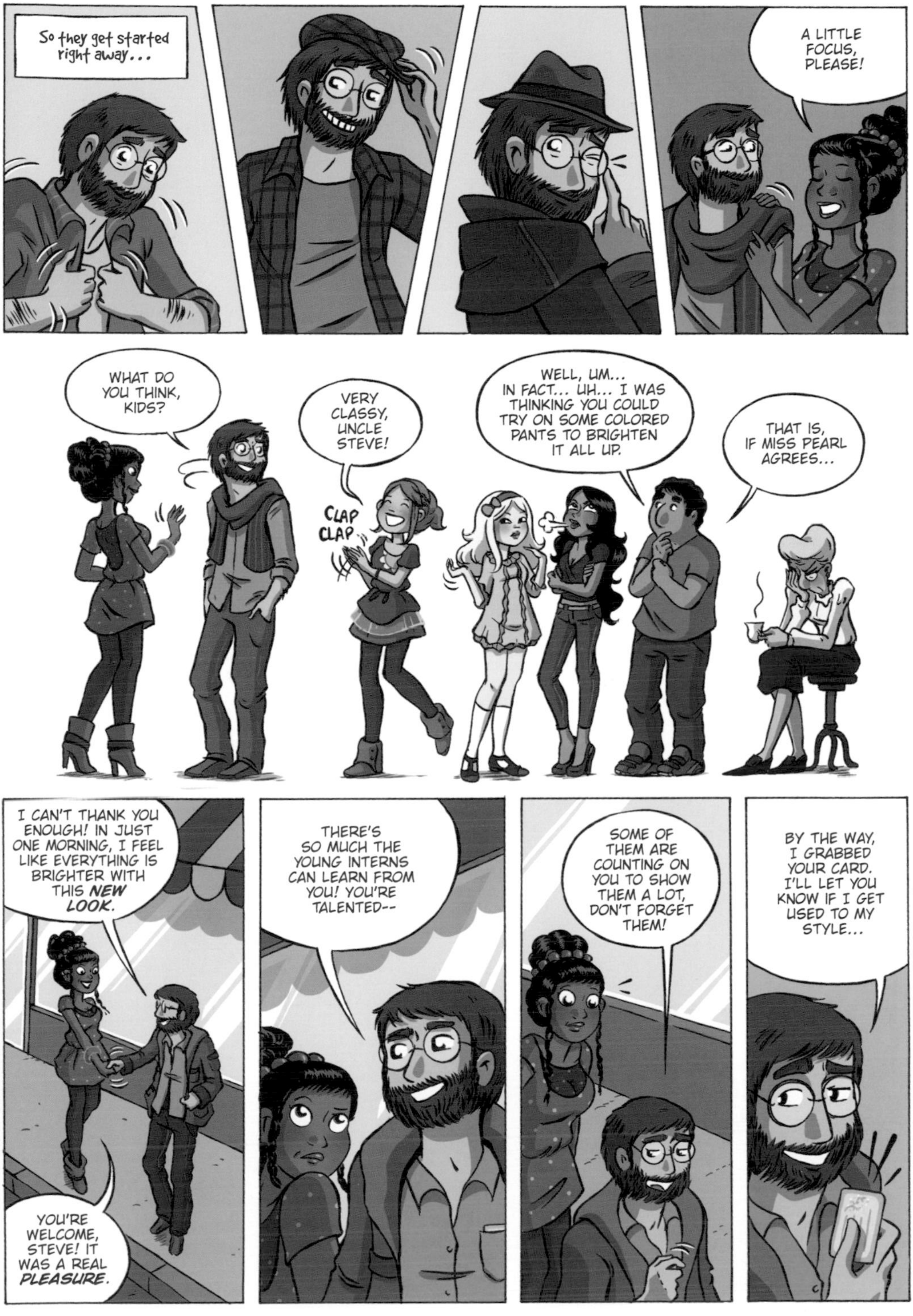
So they get started right away...
A LITTLE FOCUS, PLEASE!
WHAT DO YOU THINK, KIDS?
VERY CLASSY, UNCLE STEVE!
CLAP CLAP
WELL, UM... IN FACT... UH... I WAS THINKING YOU COULD TRY ON SOME COLORED PANTS TO BRIGHTEN IT ALL UP.
THAT IS, IF MISS PEARL AGREES...
I CAN'T THANK YOU ENOUGH! IN JUST ONE MORNING, I FEEL LIKE EVERYTHING IS BRIGHTER WITH THIS NEW LOOK.
YOU'RE WELCOME, STEVE! IT WAS A REAL PLEASURE.
THERE'S SO MUCH THE YOUNG INTERNS CAN LEARN FROM YOU! YOU'RE TALENTED--
SOME OF THEM ARE COUNTING ON YOU TO SHOW THEM A LOT, DON'T FORGET THEM!
BY THE WAY, I GRABBED YOUR CARD. I'LL LET YOU KNOW IF I GET USED TO MY STYLE...

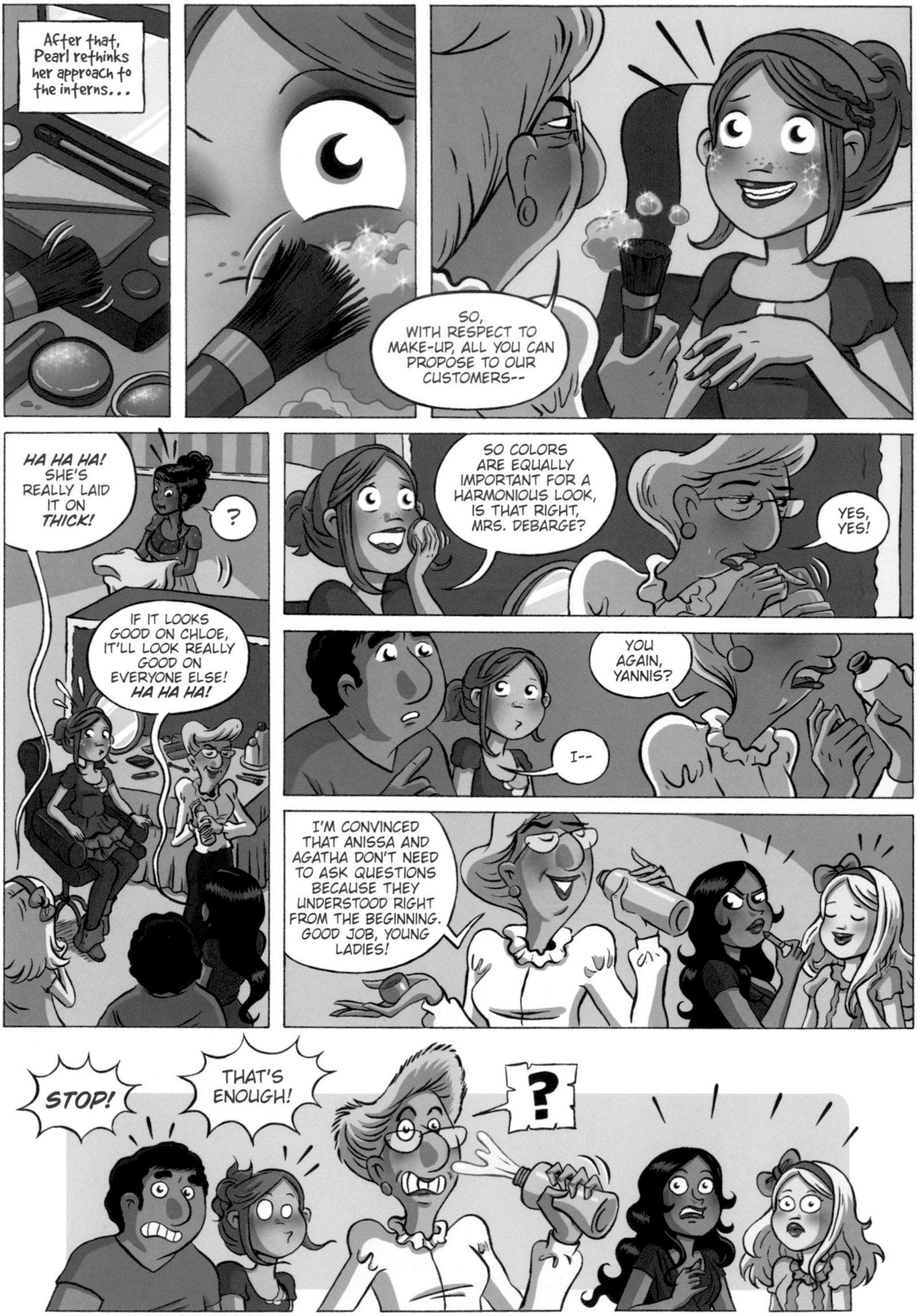
After that, Pearl rethinks her approach to the interns...
SO, WITH RESPECT TO MAKE-UP, ALL YOU CAN PROPOSE TO OUR CUSTOMERS--
HA HA HA! SHE'S REALLY LAID IT ON THICK!
?
IF IT LOOKS GOOD ON CHLOE, IT'LL LOOK REALLY GOOD ON EVERYONE ELSE! HA HA HA!
SO COLORS ARE EQUALLY IMPORTANT FOR A HARMONIOUS LOOK, IS THAT RIGHT, MRS. DEBARGE?
YES, YES!
YOU AGAIN, YANNIS?
I--
I'M CONVINCED THAT ANISSA AND AGATHA DON'T NEED TO ASK QUESTIONS BECAUSE THEY UNDERSTOOD RIGHT FROM THE BEGINNING. GOOD JOB, YOUNG LADIES!
STOP!
THAT'S ENOUGH!
?

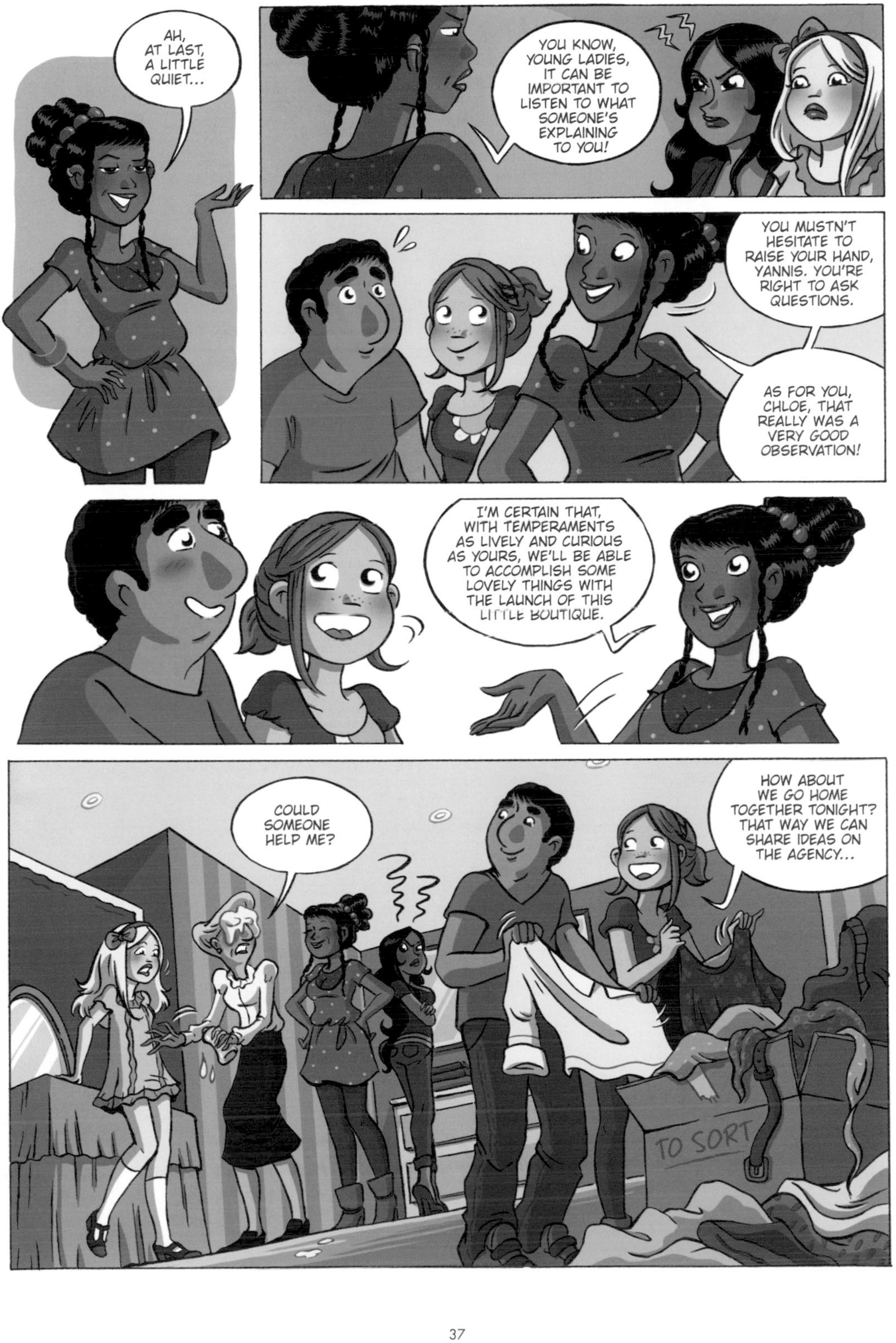
AH, AT LAST, A LITTLE QUIET...
YOU KNOW, YOUNG LADIES, IT CAN BE IMPORTANT TO LISTEN TO WHAT SOMEONE'S EXPLAINING TO YOU!
YOU MUSTN'T HESITATE TO RAISE YOUR HAND, YANNIS. YOU'RE RIGHT TO ASK QUESTIONS.
AS FOR YOU, CHLOE, THAT REALLY WAS A VERY GOOD OBSERVATION!
I'M CERTAIN THAT, WITH TEMPERAMENTS AS LIVELY AND CURIOUS AS YOURS, WE'LL BE ABLE TO ACCOMPLISH SOME LOVELY THINGS WITH THE LAUNCH OF THIS LITTLE BOUTIQUE.
COULD SOMEONE HELP ME?
HOW ABOUT WE GO HOME TOGETHER TONIGHT? THAT WAY WE CAN SHARE IDEAS ON THE AGENCY...
TO SORT

Last name: BLIN
First name: Chloe
Grade: 9th grade, Group B

Internship Report

School: G. Brassens Middle School
Internship supervisor: Mrs. DEBARGE

↳ *Not for much longer, it seems!* :)

What I appreciate:

(awful)

-Ditching those uniforms.
-The team spirit.
-The wise advice of "Princess."

→ *Thanks, Miss Pearl!* :)

"Princess" has a strange look, but he really helped me.
OH YEAH! →

Long live Princess

(+ Uncle Steve & others, of course!)

What I don't like:

-Uninteresting tasks:

 +  +

Emptying boxes — Hanging clothing — Sweeping

= *the three winners*

-Gratuitous meanness.

 +  +

= *The three winners, redux!*

What I'd have liked to have done:

-Get move involved.
-Help Yannis more.

} *I just have to get all of this organized!*
Hard work always ends up paying off!
LET'S GO !!!

Certainties

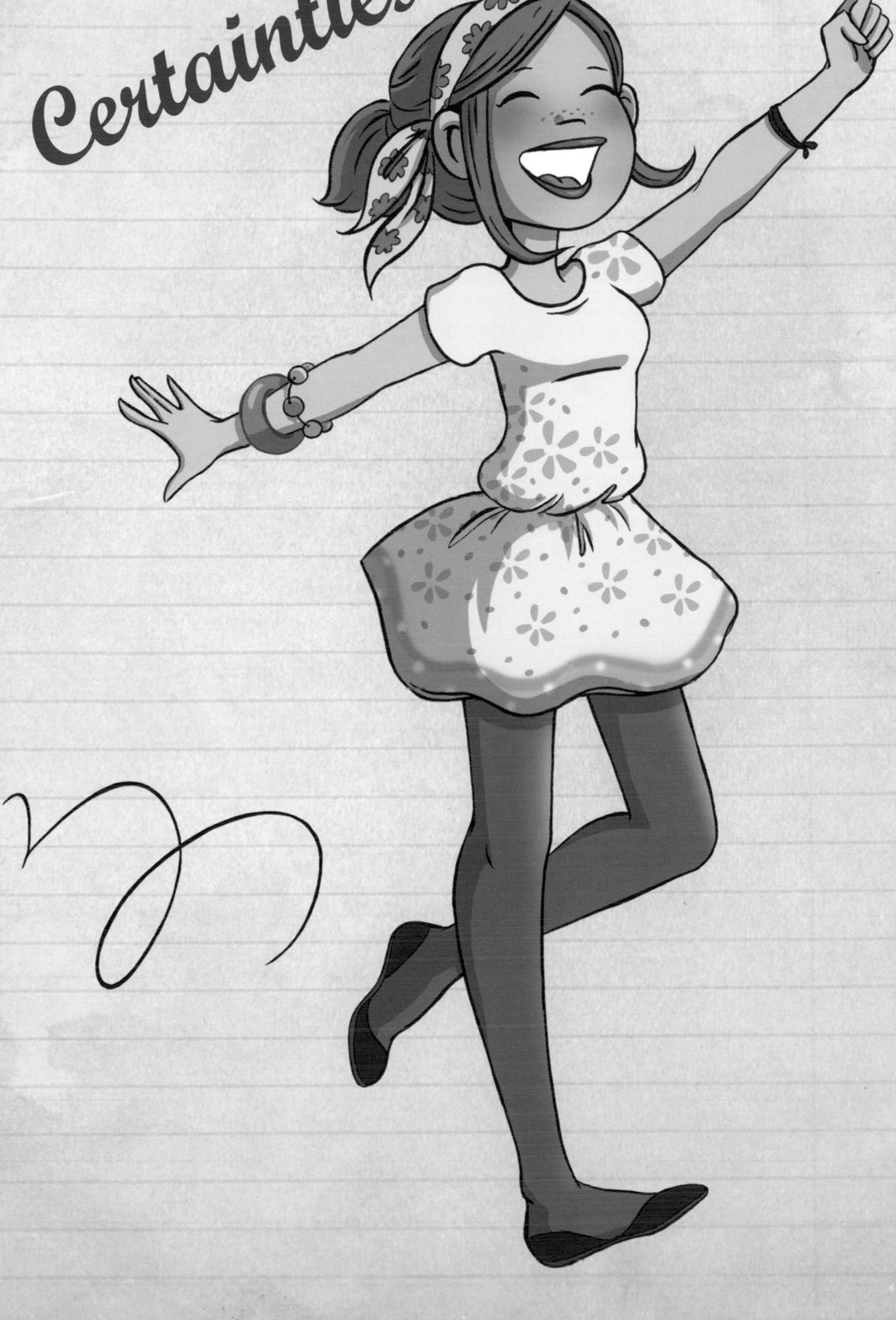

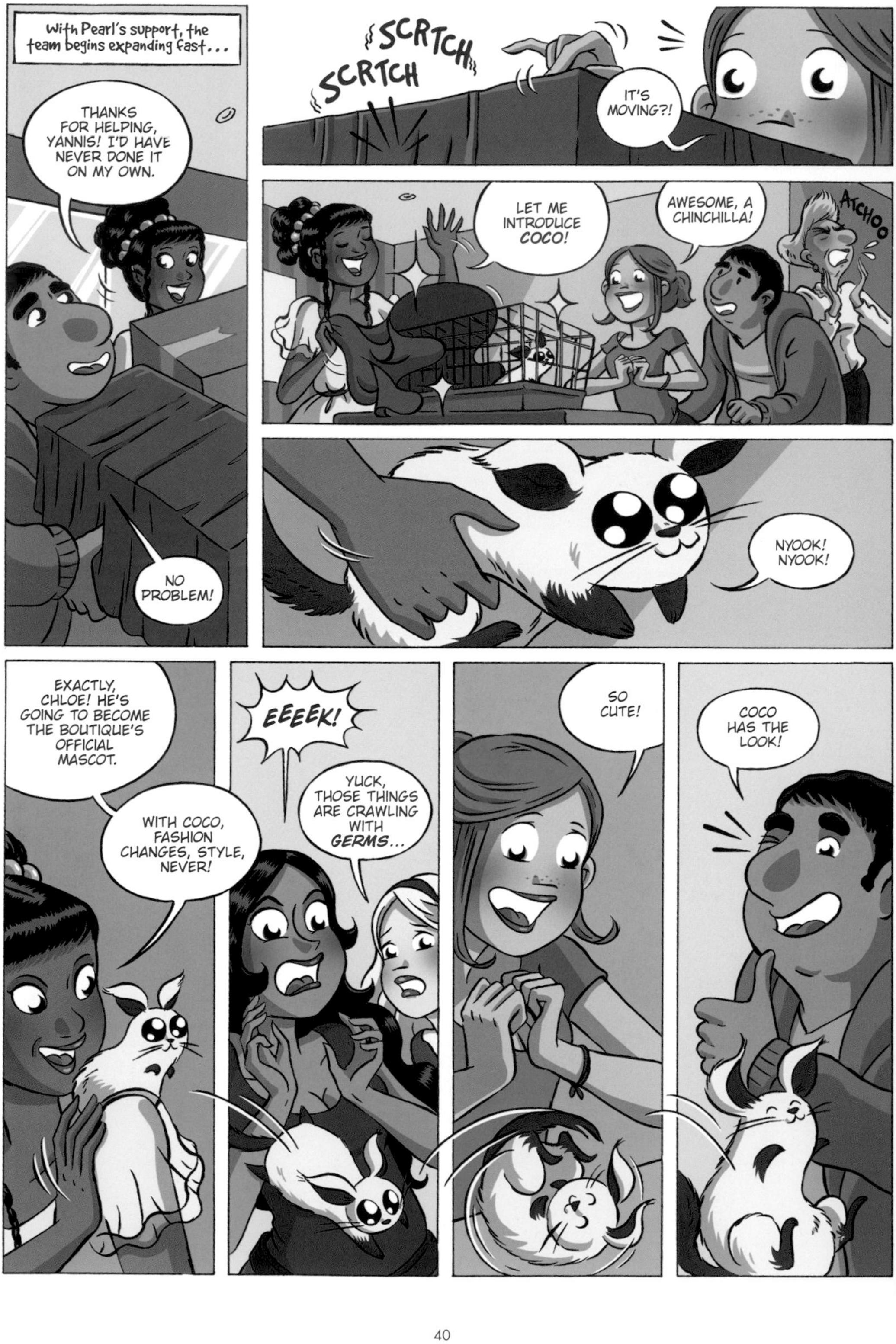
With Pearl's support, the team begins expanding fast...
THANKS FOR HELPING, YANNIS! I'D HAVE NEVER DONE IT ON MY OWN.
NO PROBLEM!
SCRTCH
SCRTCH
IT'S MOVING?!
LET ME INTRODUCE COCO!
AWESOME, A CHINCHILLA!
ATCHOO
NYOOK! NYOOK!
EXACTLY, CHLOE! HE'S GOING TO BECOME THE BOUTIQUE'S OFFICIAL MASCOT.
WITH COCO, FASHION CHANGES, STYLE, NEVER!
EEEEK!
YUCK, THOSE THINGS ARE CRAWLING WITH GERMS...
SO CUTE!
COCO HAS THE LOOK!

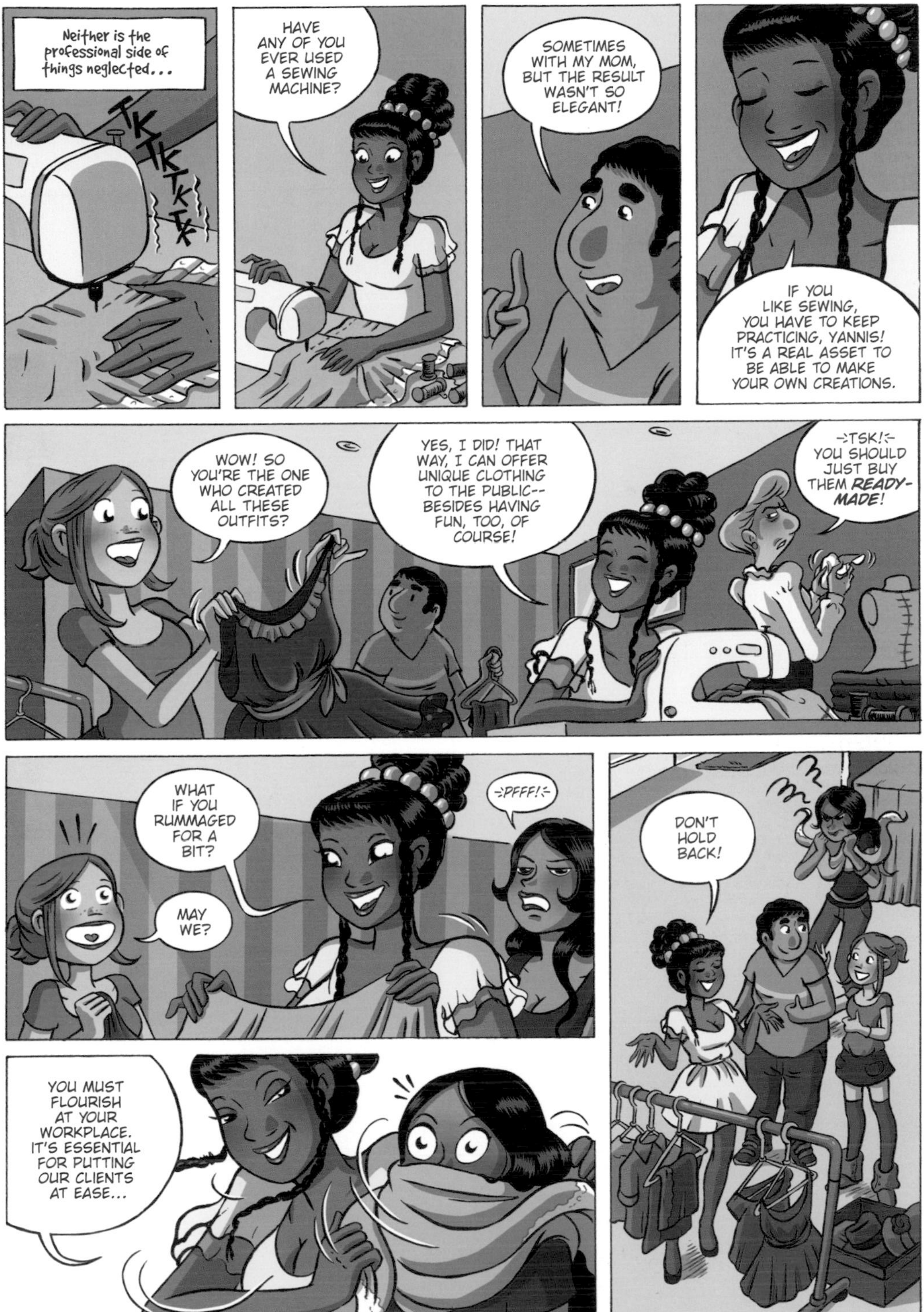
Neither is the professional side of things neglected...
TKTKTKTK
HAVE ANY OF YOU EVER USED A SEWING MACHINE?
SOMETIMES WITH MY MOM, BUT THE RESULT WASN'T SO ELEGANT!
IF YOU LIKE SEWING, YOU HAVE TO KEEP PRACTICING, YANNIS! IT'S A REAL ASSET TO BE ABLE TO MAKE YOUR OWN CREATIONS.
WOW! SO YOU'RE THE ONE WHO CREATED ALL THESE OUTFITS?
YES, I DID! THAT WAY, I CAN OFFER UNIQUE CLOTHING TO THE PUBLIC-- BESIDES HAVING FUN, TOO, OF COURSE!
TSK! YOU SHOULD JUST BUY THEM READY-MADE!
WHAT IF YOU RUMMAGED FOR A BIT?
MAY WE?
PFFF!
DON'T HOLD BACK!
YOU MUST FLOURISH AT YOUR WORKPLACE. IT'S ESSENTIAL FOR PUTTING OUR CLIENTS AT EASE...

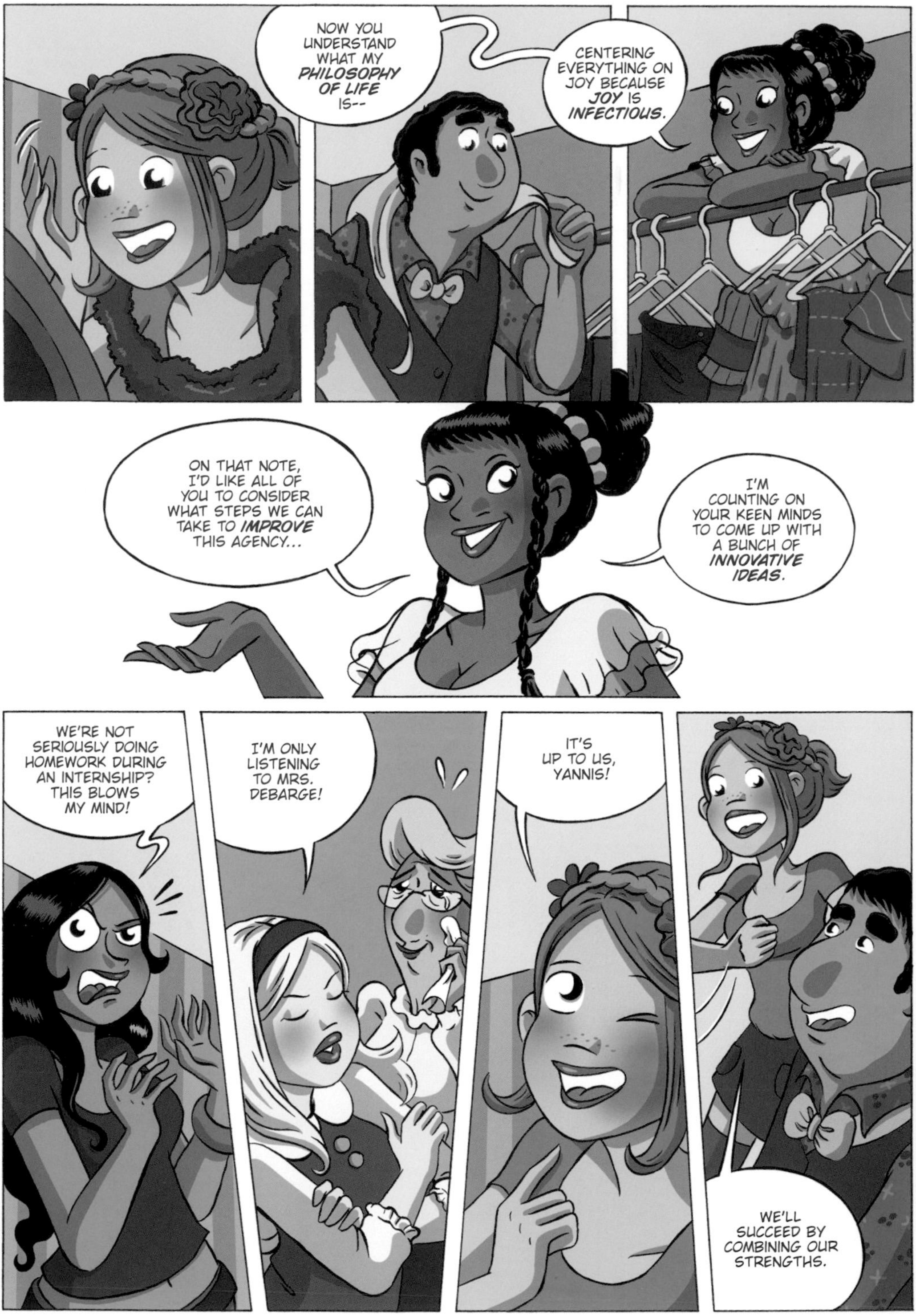
NOW YOU UNDERSTAND WHAT MY PHILOSOPHY OF LIFE IS--
CENTERING EVERYTHING ON JOY BECAUSE JOY IS INFECTIOUS.
ON THAT NOTE, I'D LIKE ALL OF YOU TO CONSIDER WHAT STEPS WE CAN TAKE TO IMPROVE THIS AGENCY...
I'M COUNTING ON YOUR KEEN MINDS TO COME UP WITH A BUNCH OF INNOVATIVE IDEAS.
WE'RE NOT SERIOUSLY DOING HOMEWORK DURING AN INTERNSHIP? THIS BLOWS MY MIND!
I'M ONLY LISTENING TO MRS. DEBARGE!
IT'S UP TO US, YANNIS!
WE'LL SUCCEED BY COMBINING OUR STRENGTHS.

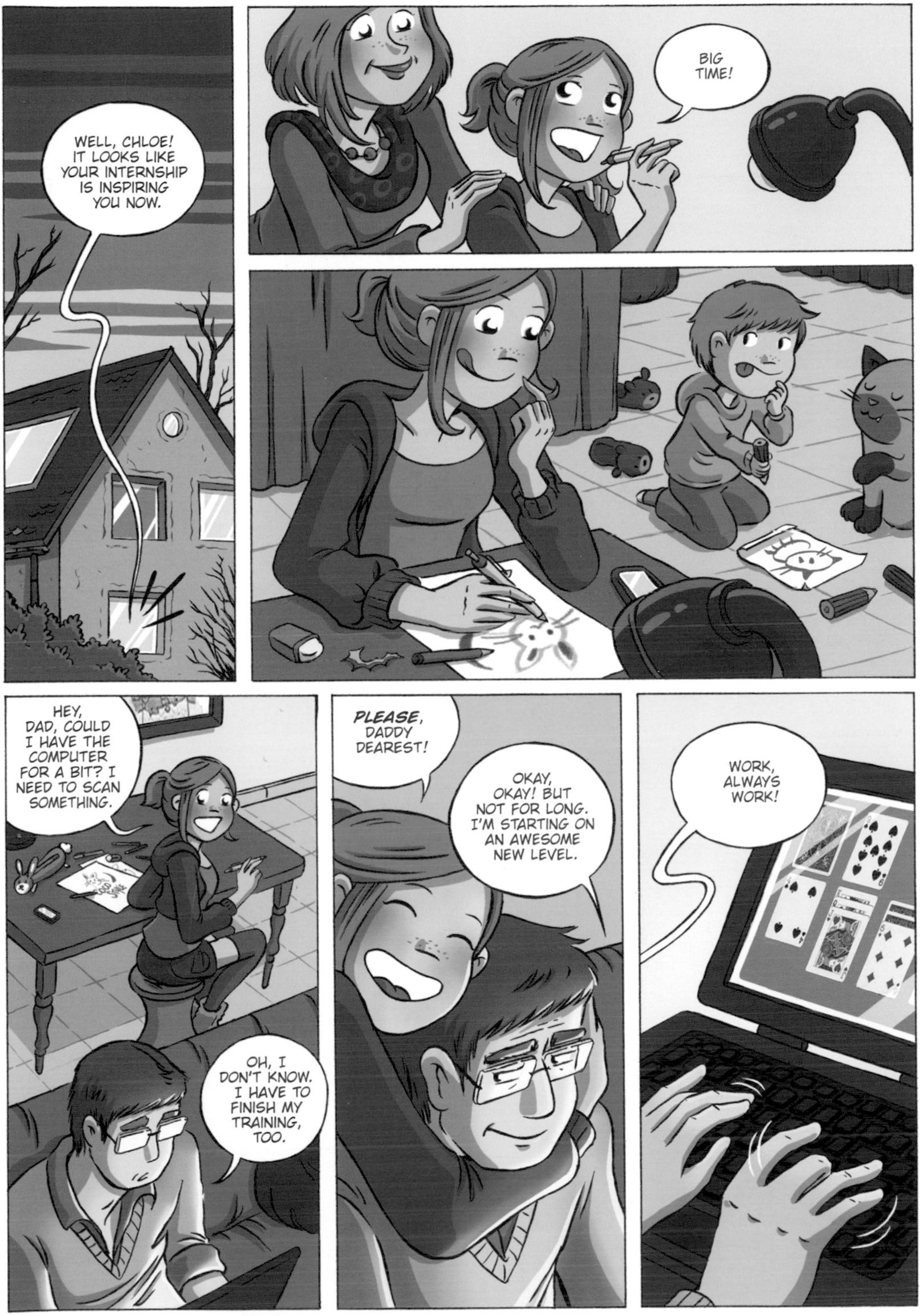
WELL, CHLOE! IT LOOKS LIKE YOUR INTERNSHIP IS INSPIRING YOU NOW.
BIG TIME!
HEY, DAD, COULD I HAVE THE COMPUTER FOR A BIT? I NEED TO SCAN SOMETHING.
OH, I DON'T KNOW. I HAVE TO FINISH MY TRAINING, TOO.
PLEASE, DADDY DEAREST!
OKAY, OKAY! BUT NOT FOR LONG. I'M STARTING ON AN AWESOME NEW LEVEL.
WORK, ALWAYS WORK!

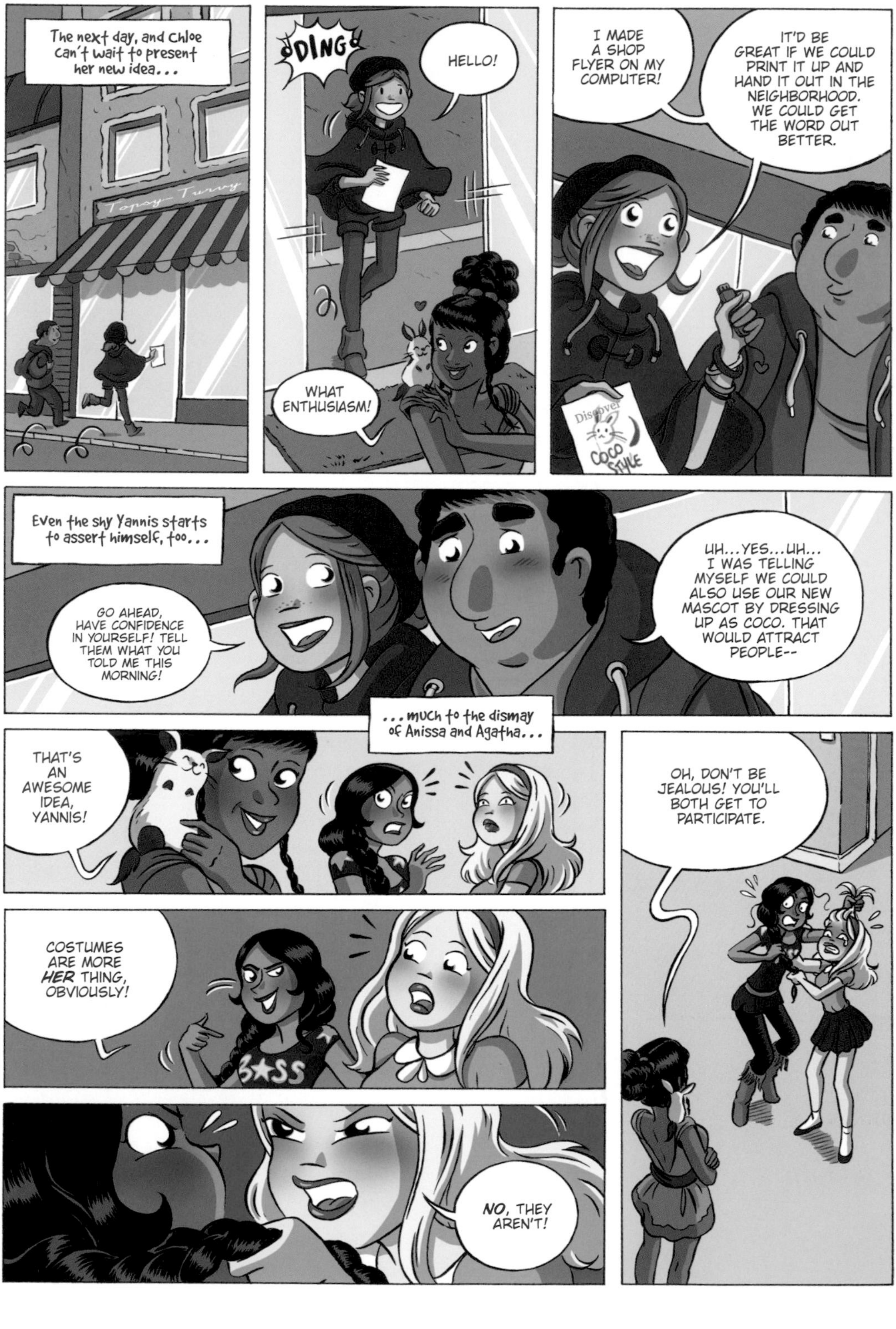

The next day, and Chloe can't wait to present her new idea...
DING
HELLO!
WHAT ENTHUSIASM!
Topsy-Turvy
I MADE A SHOP FLYER ON MY COMPUTER!
IT'D BE GREAT IF WE COULD PRINT IT UP AND HAND IT OUT IN THE NEIGHBORHOOD. WE COULD GET THE WORD OUT BETTER.
Discover COCO STYLE
Even the shy Yannis starts to assert himself, too...
GO AHEAD, HAVE CONFIDENCE IN YOURSELF! TELL THEM WHAT YOU TOLD ME THIS MORNING!
UH...YES...UH... I WAS TELLING MYSELF WE COULD ALSO USE OUR NEW MASCOT BY DRESSING UP AS COCO. THAT WOULD ATTRACT PEOPLE--
...much to the dismay of Anissa and Agatha...
THAT'S AN AWESOME IDEA, YANNIS!
COSTUMES ARE MORE *HER* THING, OBVIOUSLY!
B★SS
NO, THEY AREN'T!
OH, DON'T BE JEALOUS! YOU'LL BOTH GET TO PARTICIPATE.

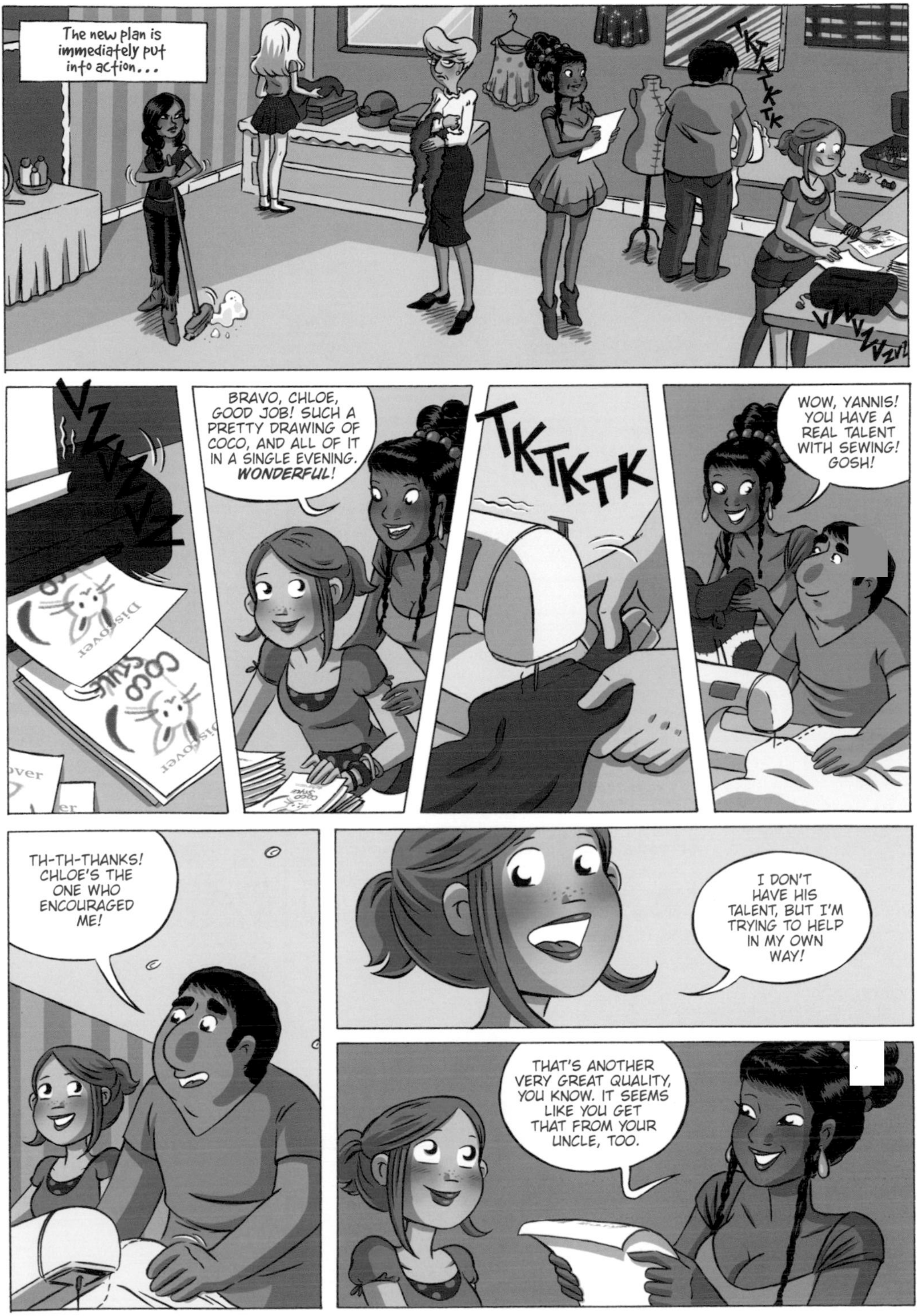
The new plan is immediately put into action...
TKTKTKTK
VVVVZVZ
VZZVVZZ
COCO STYLE
Discover
BRAVO, CHLOE, GOOD JOB! SUCH A PRETTY DRAWING OF COCO, AND ALL OF IT IN A SINGLE EVENING. WONDERFUL!
TKTKTK
WOW, YANNIS! YOU HAVE A REAL TALENT WITH SEWING! GOSH!
TH-TH-THANKS! CHLOE'S THE ONE WHO ENCOURAGED ME!
I DON'T HAVE HIS TALENT, BUT I'M TRYING TO HELP IN MY OWN WAY!
THAT'S ANOTHER VERY GREAT QUALITY, YOU KNOW. IT SEEMS LIKE YOU GET THAT FROM YOUR UNCLE, TOO.

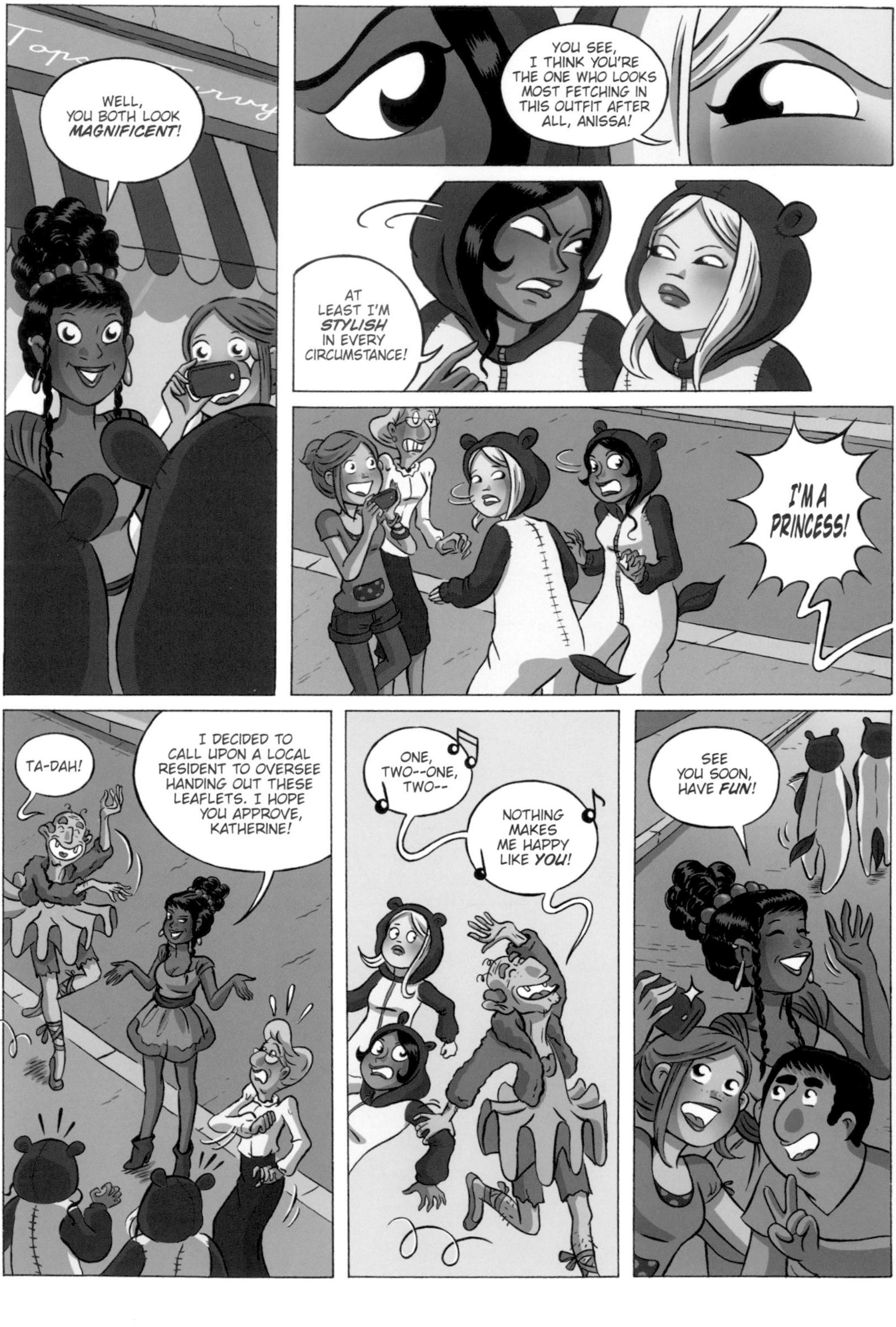
WELL, YOU BOTH LOOK MAGNIFICENT!
YOU SEE, I THINK YOU'RE THE ONE WHO LOOKS MOST FETCHING IN THIS OUTFIT AFTER ALL, ANISSA!
AT LEAST I'M STYLISH IN EVERY CIRCUMSTANCE!
I'M A PRINCESS!
TA-DAH!
I DECIDED TO CALL UPON A LOCAL RESIDENT TO OVERSEE HANDING OUT THESE LEAFLETS. I HOPE YOU APPROVE, KATHERINE!
ONE, TWO--ONE, TWO--
NOTHING MAKES ME HAPPY LIKE YOU!
SEE YOU SOON, HAVE FUN!

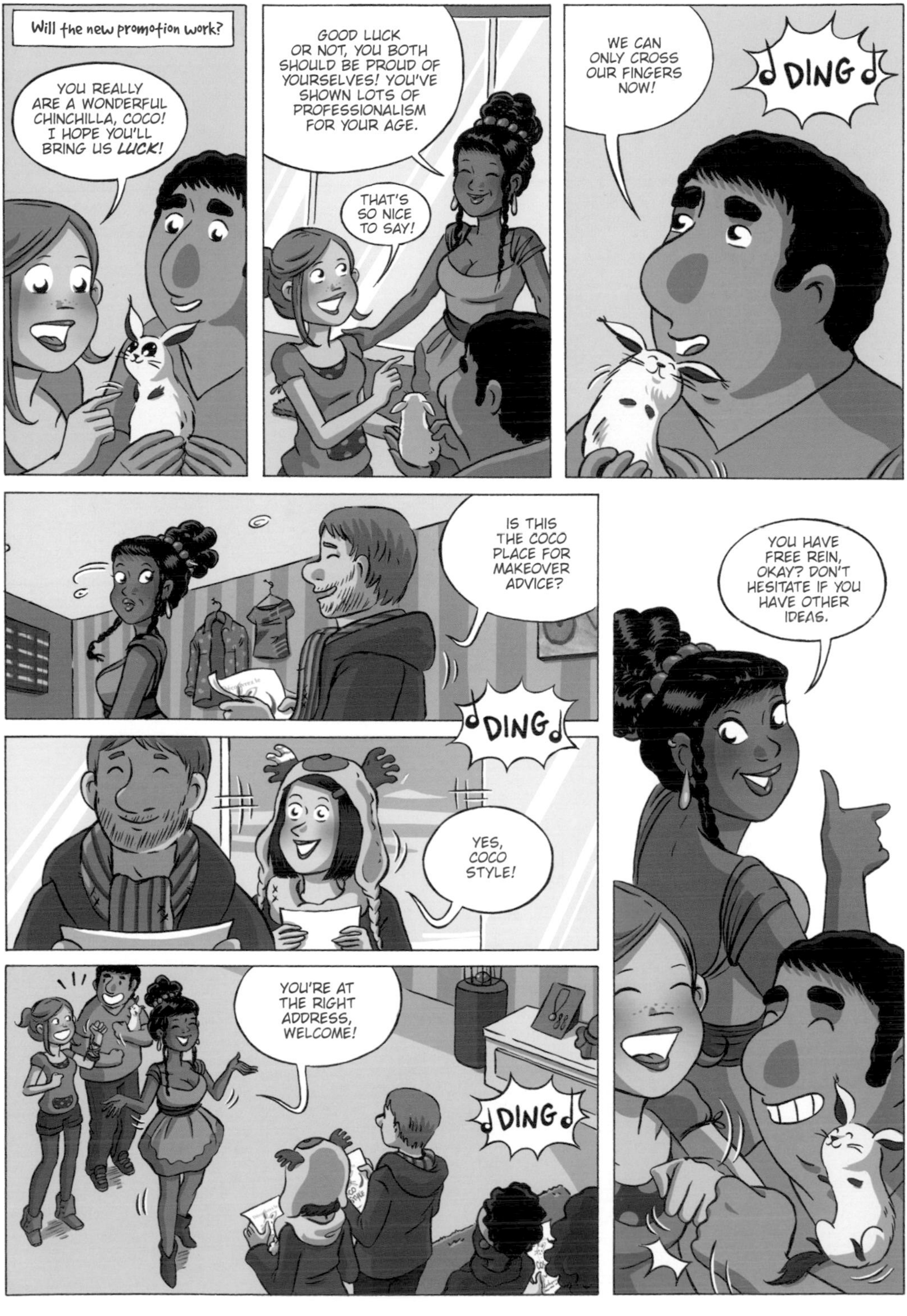
Will the new promotion work?
YOU REALLY ARE A WONDERFUL CHINCHILLA, COCO! I HOPE YOU'LL BRING US LUCK!
GOOD LUCK OR NOT, YOU BOTH SHOULD BE PROUD OF YOURSELVES! YOU'VE SHOWN LOTS OF PROFESSIONALISM FOR YOUR AGE.
THAT'S SO NICE TO SAY!
WE CAN ONLY CROSS OUR FINGERS NOW!
DING
IS THIS THE COCO PLACE FOR MAKEOVER ADVICE?
DING
YES, COCO STYLE!
YOU'RE AT THE RIGHT ADDRESS, WELCOME!
DING
YOU HAVE FREE REIN, OKAY? DON'T HESITATE IF YOU HAVE OTHER IDEAS.

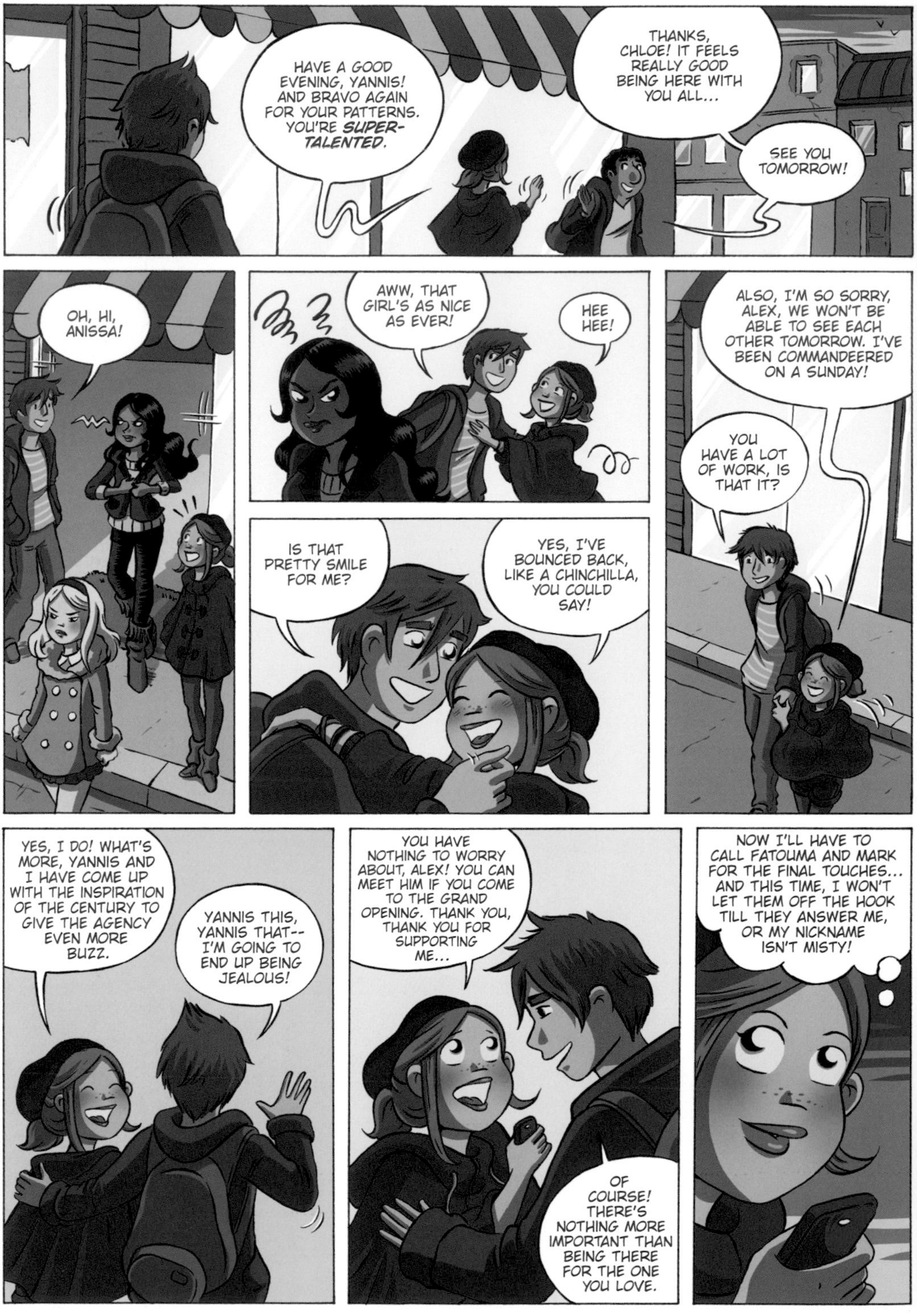
HAVE A GOOD EVENING, YANNIS! AND BRAVO AGAIN FOR YOUR PATTERNS. YOU'RE **SUPER-TALENTED**.
THANKS, CHLOE! IT FEELS REALLY GOOD BEING HERE WITH YOU ALL...
SEE YOU TOMORROW!
OH, HI, ANISSA!
AWW, THAT GIRL'S AS NICE AS EVER!
HEE HEE!
IS THAT PRETTY SMILE FOR ME?
YES, I'VE BOUNCED BACK, LIKE A CHINCHILLA, YOU COULD SAY!
ALSO, I'M SO SORRY, ALEX, WE WON'T BE ABLE TO SEE EACH OTHER TOMORROW. I'VE BEEN COMMANDEERED ON A SUNDAY!
YOU HAVE A LOT OF WORK, IS THAT IT?
YES, I DO! WHAT'S MORE, YANNIS AND I HAVE COME UP WITH THE INSPIRATION OF THE CENTURY TO GIVE THE AGENCY EVEN MORE BUZZ.
YANNIS THIS, YANNIS THAT-- I'M GOING TO END UP BEING JEALOUS!
YOU HAVE NOTHING TO WORRY ABOUT, ALEX! YOU CAN MEET HIM IF YOU COME TO THE GRAND OPENING. THANK YOU, THANK YOU FOR SUPPORTING ME...
OF COURSE! THERE'S NOTHING MORE IMPORTANT THAN BEING THERE FOR THE ONE YOU LOVE.
NOW I'LL HAVE TO CALL FATOUMA AND MARK FOR THE FINAL TOUCHES... AND THIS TIME, I WON'T LET THEM OFF THE HOOK TILL THEY ANSWER ME, OR MY NICKNAME ISN'T MISTY!

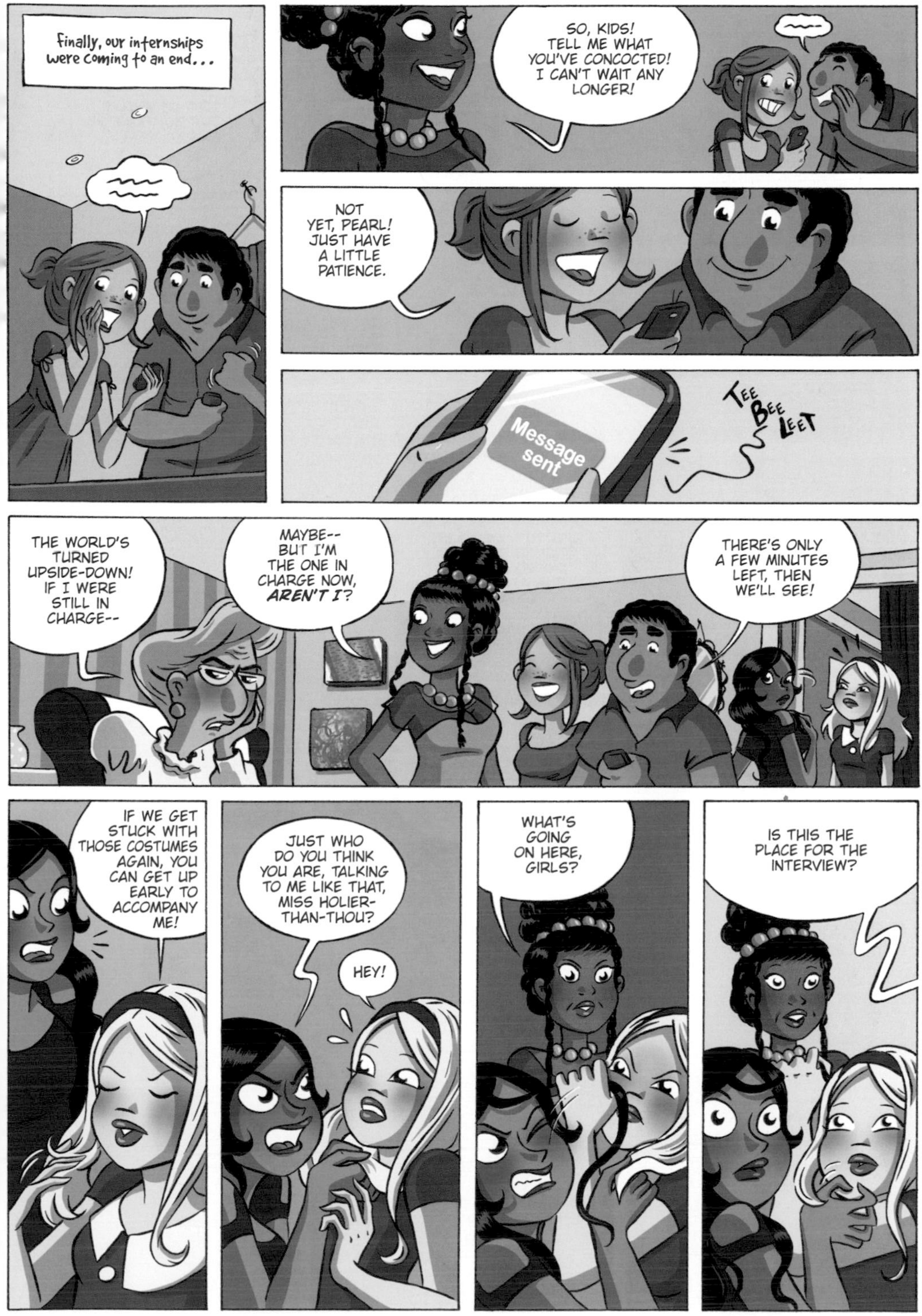
Finally, our internships were coming to an end...
SO, KIDS! TELL ME WHAT YOU'VE CONCOCTED! I CAN'T WAIT ANY LONGER!
NOT YET, PEARL! JUST HAVE A LITTLE PATIENCE.
Message sent
TEE BEE LEET
THE WORLD'S TURNED UPSIDE-DOWN! IF I WERE STILL IN CHARGE--
MAYBE-- BUT I'M THE ONE IN CHARGE NOW, AREN'T I?
THERE'S ONLY A FEW MINUTES LEFT, THEN WE'LL SEE!
IF WE GET STUCK WITH THOSE COSTUMES AGAIN, YOU CAN GET UP EARLY TO ACCOMPANY ME!
JUST WHO DO YOU THINK YOU ARE, TALKING TO ME LIKE THAT, MISS HOLIER-THAN-THOU?
HEY!
WHAT'S GOING ON HERE, GIRLS?
IS THIS THE PLACE FOR THE INTERVIEW?

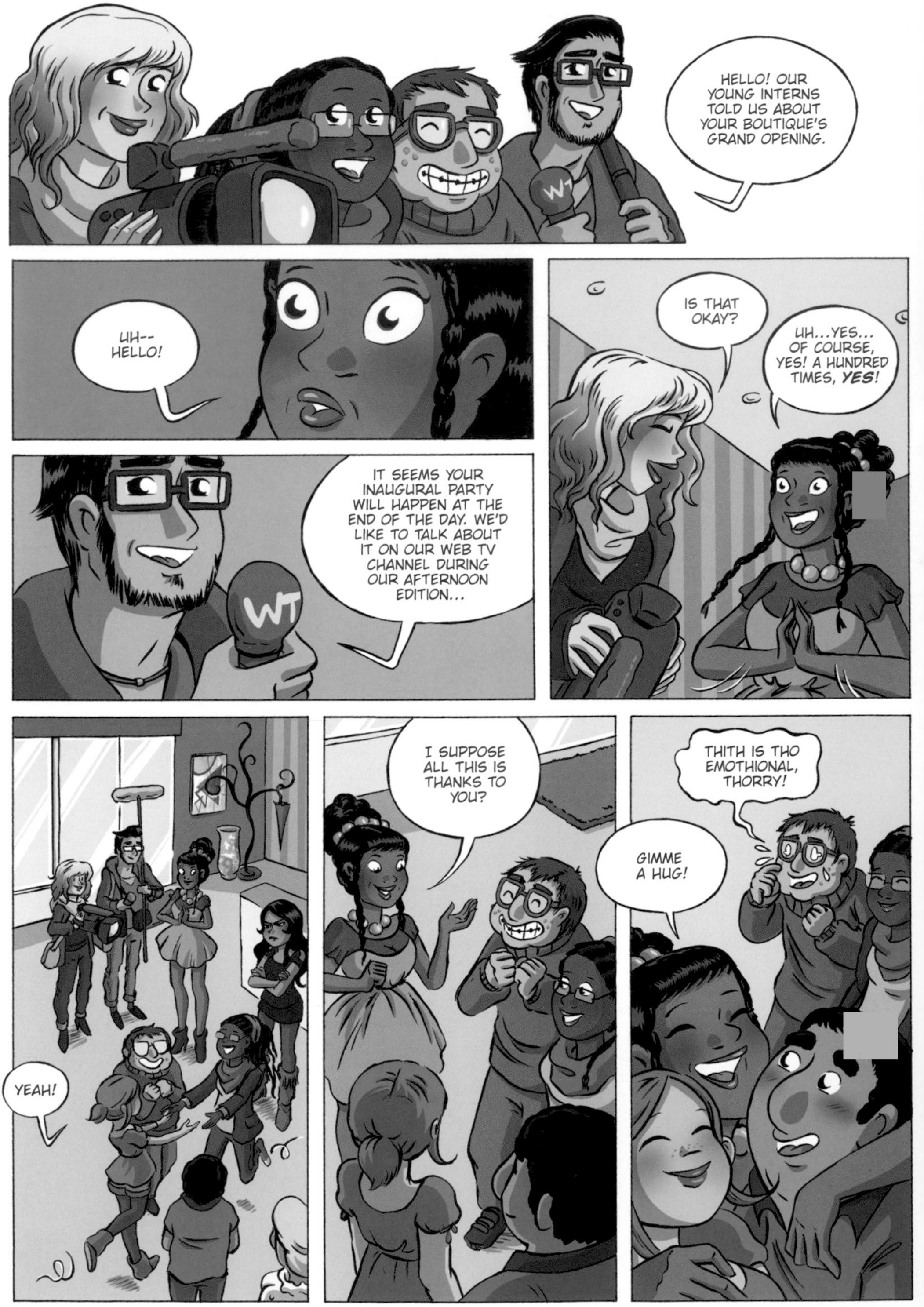
HELLO! OUR YOUNG INTERNS TOLD US ABOUT YOUR BOUTIQUE'S GRAND OPENING.
UH-- HELLO!
IS THAT OKAY?
UH...YES... OF COURSE, YES! A HUNDRED TIMES, YES!
IT SEEMS YOUR INAUGURAL PARTY WILL HAPPEN AT THE END OF THE DAY. WE'D LIKE TO TALK ABOUT IT ON OUR WEB TV CHANNEL DURING OUR AFTERNOON EDITION...
YEAH!
I SUPPOSE ALL THIS IS THANKS TO YOU?
THITH IS THO EMOTHIONAL, THORRY!
GIMME A HUG!

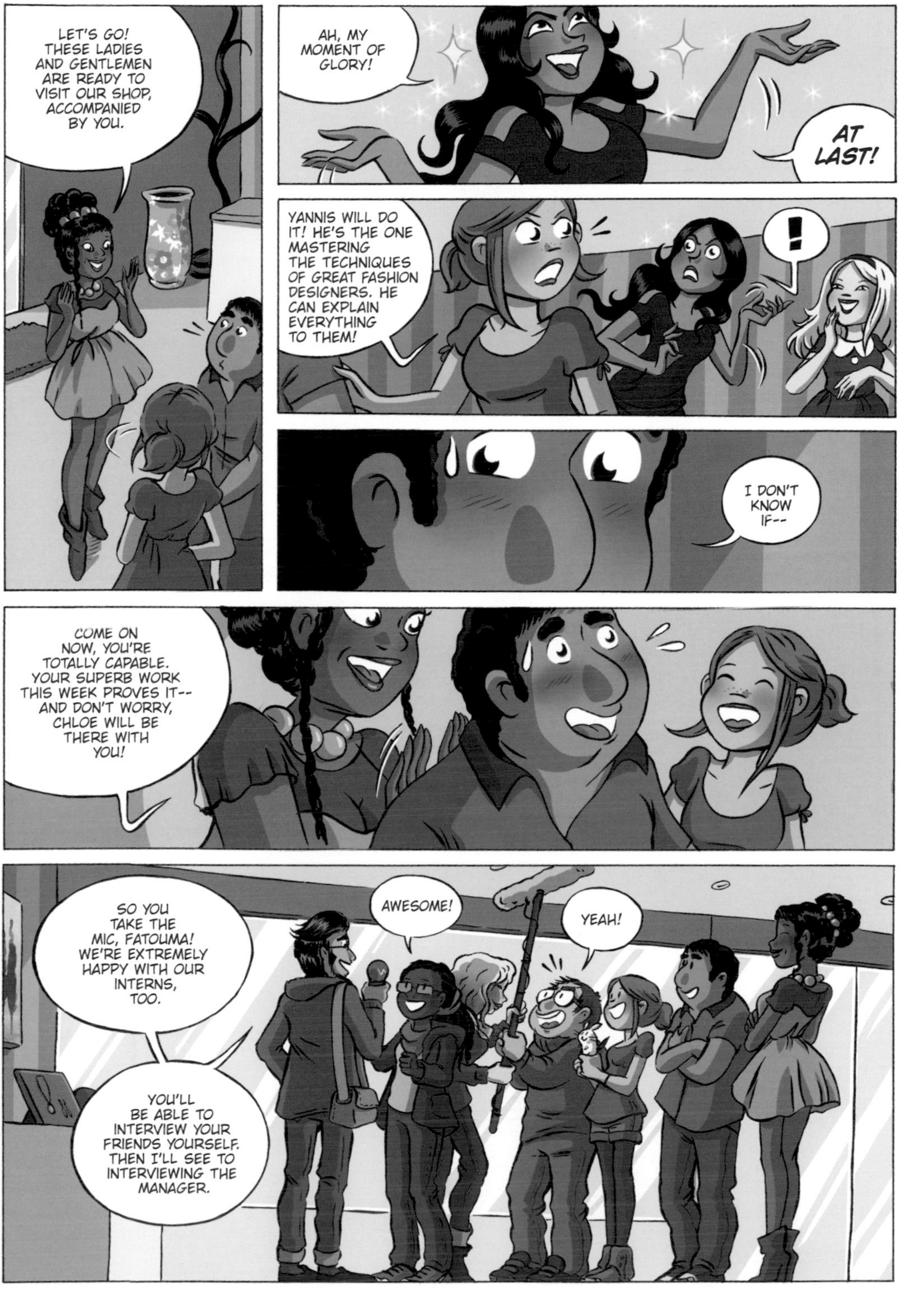
LET'S GO! THESE LADIES AND GENTLEMEN ARE READY TO VISIT OUR SHOP, ACCOMPANIED BY YOU.
AH, MY MOMENT OF GLORY!
AT LAST!
YANNIS WILL DO IT! HE'S THE ONE MASTERING THE TECHNIQUES OF GREAT FASHION DESIGNERS. HE CAN EXPLAIN EVERYTHING TO THEM!
!
I DON'T KNOW IF--
COME ON NOW, YOU'RE TOTALLY CAPABLE. YOUR SUPERB WORK THIS WEEK PROVES IT--AND DON'T WORRY, CHLOE WILL BE THERE WITH YOU!
SO YOU TAKE THE MIC, FATOUMA! WE'RE EXTREMELY HAPPY WITH OUR INTERNS, TOO.
AWESOME!
YEAH!
YOU'LL BE ABLE TO INTERVIEW YOUR FRIENDS YOURSELF. THEN I'LL SEE TO INTERVIEWING THE MANAGER.

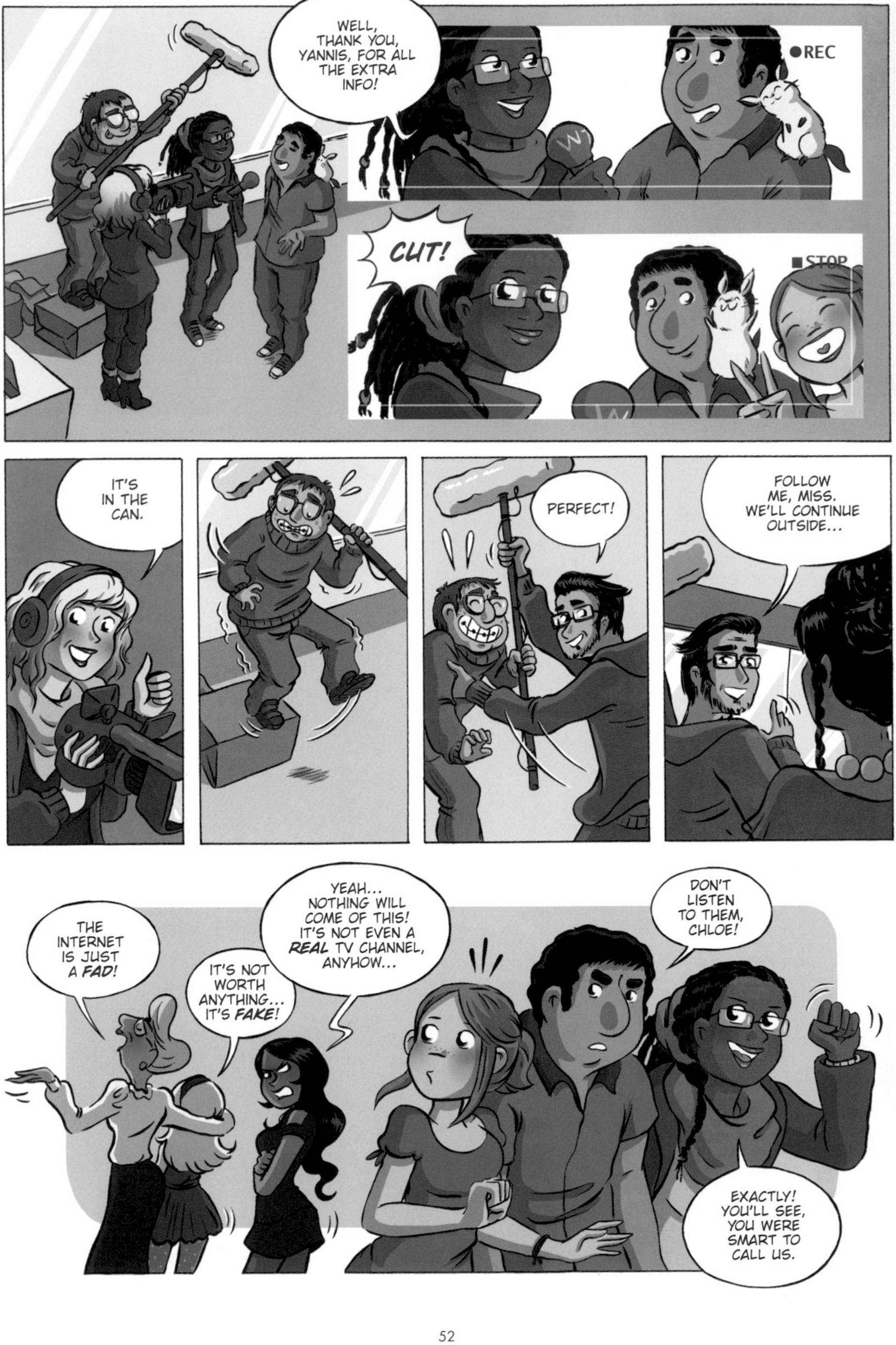
WELL, THANK YOU, YANNIS, FOR ALL THE EXTRA INFO!
●REC
CUT!
■STOP
IT'S IN THE CAN.
PERFECT!
FOLLOW ME, MISS. WE'LL CONTINUE OUTSIDE...
THE INTERNET IS JUST A **FAD**!
IT'S NOT WORTH ANYTHING... IT'S **FAKE**!
YEAH... NOTHING WILL COME OF THIS! IT'S NOT EVEN A **REAL** TV CHANNEL, ANYHOW...
DON'T LISTEN TO THEM, CHLOE!
EXACTLY! YOU'LL SEE, YOU WERE SMART TO CALL US.

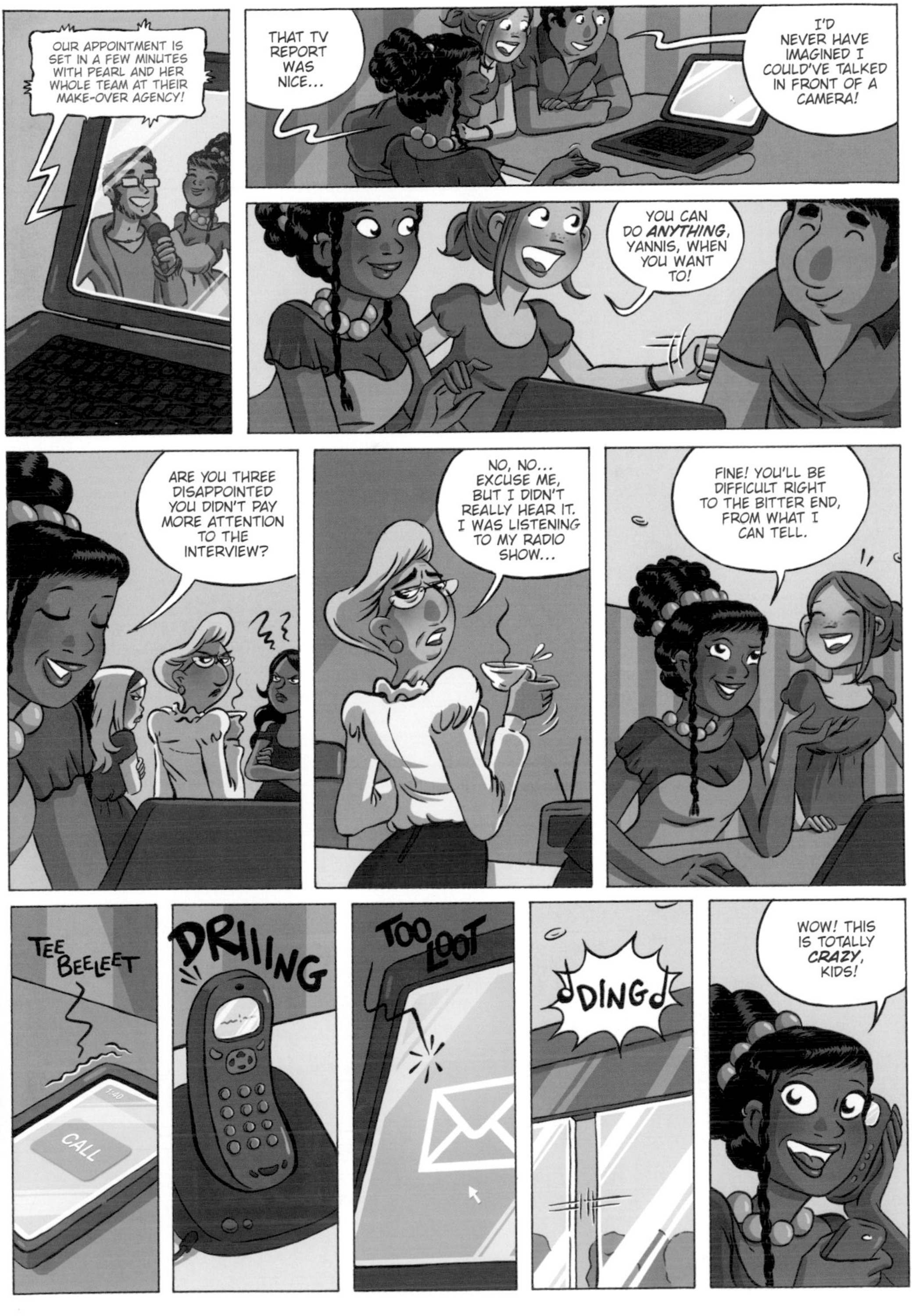
OUR APPOINTMENT IS SET IN A FEW MINUTES WITH PEARL AND HER WHOLE TEAM AT THEIR MAKE-OVER AGENCY!
THAT TV REPORT WAS NICE...
I'D NEVER HAVE IMAGINED I COULD'VE TALKED IN FRONT OF A CAMERA!
YOU CAN DO ANYTHING, YANNIS, WHEN YOU WANT TO!
ARE YOU THREE DISAPPOINTED YOU DIDN'T PAY MORE ATTENTION TO THE INTERVIEW?
NO, NO... EXCUSE ME, BUT I DIDN'T REALLY HEAR IT. I WAS LISTENING TO MY RADIO SHOW...
FINE! YOU'LL BE DIFFICULT RIGHT TO THE BITTER END, FROM WHAT I CAN TELL.
TEE BEELEET
CALL
DRIIING
TOO LOOT
DING
WOW! THIS IS TOTALLY CRAZY, KIDS!

Last name: BLIN
First name: Chloe
Grade: 9th, group B

Internship Report

School: G. Brassens Middle School
Internship Supervisor: ~~Mrs. DEBARGE~~
Miss Pearl (woo-hoo!)

Presentation of a career:

A fashion designer creates the designs that will become the collections in the coming seasons. Curious and observant, a designer knows how to anticipate customers' desires and to divine the trends of tomorrow. The initial training courses after high school will let you start as an assistant. To further develop your artistic and creative potential, it's best to continue training for a few additional years.

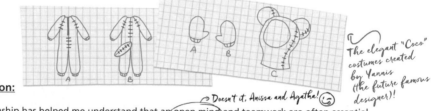

The elegant "Coco" costumes created by Yannis (the future famous designer)!

Conclusion:

Doesn't it, Anissa and Agatha!

This internship has helped me understand that an open mind and teamwork are often essential. In fact, there's nothing better to make you smile.

You also have to be able to remain modest, but not hesitate to express yourself. It's not easy! In my case, I really loved helping my friend Yannis be able to come out of his shell.
By making use of each individual's talents, you can go farther! Be passionate and you'll do it!

Acknowledgments:

A huge thanks to Miss Pearl for letting us express ourselves to the best of our ability, to Coco because he's so cute, and to Mrs. Debarge because, without her, maybe I'd have never found out that being mindful of others is so important.

Hee hee!

Hurray for the Topsy-Turvy boutique's super team! XOXOXO!

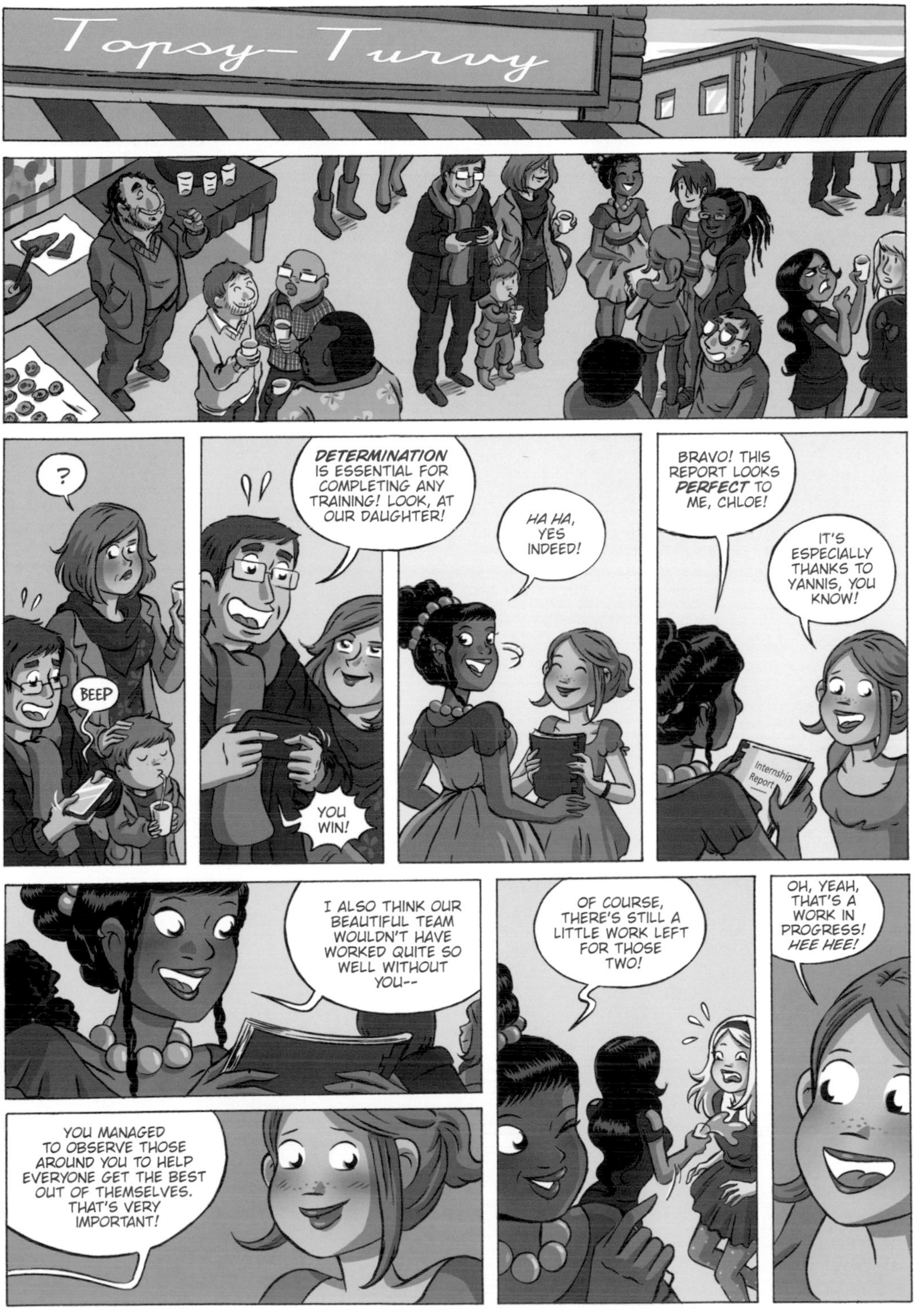
Topsy-Turvy
?
DETERMINATION IS ESSENTIAL FOR COMPLETING ANY TRAINING! LOOK, AT OUR DAUGHTER!
BEEP
YOU WIN!
HA HA, YES INDEED!
BRAVO! THIS REPORT LOOKS PERFECT TO ME, CHLOE!
IT'S ESPECIALLY THANKS TO YANNIS, YOU KNOW!
Internship Report
I ALSO THINK OUR BEAUTIFUL TEAM WOULDN'T HAVE WORKED QUITE SO WELL WITHOUT YOU--
YOU MANAGED TO OBSERVE THOSE AROUND YOU TO HELP EVERYONE GET THE BEST OUT OF THEMSELVES. THAT'S VERY IMPORTANT!
OF COURSE, THERE'S STILL A LITTLE WORK LEFT FOR THOSE TWO!
OH, YEAH, THAT'S A WORK IN PROGRESS! HEE HEE!

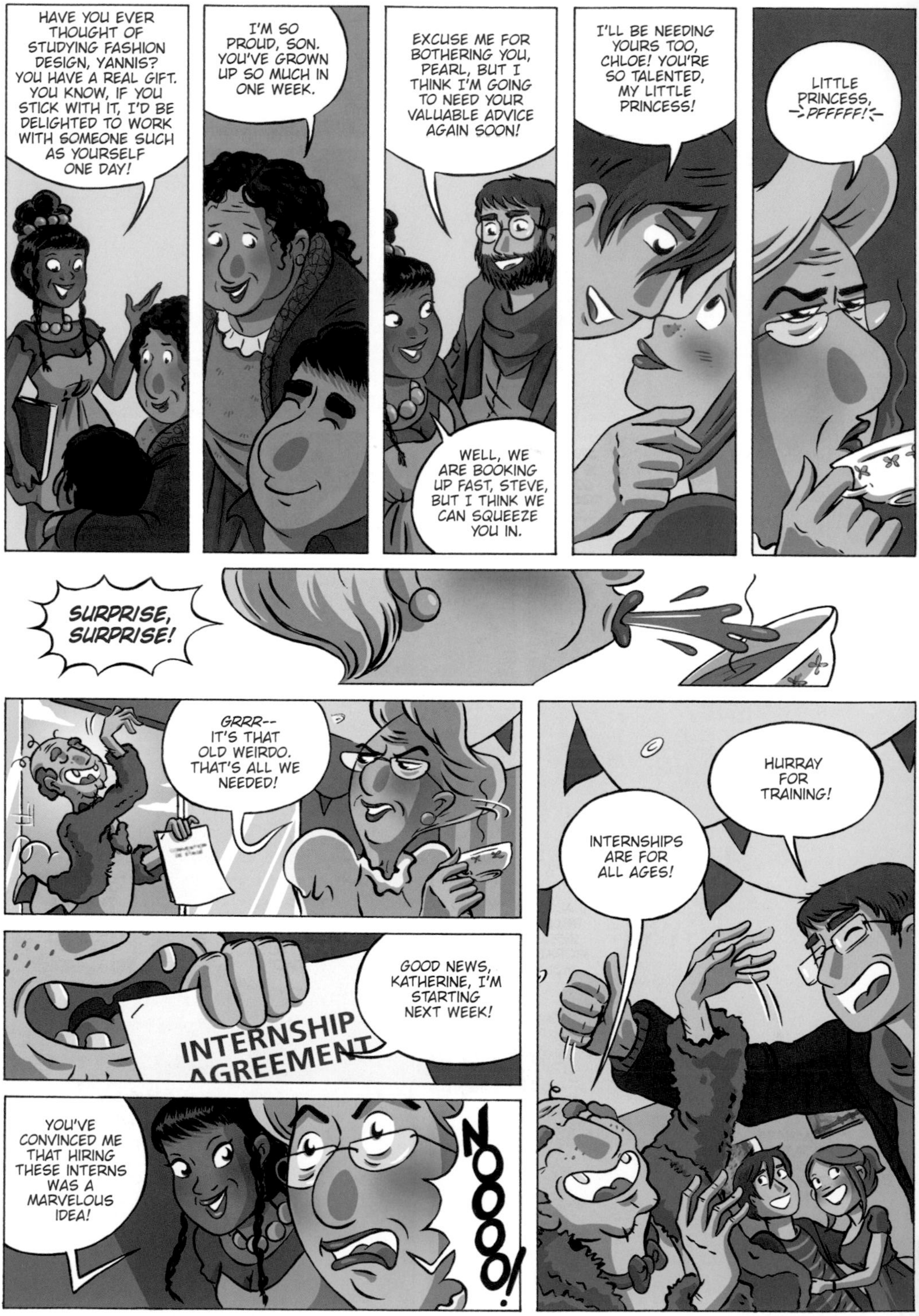
HAVE YOU EVER THOUGHT OF STUDYING FASHION DESIGN, YANNIS? YOU HAVE A REAL GIFT. YOU KNOW, IF YOU STICK WITH IT, I'D BE DELIGHTED TO WORK WITH SOMEONE SUCH AS YOURSELF ONE DAY!
I'M SO PROUD, SON. YOU'VE GROWN UP SO MUCH IN ONE WEEK.
EXCUSE ME FOR BOTHERING YOU, PEARL, BUT I THINK I'M GOING TO NEED YOUR VALUABLE ADVICE AGAIN SOON!
WELL, WE ARE BOOKING UP FAST, STEVE, BUT I THINK WE CAN SQUEEZE YOU IN.
I'LL BE NEEDING YOURS TOO, CHLOE! YOU'RE SO TALENTED, MY LITTLE PRINCESS!
LITTLE PRINCESS, PFFFFF!
SURPRISE, SURPRISE!
GRRR-- IT'S THAT OLD WEIRDO. THAT'S ALL WE NEEDED!
GOOD NEWS, KATHERINE, I'M STARTING NEXT WEEK!
INTERNSHIP AGREEMENT
YOU'VE CONVINCED ME THAT HIRING THESE INTERNS WAS A MARVELOUS IDEA!
NOOOO!
INTERNSHIPS ARE FOR ALL AGES!
HURRAY FOR TRAINING!

S.O.S. Heart in Distress

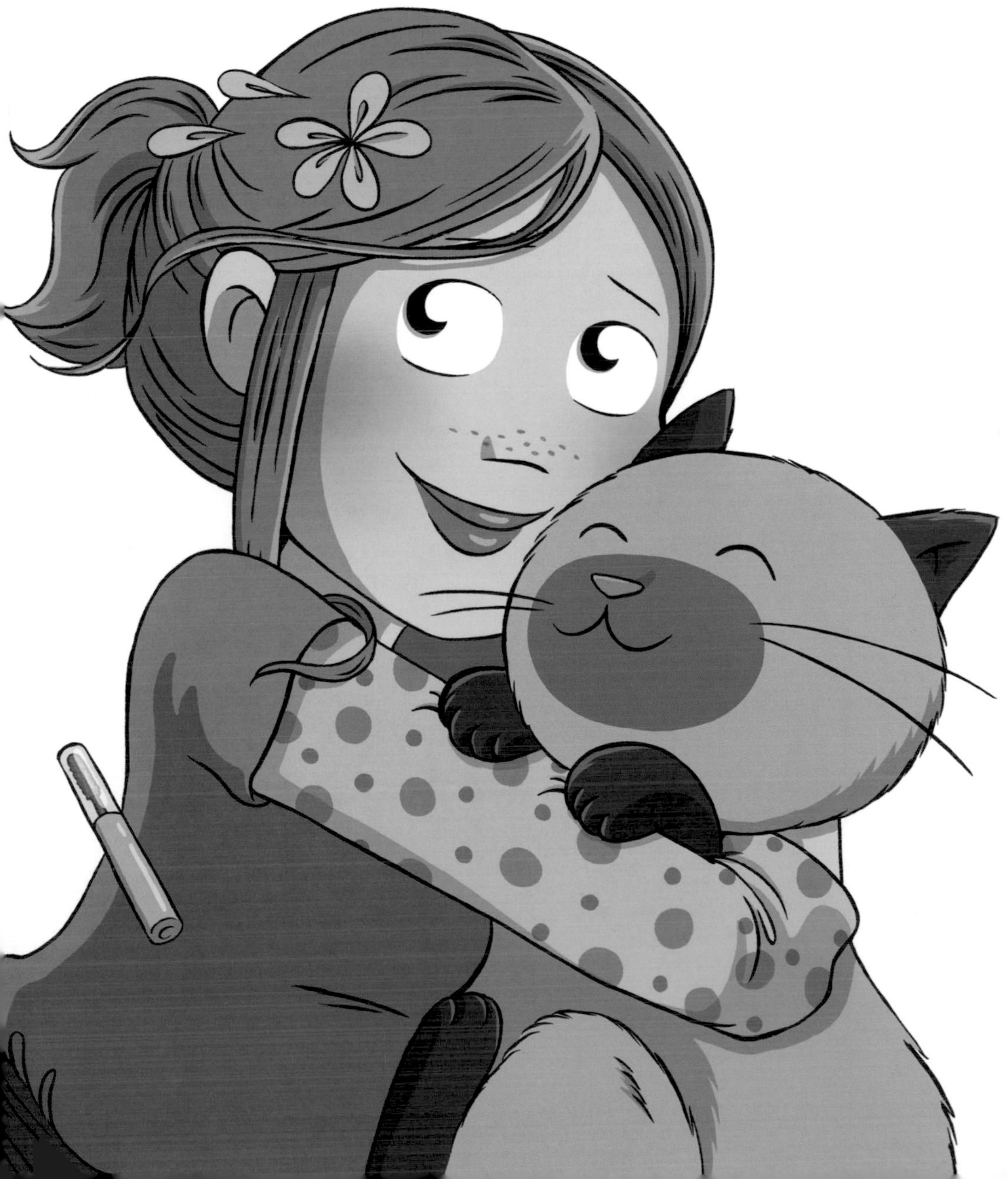

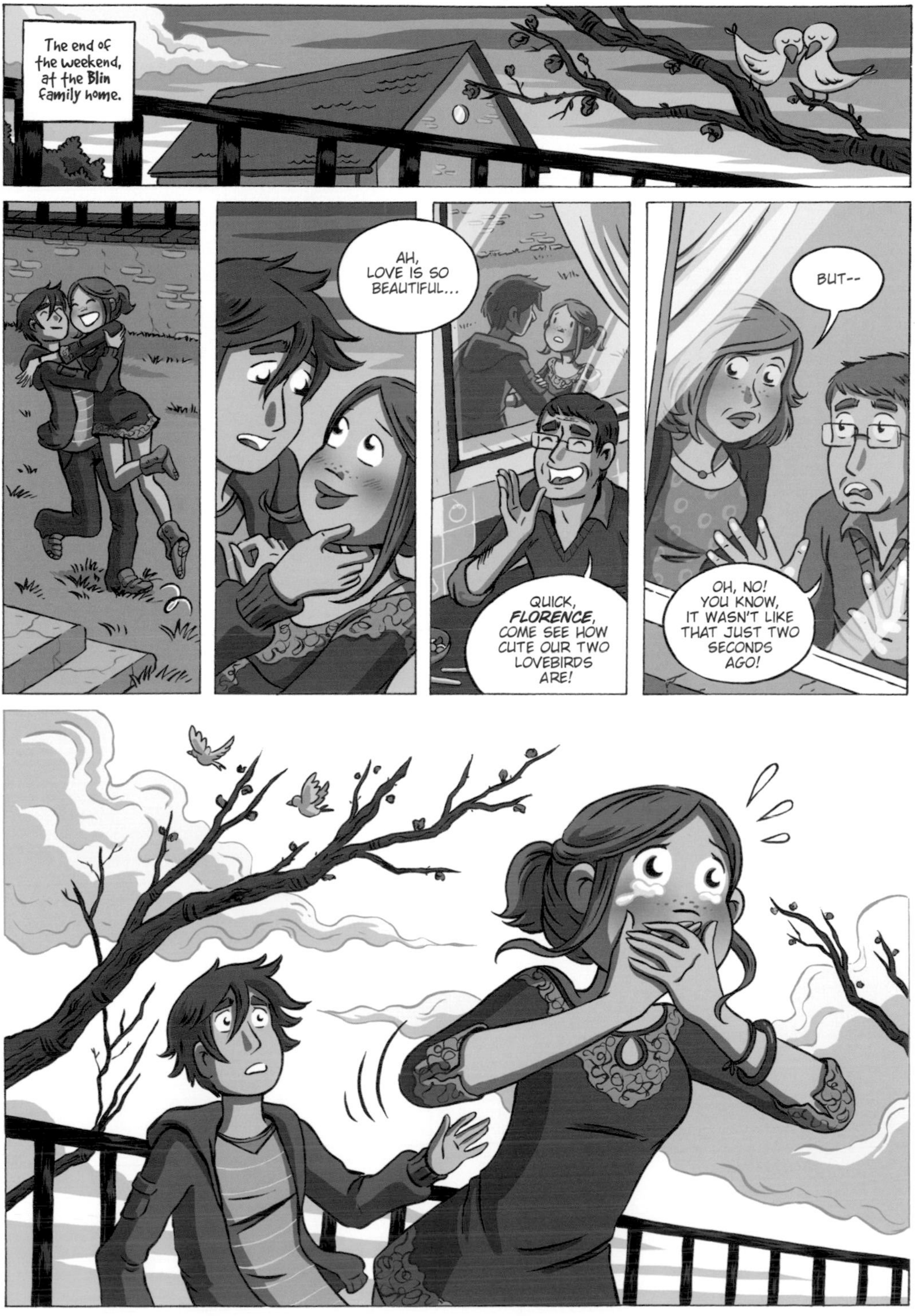
The end of the weekend, at the Blin family home.
AH, LOVE IS SO BEAUTIFUL...
QUICK, FLORENCE, COME SEE HOW CUTE OUR TWO LOVEBIRDS ARE!
BUT--
OH, NO! YOU KNOW, IT WASN'T LIKE THAT JUST TWO SECONDS AGO!

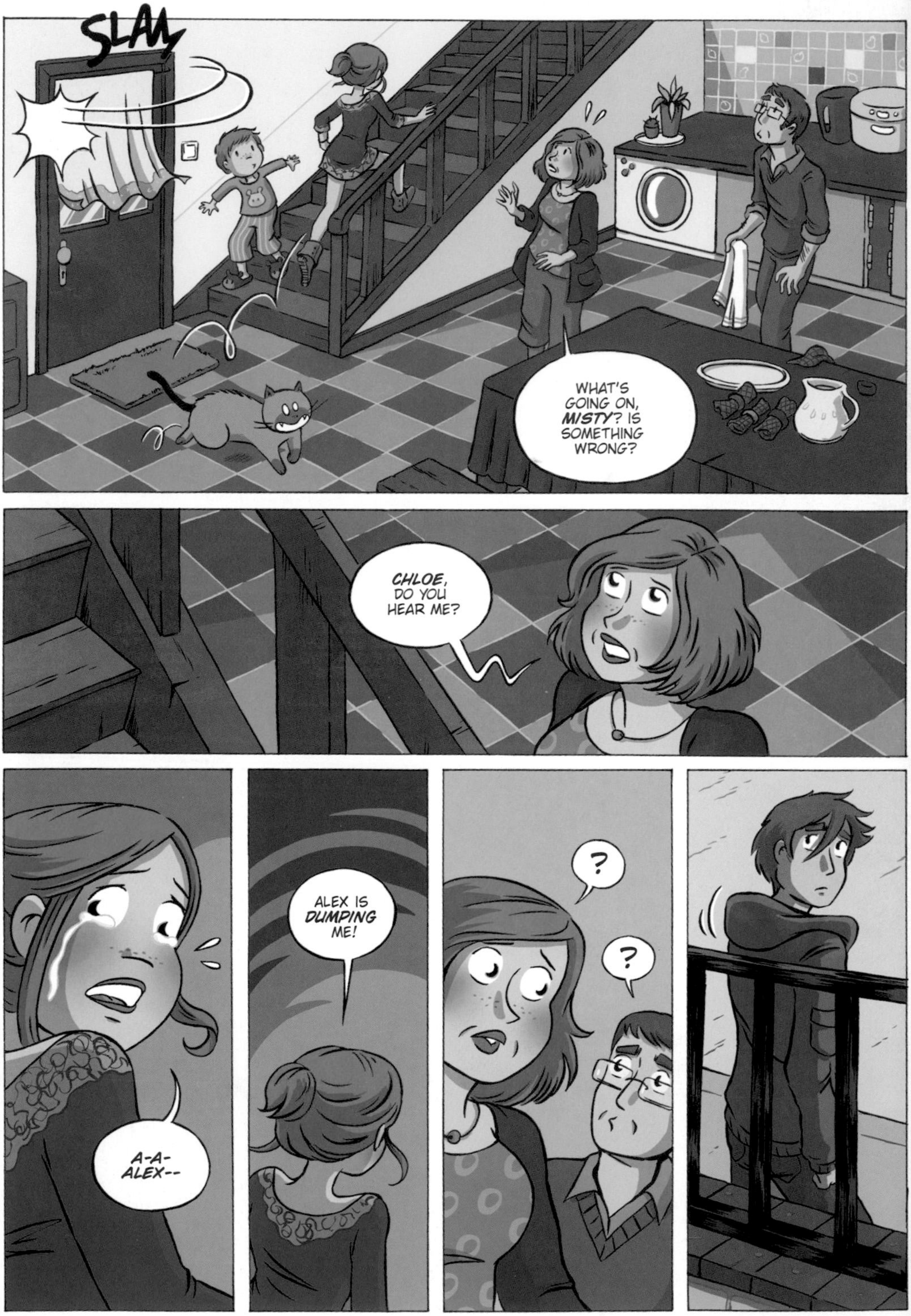
SLAM
WHAT'S GOING ON, MISTY? IS SOMETHING WRONG?
CHLOE, DO YOU HEAR ME?
A-A-ALEX--
ALEX IS DUMPING ME!
?
?

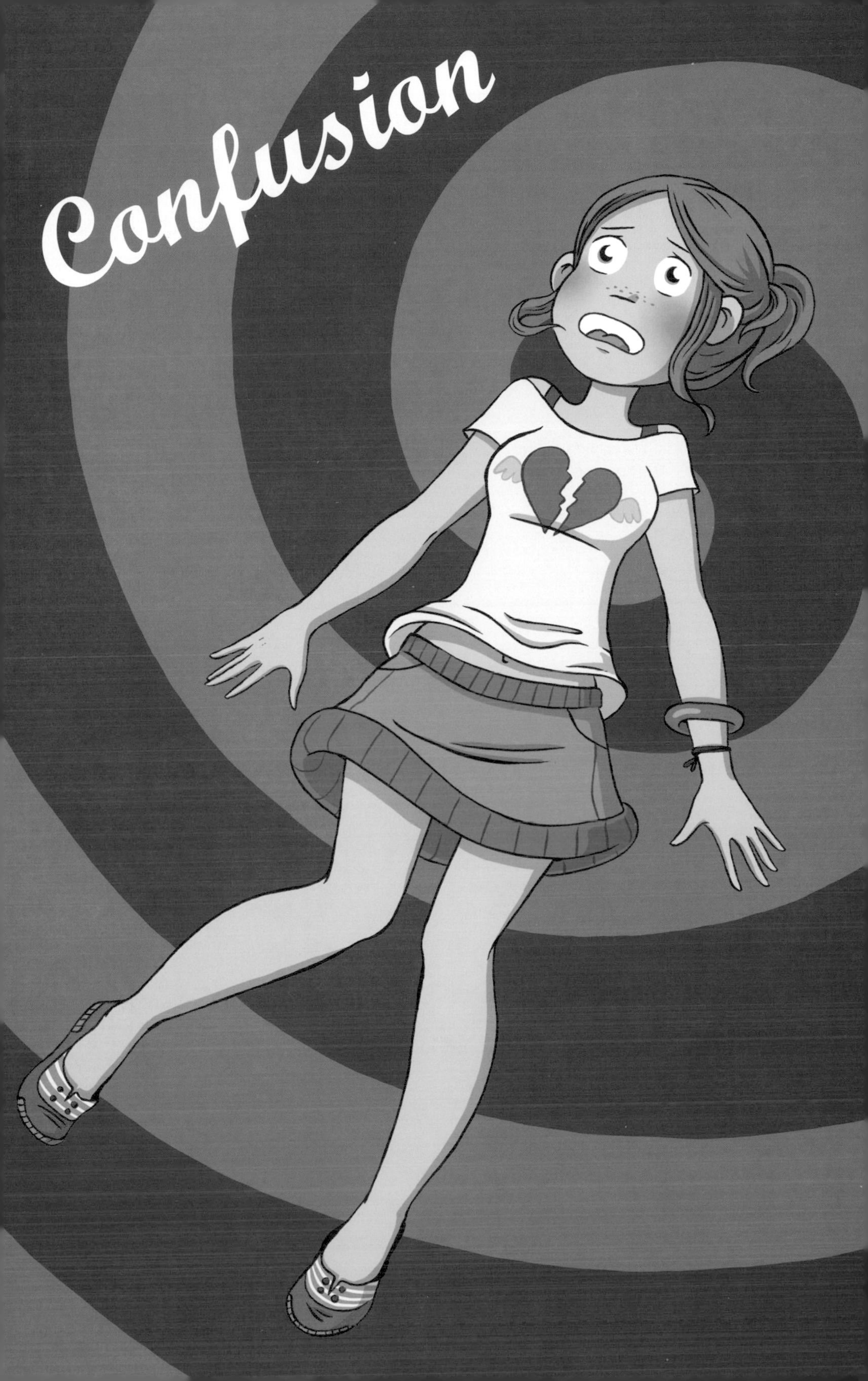
Confusion

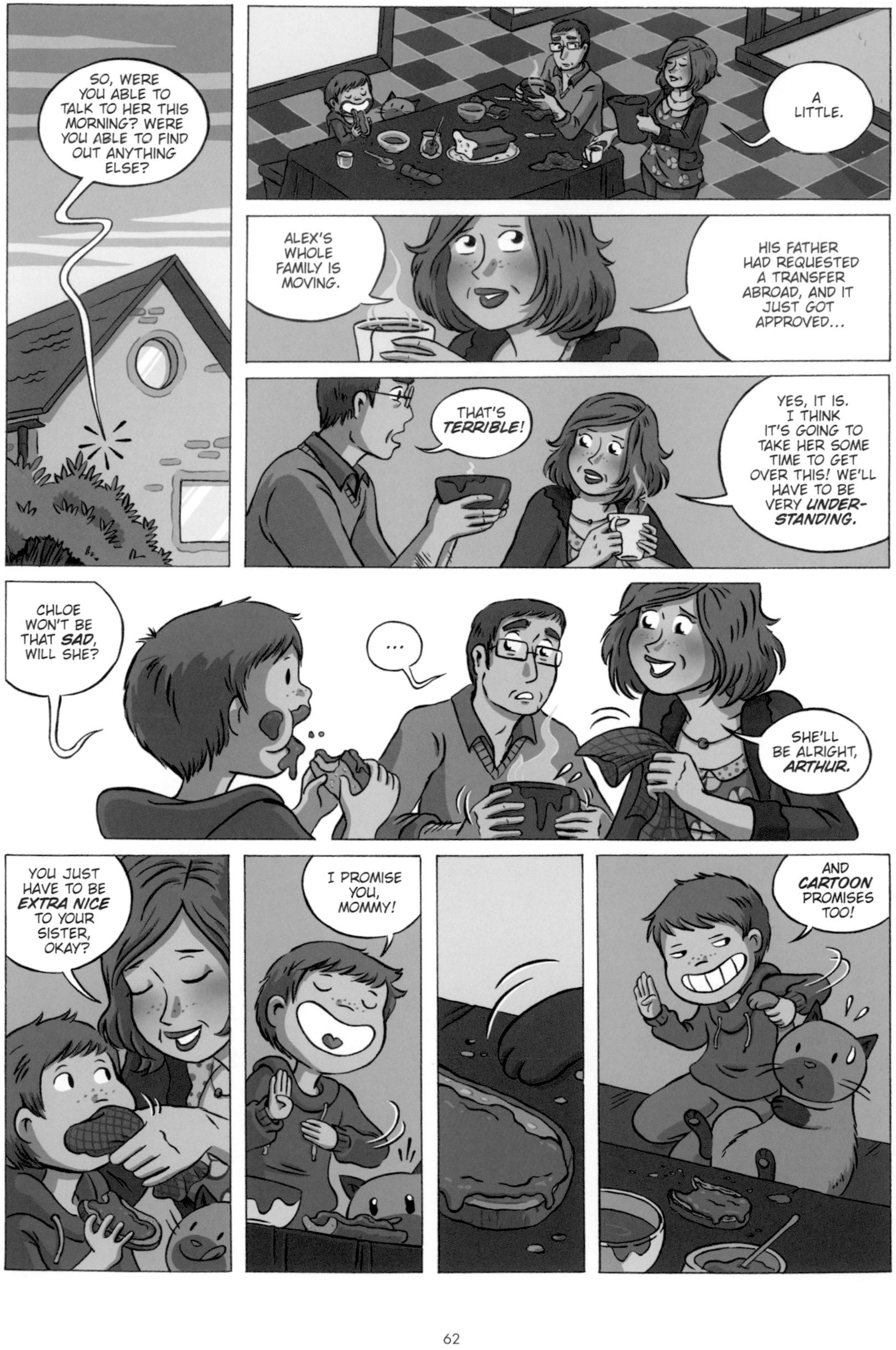
SO, WERE YOU ABLE TO TALK TO HER THIS MORNING? WERE YOU ABLE TO FIND OUT ANYTHING ELSE?
A LITTLE.
ALEX'S WHOLE FAMILY IS MOVING.
HIS FATHER HAD REQUESTED A TRANSFER ABROAD, AND IT JUST GOT APPROVED...
THAT'S TERRIBLE!
YES, IT IS. I THINK IT'S GOING TO TAKE HER SOME TIME TO GET OVER THIS! WE'LL HAVE TO BE VERY UNDER-STANDING.
CHLOE WON'T BE THAT SAD, WILL SHE?
...
SHE'LL BE ALRIGHT, ARTHUR.
YOU JUST HAVE TO BE EXTRA NICE TO YOUR SISTER, OKAY?
I PROMISE YOU, MOMMY!
AND CARTOON PROMISES TOO!

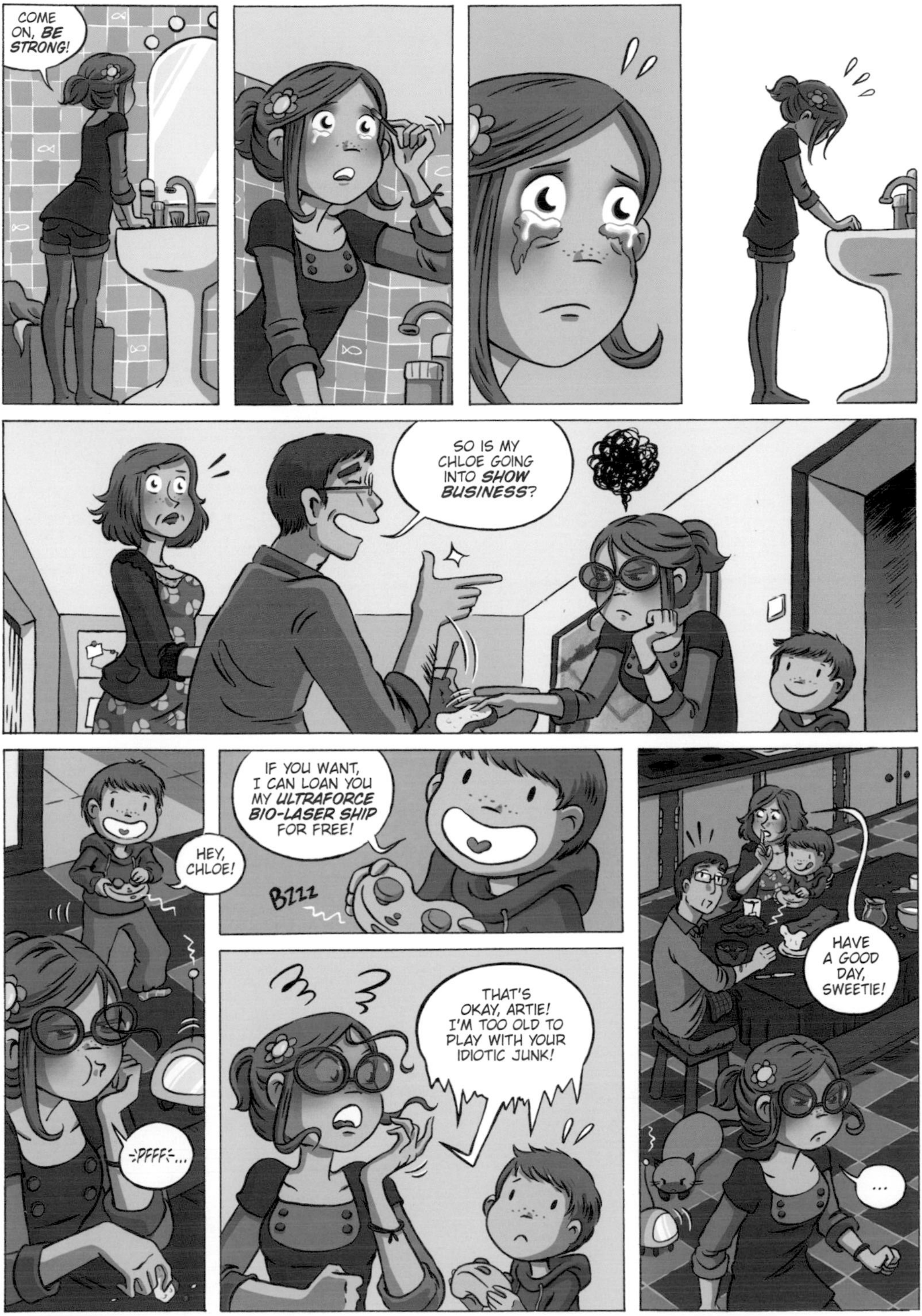
COME ON, BE STRONG!
SO IS MY CHLOE GOING INTO SHOW BUSINESS?
HEY, CHLOE!
IF YOU WANT, I CAN LOAN YOU MY ULTRAFORCE BIO-LASER SHIP FOR FREE!
BZZZ
PFFF...
THAT'S OKAY, ARTIE! I'M TOO OLD TO PLAY WITH YOUR IDIOTIC JUNK!
HAVE A GOOD DAY, SWEETIE!
...

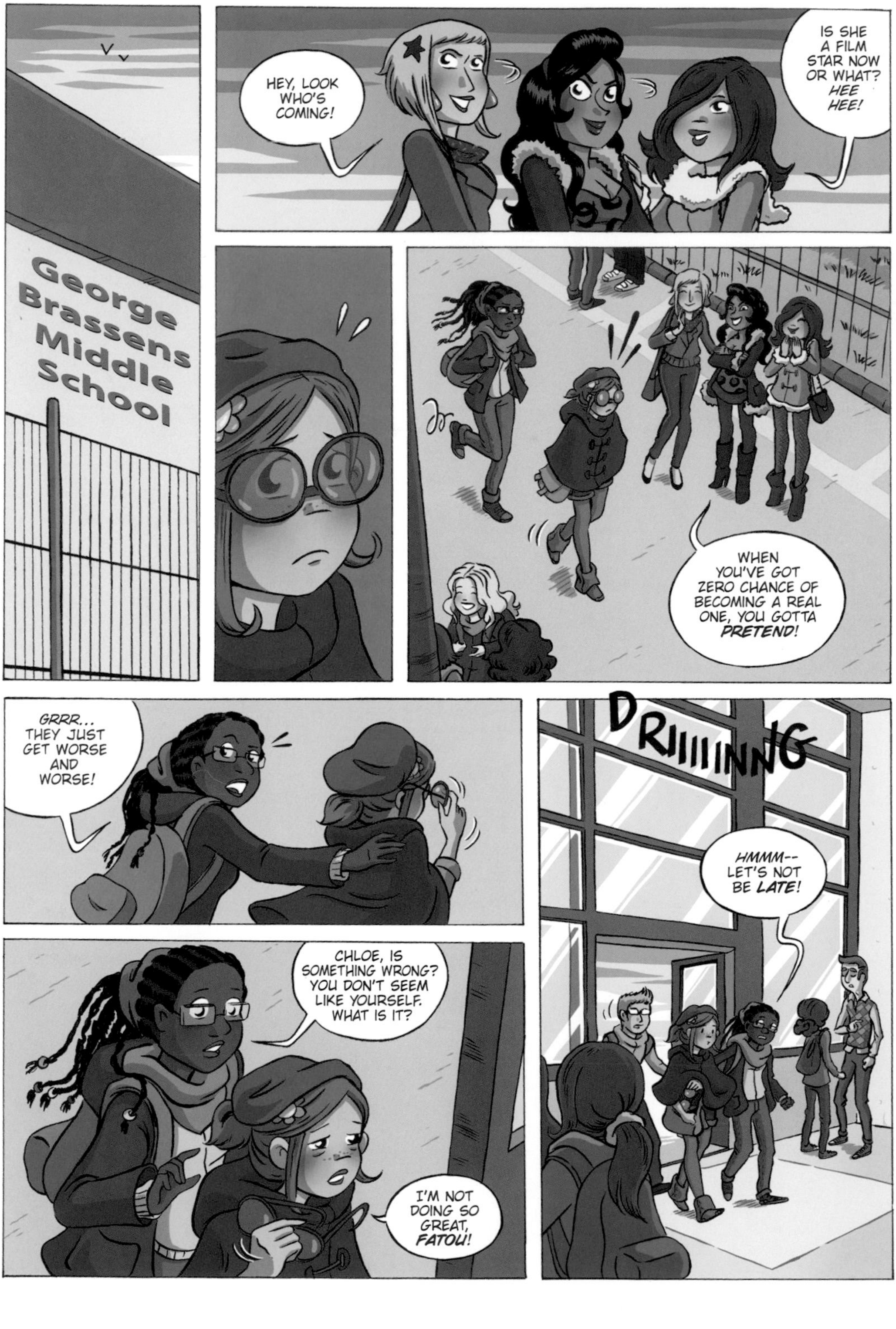
George Brassens Middle School
HEY, LOOK WHO'S COMING!
IS SHE A FILM STAR NOW OR WHAT? HEE HEE!
WHEN YOU'VE GOT ZERO CHANCE OF BECOMING A REAL ONE, YOU GOTTA PRETEND!
GRRR... THEY JUST GET WORSE AND WORSE!
DRIIIIINNG
HMMM-- LET'S NOT BE LATE!
CHLOE, IS SOMETHING WRONG? YOU DON'T SEEM LIKE YOURSELF. WHAT IS IT?
I'M NOT DOING SO GREAT, FATOU!

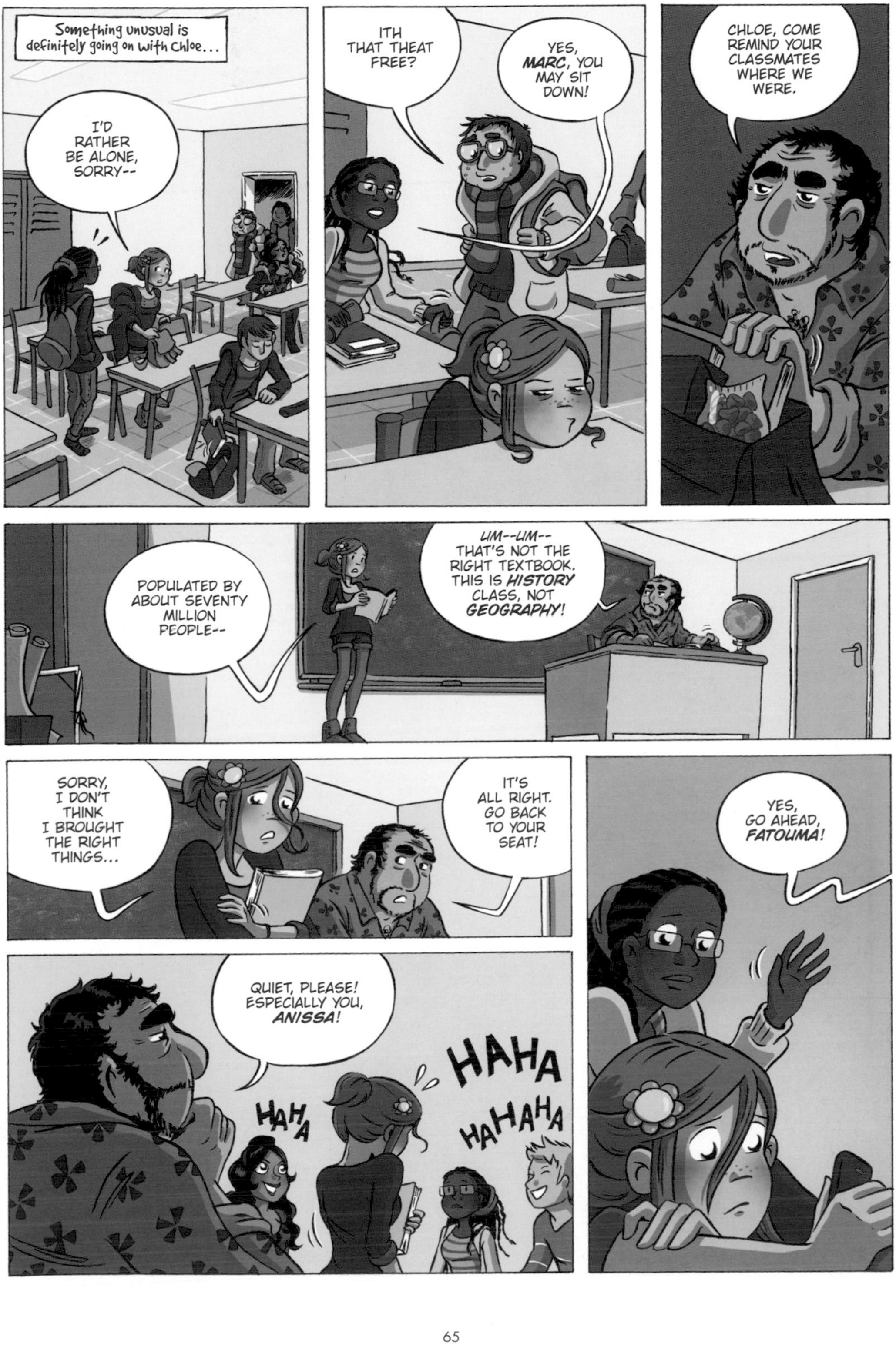
Something unusual is definitely going on with Chloe...
I'D RATHER BE ALONE, SORRY--
ITH THAT THEAT FREE?
YES, MARC, YOU MAY SIT DOWN!
CHLOE, COME REMIND YOUR CLASSMATES WHERE WE WERE.
POPULATED BY ABOUT SEVENTY MILLION PEOPLE--
UM--UM-- THAT'S NOT THE RIGHT TEXTBOOK. THIS IS HISTORY CLASS, NOT GEOGRAPHY!
SORRY, I DON'T THINK I BROUGHT THE RIGHT THINGS...
IT'S ALL RIGHT. GO BACK TO YOUR SEAT!
QUIET, PLEASE! ESPECIALLY YOU, ANISSA!
HAHA
HAHA
HAHAHA
YES, GO AHEAD, FATOUMA!

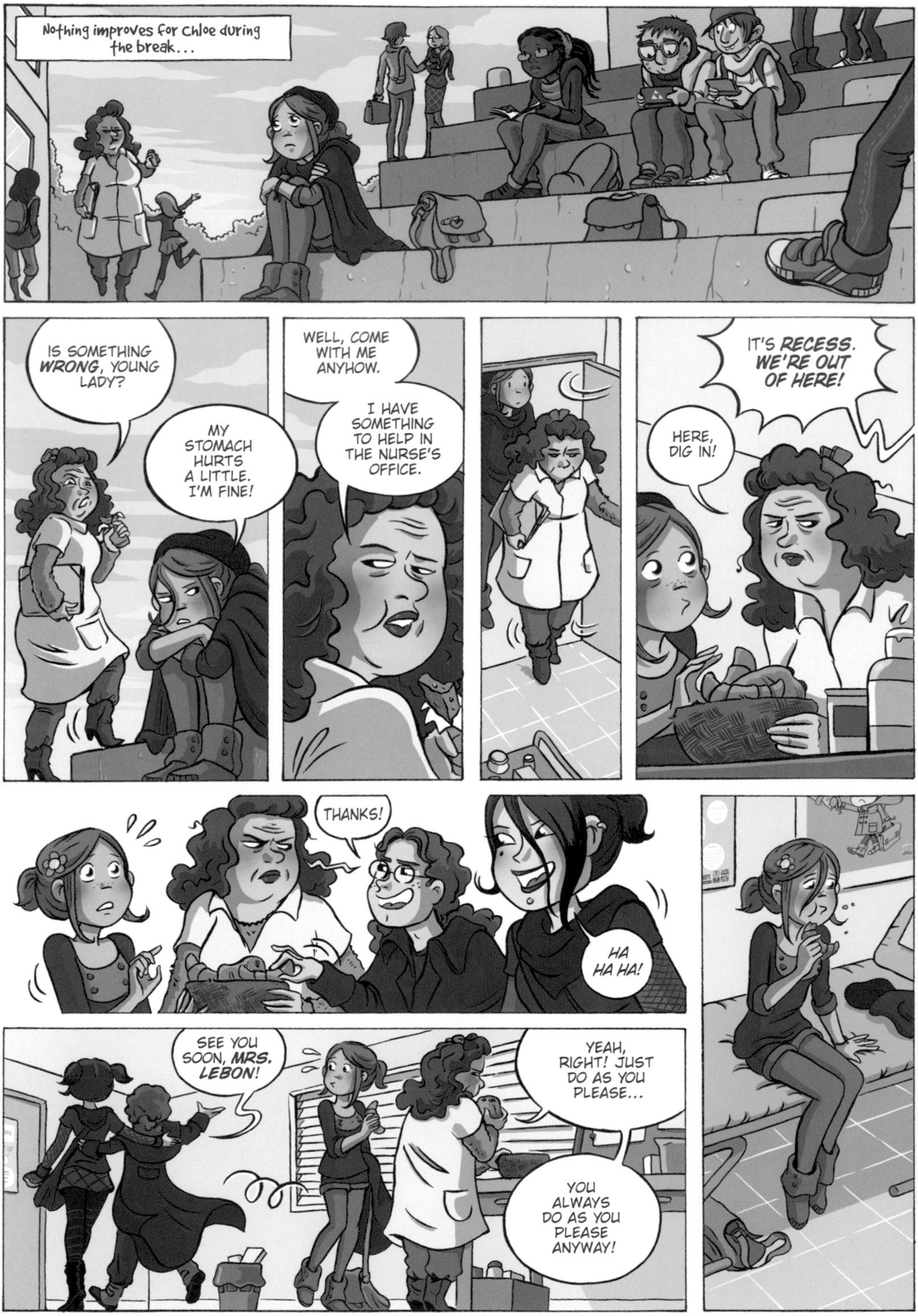
Nothing improves for Chloe during the break...
IS SOMETHING *WRONG*, YOUNG LADY?
MY STOMACH HURTS A LITTLE. I'M FINE!
WELL, COME WITH ME ANYHOW.
I HAVE SOMETHING TO HELP IN THE NURSE'S OFFICE.
IT'S *RECESS. WE'RE OUT OF HERE!*
HERE, DIG IN!
THANKS!
HA HA HA!
SEE YOU SOON, *MRS. LEBON!*
YEAH, RIGHT! JUST DO AS YOU PLEASE...
YOU ALWAYS DO AS YOU PLEASE ANYWAY!

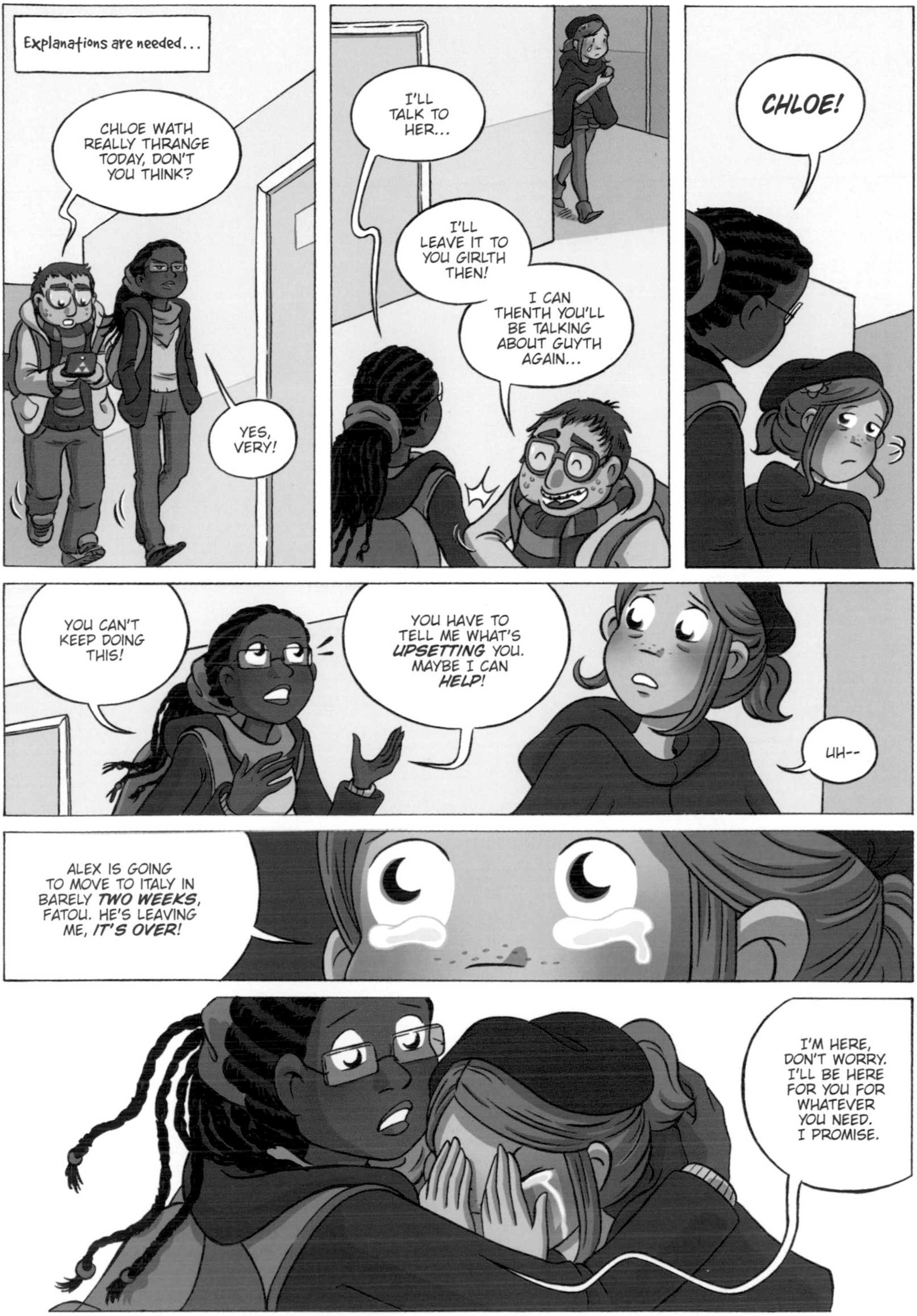
Explanations are needed...
CHLOE WATH REALLY THRANGE TODAY, DON'T YOU THINK?
YES, VERY!
I'LL TALK TO HER...
I'LL LEAVE IT TO YOU GIRLTH THEN!
I CAN THENTH YOU'LL BE TALKING ABOUT GUYTH AGAIN...
CHLOE!
YOU CAN'T KEEP DOING THIS!
YOU HAVE TO TELL ME WHAT'S UPSETTING YOU. MAYBE I CAN HELP!
UH--
ALEX IS GOING TO MOVE TO ITALY IN BARELY TWO WEEKS, FATOU. HE'S LEAVING ME, IT'S OVER!
I'M HERE, DON'T WORRY. I'LL BE HERE FOR YOU FOR WHATEVER YOU NEED. I PROMISE.

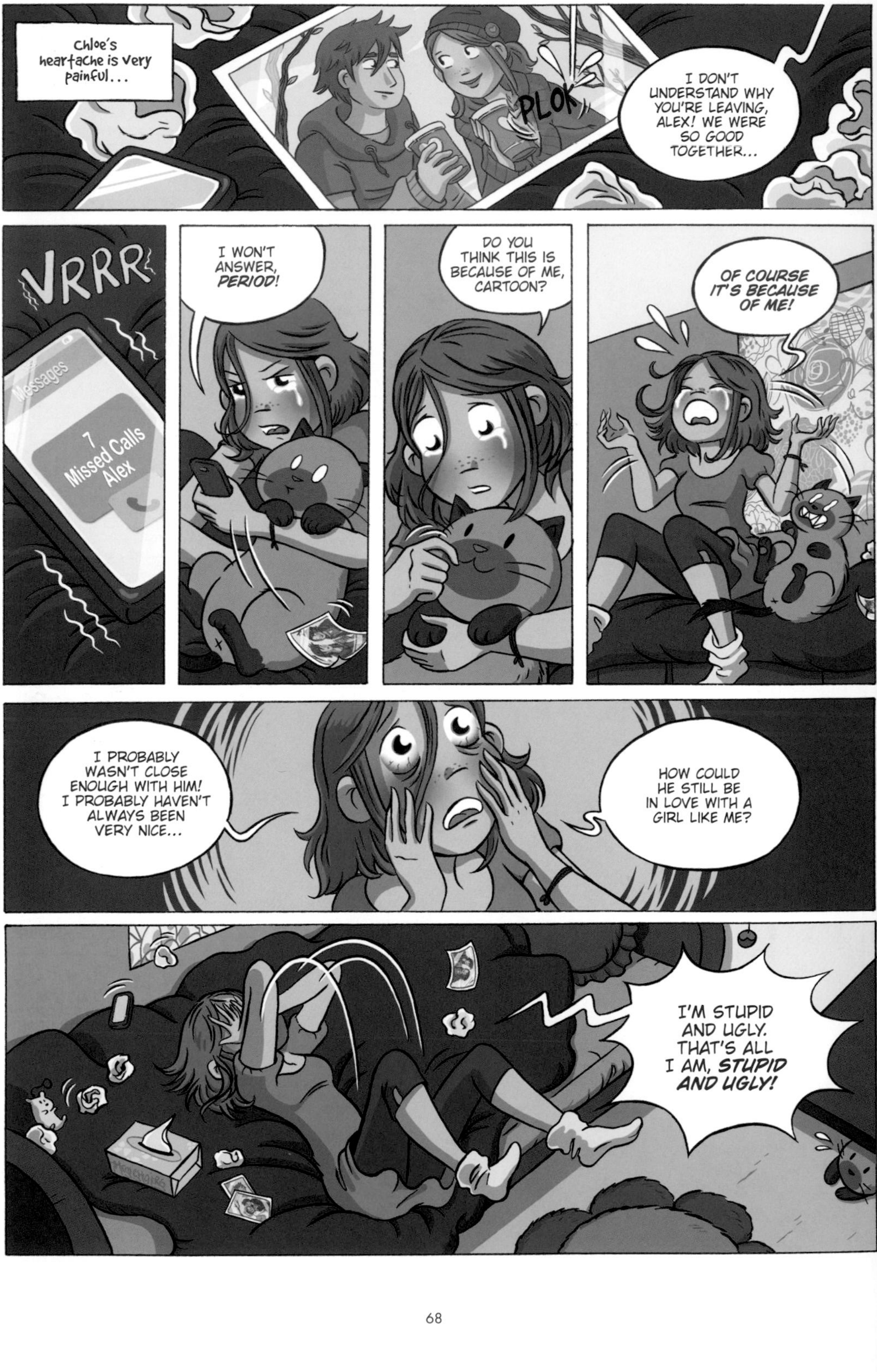
Chloe's heartache is very painful...
PLOK
I DON'T UNDERSTAND WHY YOU'RE LEAVING, ALEX! WE WERE SO GOOD TOGETHER...
VRRR
Messages
7 Missed Calls Alex
I WON'T ANSWER, *PERIOD!*
DO YOU THINK THIS IS BECAUSE OF ME, CARTOON?
OF COURSE IT'S BECAUSE OF ME!
I PROBABLY WASN'T CLOSE ENOUGH WITH HIM! I PROBABLY HAVEN'T ALWAYS BEEN VERY NICE...
HOW COULD HE STILL BE IN LOVE WITH A GIRL LIKE ME?
I'M STUPID AND UGLY. THAT'S ALL I AM, *STUPID AND UGLY!*

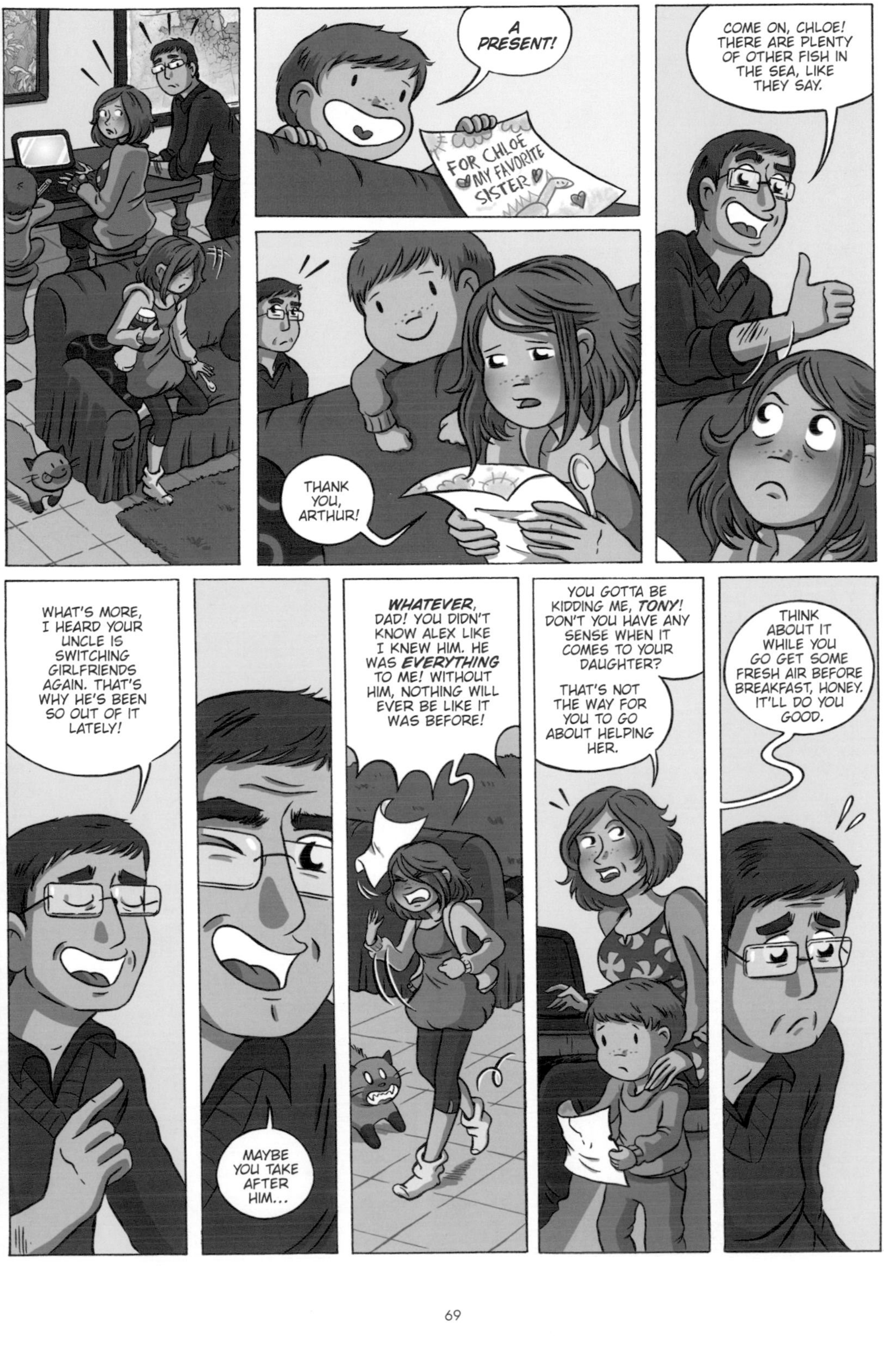
A PRESENT!
FOR CHLOE MY FAVORITE SISTER
THANK YOU, ARTHUR!
COME ON, CHLOE! THERE ARE PLENTY OF OTHER FISH IN THE SEA, LIKE THEY SAY.
WHAT'S MORE, I HEARD YOUR UNCLE IS SWITCHING GIRLFRIENDS AGAIN. THAT'S WHY HE'S BEEN SO OUT OF IT LATELY!
MAYBE YOU TAKE AFTER HIM...
WHATEVER, DAD! YOU DIDN'T KNOW ALEX LIKE I KNEW HIM. HE WAS EVERYTHING TO ME! WITHOUT HIM, NOTHING WILL EVER BE LIKE IT WAS BEFORE!
YOU GOTTA BE KIDDING ME, TONY! DON'T YOU HAVE ANY SENSE WHEN IT COMES TO YOUR DAUGHTER?
THAT'S NOT THE WAY FOR YOU TO GO ABOUT HELPING HER.
THINK ABOUT IT WHILE YOU GO GET SOME FRESH AIR BEFORE BREAKFAST, HONEY. IT'LL DO YOU GOOD.

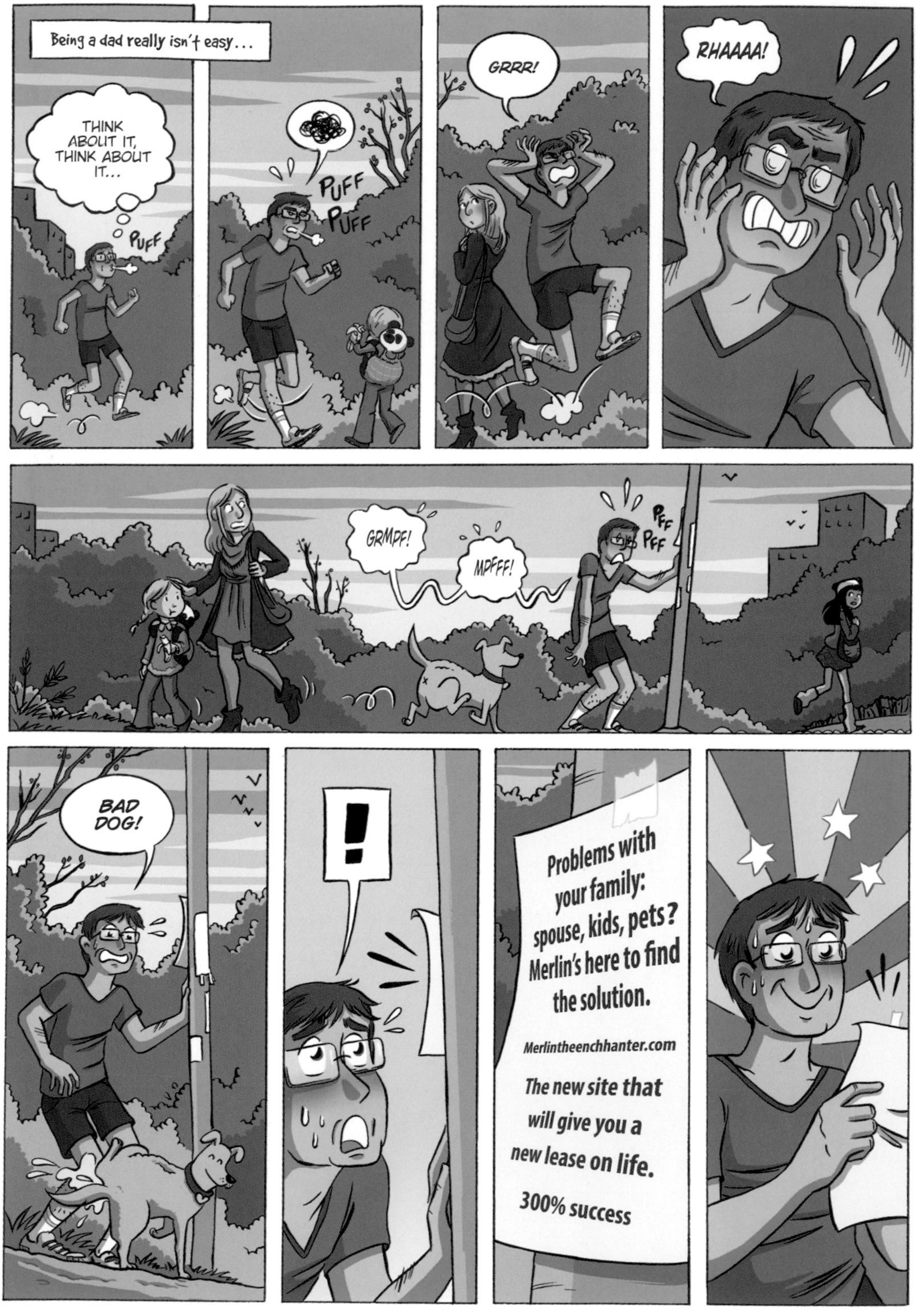
Being a dad really isn't easy...
THINK ABOUT IT, THINK ABOUT IT...
PUFF
PUFF PUFF
GRRR!
RHAAAA!
GRMPF!
MPFFF!
PFF PFF
BAD DOG!
!
Problems with your family: spouse, kids, pets? Merlin's here to find the solution.
Merlintheenchhanter.com
The new site that will give you a new lease on life.
300% success

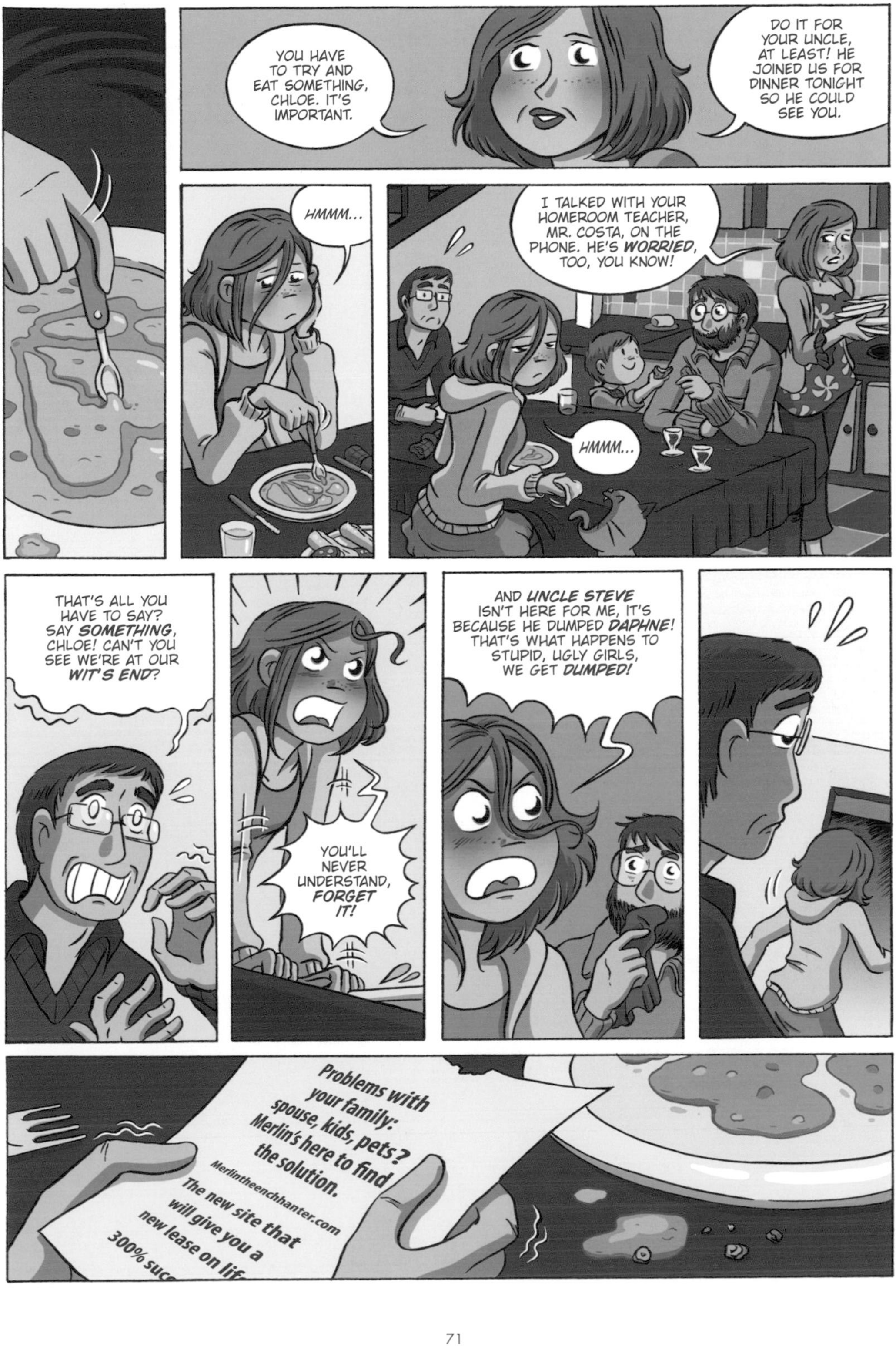
YOU HAVE TO TRY AND EAT SOMETHING, CHLOE. IT'S IMPORTANT.
DO IT FOR YOUR UNCLE, AT LEAST! HE JOINED US FOR DINNER TONIGHT SO HE COULD SEE YOU.
HMMM...
I TALKED WITH YOUR HOMEROOM TEACHER, MR. COSTA, ON THE PHONE. HE'S WORRIED, TOO, YOU KNOW!
HMMM...
THAT'S ALL YOU HAVE TO SAY? SAY SOMETHING, CHLOE! CAN'T YOU SEE WE'RE AT OUR WIT'S END?
YOU'LL NEVER UNDERSTAND, FORGET IT!
AND UNCLE STEVE ISN'T HERE FOR ME, IT'S BECAUSE HE DUMPED DAPHNE! THAT'S WHAT HAPPENS TO STUPID, UGLY GIRLS, WE GET DUMPED!
Problems with your family: spouse, kids, pets? Merlin's here to find the solution.
Merlintheenchhanter.com
The new site that will give you a new lease on lif
300% succ

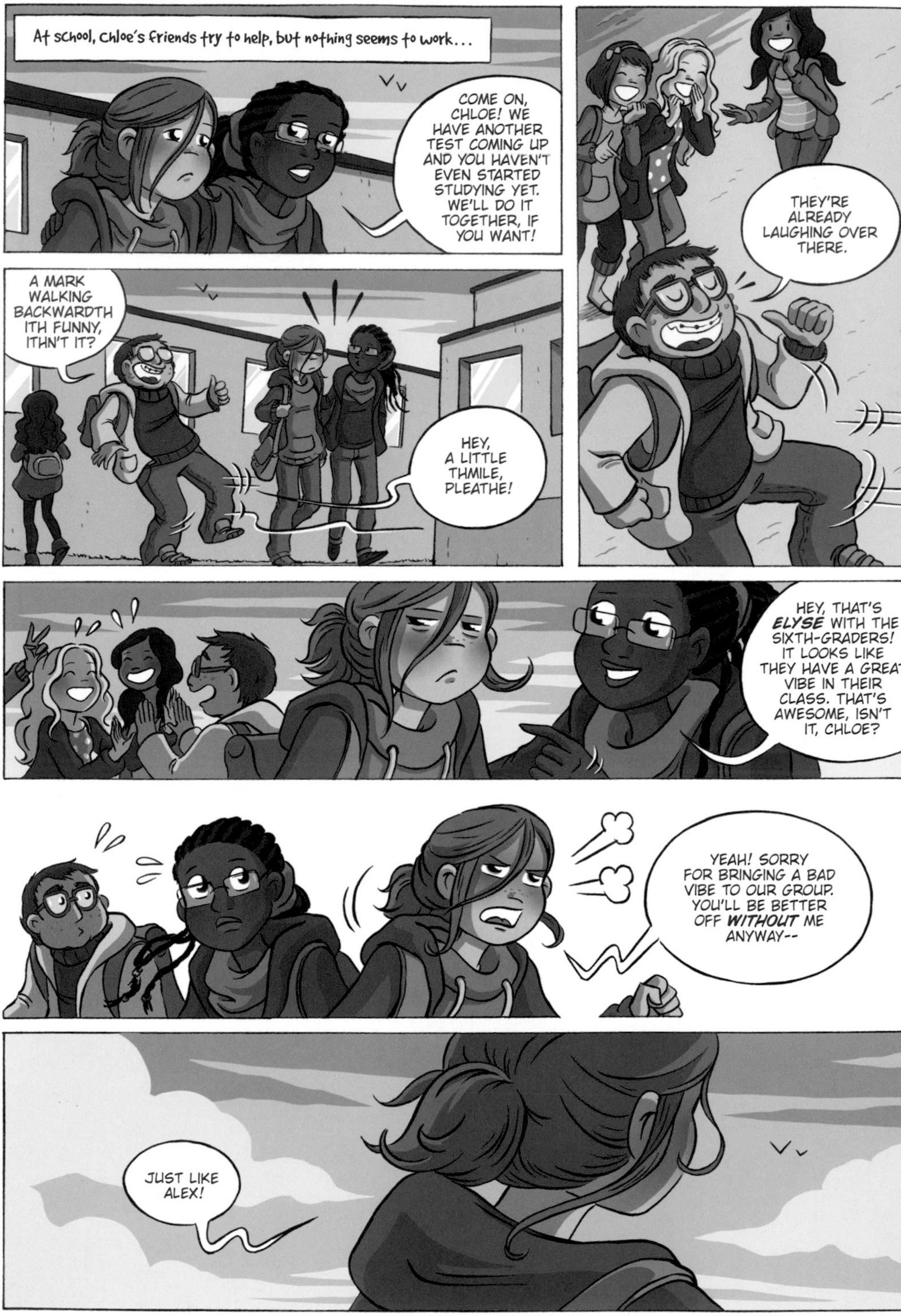
At school, Chloe's friends try to help, but nothing seems to work...
COME ON, CHLOE! WE HAVE ANOTHER TEST COMING UP AND YOU HAVEN'T EVEN STARTED STUDYING YET. WE'LL DO IT TOGETHER, IF YOU WANT!
A MARK WALKING BACKWARDTH ITH FUNNY, ITHN'T IT?
HEY, A LITTLE THMILE, PLEATHE!
THEY'RE ALREADY LAUGHING OVER THERE.
HEY, THAT'S ELYSE WITH THE SIXTH-GRADERS! IT LOOKS LIKE THEY HAVE A GREAT VIBE IN THEIR CLASS. THAT'S AWESOME, ISN'T IT, CHLOE?
YEAH! SORRY FOR BRINGING A BAD VIBE TO OUR GROUP. YOU'LL BE BETTER OFF WITHOUT ME ANYWAY--
JUST LIKE ALEX!

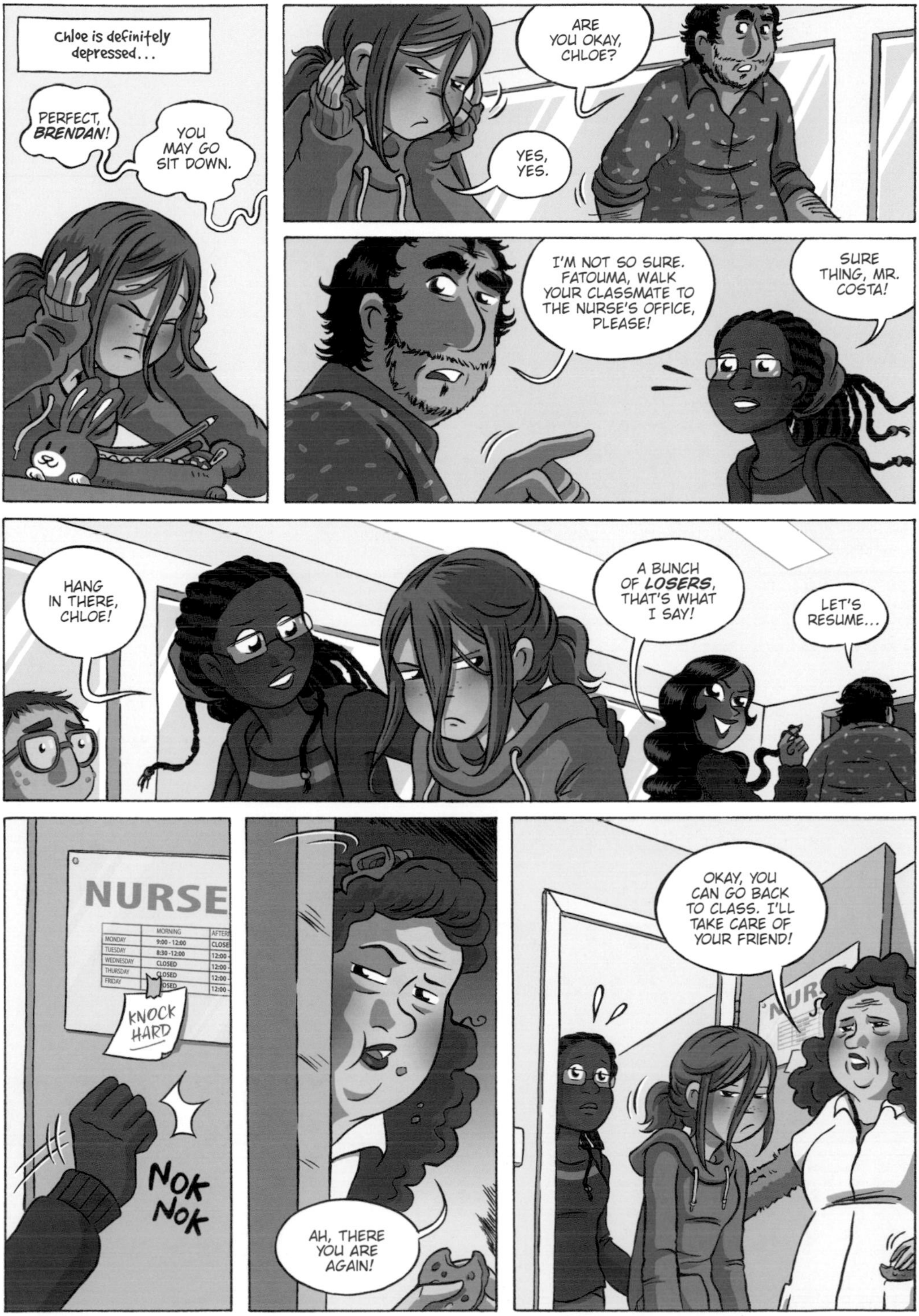

Chloe is definitely depressed...
PERFECT, BRENDAN!
YOU MAY GO SIT DOWN.
ARE YOU OKAY, CHLOE?
YES, YES.
I'M NOT SO SURE. FATOUMA, WALK YOUR CLASSMATE TO THE NURSE'S OFFICE, PLEASE!
SURE THING, MR. COSTA!
HANG IN THERE, CHLOE!
A BUNCH OF LOSERS, THAT'S WHAT I SAY!
LET'S RESUME...
NURSE
KNOCK HARD
NOK NOK
AH, THERE YOU ARE AGAIN!
OKAY, YOU CAN GO BACK TO CLASS. I'LL TAKE CARE OF YOUR FRIEND!

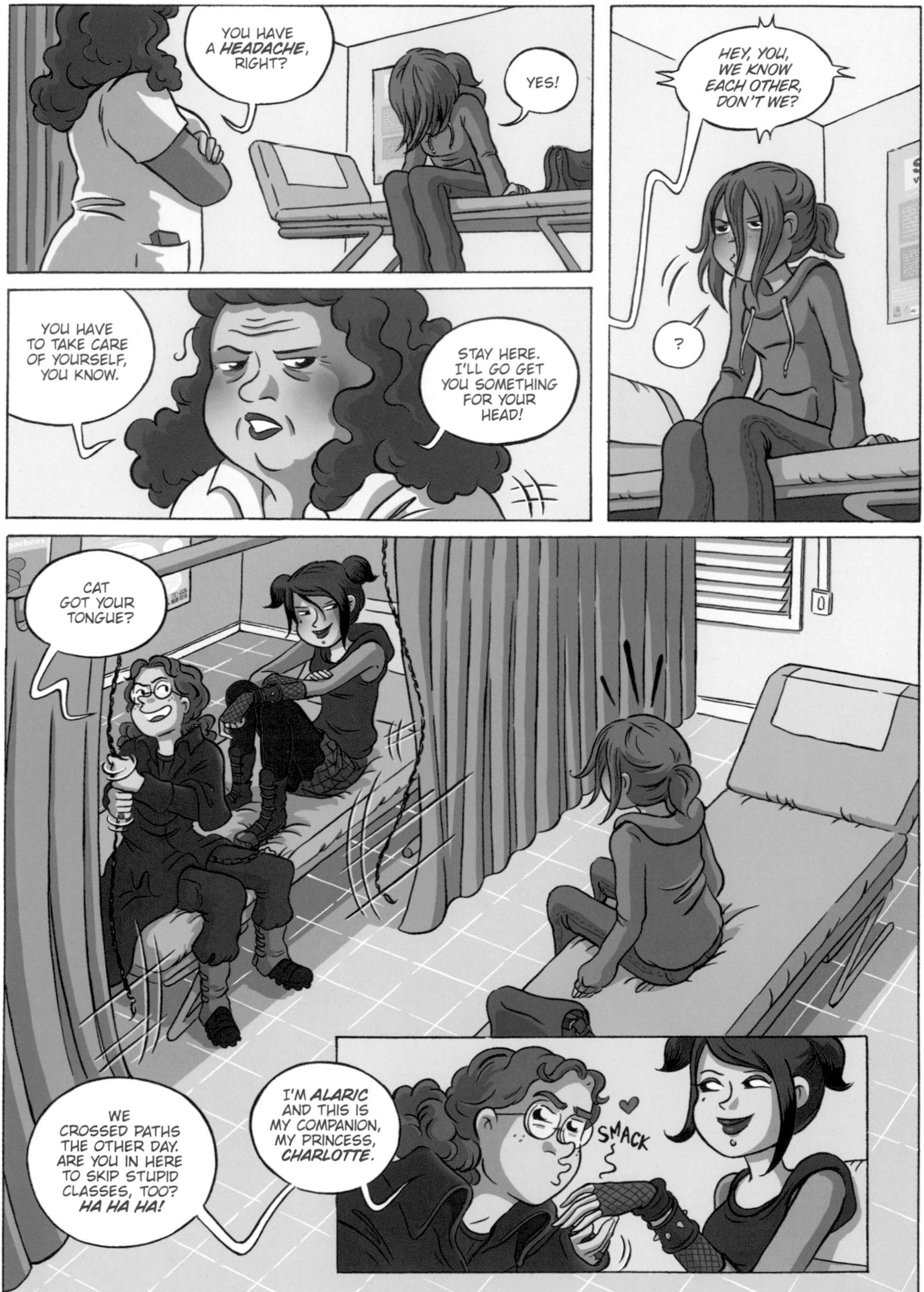
YOU HAVE A HEADACHE, RIGHT?
YES!
HEY, YOU, WE KNOW EACH OTHER, DON'T WE?
?
YOU HAVE TO TAKE CARE OF YOURSELF, YOU KNOW.
STAY HERE. I'LL GO GET YOU SOMETHING FOR YOUR HEAD!
CAT GOT YOUR TONGUE?
WE CROSSED PATHS THE OTHER DAY. ARE YOU IN HERE TO SKIP STUPID CLASSES, TOO? HA HA HA!
I'M ALARIC AND THIS IS MY COMPANION, MY PRINCESS, CHARLOTTE.
SMACK

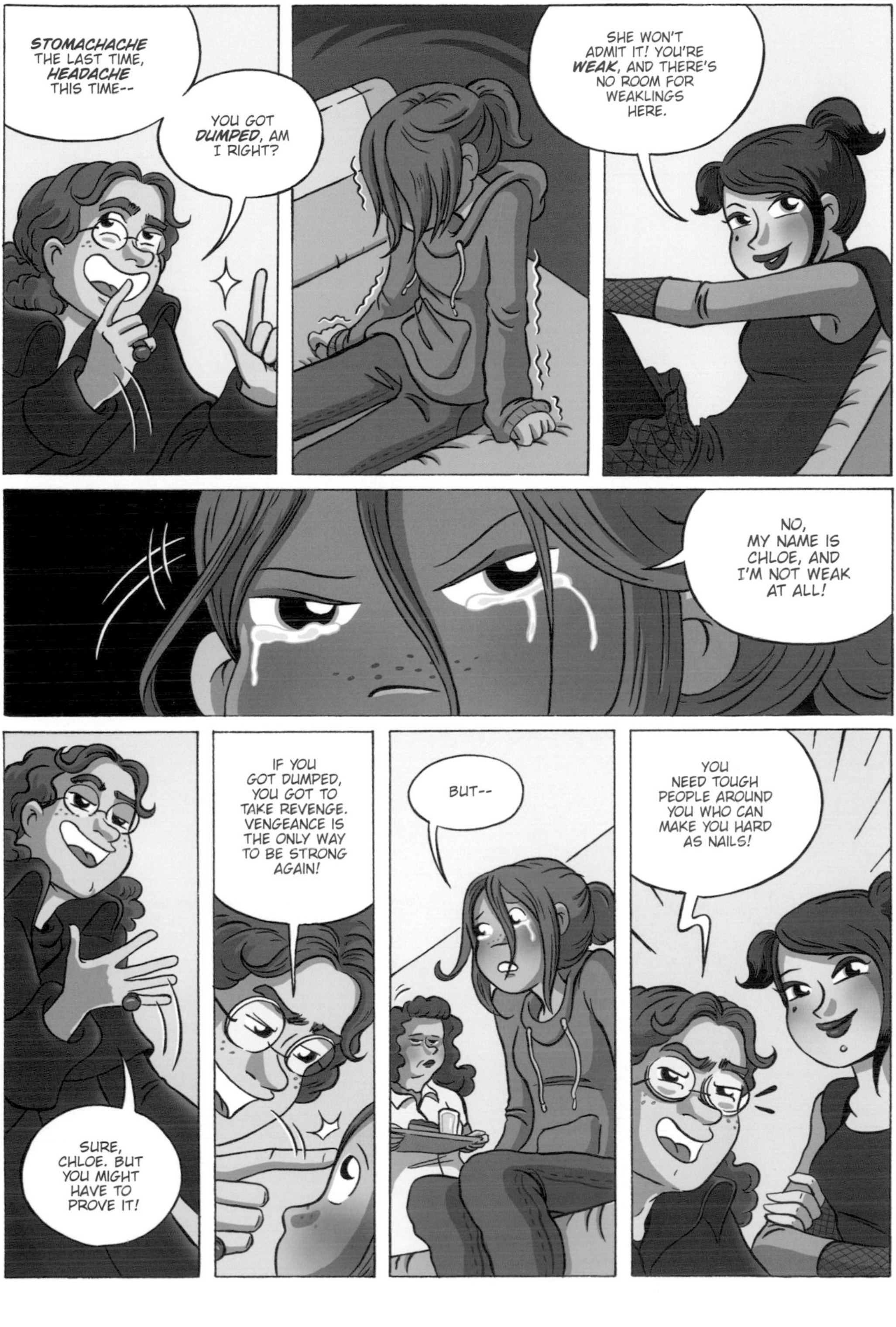
STOMACHACHE THE LAST TIME, HEADACHE THIS TIME--
YOU GOT DUMPED, AM I RIGHT?
SHE WON'T ADMIT IT! YOU'RE WEAK, AND THERE'S NO ROOM FOR WEAKLINGS HERE.
NO, MY NAME IS CHLOE, AND I'M NOT WEAK AT ALL!
SURE, CHLOE. BUT YOU MIGHT HAVE TO PROVE IT!
IF YOU GOT DUMPED, YOU GOT TO TAKE REVENGE. VENGEANCE IS THE ONLY WAY TO BE STRONG AGAIN!
BUT--
YOU NEED TOUGH PEOPLE AROUND YOU WHO CAN MAKE YOU HARD AS NAILS!

SNIFF
breakup notebook
WHY, ALEX?
We were so one-of-a-kind!
Italy is so far away!
C+A=
It's ALL MY fault!!!
I couldn't even keep you with me, Alex.
With you, I'm weeping,
my heart cries out pained
Was our love ever only feigned?
Nobody, nothing around me is normal,
Now everything around me seems so banal.
Totally lost, who I am anymore?
The two of us are done for!
Once in love, my joy has taken flight,
It probably serves me right...
Chloe
SYMPTOMS:
-stomach and head aches
-feeling apathetic
-INFINITE SADNESS
SNIFF
Here's where I am now!
All alone with myself...

Rebellion

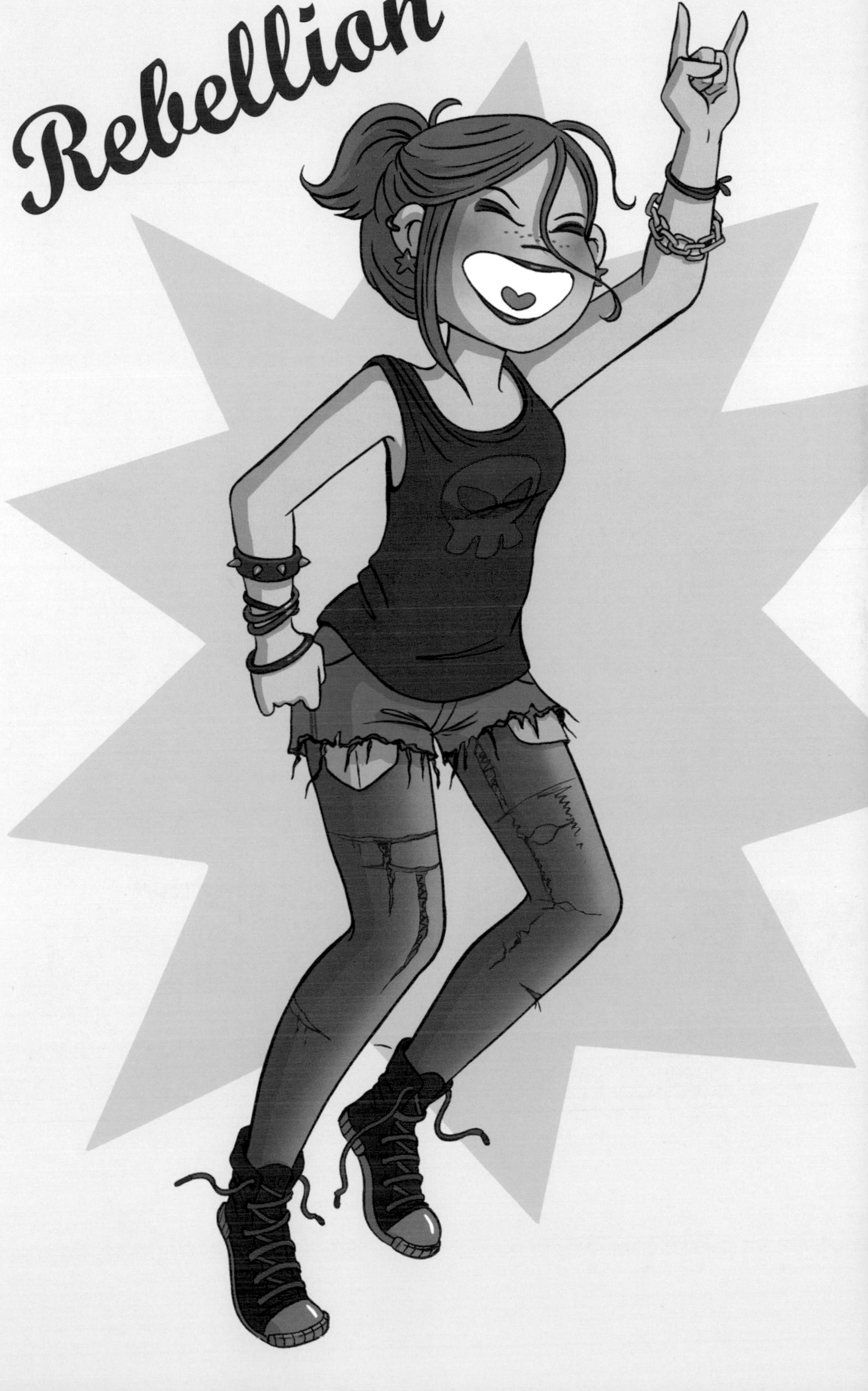

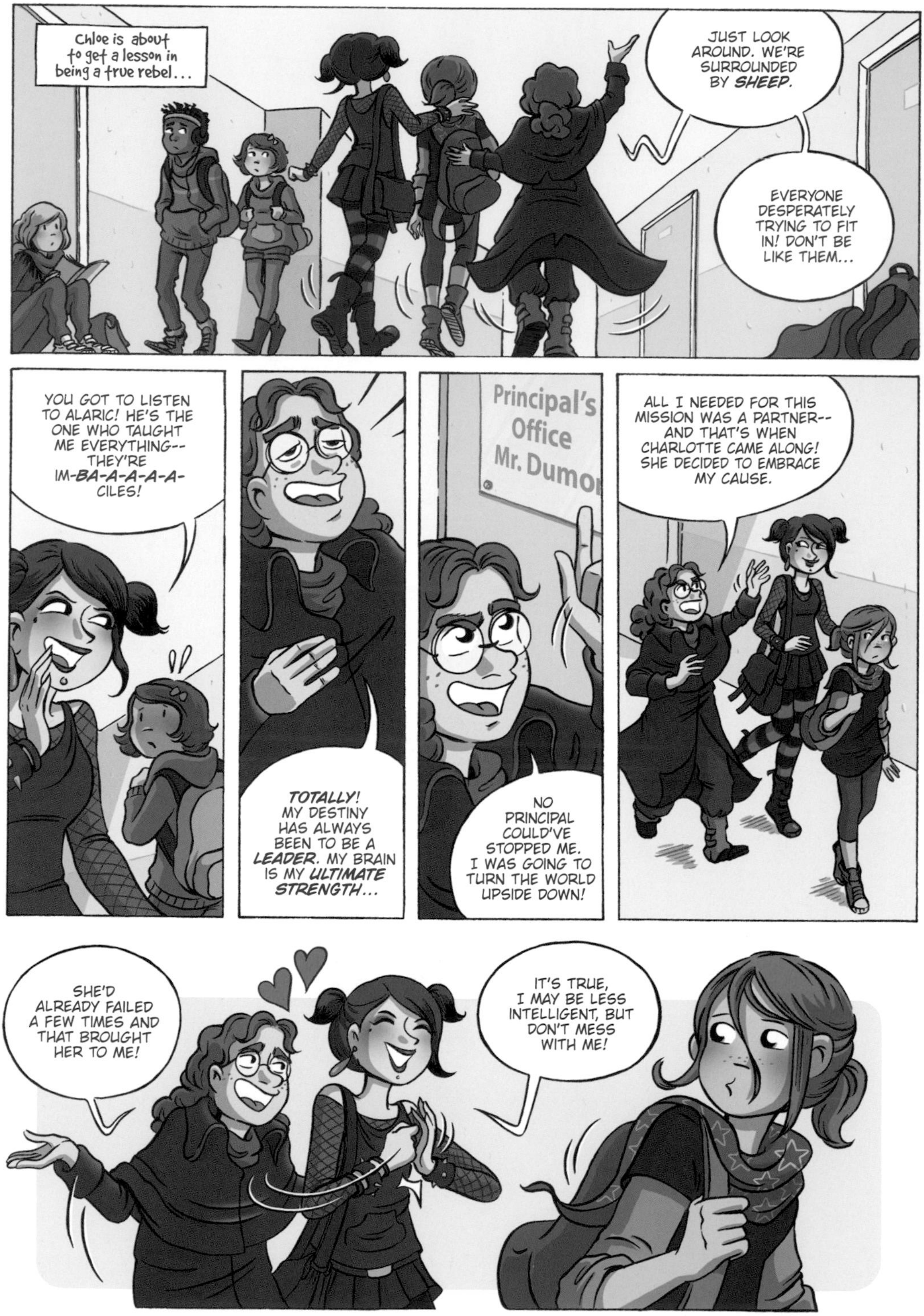
Chloe is about to get a lesson in being a true rebel...
JUST LOOK AROUND. WE'RE SURROUNDED BY SHEEP.
EVERYONE DESPERATELY TRYING TO FIT IN! DON'T BE LIKE THEM...
YOU GOT TO LISTEN TO ALARIC! HE'S THE ONE WHO TAUGHT ME EVERYTHING-- THEY'RE IM-BA-A-A-A-CILES!
TOTALLY! MY DESTINY HAS ALWAYS BEEN TO BE A LEADER. MY BRAIN IS MY ULTIMATE STRENGTH...
Principal's Office Mr. Dumor
NO PRINCIPAL COULD'VE STOPPED ME. I WAS GOING TO TURN THE WORLD UPSIDE DOWN!
ALL I NEEDED FOR THIS MISSION WAS A PARTNER-- AND THAT'S WHEN CHARLOTTE CAME ALONG! SHE DECIDED TO EMBRACE MY CAUSE.
SHE'D ALREADY FAILED A FEW TIMES AND THAT BROUGHT HER TO ME!
IT'S TRUE, I MAY BE LESS INTELLIGENT, BUT DON'T MESS WITH ME!

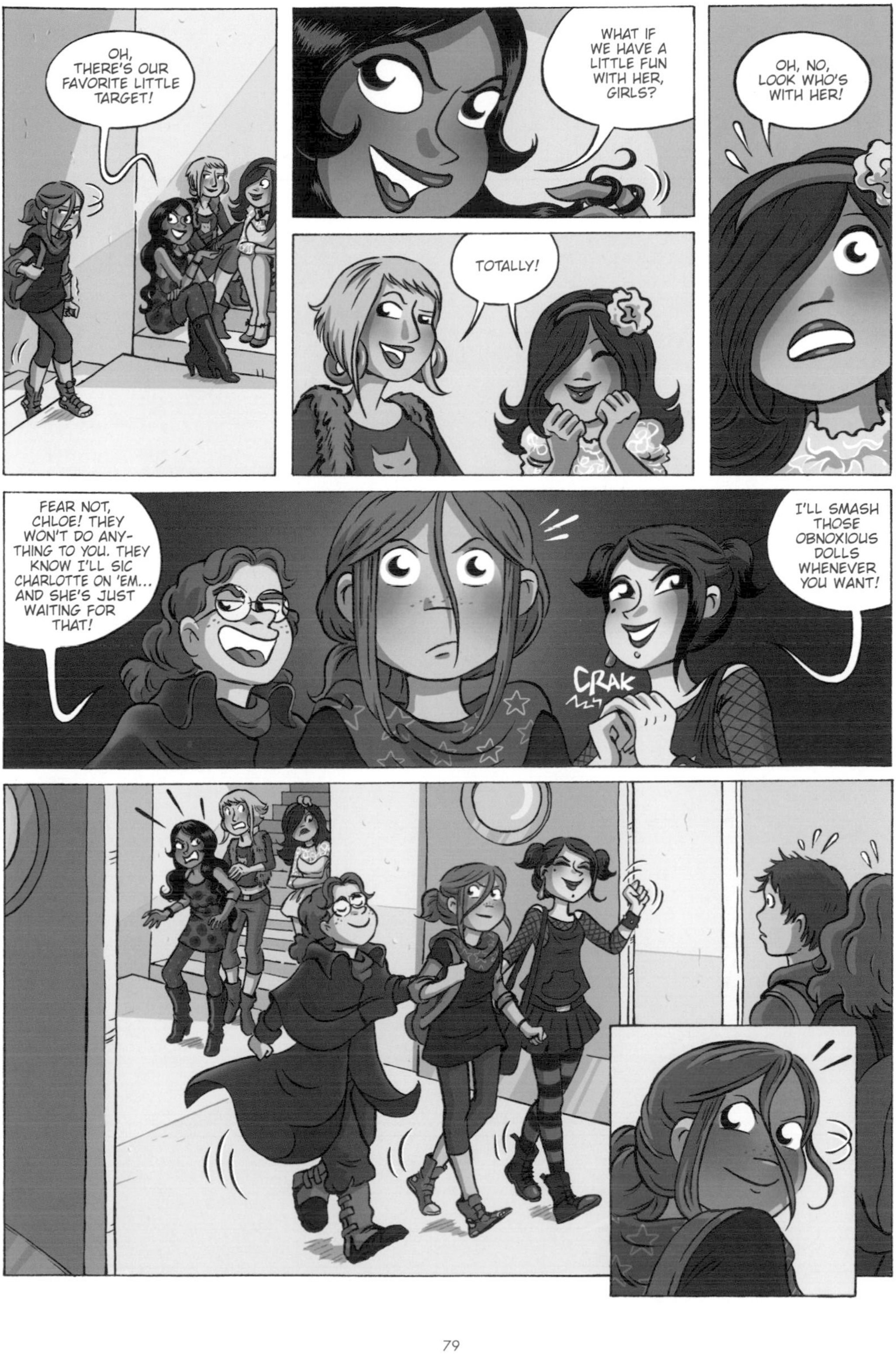
OH, THERE'S OUR FAVORITE LITTLE TARGET!
WHAT IF WE HAVE A LITTLE FUN WITH HER, GIRLS?
TOTALLY!
OH, NO, LOOK WHO'S WITH HER!
FEAR NOT, CHLOE! THEY WON'T DO ANYTHING TO YOU. THEY KNOW I'LL SIC CHARLOTTE ON 'EM... AND SHE'S JUST WAITING FOR THAT!
CRAK
I'LL SMASH THOSE OBNOXIOUS DOLLS WHENEVER YOU WANT!

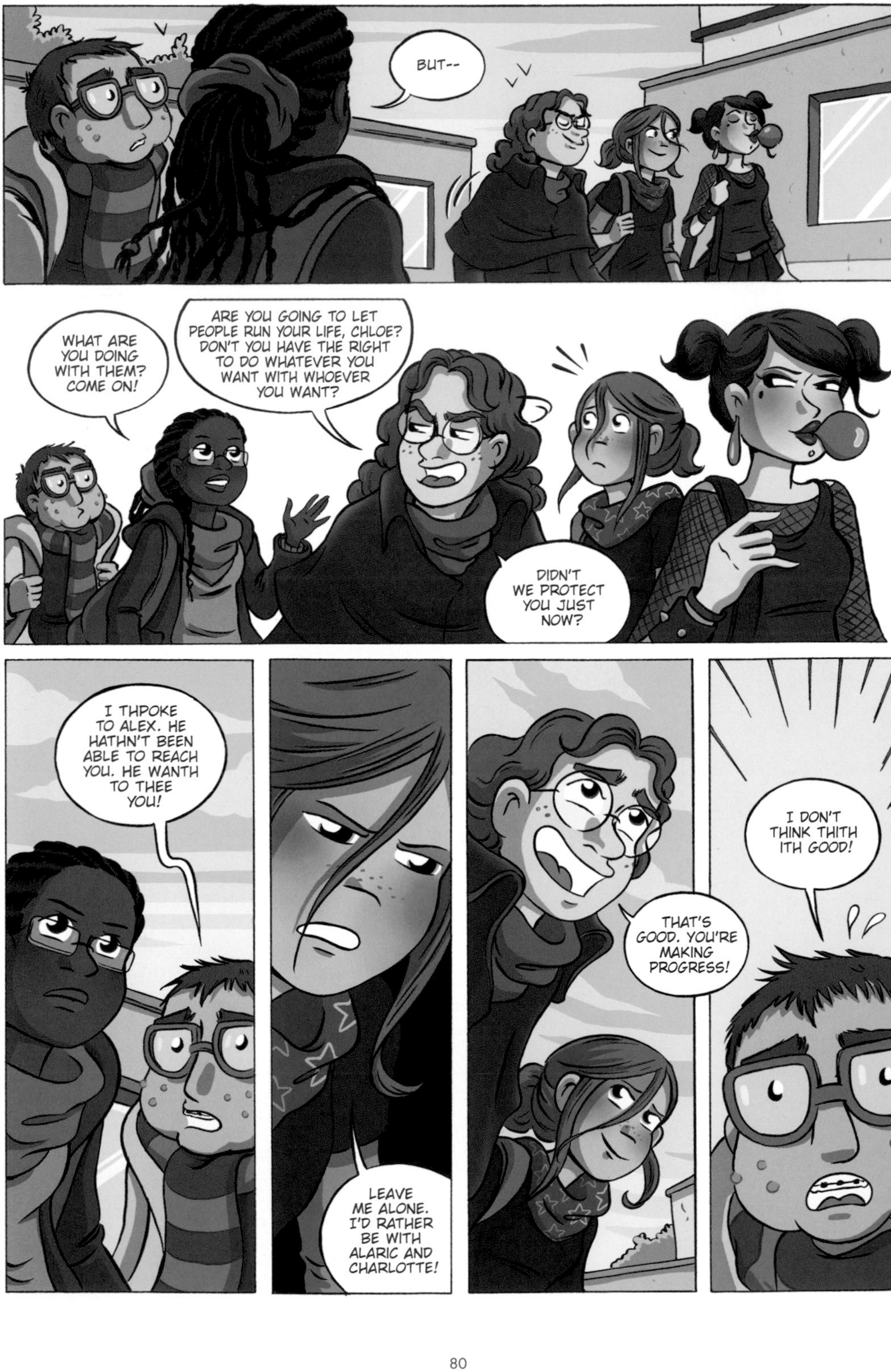
BUT--
WHAT ARE YOU DOING WITH THEM? COME ON!
ARE YOU GOING TO LET PEOPLE RUN YOUR LIFE, CHLOE? DON'T YOU HAVE THE RIGHT TO DO WHATEVER YOU WANT WITH WHOEVER YOU WANT?
DIDN'T WE PROTECT YOU JUST NOW?
I THPOKE TO ALEX. HE HATHN'T BEEN ABLE TO REACH YOU. HE WANTH TO THEE YOU!
LEAVE ME ALONE. I'D RATHER BE WITH ALARIC AND CHARLOTTE!
THAT'S GOOD. YOU'RE MAKING PROGRESS!
I DON'T THINK THITH ITH GOOD!

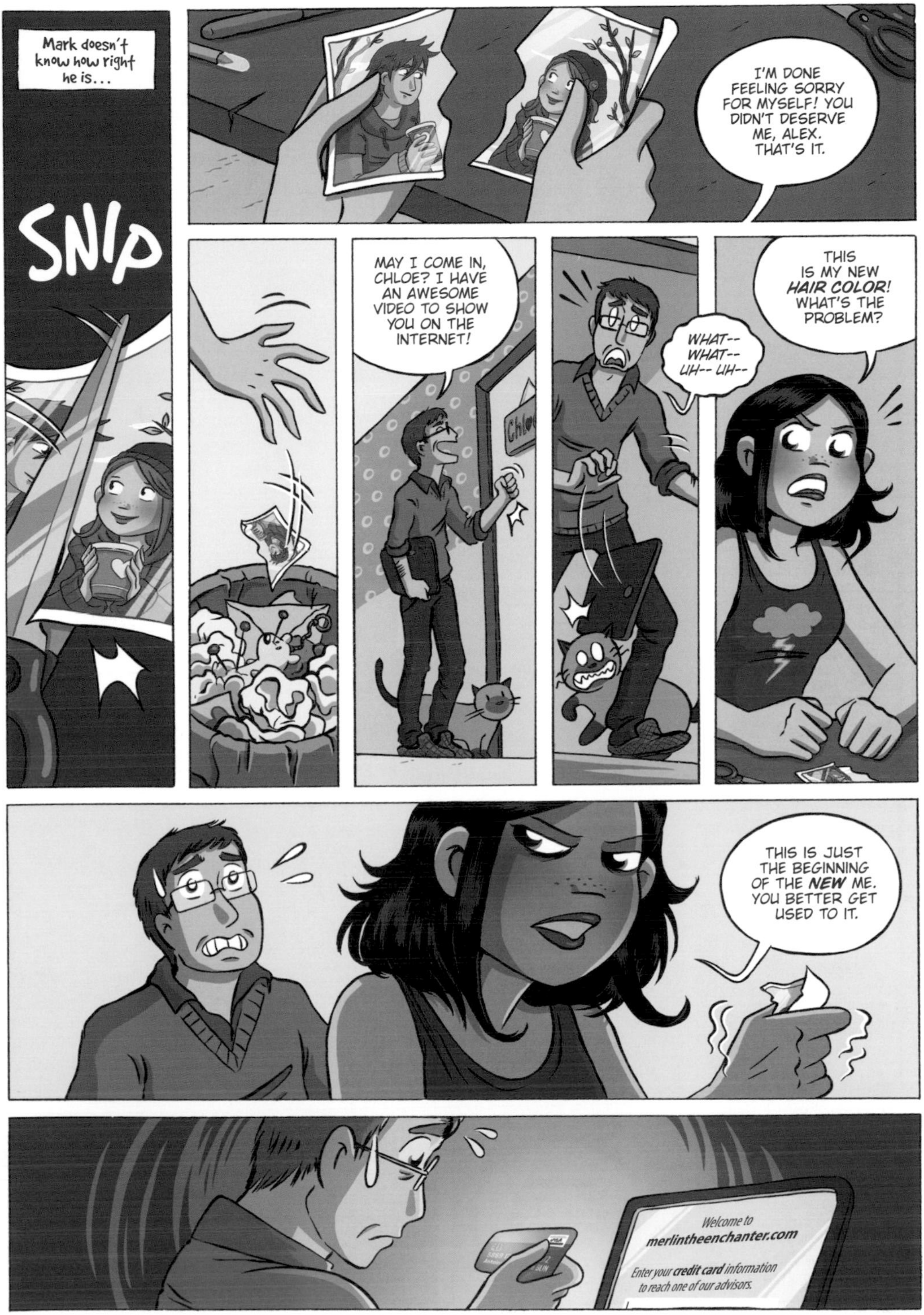
Mark doesn't know how right he is...
SNIP
I'M DONE FEELING SORRY FOR MYSELF! YOU DIDN'T DESERVE ME, ALEX. THAT'S IT.
MAY I COME IN, CHLOE? I HAVE AN AWESOME VIDEO TO SHOW YOU ON THE INTERNET!
Chloe
WHAT-- WHAT-- UH-- UH--
THIS IS MY NEW HAIR COLOR! WHAT'S THE PROBLEM?
THIS IS JUST THE BEGINNING OF THE NEW ME. YOU BETTER GET USED TO IT.
Welcome to
merlintheenchanter.com
Enter your credit card information to reach one of our advisors.

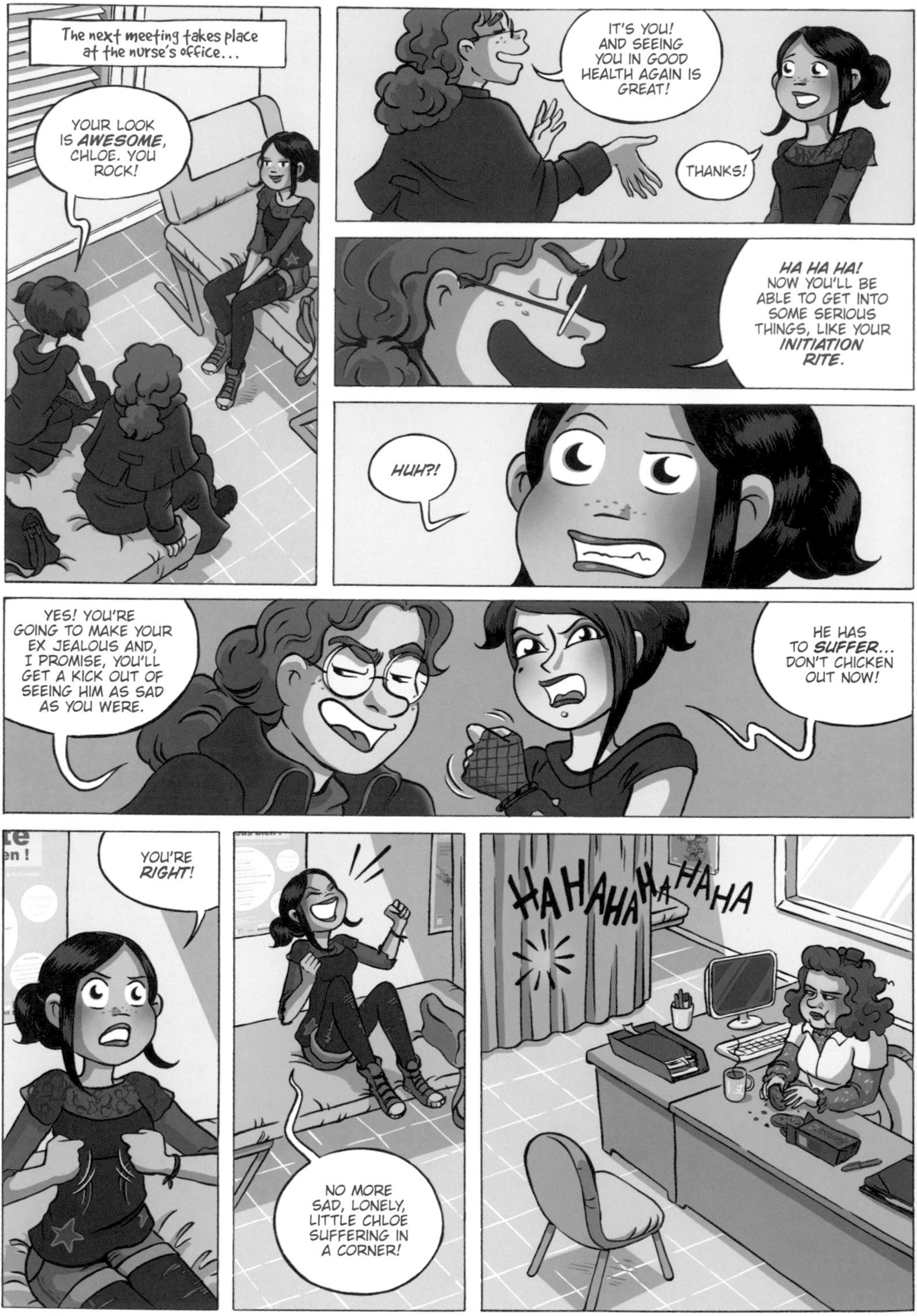
The next meeting takes place at the nurse's office...
YOUR LOOK IS **AWESOME**, CHLOE. YOU ROCK!
IT'S YOU! AND SEEING YOU IN GOOD HEALTH AGAIN IS GREAT!
THANKS!
HA HA HA! NOW YOU'LL BE ABLE TO GET INTO SOME SERIOUS THINGS, LIKE YOUR **INITIATION RITE**.
HUH?!
YES! YOU'RE GOING TO MAKE YOUR EX JEALOUS AND, I PROMISE, YOU'LL GET A KICK OUT OF SEEING HIM AS SAD AS YOU WERE.
HE HAS TO **SUFFER**... DON'T CHICKEN OUT NOW!
YOU'RE **RIGHT**!
NO MORE SAD, LONELY, LITTLE CHLOE SUFFERING IN A CORNER!
HAHAHAHAHAHA

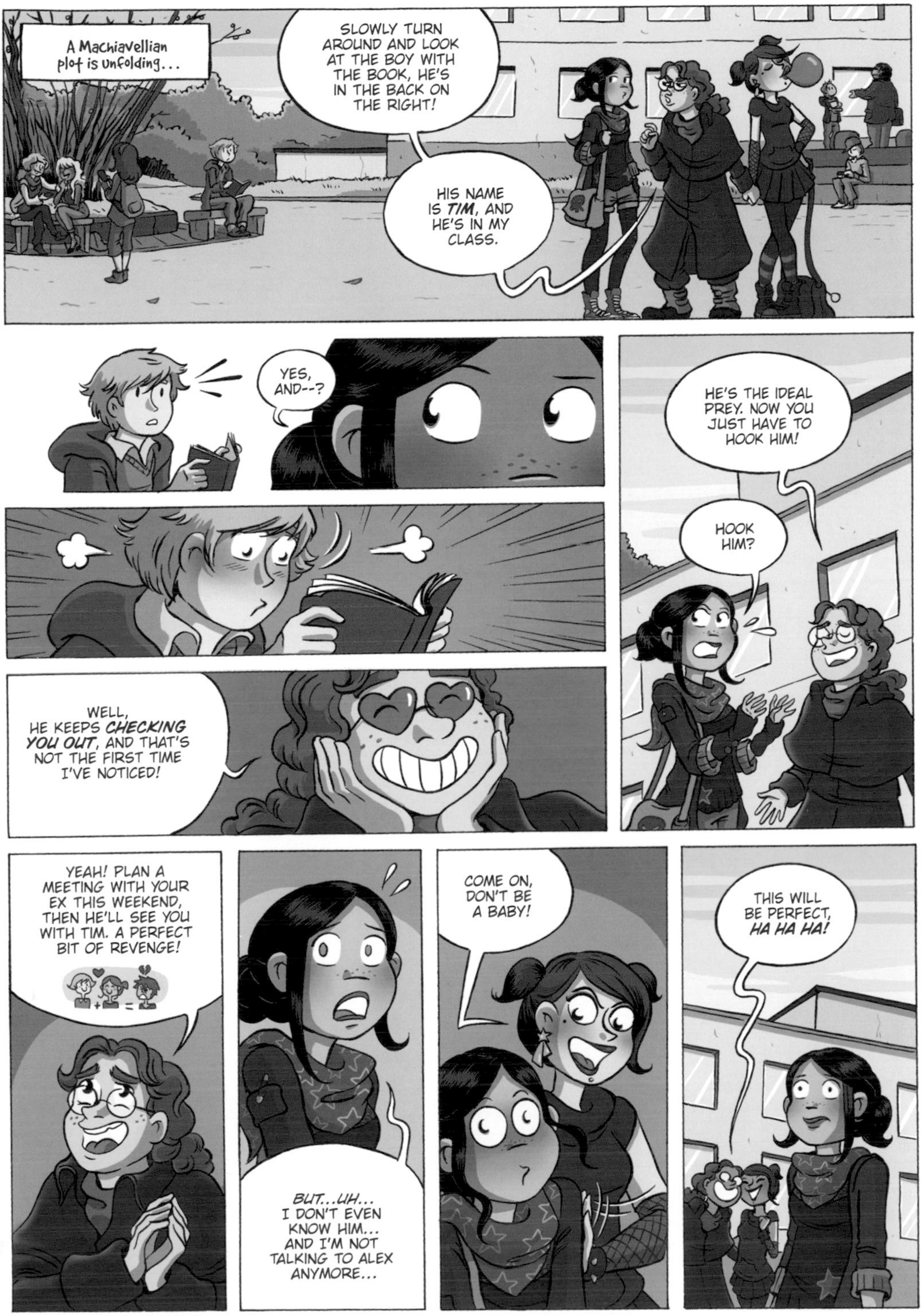
A Machiavellian plot is unfolding...
SLOWLY TURN AROUND AND LOOK AT THE BOOK, HE'S IN THE BACK ON THE RIGHT!
HIS NAME IS TIM, AND HE'S IN MY CLASS.
YES, AND--?
HE'S THE IDEAL PREY. NOW YOU JUST HAVE TO HOOK HIM!
HOOK HIM?
WELL, HE KEEPS CHECKING YOU OUT, AND THAT'S NOT THE FIRST TIME I'VE NOTICED!
YEAH! PLAN A MEETING WITH YOUR EX THIS WEEKEND, THEN HE'LL SEE YOU WITH TIM. A PERFECT BIT OF REVENGE!
BUT...UH... I DON'T EVEN KNOW HIM... AND I'M NOT TALKING TO ALEX ANYMORE...
COME ON, DON'T BE A BABY!
THIS WILL BE PERFECT, HA HA HA!

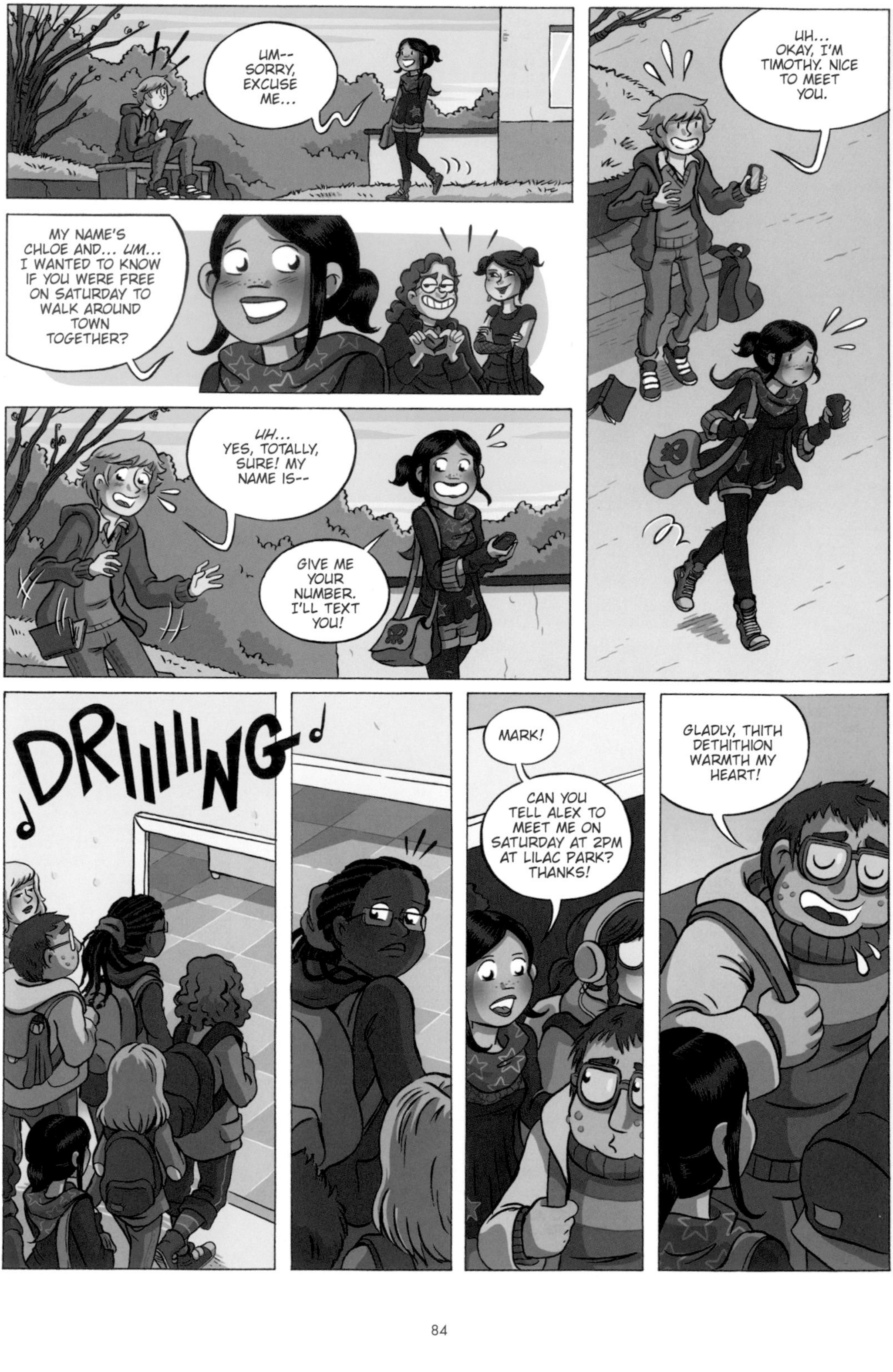
UM--
SORRY,
EXCUSE
ME...
MY NAME'S CHLOE AND... UM... I WANTED TO KNOW IF YOU WERE FREE ON SATURDAY TO WALK AROUND TOWN TOGETHER?
UH... YES, TOTALLY, SURE! MY NAME IS--
GIVE ME YOUR NUMBER. I'LL TEXT YOU!
UH... OKAY, I'M TIMOTHY. NICE TO MEET YOU.
DRIIIING
MARK!
CAN YOU TELL ALEX TO MEET ME ON SATURDAY AT 2PM AT LILAC PARK? THANKS!
GLADLY, THITH DETHITHION WARMTH MY HEART!

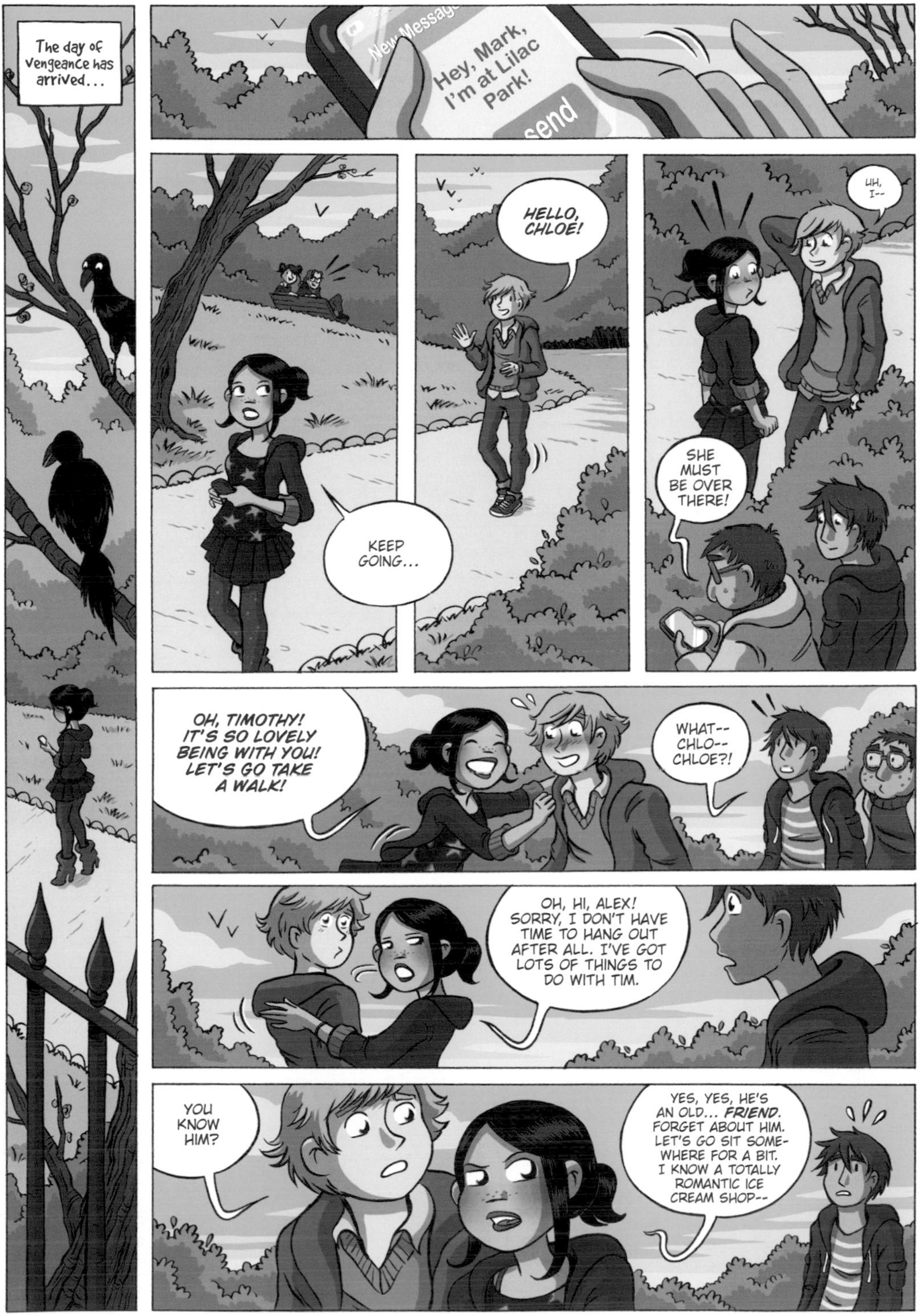

The day of vengeance has arrived...
New Message
Hey, Mark, I'm at Lilac Park!
send
KEEP GOING...
HELLO, CHLOE!
UH, I--
SHE MUST BE OVER THERE!
OH, TIMOTHY! IT'S SO LOVELY BEING WITH YOU! LET'S GO TAKE A WALK!
WHAT-- CHLO-- CHLOE?!
OH, HI, ALEX! SORRY, I DON'T HAVE TIME TO HANG OUT AFTER ALL. I'VE GOT LOTS OF THINGS TO DO WITH TIM.
YOU KNOW HIM?
YES, YES, HE'S AN OLD... FRIEND. FORGET ABOUT HIM. LET'S GO SIT SOME-WHERE FOR A BIT. I KNOW A TOTALLY ROMANTIC ICE CREAM SHOP--

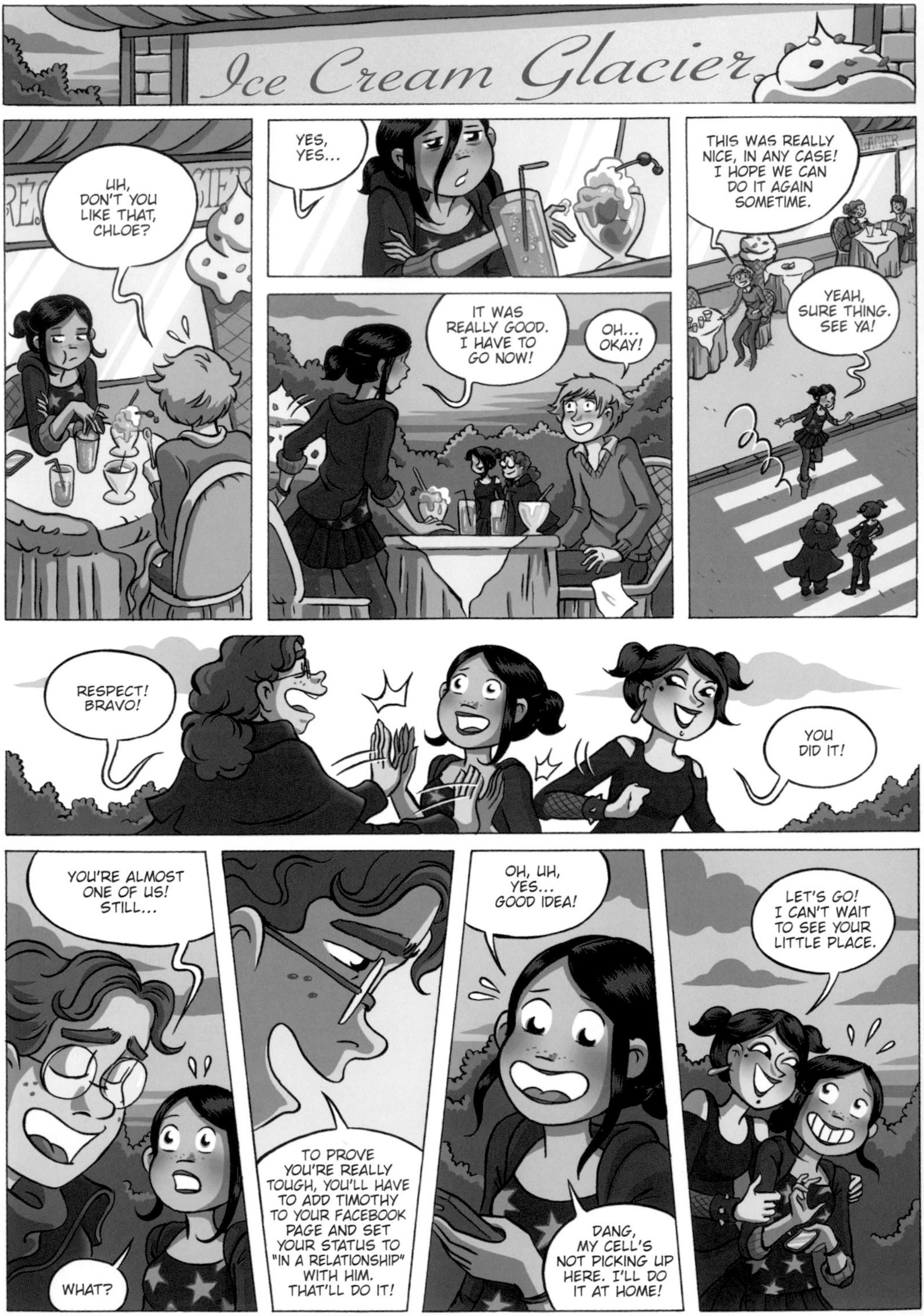
Ice Cream Glacier
UH, DON'T YOU LIKE THAT, CHLOE?
YES, YES...
IT WAS REALLY GOOD. I HAVE TO GO NOW!
OH... OKAY!
THIS WAS REALLY NICE, IN ANY CASE! I HOPE WE CAN DO IT AGAIN SOMETIME.
YEAH, SURE THING. SEE YA!
RESPECT! BRAVO!
YOU DID IT!
YOU'RE ALMOST ONE OF US! STILL...
WHAT?
TO PROVE YOU'RE REALLY TOUGH, YOU'LL HAVE TO ADD TIMOTHY TO YOUR FACEBOOK PAGE AND SET YOUR STATUS TO "IN A RELATIONSHIP" WITH HIM. THAT'LL DO IT!
OH, UH, YES... GOOD IDEA!
DANG, MY CELL'S NOT PICKING UP HERE. I'LL DO IT AT HOME!
LET'S GO! I CAN'T WAIT TO SEE YOUR LITTLE PLACE.

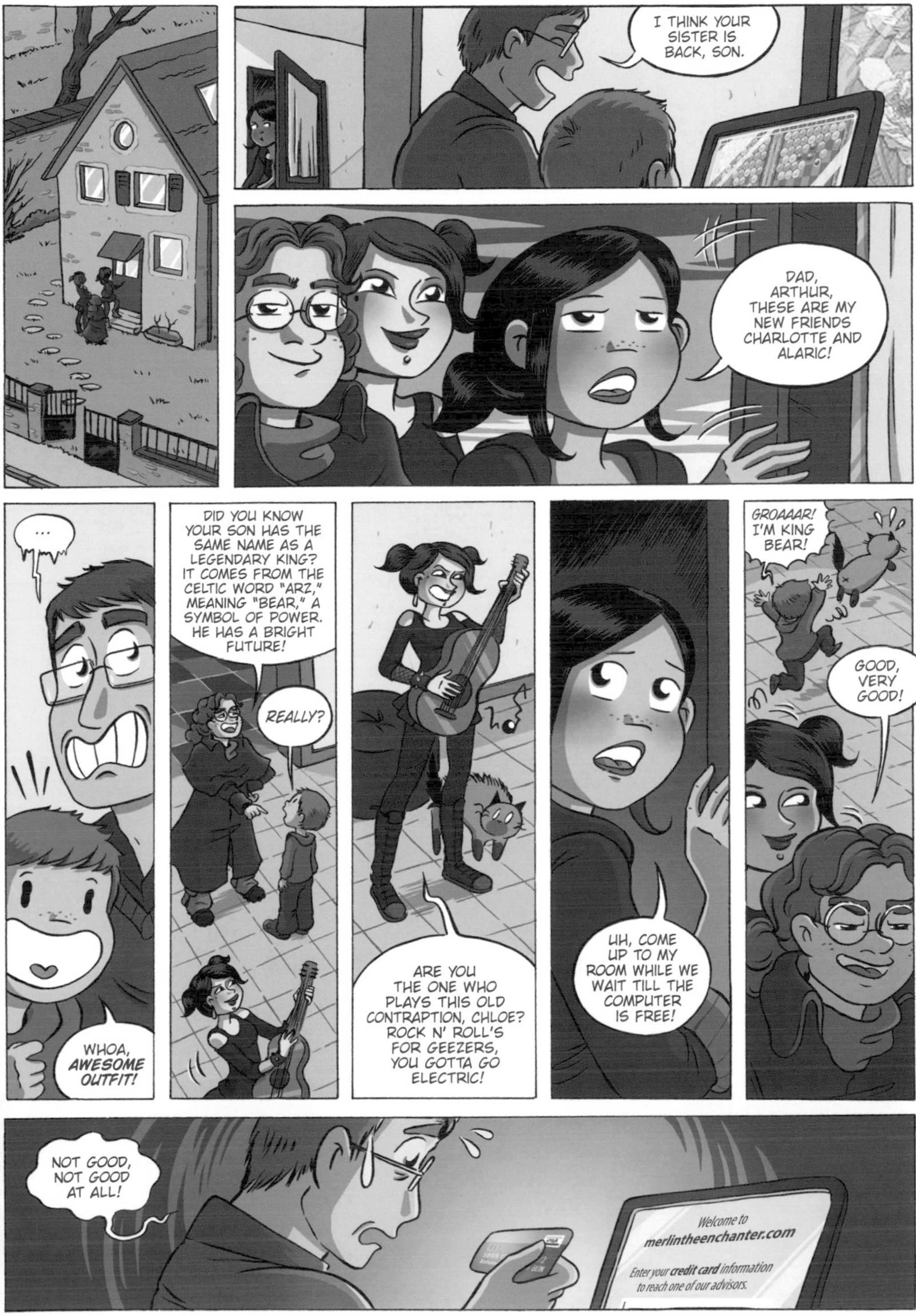
I THINK YOUR SISTER IS BACK, SON.
DAD, ARTHUR, THESE ARE MY NEW FRIENDS CHARLOTTE AND ALARIC!
...
WHOA, AWESOME OUTFIT!
DID YOU KNOW YOUR SON HAS THE SAME NAME AS A LEGENDARY KING? IT COMES FROM THE CELTIC WORD "ARZ," MEANING "BEAR," A SYMBOL OF POWER. HE HAS A BRIGHT FUTURE!
REALLY?
ARE YOU THE ONE WHO PLAYS THIS OLD CONTRAPTION, CHLOE? ROCK N' ROLL'S FOR GEEZERS, YOU GOTTA GO ELECTRIC!
UH, COME UP TO MY ROOM WHILE WE WAIT TILL THE COMPUTER IS FREE!
GROAAAR! I'M KING BEAR!
GOOD, VERY GOOD!
NOT GOOD, NOT GOOD AT ALL!
Welcome to merlintheenchanter.com
Enter your credit card information to reach one of our advisors.

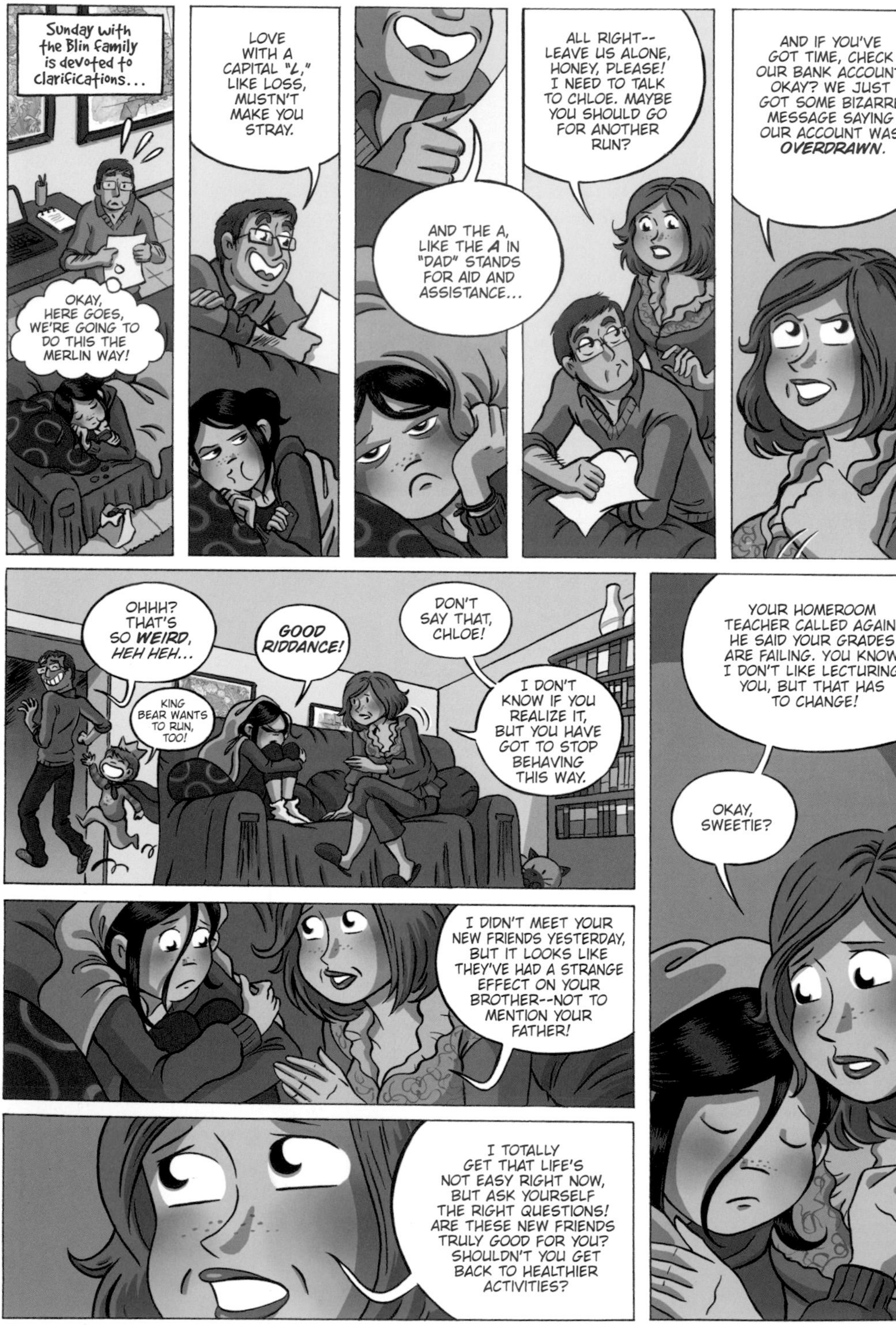
Sunday with the Blin family is devoted to clarifications...
OKAY, HERE GOES, WE'RE GOING TO DO THIS THE MERLIN WAY!
LOVE WITH A CAPITAL "L," LIKE LOSS, MUSTN'T MAKE YOU STRAY.
AND THE A, LIKE THE A IN "DAD" STANDS FOR AID AND ASSISTANCE...
ALL RIGHT-- LEAVE US ALONE, HONEY, PLEASE! I NEED TO TALK TO CHLOE. MAYBE YOU SHOULD GO FOR ANOTHER RUN?
AND IF YOU'VE GOT TIME, CHECK OUR BANK ACCOUNT, OKAY? WE JUST GOT SOME BIZARRE MESSAGE SAYING OUR ACCOUNT WAS OVERDRAWN.
OHHH? THAT'S SO WEIRD, HEH HEH...
KING BEAR WANTS TO RUN, TOO!
GOOD RIDDANCE!
DON'T SAY THAT, CHLOE!
I DON'T KNOW IF YOU REALIZE IT, BUT YOU HAVE GOT TO STOP BEHAVING THIS WAY.
I DIDN'T MEET YOUR NEW FRIENDS YESTERDAY, BUT IT LOOKS LIKE THEY'VE HAD A STRANGE EFFECT ON YOUR BROTHER--NOT TO MENTION YOUR FATHER!
I TOTALLY GET THAT LIFE'S NOT EASY RIGHT NOW, BUT ASK YOURSELF THE RIGHT QUESTIONS! ARE THESE NEW FRIENDS TRULY GOOD FOR YOU? SHOULDN'T YOU GET BACK TO HEALTHIER ACTIVITIES?
YOUR HOMEROOM TEACHER CALLED AGAIN, HE SAID YOUR GRADES ARE FAILING. YOU KNOW I DON'T LIKE LECTURING YOU, BUT THAT HAS TO CHANGE!
OKAY, SWEETIE?

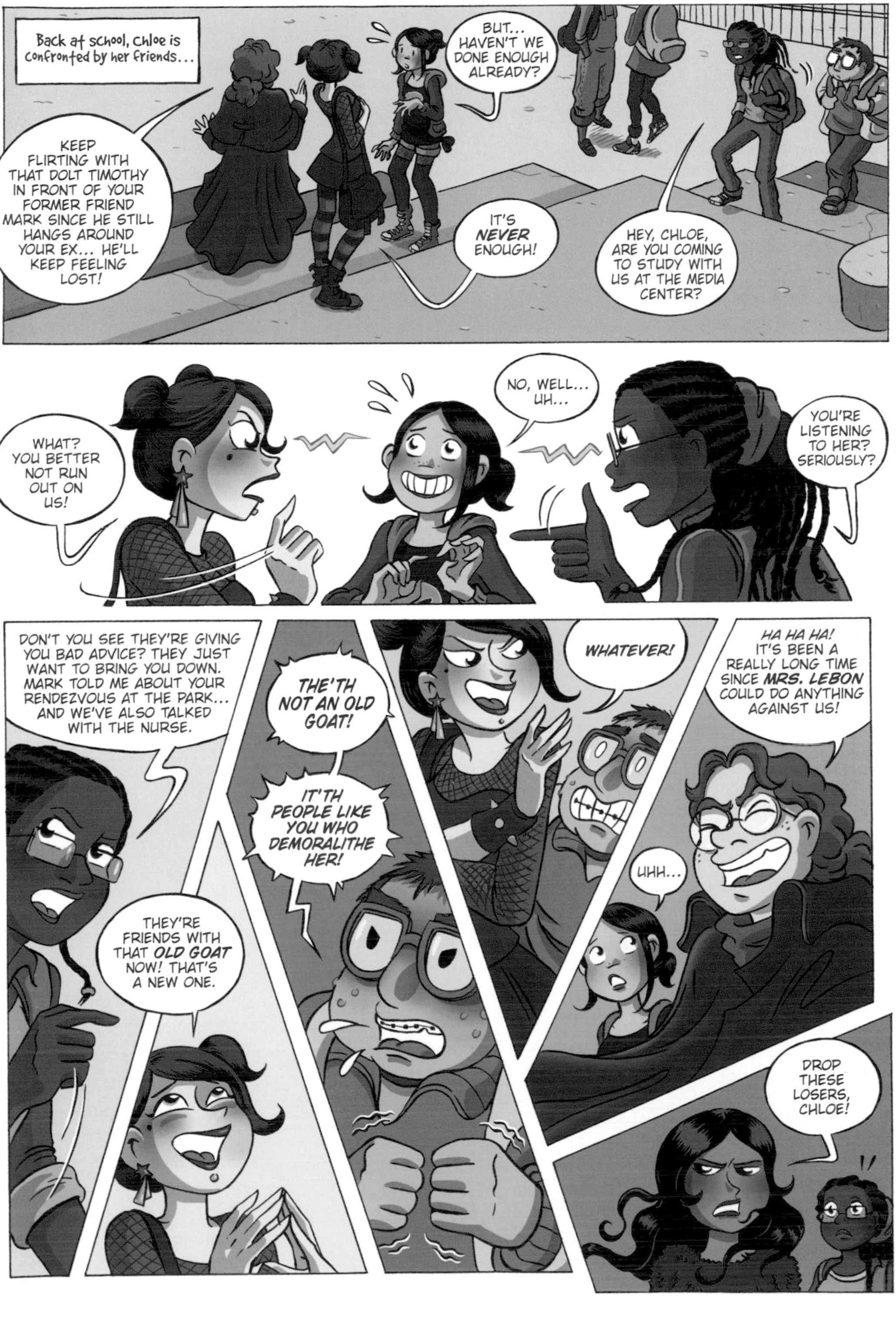

Back at school, Chloe is confronted by her friends...
KEEP FLIRTING WITH THAT DOLT TIMOTHY IN FRONT OF YOUR FORMER FRIEND MARK SINCE HE STILL HANGS AROUND YOUR EX... HE'LL KEEP FEELING LOST!
BUT... HAVEN'T WE DONE ENOUGH ALREADY?
IT'S NEVER ENOUGH!
HEY, CHLOE, ARE YOU COMING TO STUDY WITH US AT THE MEDIA CENTER?
WHAT? YOU BETTER NOT RUN OUT ON US!
NO, WELL... UH...
YOU'RE LISTENING TO HER? SERIOUSLY?
DON'T YOU SEE THEY'RE GIVING YOU BAD ADVICE? THEY JUST WANT TO BRING YOU DOWN. MARK TOLD ME ABOUT YOUR RENDEZVOUS AT THE PARK... AND WE'VE ALSO TALKED WITH THE NURSE.
THEY'RE FRIENDS WITH THAT OLD GOAT NOW! THAT'S A NEW ONE.
THE'TH NOT AN OLD GOAT!
IT'TH PEOPLE LIKE YOU WHO DEMORALITHE HER!
WHATEVER!
HA HA HA! IT'S BEEN A REALLY LONG TIME SINCE MRS. LEBON COULD DO ANYTHING AGAINST US!
UHH...
DROP THESE LOSERS, CHLOE!

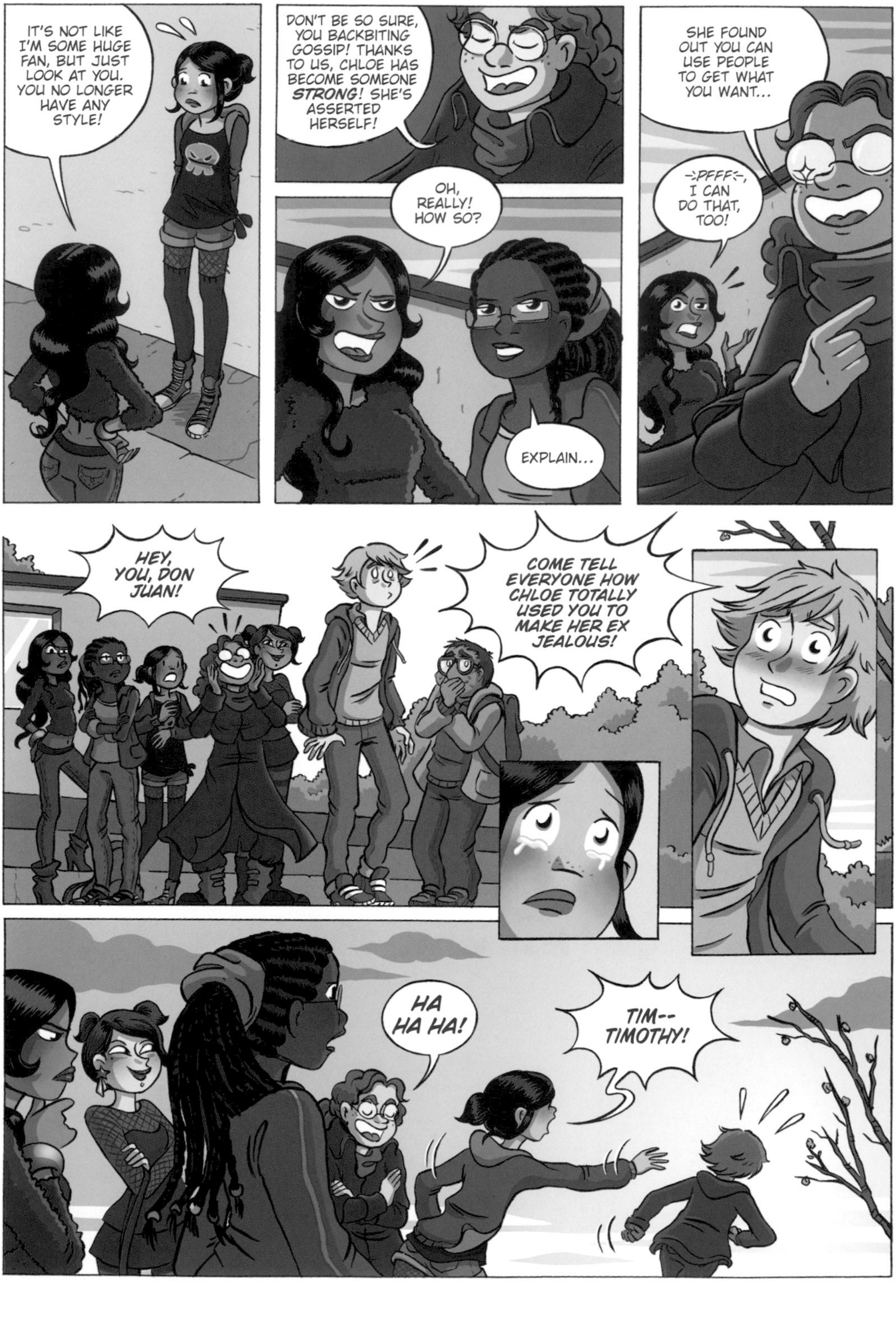
IT'S NOT LIKE I'M SOME HUGE FAN, BUT JUST LOOK AT YOU. YOU NO LONGER HAVE ANY STYLE!
DON'T BE SO SURE, YOU BACKBITING GOSSIP! THANKS TO US, CHLOE HAS BECOME SOMEONE STRONG! SHE'S ASSERTED HERSELF!
OH, REALLY! HOW SO?
EXPLAIN...
SHE FOUND OUT YOU CAN USE PEOPLE TO GET WHAT YOU WANT...
PFFF, I CAN DO THAT, TOO!
HEY, YOU, DON JUAN!
COME TELL EVERYONE HOW CHLOE TOTALLY USED YOU TO MAKE HER EX JEALOUS!
HA HA HA!
TIM-- TIMOTHY!

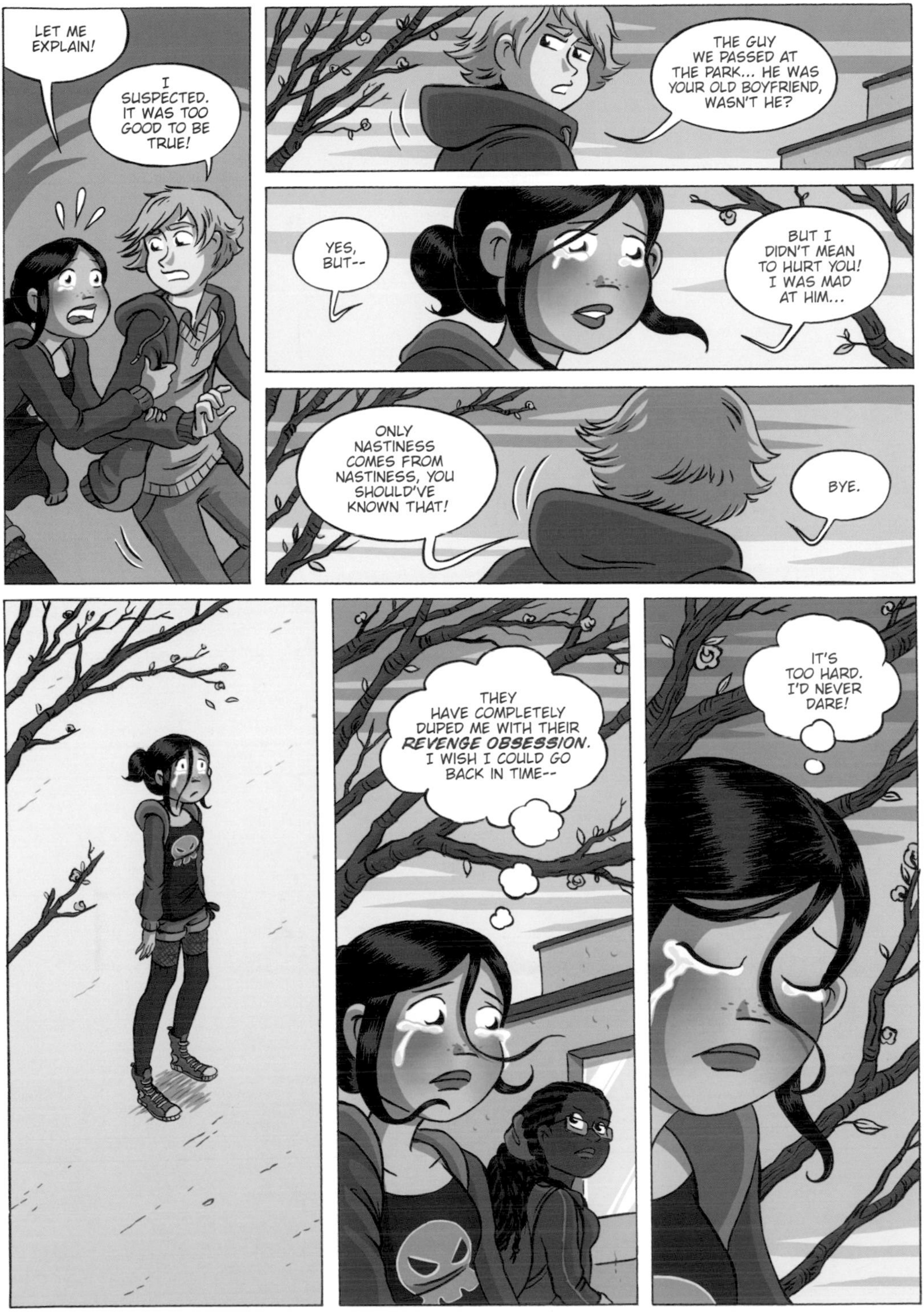
LET ME EXPLAIN!
I SUSPECTED. IT WAS TOO GOOD TO BE TRUE!
THE GUY WE PASSED AT THE PARK... HE WAS YOUR OLD BOYFRIEND, WASN'T HE?
YES, BUT--
BUT I DIDN'T MEAN TO HURT YOU! I WAS MAD AT HIM...
ONLY NASTINESS COMES FROM NASTINESS, YOU SHOULD'VE KNOWN THAT!
BYE.
THEY HAVE COMPLETELY DUPED ME WITH THEIR ***REVENGE OBSESSION***. I WISH I COULD GO BACK IN TIME--
IT'S TOO HARD. I'D NEVER DARE!

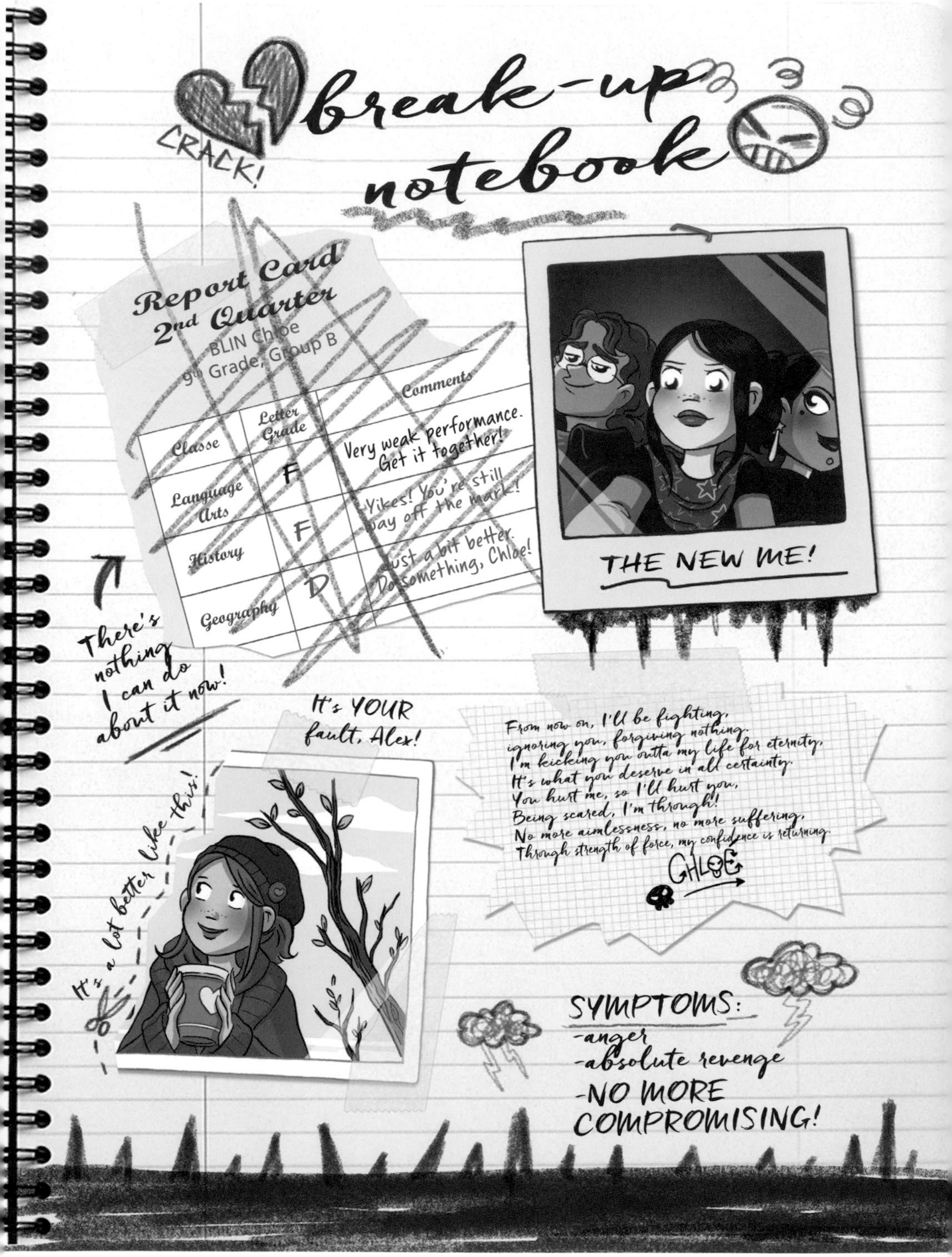
break-up notebook
CRACK!
Report Card
2nd Quarter
BLIN Chloe
9th Grade, Group B
Classe | Letter Grade | Comments
Language Arts | F | Very weak performance. Get it together!
History | F | Yikes! You're still way off the mark!
Geography | D | Just a bit better. Do something, Chloe!
There's nothing I can do about it now!
THE NEW ME!
It's YOUR fault, Alex!
It's a lot better like this!
From now on, I'll be fighting,
ignoring you, forgiving nothing.
I'm kicking you outta my life for eternity,
It's what you deserve in all certainty.
You hurt me, so I'll hurt you,
Being scared, I'm through!
No more aimlessness, no more suffering,
Through strength of force, my confidence is returning.
CHLOE
SYMPTOMS:
-anger
-absolute revenge
-NO MORE COMPROMISING!

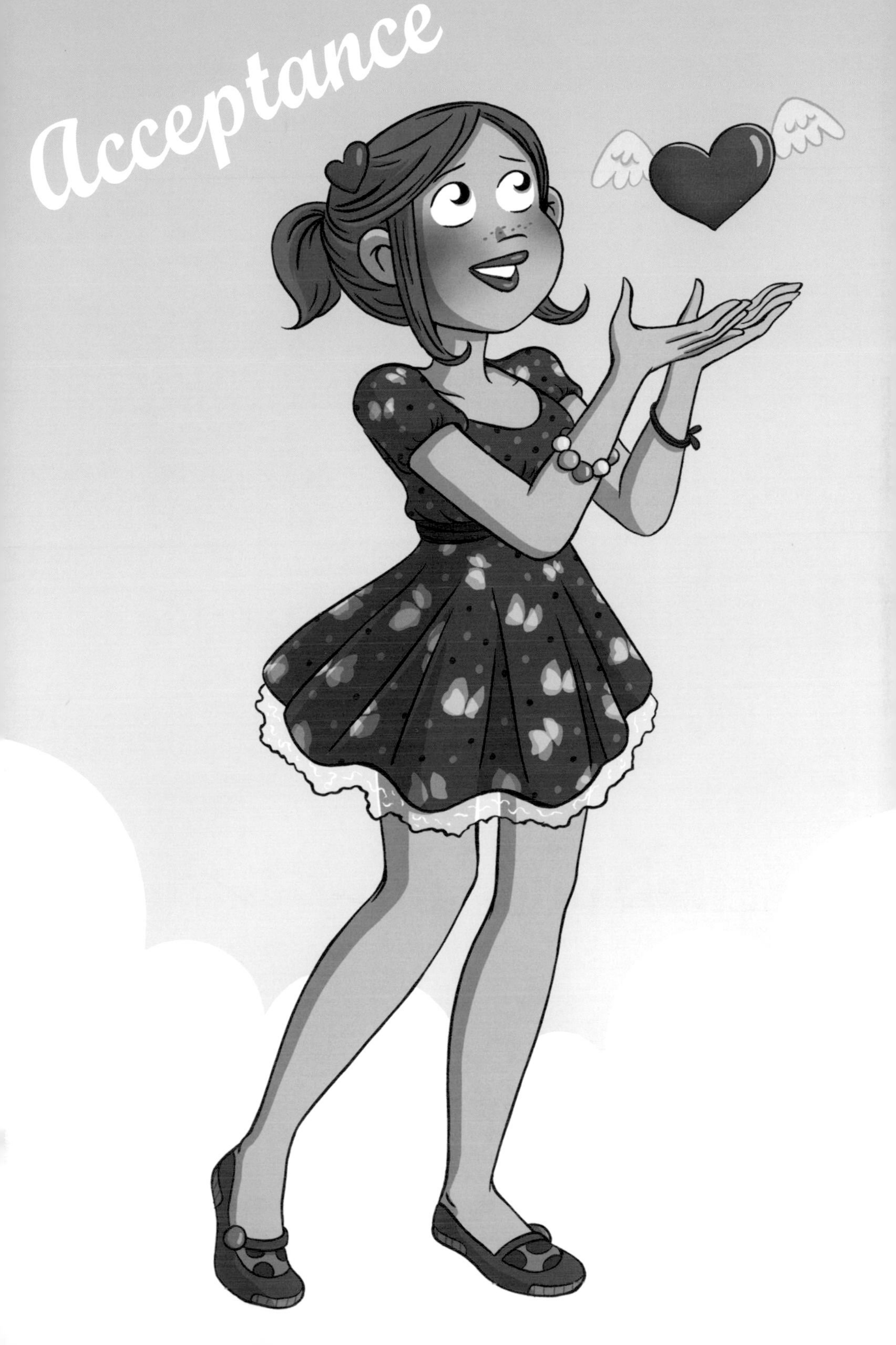
Acceptance

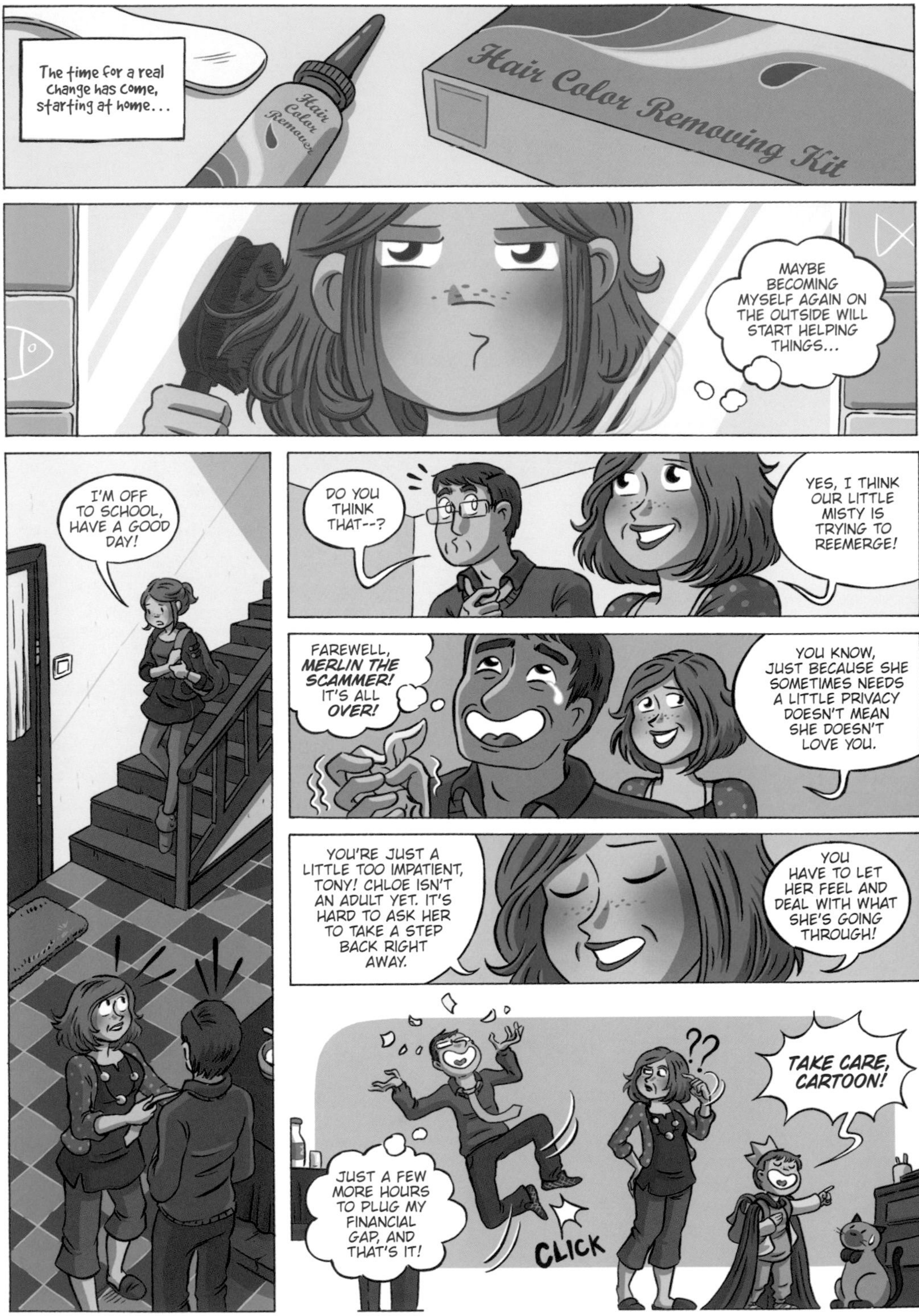
The time for a real change has come, starting at home...
Hair Color Remover
Hair Color Removing Kit
MAYBE BECOMING MYSELF AGAIN ON THE OUTSIDE WILL START HELPING THINGS...
I'M OFF TO SCHOOL, HAVE A GOOD DAY!
DO YOU THINK THAT--?
YES, I THINK OUR LITTLE MISTY IS TRYING TO REEMERGE!
FAREWELL, MERLIN THE SCAMMER! IT'S ALL OVER!
YOU KNOW, JUST BECAUSE SHE SOMETIMES NEEDS A LITTLE PRIVACY DOESN'T MEAN SHE DOESN'T LOVE YOU.
YOU'RE JUST A LITTLE TOO IMPATIENT, TONY! CHLOE ISN'T AN ADULT YET. IT'S HARD TO ASK HER TO TAKE A STEP BACK RIGHT AWAY.
YOU HAVE TO LET HER FEEL AND DEAL WITH WHAT SHE'S GOING THROUGH!
JUST A FEW MORE HOURS TO PLUG MY FINANCIAL GAP, AND THAT'S IT!
CLICK
??
TAKE CARE, CARTOON!

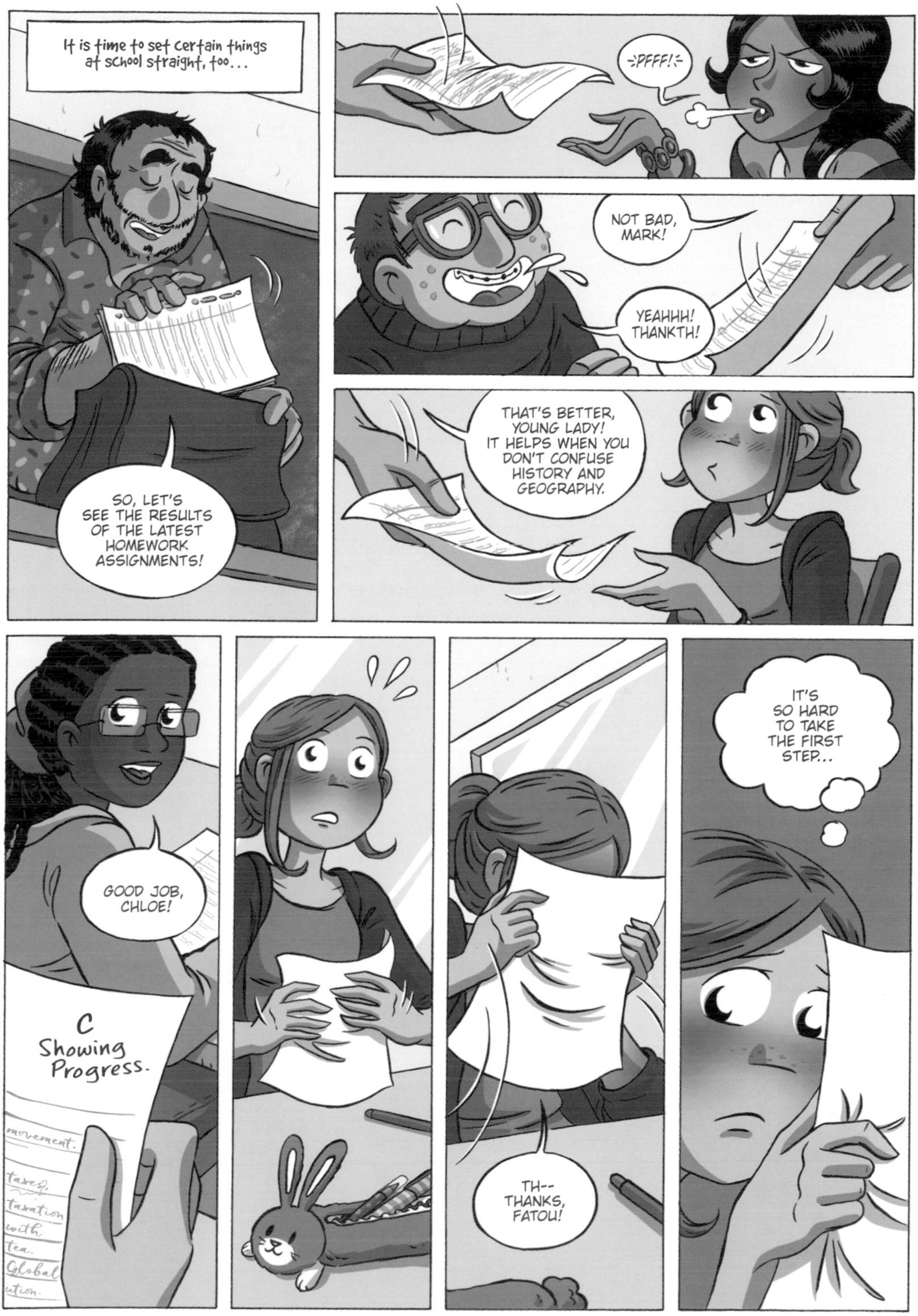
It is time to set certain things at school straight, too...
SO, LET'S SEE THE RESULTS OF THE LATEST HOMEWORK ASSIGNMENTS!
-PFFF!-
NOT BAD, MARK!
YEAHHH! THANKTH!
THAT'S BETTER, YOUNG LADY! IT HELPS WHEN YOU DON'T CONFUSE HISTORY AND GEOGRAPHY.
GOOD JOB, CHLOE!
C Showing Progress.
TH-- THANKS, FATOU!
IT'S SO HARD TO TAKE THE FIRST STEP...

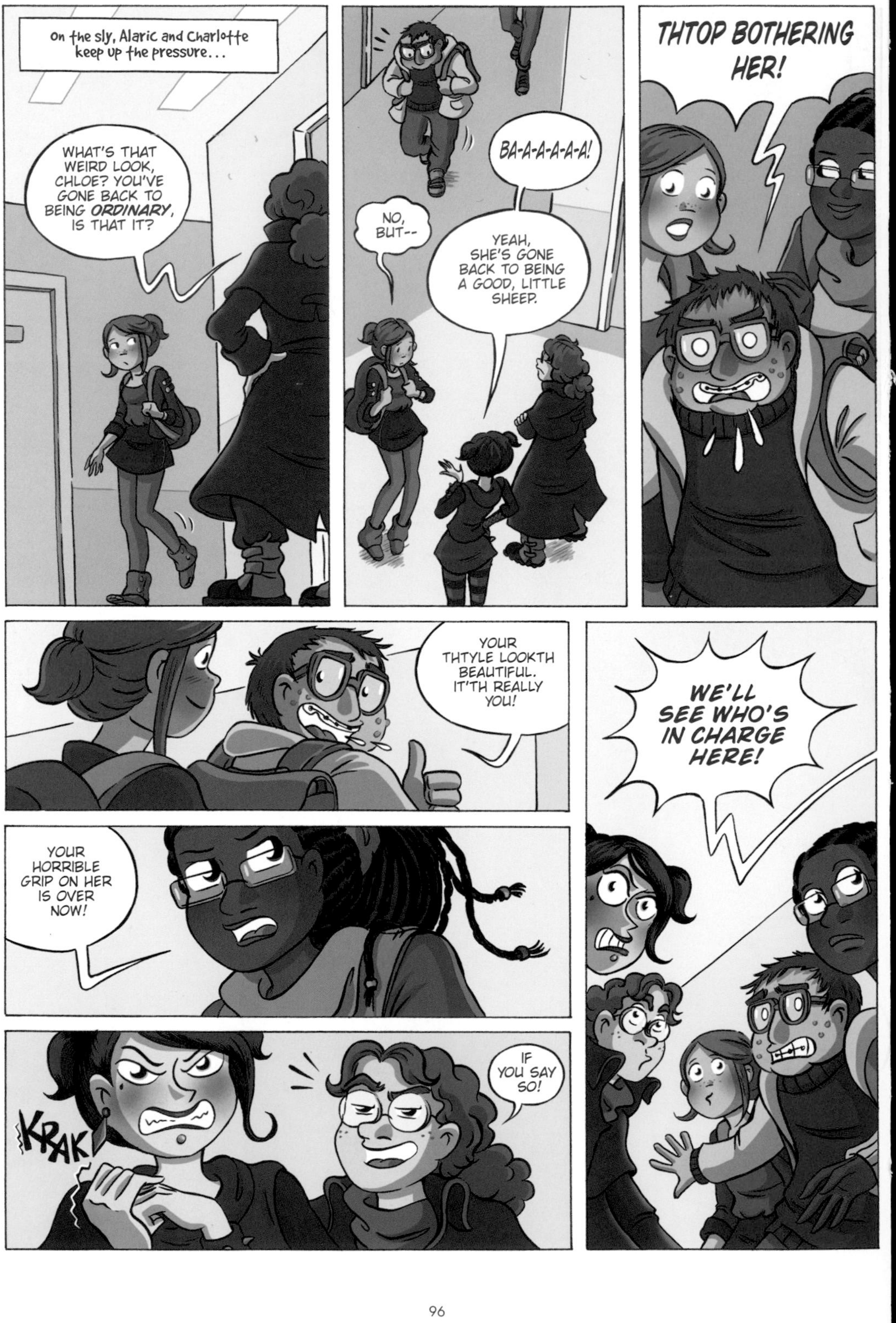

On the sly, Alaric and Charlotte keep up the pressure...
WHAT'S THAT WEIRD LOOK, CHLOE? YOU'VE GONE BACK TO BEING ORDINARY, IS THAT IT?
BA-A-A-A-A-A!
NO, BUT--
YEAH, SHE'S GONE BACK TO BEING A GOOD, LITTLE SHEEP.
THTOP BOTHERING HER!
YOUR THTYLE LOOKTH BEAUTIFUL. IT'TH REALLY YOU!
YOUR HORRIBLE GRIP ON HER IS OVER NOW!
KRAK
IF YOU SAY SO!
WE'LL SEE WHO'S IN CHARGE HERE!

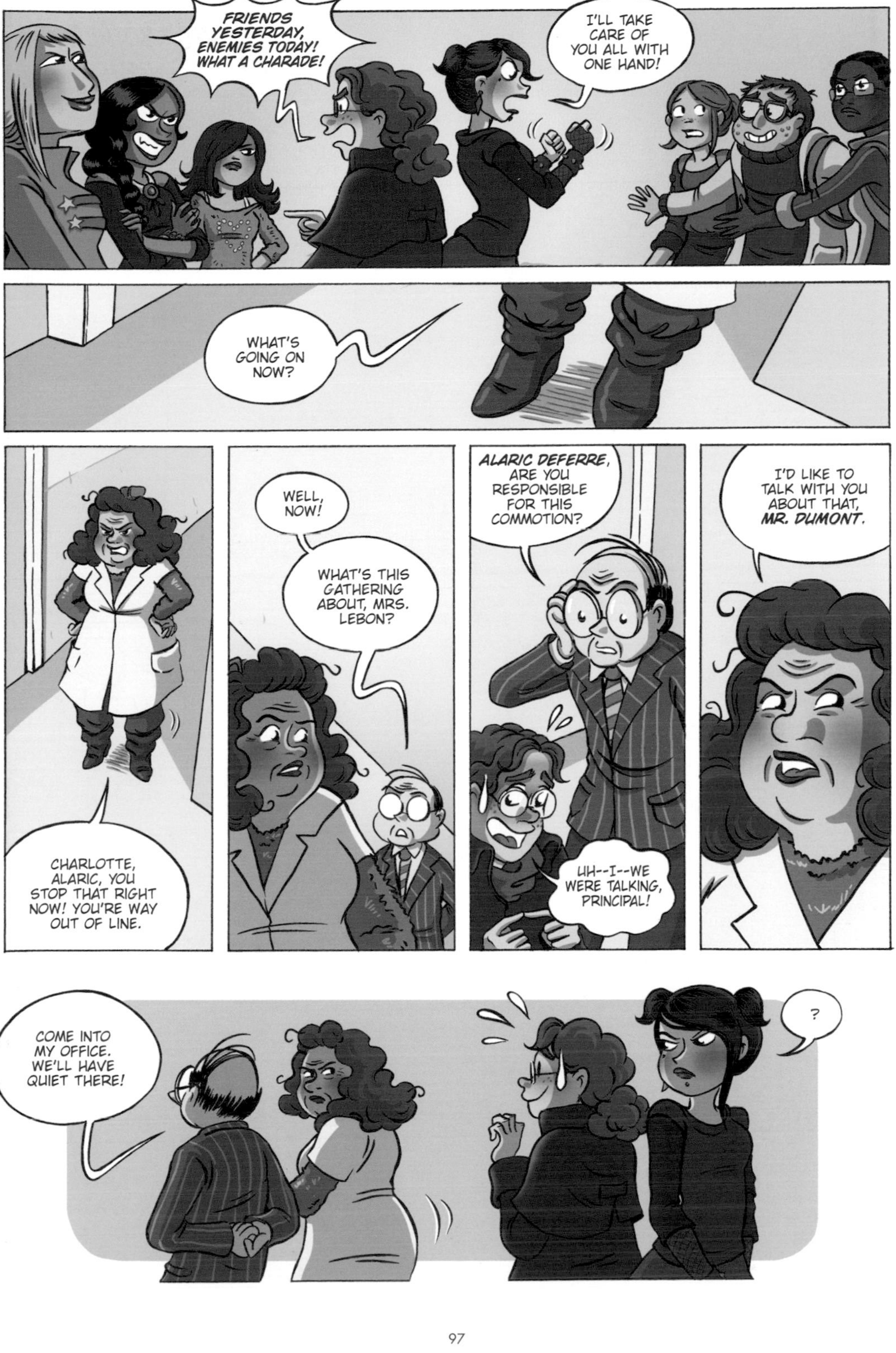
FRIENDS YESTERDAY, ENEMIES TODAY! WHAT A CHARADE!
I'LL TAKE CARE OF YOU ALL WITH ONE HAND!
WHAT'S GOING ON NOW?
CHARLOTTE, ALARIC, YOU STOP THAT RIGHT NOW! YOU'RE WAY OUT OF LINE.
WELL, NOW!
WHAT'S THIS GATHERING ABOUT, MRS. LEBON?
ALARIC DEFERRE, ARE YOU RESPONSIBLE FOR THIS COMMOTION?
UH--I--WE WERE TALKING, PRINCIPAL!
I'D LIKE TO TALK WITH YOU ABOUT THAT, MR. DUMONT.
COME INTO MY OFFICE. WE'LL HAVE QUIET THERE!
?

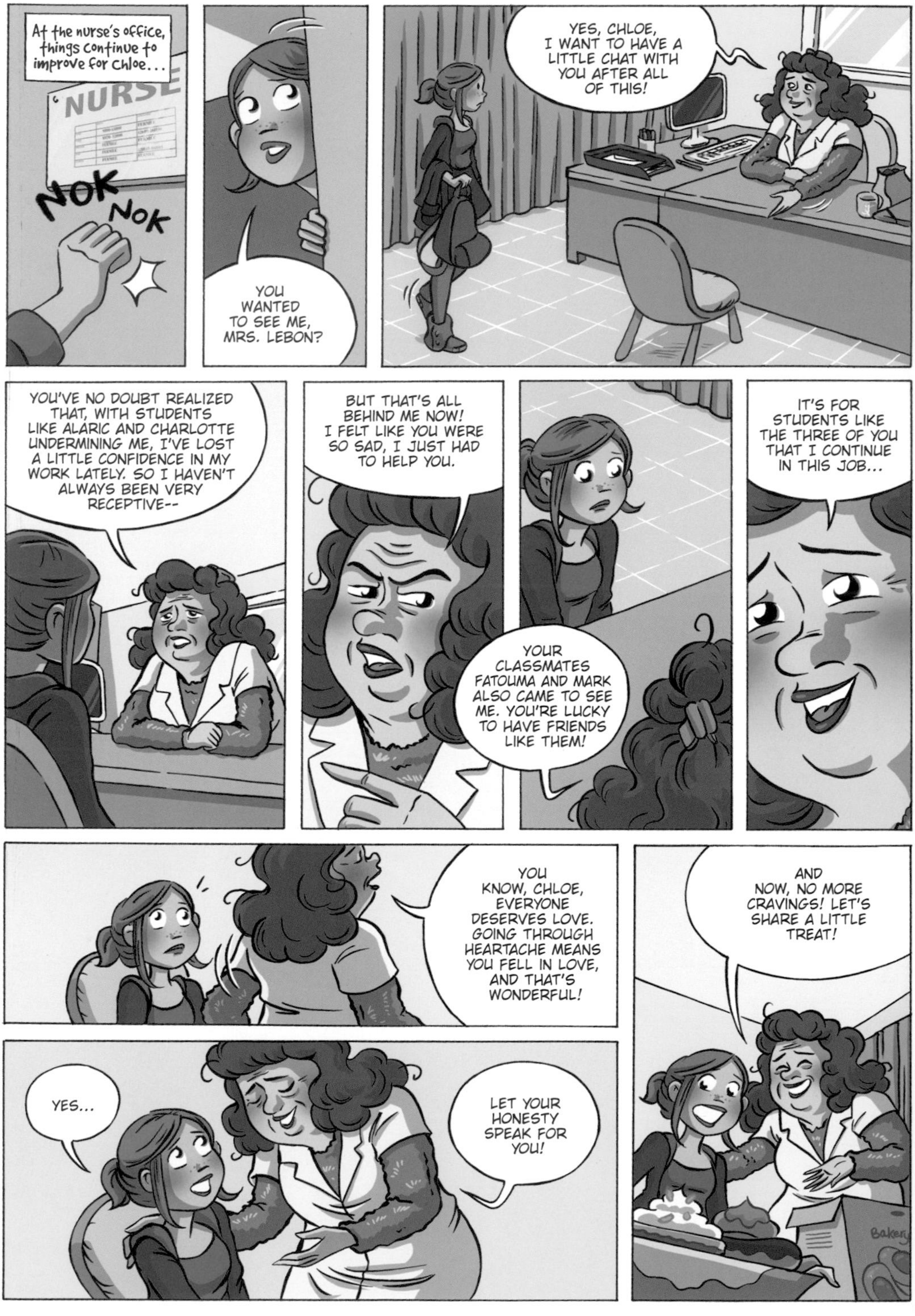
At the nurse's office, things continue to improve for Chloe...
NURSE
NOK
NOK
YOU WANTED TO SEE ME, MRS. LEBON?
YES, CHLOE, I WANT TO HAVE A LITTLE CHAT WITH YOU AFTER ALL OF THIS!
YOU'VE NO DOUBT REALIZED THAT, WITH STUDENTS LIKE ALARIC AND CHARLOTTE UNDERMINING ME, I'VE LOST A LITTLE CONFIDENCE IN MY WORK LATELY. SO I HAVEN'T ALWAYS BEEN VERY RECEPTIVE--
BUT THAT'S ALL BEHIND ME NOW! I FELT LIKE YOU WERE SO SAD, I JUST HAD TO HELP YOU.
YOUR CLASSMATES FATOUMA AND MARK ALSO CAME TO SEE ME. YOU'RE LUCKY TO HAVE FRIENDS LIKE THEM!
IT'S FOR STUDENTS LIKE THE THREE OF YOU THAT I CONTINUE IN THIS JOB...
YOU KNOW, CHLOE, EVERYONE DESERVES LOVE. GOING THROUGH HEARTACHE MEANS YOU FELL IN LOVE, AND THAT'S WONDERFUL!
YES...
LET YOUR HONESTY SPEAK FOR YOU!
AND NOW, NO MORE CRAVINGS! LET'S SHARE A LITTLE TREAT!
Bakery

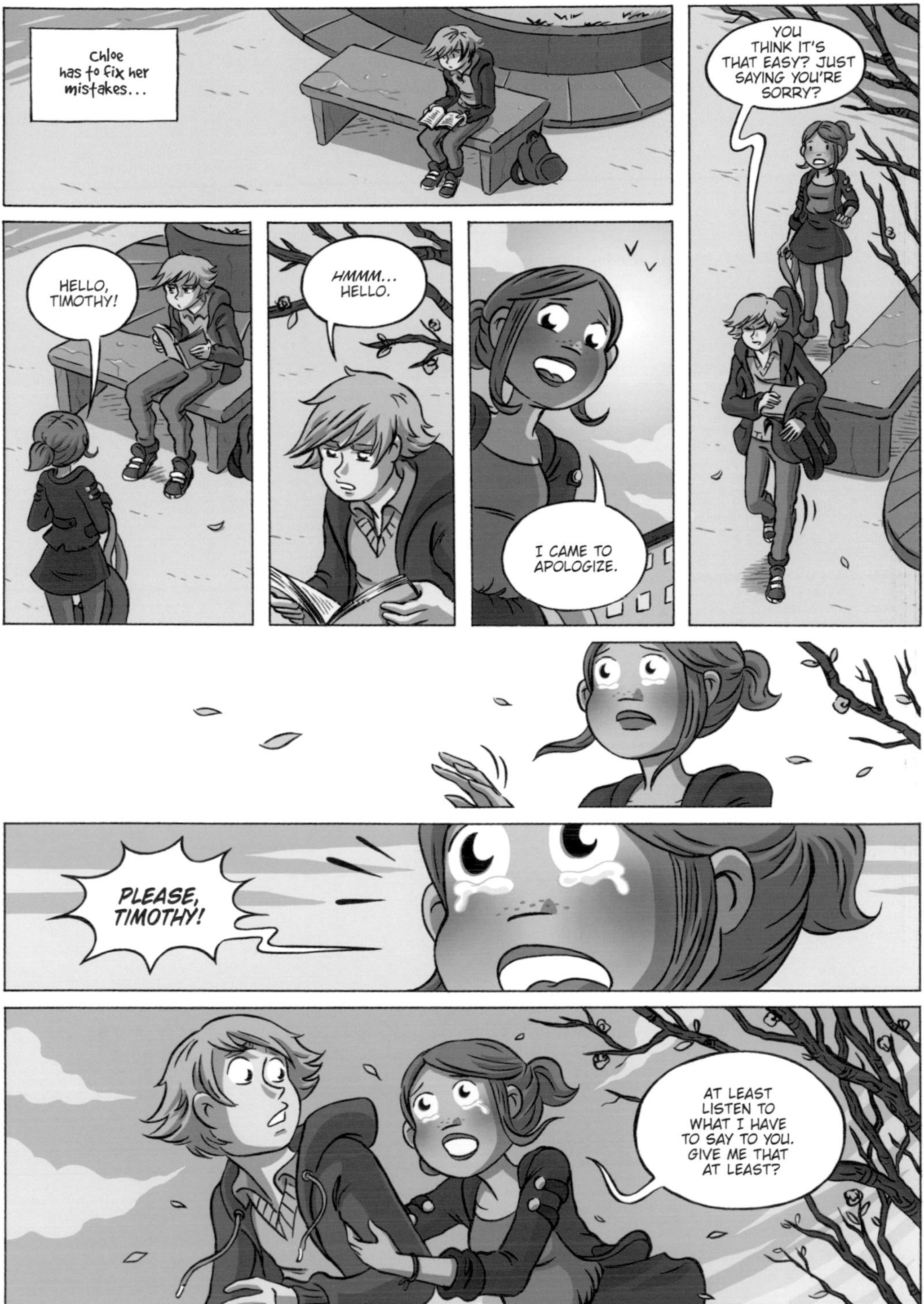
Chloe has to fix her mistakes...
HELLO, TIMOTHY!
HMMM... HELLO.
I CAME TO APOLOGIZE.
YOU THINK IT'S THAT EASY? JUST SAYING YOU'RE SORRY?
PLEASE, TIMOTHY!
AT LEAST LISTEN TO WHAT I HAVE TO SAY TO YOU. GIVE ME THAT AT LEAST?

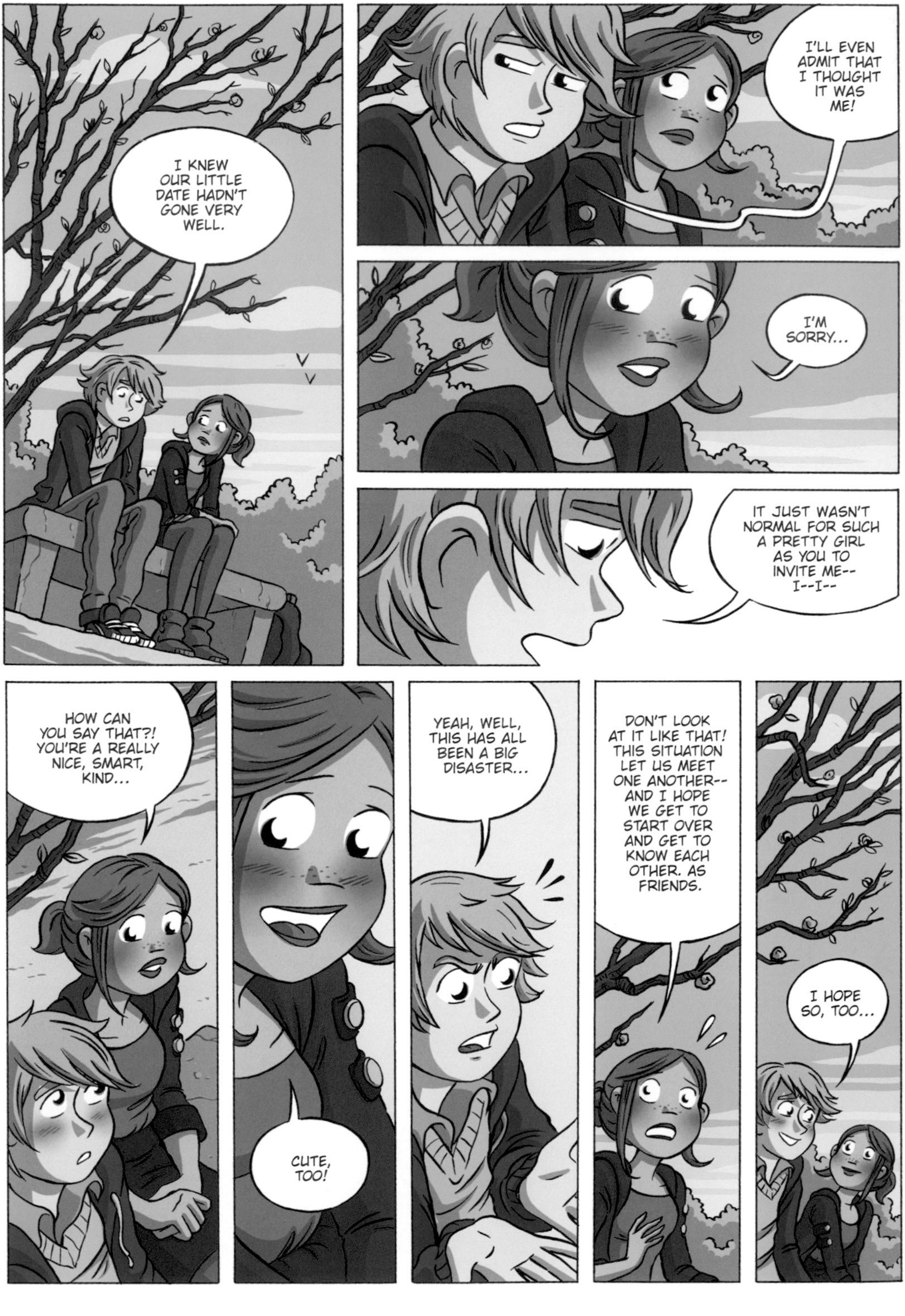
I KNEW OUR LITTLE DATE HADN'T GONE VERY WELL.
I'LL EVEN ADMIT THAT I THOUGHT IT WAS ME!
I'M SORRY...
IT JUST WASN'T NORMAL FOR SUCH A PRETTY GIRL AS YOU TO INVITE ME-- I--I--
HOW CAN YOU SAY THAT?! YOU'RE A REALLY NICE, SMART, KIND...
CUTE, TOO!
YEAH, WELL, THIS HAS ALL BEEN A BIG DISASTER...
DON'T LOOK AT IT LIKE THAT! THIS SITUATION LET US MEET ONE ANOTHER-- AND I HOPE WE GET TO START OVER AND GET TO KNOW EACH OTHER. AS FRIENDS.
I HOPE SO, TOO...

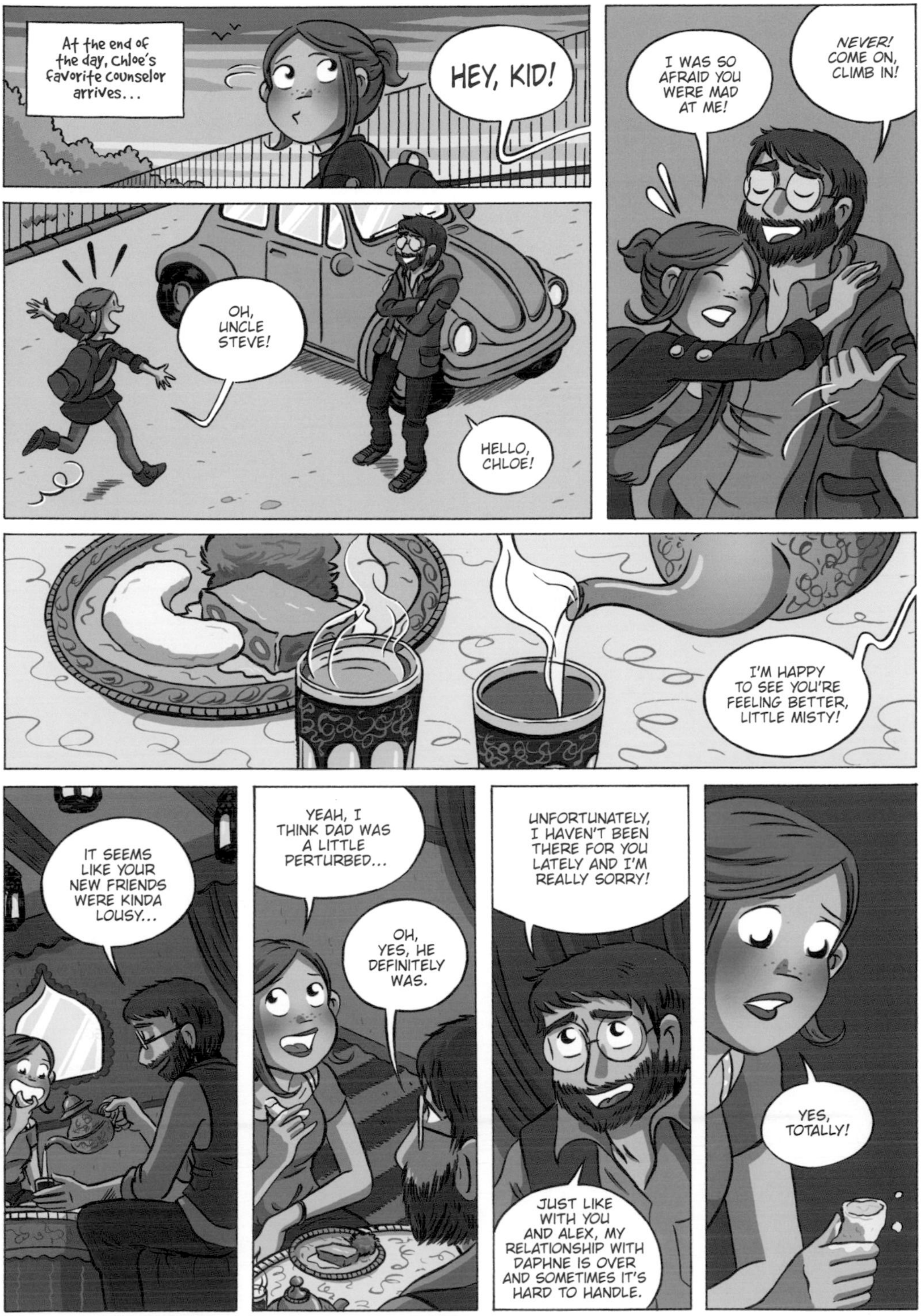
At the end of the day, Chloe's favorite counselor arrives...
HEY, KID!
I WAS SO AFRAID YOU WERE MAD AT ME!
NEVER! COME ON, CLIMB IN!
OH, UNCLE STEVE!
HELLO, CHLOE!
I'M HAPPY TO SEE YOU'RE FEELING BETTER, LITTLE MISTY!
IT SEEMS LIKE YOUR NEW FRIENDS WERE KINDA LOUSY...
YEAH, I THINK DAD WAS A LITTLE PERTURBED...
OH, YES, HE DEFINITELY WAS.
UNFORTUNATELY, I HAVEN'T BEEN THERE FOR YOU LATELY AND I'M REALLY SORRY!
JUST LIKE WITH YOU AND ALEX, MY RELATIONSHIP WITH DAPHNE IS OVER AND SOMETIMES IT'S HARD TO HANDLE.
YES, TOTALLY!

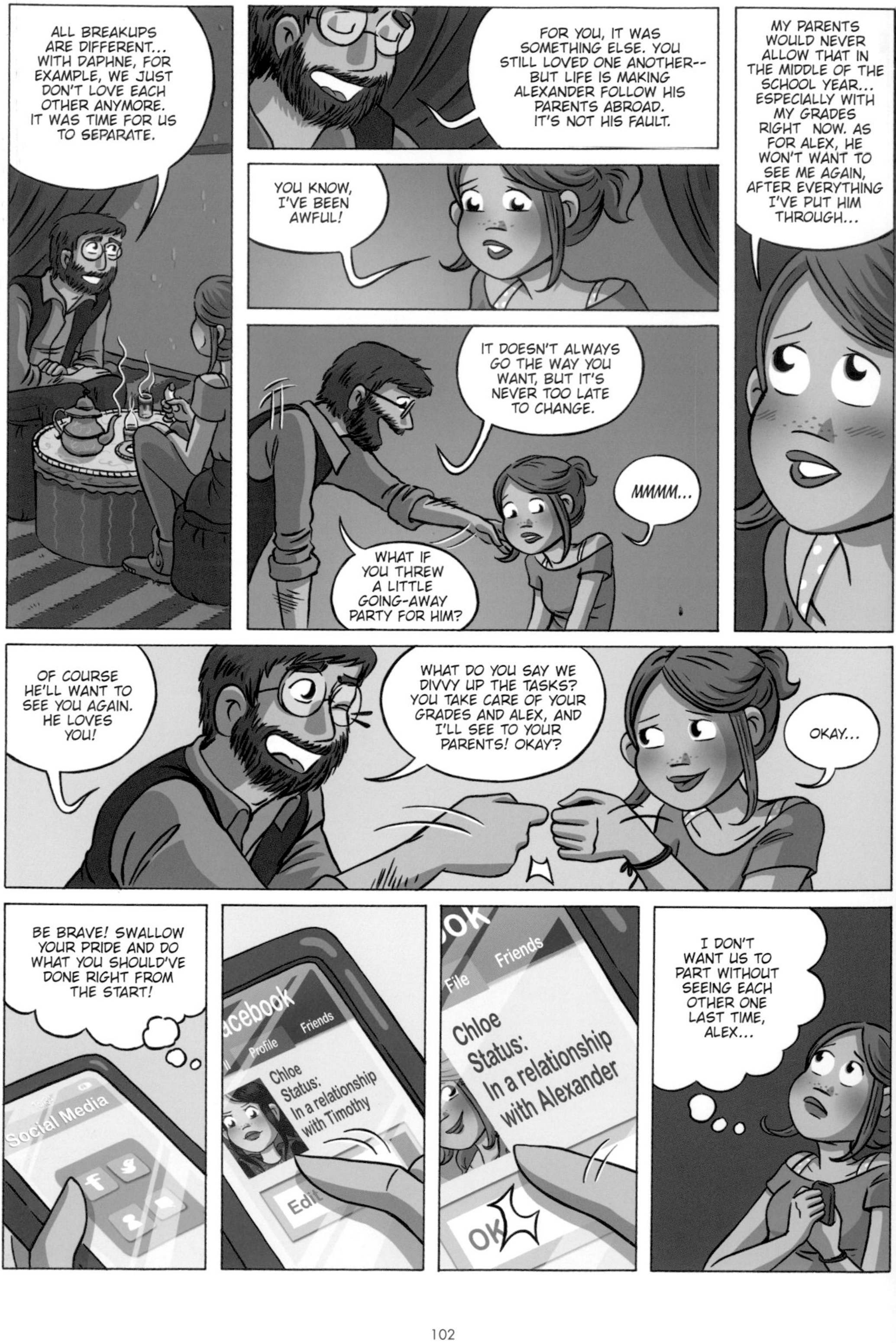
ALL BREAKUPS ARE DIFFERENT... WITH DAPHNE, FOR EXAMPLE, WE JUST DON'T LOVE EACH OTHER ANYMORE. IT WAS TIME FOR US TO SEPARATE.
FOR YOU, IT WAS SOMETHING ELSE. YOU STILL LOVED ONE ANOTHER-- BUT LIFE IS MAKING ALEXANDER FOLLOW HIS PARENTS ABROAD. IT'S NOT HIS FAULT.
YOU KNOW, I'VE BEEN AWFUL!
IT DOESN'T ALWAYS GO THE WAY YOU WANT, BUT IT'S NEVER TOO LATE TO CHANGE.
MMMM...
WHAT IF YOU THREW A LITTLE GOING-AWAY PARTY FOR HIM?
MY PARENTS WOULD NEVER ALLOW THAT IN THE MIDDLE OF THE SCHOOL YEAR... ESPECIALLY WITH MY GRADES RIGHT NOW. AS FOR ALEX, HE WON'T WANT TO SEE ME AGAIN, AFTER EVERYTHING I'VE PUT HIM THROUGH...
OF COURSE HE'LL WANT TO SEE YOU AGAIN. HE LOVES YOU!
WHAT DO YOU SAY WE DIVVY UP THE TASKS? YOU TAKE CARE OF YOUR GRADES AND ALEX, AND I'LL SEE TO YOUR PARENTS! OKAY?
OKAY...
BE BRAVE! SWALLOW YOUR PRIDE AND DO WHAT YOU SHOULD'VE DONE RIGHT FROM THE START!
Social Media
acebook
Profile
Friends
Chloe
Status:
In a relationship with Timothy
Edit
File
Friends
Chloe
Status:
In a relationship with Alexander
OK
I DON'T WANT US TO PART WITHOUT SEEING EACH OTHER ONE LAST TIME, ALEX...

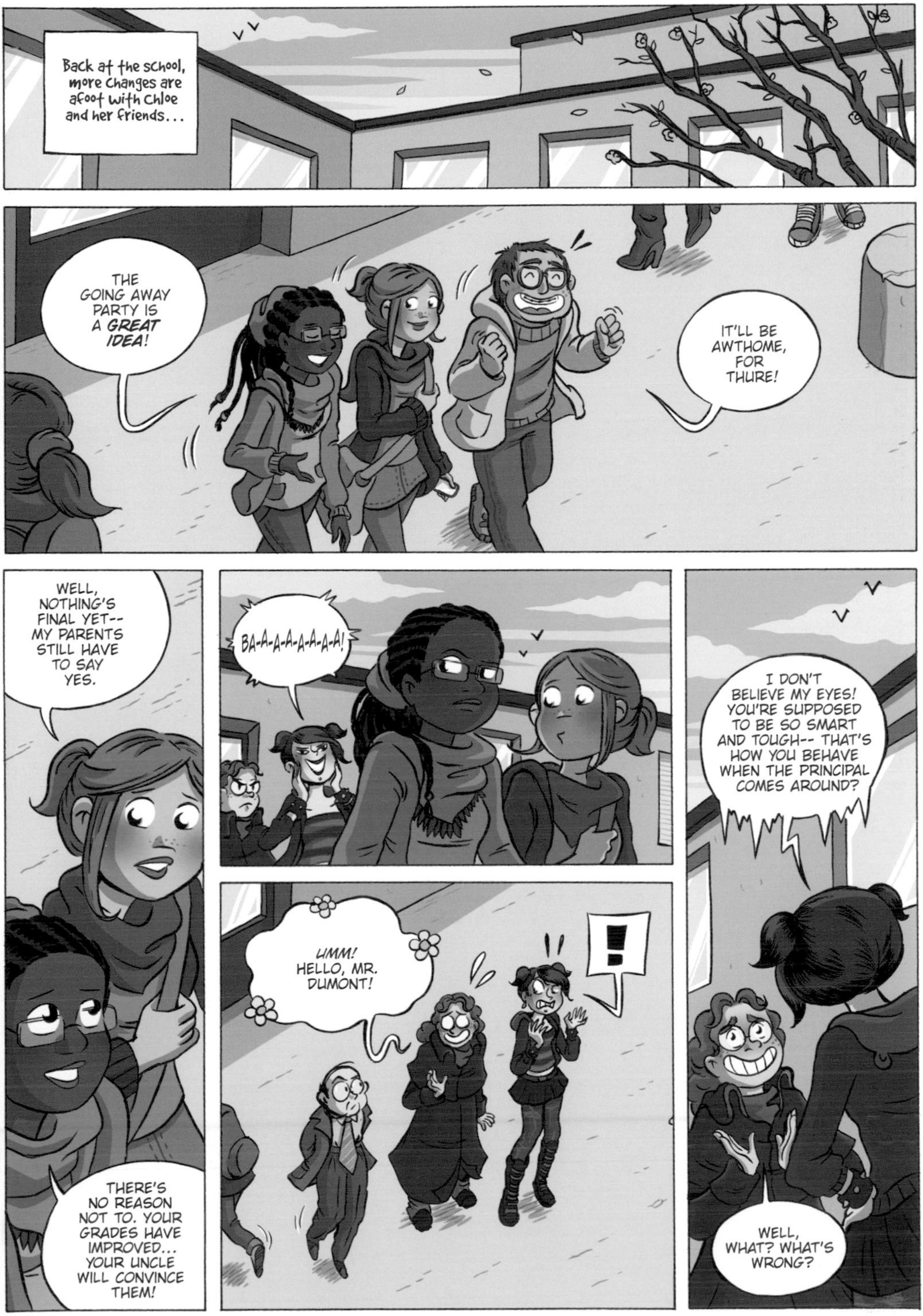
Back at the school, more changes are afoot with Chloe and her friends...
THE GOING AWAY PARTY IS A **GREAT IDEA**!
IT'LL BE AWTHOME, FOR THURE!
WELL, NOTHING'S FINAL YET-- MY PARENTS STILL HAVE TO SAY YES.
THERE'S NO REASON NOT TO. YOUR GRADES HAVE IMPROVED... YOUR UNCLE WILL CONVINCE THEM!
BA-A-A-A-A-A-A-A!
UMM! HELLO, MR. DUMONT!
!
I DON'T BELIEVE MY EYES! YOU'RE SUPPOSED TO BE SO SMART AND TOUGH-- THAT'S HOW YOU BEHAVE WHEN THE PRINCIPAL COMES AROUND?
WELL, WHAT? WHAT'S WRONG?

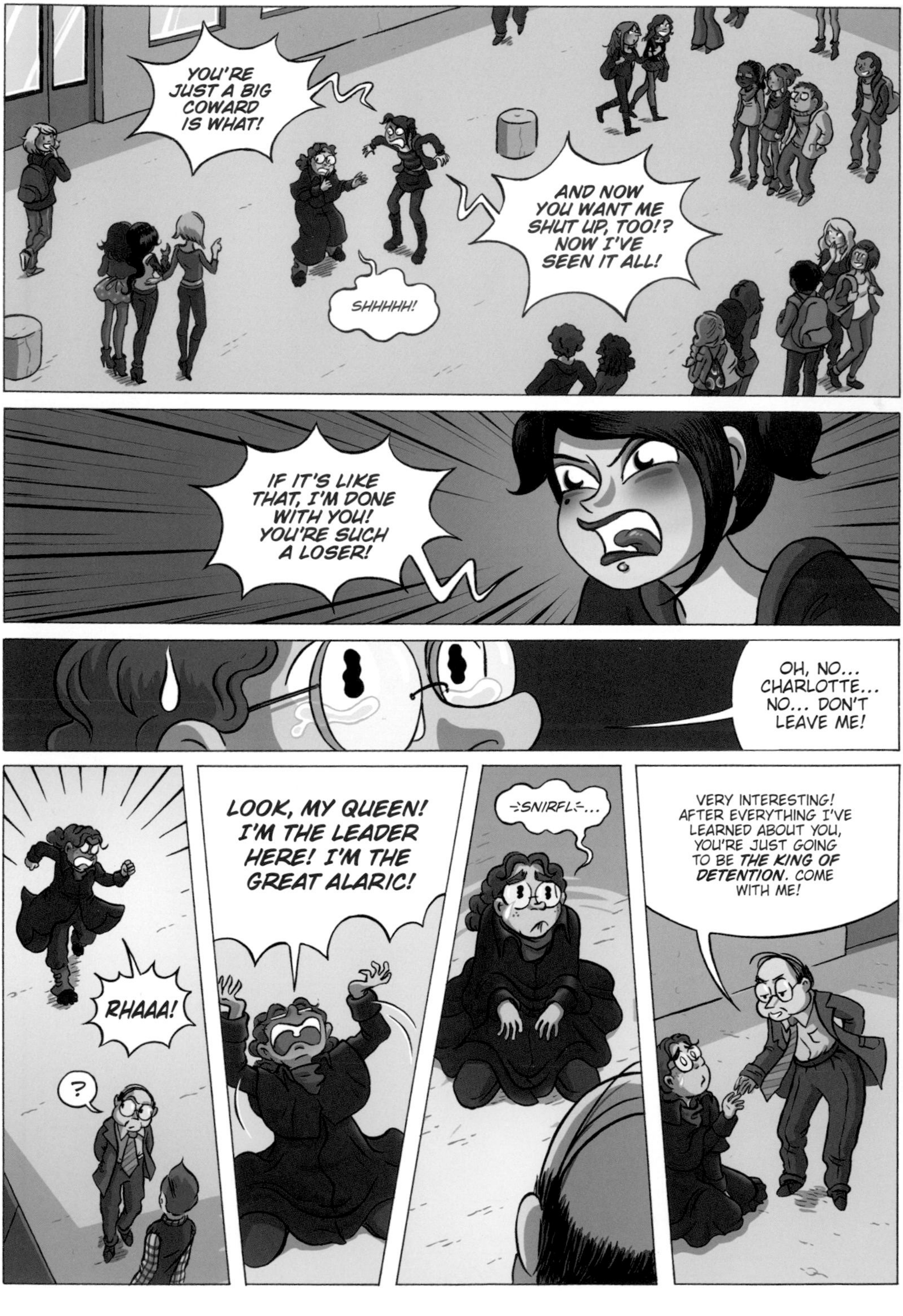

YOU'RE JUST A BIG COWARD IS WHAT!
AND NOW YOU WANT ME SHUT UP, TOO!? NOW I'VE SEEN IT ALL!
SHHHHH!
IF IT'S LIKE THAT, I'M DONE WITH YOU! YOU'RE SUCH A LOSER!
OH, NO... CHARLOTTE... NO... DON'T LEAVE ME!
RHAAA!
?
LOOK, MY QUEEN! I'M THE LEADER HERE! I'M THE GREAT ALARIC!
SNIRFL...
VERY INTERESTING! AFTER EVERYTHING I'VE LEARNED ABOUT YOU, YOU'RE JUST GOING TO BE THE KING OF DETENTION. COME WITH ME!

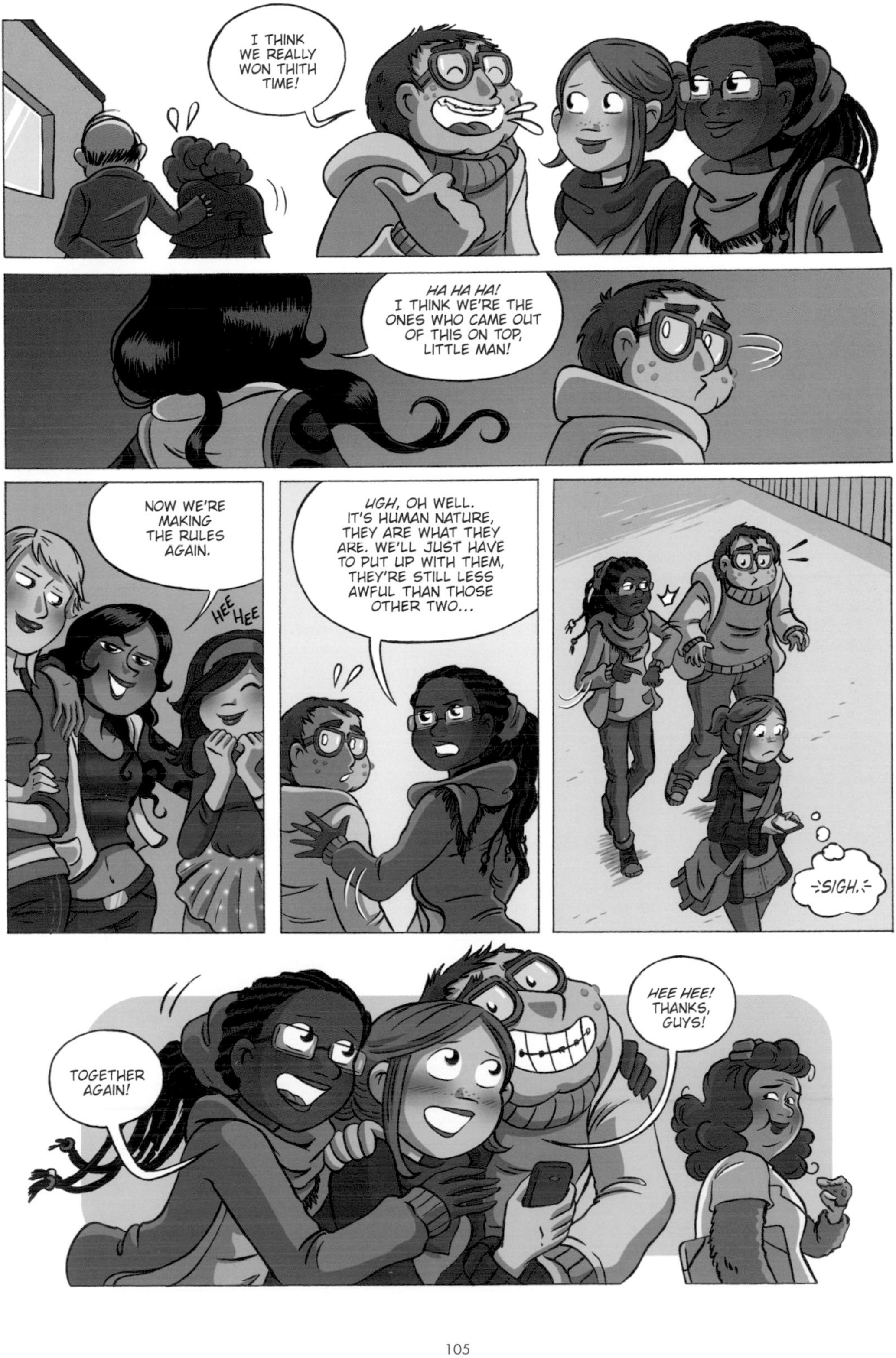

I THINK WE REALLY WON THITH TIME!
HA HA HA! I THINK WE'RE THE ONES WHO CAME OUT OF THIS ON TOP, LITTLE MAN!
NOW WE'RE MAKING THE RULES AGAIN.
HEE HEE
UGH, OH WELL. IT'S HUMAN NATURE, THEY ARE WHAT THEY ARE. WE'LL JUST HAVE TO PUT UP WITH THEM, THEY'RE STILL LESS AWFUL THAN THOSE OTHER TWO...
SIGH.
TOGETHER AGAIN!
HEE HEE! THANKS, GUYS!

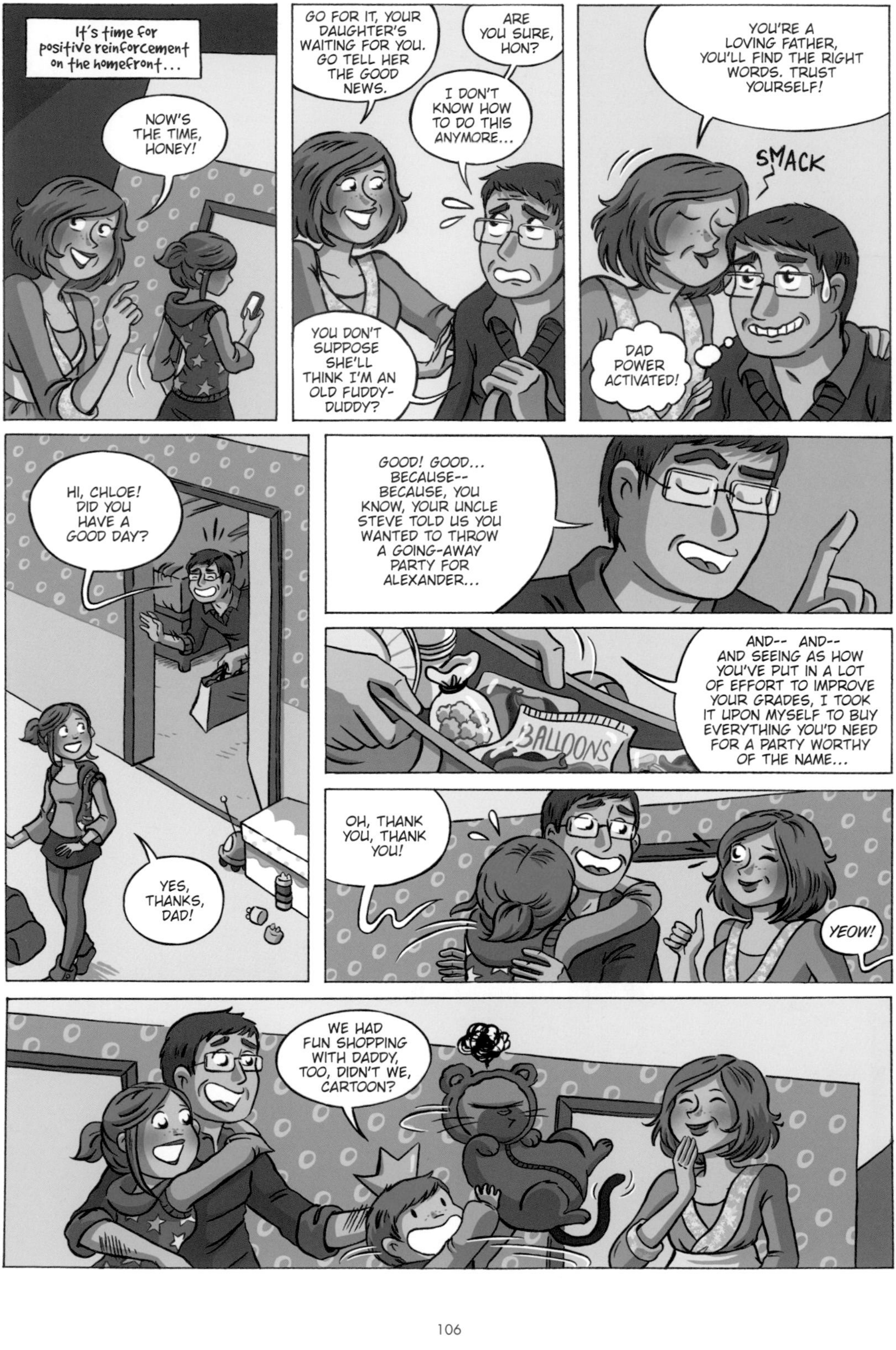
It's time for positive reinforcement on the homefront...
NOW'S THE TIME, HONEY!
GO FOR IT, YOUR DAUGHTER'S WAITING FOR YOU. GO TELL HER THE GOOD NEWS.
ARE YOU SURE, HON?
I DON'T KNOW HOW TO DO THIS ANYMORE...
YOU DON'T SUPPOSE SHE'LL THINK I'M AN OLD FUDDY-DUDDY?
YOU'RE A LOVING FATHER, YOU'LL FIND THE RIGHT WORDS. TRUST YOURSELF!
SMACK
DAD POWER ACTIVATED!
HI, CHLOE! DID YOU HAVE A GOOD DAY?
YES, THANKS, DAD!
GOOD! GOOD... BECAUSE-- BECAUSE, YOU KNOW, YOUR UNCLE STEVE TOLD US YOU WANTED TO THROW A GOING-AWAY PARTY FOR ALEXANDER...
BALLOONS
AND-- AND-- AND SEEING AS HOW YOU'VE PUT IN A LOT OF EFFORT TO IMPROVE YOUR GRADES, I TOOK IT UPON MYSELF TO BUY EVERYTHING YOU'D NEED FOR A PARTY WORTHY OF THE NAME...
OH, THANK YOU, THANK YOU!
YEOW!
WE HAD FUN SHOPPING WITH DADDY, TOO, DIDN'T WE, CARTOON?

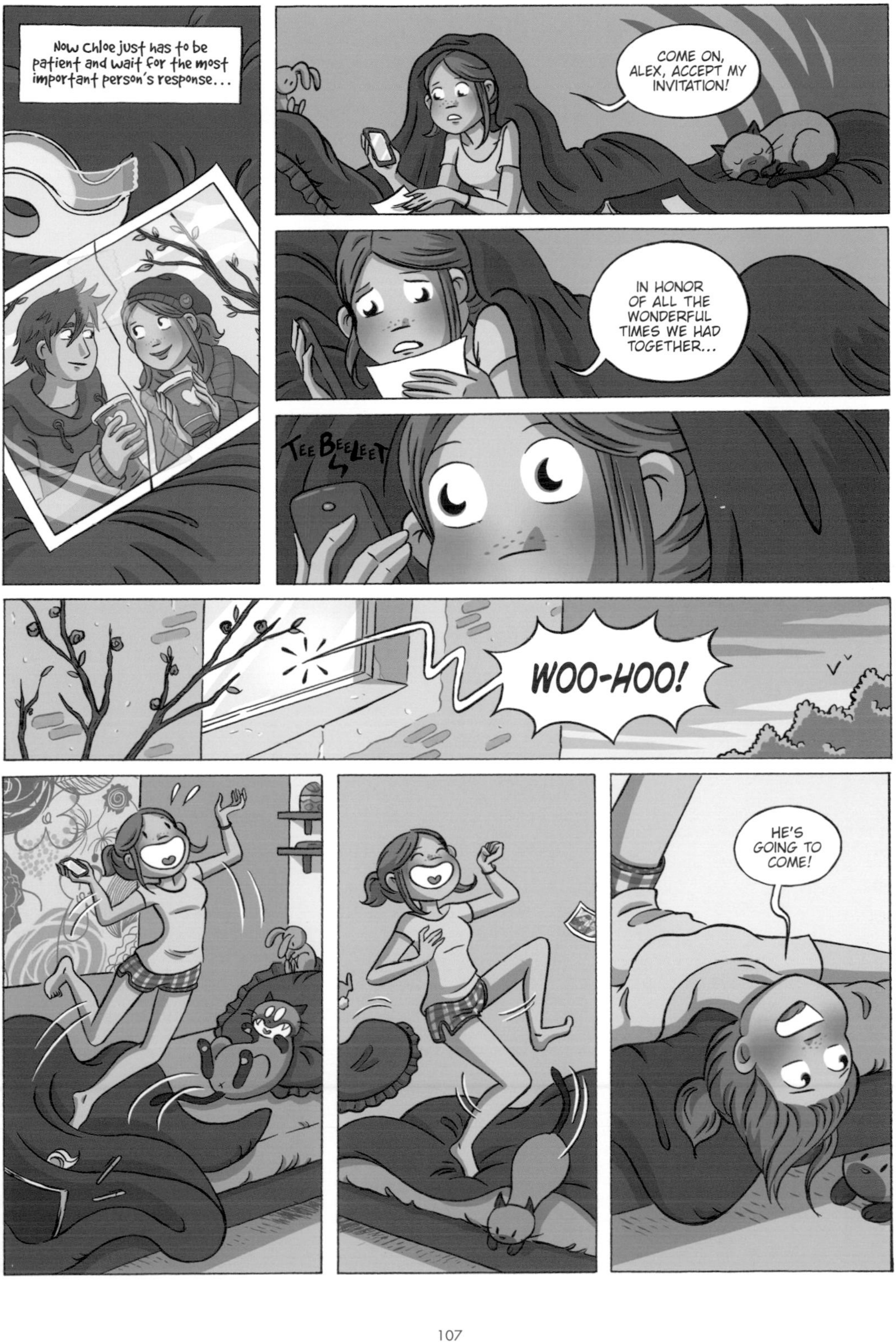
Now Chloe just has to be patient and wait for the most important person's response...
COME ON, ALEX, ACCEPT MY INVITATION!
IN HONOR OF ALL THE WONDERFUL TIMES WE HAD TOGETHER...
TEE BEELEET
WOO-HOO!
HE'S GOING TO COME!

break-up notebook

The two of us will never forget one another!

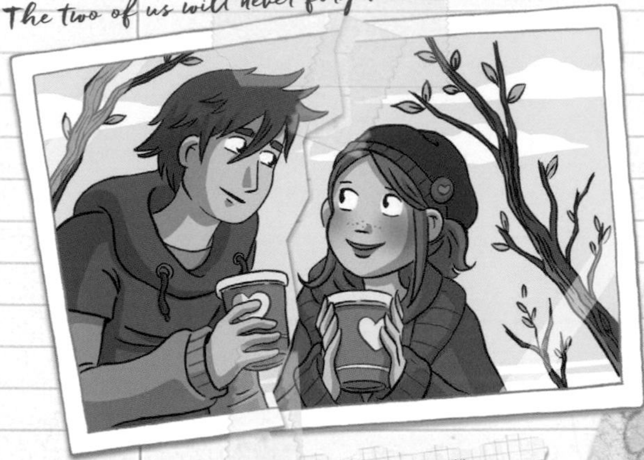

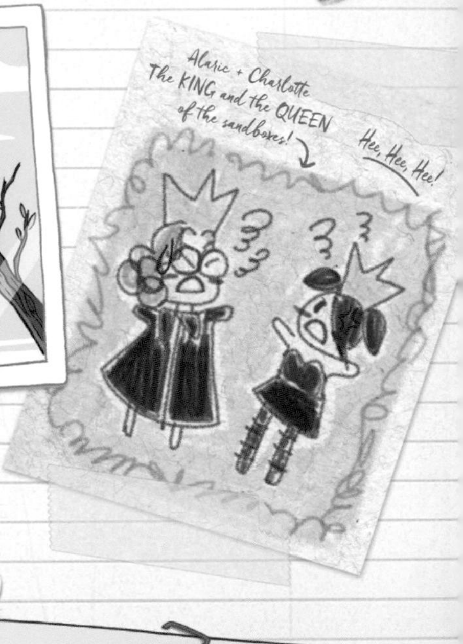
Alaric + Charlotte
The KING and the QUEEN
of the sandboxes!
Hee, Hee, Hee!

In the depths of my soul, I've found my flame again.
No longer is life drama and pain!
Memories and smiles to piece myself together right,
Keeping it all in line of sight.

Seeing you again, finally letting go, the end of my despair,
Can there be a friendship there?
One last look braved,
In my heart engraved,
My love for you saved.

~ Chloe ~

SYMPTOMS:
- unforgettable memories
- a zest for life
- I CAN'T WAIT FOR TOMORROW!

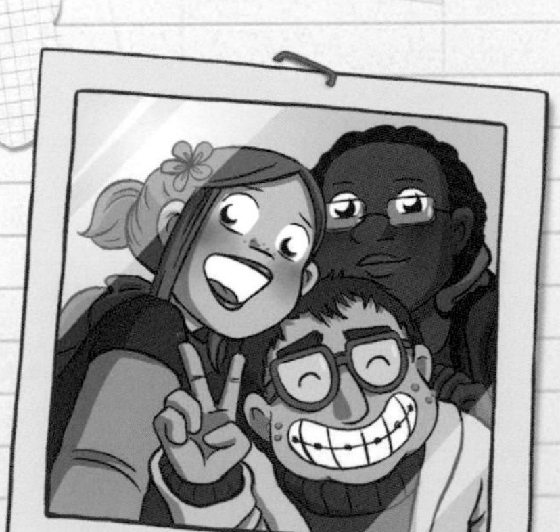

Friends for life!

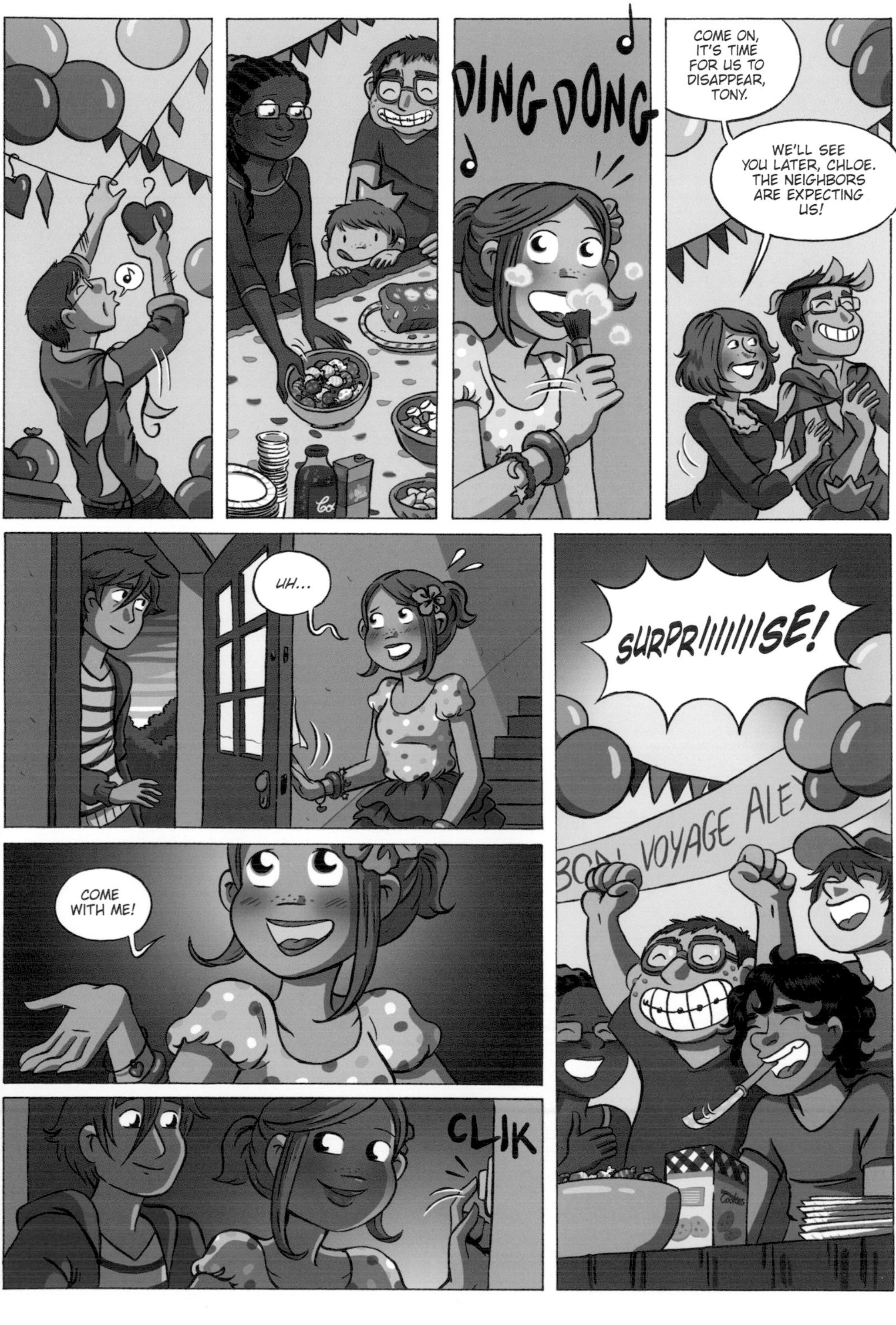
DING-DONG
COME ON, IT'S TIME FOR US TO DISAPPEAR, TONY.
WE'LL SEE YOU LATER, CHLOE. THE NEIGHBORS ARE EXPECTING US!
UH...
COME WITH ME!
CLIK
SURPRIIIIIIIISE!
BON VOYAGE ALEX

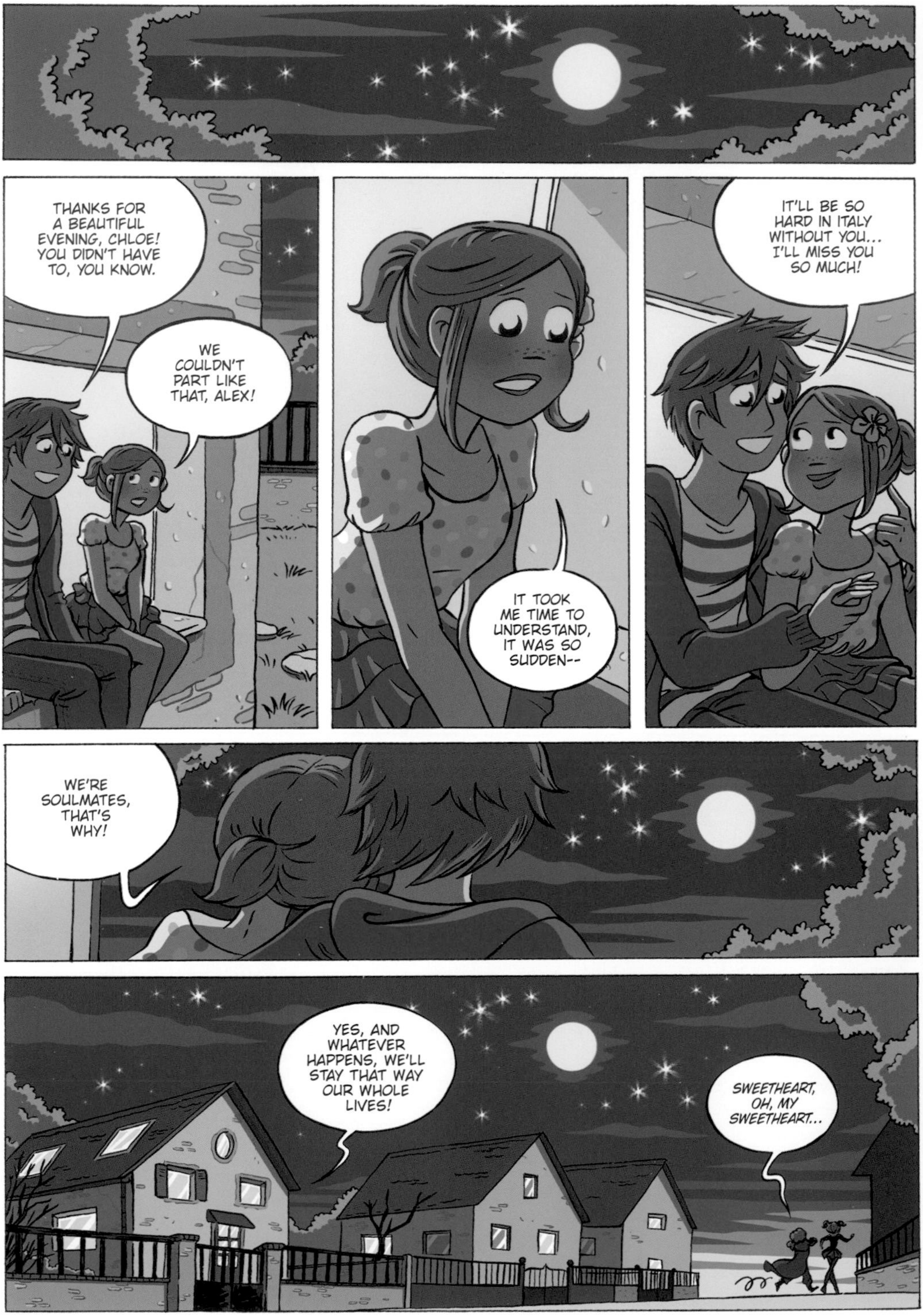
THANKS FOR A BEAUTIFUL EVENING, CHLOE! YOU DIDN'T HAVE TO, YOU KNOW.
WE COULDN'T PART LIKE THAT, ALEX!
IT TOOK ME TIME TO UNDERSTAND, IT WAS SO SUDDEN--
IT'LL BE SO HARD IN ITALY WITHOUT YOU... I'LL MISS YOU SO MUCH!
WE'RE SOULMATES, THAT'S WHY!
YES, AND WHATEVER HAPPENS, WE'LL STAY THAT WAY OUR WHOLE LIVES!
SWEETHEART, OH, MY SWEETHEART...

TEST

HOW WOULD YOU REACT TO HEARTACHE?

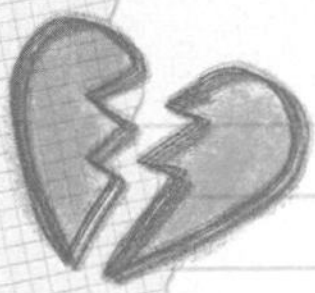

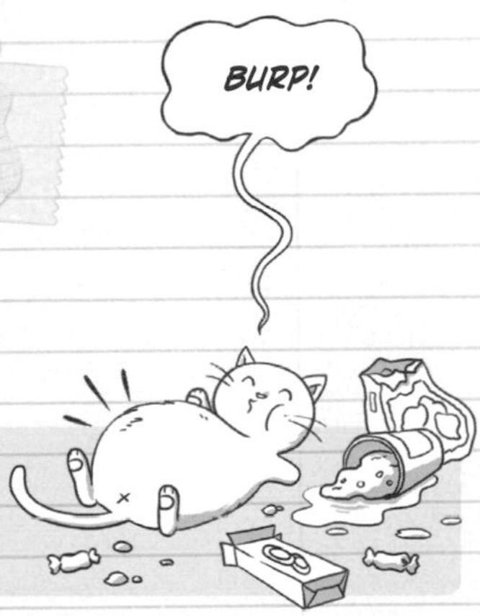
BURP!

1 **When you're sad, you find comfort in:**

- **Solitude**, a tub of ice cream is your best friend.
- **Criticism**, there's nothing better than firing off a few jabs.
- **Company**, the time has come to find some new friends.

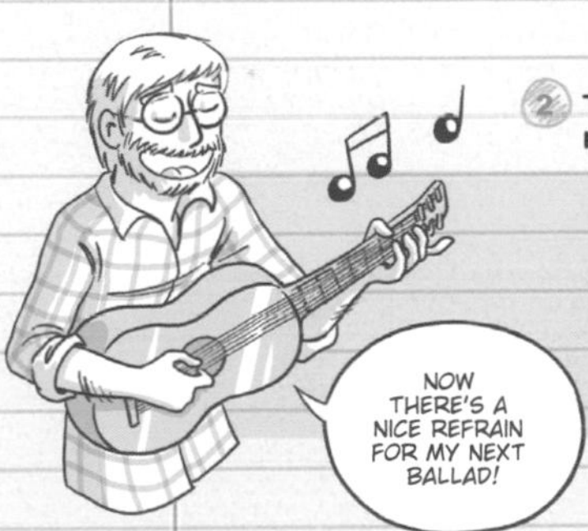
NOW THERE'S A NICE REFRAIN FOR MY NEXT BALLAD!

2 **The phrase "The two of us for life!" makes you think of:**

- **A sweet dream**, it's hard to hold onto it.
- **A self-evident fact**, you never really forget the ones you love.
- **A nightmare**, it's important to switch up your experiences.

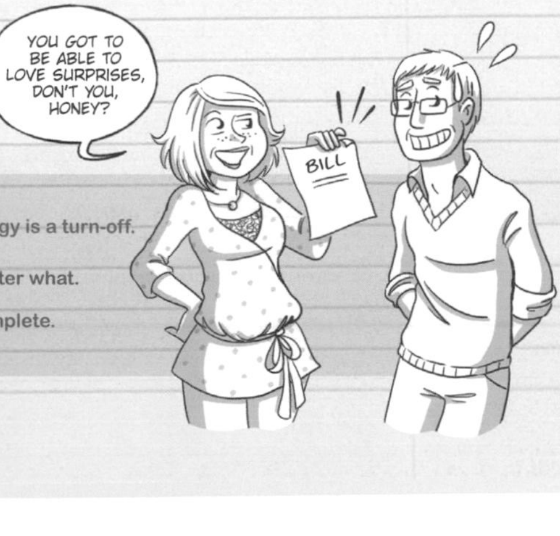
YOU GOT TO BE ABLE TO LOVE SURPRISES, DON'T YOU, HONEY?
BILL

3 **According to you, being a couple means:**

- **Being together occasionally**, being clingy is a turn-off.
- **Sharing the same point of view**, no matter what.
- **Being as one**, the merging must be complete.

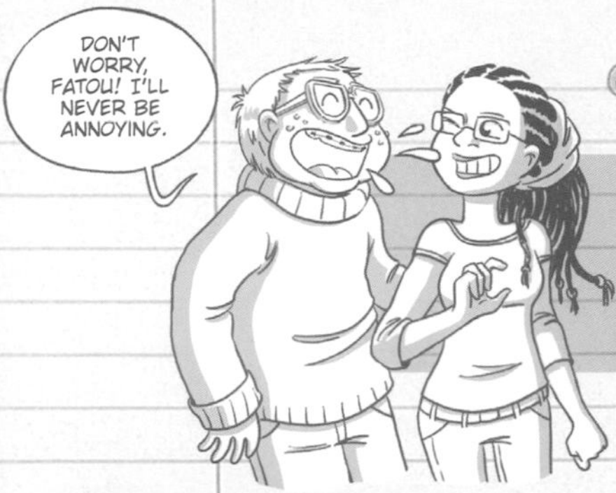
DON'T WORRY, FATOU! I'LL NEVER BE ANNOYING.

4 If someone close to you becomes increasingly unpleasant, you decide:

- To wait for it to pass, sometimes you just have to be patient.
- To talk to her or him one-on-one, you have to set things straight.
- To delete them from your life, you're not kidding around.

5 Staying friends with your ex is:

- Unthinkable, once disappointed, you never want to look backwards.
- Essential, that person will always be part of you.
- Weird, you won't know what you'd have to say to each other.

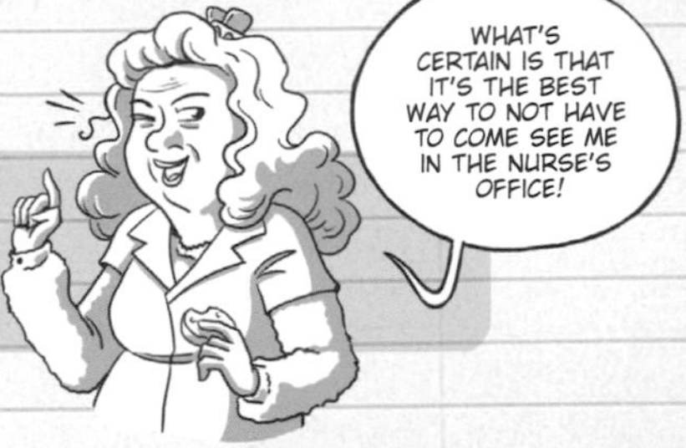
WHAT'S CERTAIN IS THAT IT'S THE BEST WAY TO NOT HAVE TO COME SEE ME IN THE NURSE'S OFFICE!

ANSWERS

You mostly have ♥:

It's never easy to come to terms with heartache, especially when you're of a sensitive nature. All the sweets that you eat during hard times tend to prove that! A little patience will get you through it. This rebuilding phase is just a bad spell. And don't forget, you're not alone. You can confide in your friends or family. Talking often does lots of good.

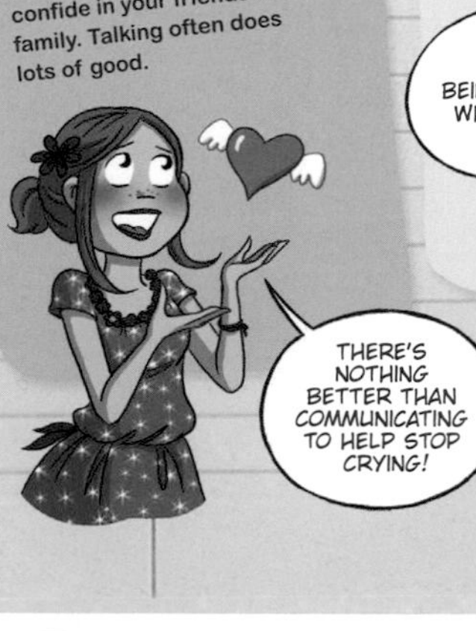
THERE'S NOTHING BETTER THAN COMMUNICATING TO HELP STOP CRYING!

You mostly have ♥:

You know about boys! What's more, you have a tendency to lead them around by the nose. Independent, in general, you're slow to get invested in relationships, so you're not at all scared of a breakup. Everyone's different, though, so be careful not to hurt your current significant other too much. By relying on your intelligence and honesty to avoid mistakes of that kind, you'll come out all the better for it.

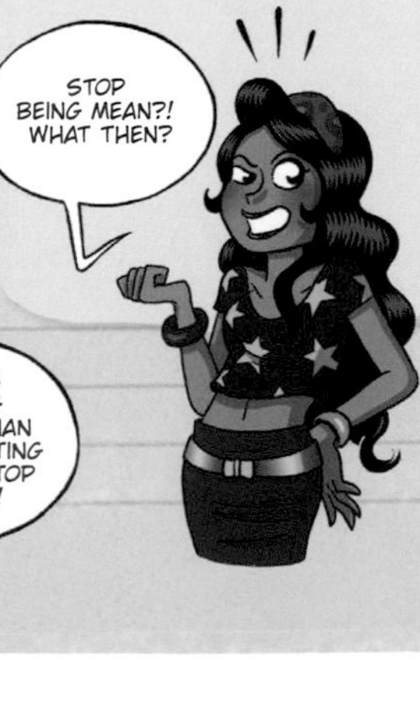
STOP BEING MEAN?! WHAT THEN?

You mostly have ♥:

Uncompromising, you never mope around. This strength, which allows you to bounce right back, mustn't keep you from what you could feel in the deepest part of yourself. Shedding a few tears never hurt anybody. Also, listening to your heart will often help you. Just express your feelings a little more! Considering all the benefits they bring, it would be a shame to deprive yourself of them.

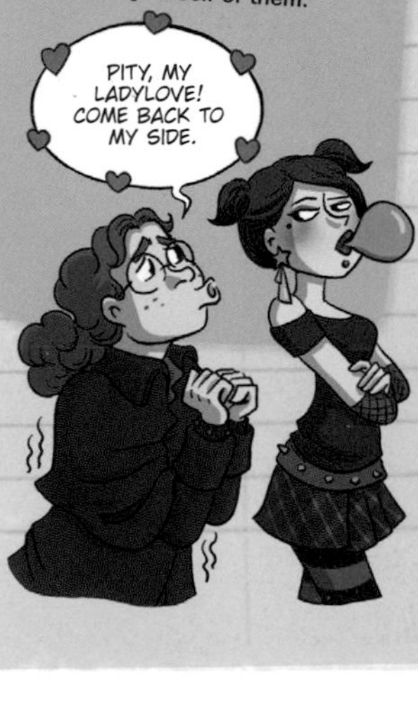
PITY, MY LADYLOVE! COME BACK TO MY SIDE.